The Samurai's Wife

to

ray

Also by Laura Joh Rowland

The Concubine's Tattoo
The Way of the Traitor
Bundori
Shinjū

The Samurai's Wife

Laura Joh Rowland

 ST. MARTIN'S MINOTAUR ✖ NEW YORK

Library of Congress Cataloging-in-Publication Data

Rowland, Laura Joh.
    The samurai's wife / Laura Joh Rowland—1st U.S. ed.
        p. cm.
    ISBN 978-1-250-03578-3
        1. Ichiro, Sano (Fictitious character)—Fiction. 2. Samurai—Japan—Fiction.
    3. Kyoto (Japan)—Fiction. 4. Japan—History—Genroku period, 1688–1704—
    Fiction. I. Title

    PS3568.O934 S26 2000
    813'.54—dc21   99-087939

First Edition: April 2000

This book is dedicated to the independent booksellers who have supported my work, especially Britton Trice and Deb Wehmeier of Garden District Book Shop, Barbara Peters of The Poisoned Pen, Tom and Enid Schantz of The Rue Morgue, Patsy Asher of Remember the Alibi, and Dean James of Murder by the Book. My sincere thanks to you all.

The Samurai's Wife

Japan

Genroku Period,
Year 4, Month 6

(July 1691)

Prologue

Nine hundred years ago, the city was Heian-kyō, Capital of Peace and Tranquillity, founded as seat of the emperors who ruled Japan. Now, long after the reigning power had passed to the Tokugawa shoguns and their stronghold in Edo far to the east, it is simply Miyako, or Kyōto—the capital. But the shadows of the past haunt the present. The Imperial Palace still dominates the city, as always, forever. There the current emperor and his court exist as though suspended in time, masters of no one, human relics of bygone splendor. After centuries of war and bloodshed, of fallen regimes and changing fortunes, the eternal antagonisms, forgotten secrets, and ancient dangers still survive. . . .

In the imperial enclosure, the palace's innermost private heart, a warm summer midnight enfolded the garden. Over flowerbeds and gravel paths, the foliage of maple, willow, cherry, and plum trees arched in dark, motionless canopies. The evening rain had ceased; a full moon glowed through vaporous cloud. The calm surface of the pond reflected the sky's luminosity. On an island in the pond's center, a rustic cottage stood amid twisted pines. Inside burned a lantern, its white globe crisscrossed by the window lattice.

West of the garden loomed the residences, ceremonial halls, offices, storehouses, and kitchens of the emperor's household. Their tile roofs gleamed in the moon's pallid radiance. From a passageway between two buildings, another lantern emerged. It swung from the hand of the left minister, chief official of the Imperial Court.

He strode along the pond toward a stone bridge leading to the island. Heat hazed the air like a moist veil. Fireflies twinkled feebly, as if the humidity quenched their light. A waterfall rippled; frogs croaked. The chirps of crickets and shrill of cicadas blended into a solid fabric of sound stretched across the night. The lantern cast the shadow of the left minister's tall figure dressed in archaic imperial style—wide trousers and a cropped jacket whose long train dragged on the ground. Beneath his broad-brimmed black hat shone the sallow face of a man in middle age, with the arched brows and haughty nose inherited from ancestors who had held his post before him. As he followed a path between the trees toward his secret rendezvous, anticipation increased his pace. A smile hovered upon his mouth; he drew deep breaths of night air.

The drowsy sweetness of lilies and clover drifted heavenward over the pond's marshy scent, masking the rich summer odors of damp earth, grass, night soil, and drains. A sense of well-being intoxicated the left minister, heady as the night's aromatic breath. He felt as vigorous as in his youth, and extraordinarily alive. Now he could look back through years of anguish with detachment.

Fifteen years ago, an unfortunate convergence of fate and deed had condemned him to serve two masters. Birthright had placed him in a station at the heart of palace affairs, in a position to know everything worth knowing. A crime committed in passion had rendered him vulnerable to persons outside the sequestered world of the court's five thousand residents. His two best qualities—intelligence and a gift for manipulating people—had doomed him to live in two worlds, an impotent slave in one, isolated from family, friends, and colleagues in the other. He'd been an actor playing two opposing roles. But now, having reclaimed the power to shape his own destiny, he stood ready to unite his two worlds, with himself at their summit.

Tonight would bring a taste of the rewards to come.

The light in the pavilion kindled the left minister's eagerness. He walked faster as a surge of sexual arousal fed his new sense of omnipotence. Although uncertainty and danger lay ahead, he was buoyed by confidence that soon he would realize his highest ambitions, his deepest desires. Tonight everything was already prepared, an advance celebration of his triumph.

Along the pond, a bamboo grove rustled in the breezeless air. The left minister paused, then dismissed it as the movement of some harmless feral creature and continued on his way. But the rustling followed him. Hearing footsteps, he frowned in puzzled annoyance.

The imperial family, their lives circumscribed by tradition, rarely ventured outside so late. Desiring privacy for his rendezvous, the left minister had ordered everyone else to stay out of the garden tonight. Who dared to disobey?

Reluctantly he stopped again. The bridge lay a hundred paces ahead; across the silvery pond, the cottage lantern beckoned. The left minister peered into the dense thicket of bamboo.

"Who's there?" he demanded. "Show yourself!"

No answer came. The moving bamboo leaves stilled. Angry now, the left minister stalked toward the intruder. "I order you to come out. Now!"

An abrupt change in atmosphere halted him ten paces short of the grove. Here the night seemed charged with energy. A soundless vibration pulsated through the left minister. The insect shrills receded to the edge of his hearing; the darkness paled within the space around him. His skin tightened, and his heart began to thud in deep, urgent beats. The will of the person in the bamboo grove seemed to close around the left minister's mind. Inexplicable fear seized him. Icy sweat broke out his face; his muscles weakened.

He knew that the person must be a member of the emperor's family, a servant, courtier, or attendant—a mortal human. But the strange force magnified the left minister's image of the intruder to gigantic size. He could hear it breathing monstrous gulps of air.

"Who are you?" His query came out sounding weak and timorous. "What do you want?" Somehow he understood, without word or gesture from the anonymous presence, its evil intent toward him.

The ominous breathing came faster, louder. The left minister turned and fled. On north and south, fences sealed off the garden. To the east, a stone wall separated the imperial enclosure from the estates of the court nobles. Vacant audience chambers, locked at night, cut him off from the shelter of the palace. There was no refuge except the island cottage. The left minister ran toward the lighted window, which promised companionship and safety, but his legs felt clumsy, his body weighted with the heavy malaise of nightmare. He stumbled, dropping his lantern. His stiff, cumbersome garments further hampered movement. Close behind, he heard the breathing, a vicious, predatory rasp. The ghostly grip on his mind crushed his courage.

"Help!" called the left minister, but his pursuer's will strangled his voice. Now he was sorry he'd banned everyone from the garden. He knew he could expect no help from the cottage's lone occupant.

As he struggled on, the eerie force enclosed him like a bubble. Desperately he zigzagged, trying to escape, but the awful pulsating sensation followed him. The weakness in his muscles increased. Glancing over his shoulder, he saw, through the force's pale halo, the indistinct silhouette of a human figure advancing on him. His heart pounded; his lungs couldn't draw enough air. He reached the bridge without the strength to run any farther. Falling to his knees, he crawled. The rough stone surface abraded his hands. He heard the chilling tap-tap of the intruder's footfalls coming closer. Reaching the island, the left minister dragged himself across sandy grass. He clutched the railing of the cottage veranda and pulled himself to a standing position. The three steps to the door loomed like towering cliffs. In the window, the lantern glowed, a mocking symbol of hope denied. The left minister turned to face his pursuer.

"No," he gasped, raising his hands in a futile attempt to ward off the undefined threat. "Please, no."

The intruder halted a few steps away. The noisy breathing stopped. Waves of panic washed over the left minister as he cowered in the sudden awful silence. Then, in the blurred oval of its face, the intruder's mouth opened—a darker void in darkness. Air rushed inward.

Then a scream shattered the night: a deafening wail that encompassed the full range of sound, from deepest groan to shrillest whine. The ghastly, inhuman voice blasted the left minister. Its low notes thundered through him with rumbles a million times stronger than an earthquake. The left minister's limbs splayed as sharp cracks like gunfire shot along his bones. As he howled in pain, sinews snapped. Terror combined with wonder.

Merciful gods, what is this terrible magic?

The scream's middle notes churned his bowels into liquid fire. The wail resonated in his heart, which beat faster and faster, swelling inside his chest. As his lungs ballooned, he breathed with harsh gasps. He fell, writhing in agony. The scream's shrillness arced along his nerves; convulsions wracked him. In the final moment before pain devoured reason, he knew he would never make his rendezvous. Nor would his dreams ever come to pass.

Now the left minister's insides erupted. Hot blood surged into his throat, filled his ears, choked off his breath, and blinded him. The scream's vibrations escalated until his brain exploded in a cataclysm of white-hot light.

Then death extinguished terror, pain, and consciousness.

The scream echoed across the city, then faded. A lull in the normal night sounds followed in its wake. For an eternal moment, time hung suspended in dead quiet. Then the doors and gates of the palace

6

slammed open; lamps lit windows. The compound came alive with the clamor of voices, of hurrying footsteps. Flaming torches, borne by guards, converged on the imperial enclosure.

A breath extinguished the flame of the lantern in the cottage. A shadowy figure crept through the garden, merging with other shadows, and disappeared.

From the attic of a shop in Edo's Nihonbashi merchant district, Sano Ichirō, the shogun's *sōsakan-sama*—Most Honorable Investigator of Events, Situations, and People—conducted a secret surveillance. He and his chief retainer, Hirata, peered through the window blinds. Below them lay Tobacco Lane, a street of tobacco shops and warehouses, restaurants and teahouses. As the summer twilight deepened, the peaked roofs turned to dark silhouettes against a rosy sky. Tobacco Lane, recently bustling with daytime commerce, was now a corridor of blank facades, its storefronts hidden behind sliding doors. Lanterns burned over gates at either end of the block. Across the city echoed the usual evening music of dogs barking, horses' neighs, the clatter of night-soil carts, and tolling temple bells. The only sign of activity came from the Good Fortune Noodle Restaurant, a tiny establishment wedged between two shops across the street. Lamplight striped its barred window. Smoke wafted from the kitchen.

"Dinner's long past," Sano said, "but I smell fish cooking over there."

Hirata nodded. "She's definitely expecting someone."

"Let's just hope it's our man," Sano said.

Nearby, Sano's wife, Reiko, stood amid bales of fragrant tobacco. Her pastel summer robes glowed in the faint light from the window and open skylight. Twenty-one years old, with eyes like bright black flower petals and long, lustrous hair worn in a knot, she was small and slender. Since their marriage last autumn, Sano had defied convention by permitting Reiko to help with his cases. Even though both of them knew that a proper wife should be waiting for him at home, he'd learned that Reiko could question witnesses and uncover evidence in places where a male detective couldn't go. Now here to witness the climax of this investigation, Reiko joined Sano and Hirata at the window. She tensed, listening, her lovely, delicate oval face alert.

"I hear someone coming," she said.

In the street below, an old man shuffled into view, leaning on a cane. The lantern at the gate illuminated his straggly white hair; a tattered kimono hung on his stooped body.

"That's the Lion of the Kantō?" Surprise lifted Reiko's voice. The notorious crime lord ruled a band of gangsters who ran gambling dens, robbed travelers, operated illegal brothels, and extorted money from merchants throughout the Kantō, the region surrounding Edo. "I expected someone more impressive."

"The Lion travels in disguise," Sano reminded her. "Few people know what he really looks like. That's one way he's managed to evade capture for so long."

His other methods included bribing police to ignore his activities, killing his enemies, and keeping on the move. Attempts by Sano's detective corps to infiltrate the gang had failed, and their informants had refused to talk. Hence, Reiko had used her special communication network, composed of wives, relatives, servants, and other women associated with powerful samurai clans. They collected gossip, spread news and rumors. From them Reiko learned that the Lion had a mistress—a widow who ran the Good Fortune Noodle Restaurant. During a month's surveillance, Sano's detectives had observed that men of different descriptions regularly visited after the restaurant closed. Guessing that these were all the Lion in various disguises, Sano had planned an ambush and taken over this shop as his headquarters.

Now he said to Reiko, "If that old man is the Lion and we catch him, we'll have you to thank."

Sano felt excitement and anxiety surging through him. While he yearned to end the Lion's reign of crime, he was worried about Reiko. He wished she were safe at home, though what possible harm could come to her from merely watching through the window?

Up a curve in the road, another watcher peered out a different window, this one in a half-timbered mansion with a tile roof and high earthen wall. From his position in the lamplit second-floor parlor, Chamberlain Yanagisawa had a perfect view of Tobacco Lane, the Good Fortune Noodle Restaurant, and the shop where Sano and his comrades hid. Over silk robes he wore an armor tunic; a golden-horned helmet framed his handsome face. Inhaling on a long silver pipe, he savored the rise of anticipation. He turned to his chief retainer, Aisu, who squatted on the tatami floor nearby.

"Are you sure they're in there?" Yanagisawa asked.

"Oh, yes, Honorable Chamberlain." A slender man several years older than Yanagisawa's own age of thirty-three, Aisu had tensely coiled grace and hooded eyes that gave him a deceptive look of perpetual drowsiness. His voice was a sibilant drawl. "I climbed on the roof and saw Sano, his wife, and Hirata through the skylight. Six detectives are in the shop below. The side window is open." Aisu grinned. "Oh, yes, it's the perfect setup. A brilliant plan, Honorable Chamberlain."

"Any sign of the Lion yet?"

Aisu shook his head.

"Is everything ready?" Yanagisawa asked.

"Oh, yes." Aisu patted the lumpy cloth sack that lay on a table beside him.

"Timing is critical," Yanagisawa reminded him. "Have you given the men their orders?"

"Oh, yes. Everyone's in place."

"How fortunate that I managed to learn about Sano's plans in time to prepare." A smug smile curved Yanagisawa's mouth.

Today he'd received a message from his spy in Sano's household, describing the ambush. Yanagisawa had quickly organized his own scheme, commandeering the mansion of a rich tobacco merchant for a lookout station. If he succeeded, he would soon see his rival destroyed. The misfortunes of the past would end.

Since his youth, Yanagisawa had been the shogun's lover, influencing the weak Tokugawa Tsunayoshi and winning his post as second-in-command. As the ruler of Japan in all but name, Yanagisawa had virtually absolute power. Then Sano, the upstart scholar, martial arts teacher, son of a *rōnin*—masterless samurai—and former police commander, had been promoted to the position of *sōsakan-sama*. The shogun had developed a high regard for Sano, who now commanded a staff of one hundred detectives and had gained influence over the *bakufu*, Japan's military government. Yanagisawa faced opposition from Sano whenever he proposed policies to Tokugawa Tsunayoshi and the Council of Elders; they sometimes took Sano's advice instead of his own. Sano's daring exploits overshadowed Yanagisawa's own importance, making him crave the adventure of detective work. And those exploits often meant serious trouble for him.

A case of double murder had led to Sano's discovery of a plot against the Tokugawa regime; he'd saved the shogun's life and won a post at Edo Castle. During his investigation of the Bundori Murders, when a madman had terrorized Edo with a series of grisly killings, Yanagisawa had been taken hostage by the murderer and nearly killed. Last year he'd exiled Sano to Nagasaki, but Sano had returned a hero. The final outrage had come when Sano, while investigating the poisoning of the shogun's concubine, had caused the death of Yanagisawa's lover.

Now Yanagisawa couldn't stand the sight of Sano and Reiko's happiness together. Tonight he would be rid of them. There'd be no more competition for the shogun's favor; no more humiliation. And as a bonus, he would steal Sano's reputation as a great detective.

A movement in the street outside caught Yanagisawa's eye. The foreshortened figure of an old man with a cane passed beneath the window. Yanagisawa beckoned Aisu, who glided swiftly to his side. They watched as the old man approached the noodle restaurant.

"Go!" Yanagisawa ordered.

"Oh, yes, Honorable Chamberlain." Aisu snatched up the cloth bundle and vanished without a sound.

Reiko said, "Look! He's stopping."

The old man beat his cane on the restaurant's door. It opened, and he disappeared inside.

"Let's go," Sano said to Hirata, then told Reiko, "We'll be back soon."

Her face shone with excitement. "I'm going with you!" She pushed up her sleeve, revealing the dagger strapped to her arm.

Consternation halted Sano. The problem with their partnership was that Reiko always wanted to do more than he could allow; to go places where a respectable woman could not be seen, risking social censure and her own life for the sake of their work. Always, Sano's desire for her assistance vied with his need to protect her. Sympathizing with Reiko's desire for adventure didn't ease his fear that their unusual marriage would provoke scandal and disgrace.

"I can't let you," he said. "You promised you would just watch if I let you come."

Reiko began to protest, then subsided in unhappy resignation: Promises between them were sacred, and she wouldn't break her word.

Sano and Hirata bounded down the staircase. In the dim shop, six detectives, waiting by the tobacco bins, sprang to attention. "The Lion is inside," Sano said. "We'll surround the place, and——"

From above the ceiling came a clatter, as though something had hit the floor upstairs, then the *whump* of a muffled explosion, followed by a scream.

"What was that?" Hirata said.

"Reiko!" Sano's heart seized. He turned to run back upstairs.

A fist-sized object flew in through the window. It landed in front of Sano and erupted in a cloud of smoke. Sulfurous fumes engulfed the shop. Coughs spasmed Sano's chest; his eyes burned. Through the dense haze, he heard the men coughing and thrashing around. Someone yelled, "A bomb!"

"This way out," Hirata cried.

Sano heard Reiko calling from the attic, but he couldn't even see the stairway. "Reiko!" he yelled. "Don't come down here. Go to the window!"

He rushed outside and saw Reiko climbing down a wooden pillar from the balcony. More smoke billowed out the window and skylight. Gasping and wheezing, Sano reached up and grabbed Reiko, who fell into his arms. Coughs wracked her body. From a nearby firewatch tower came the clang of a bell. Carrying his wife, Sano staggered down the street, where the air was fresh and a crowd had gathered. The fire brigade, dressed in leather tunics and helmets, arrived with buckets of water.

"Don't go in there!" Sano shouted. "Poison fumes!"

The crowd exclaimed. The fire brigade broke down the shop doors and hurled water inside. Sano and Reiko collapsed together on the ground. The detectives joined them, while Hirata stumbled over to the Good Fortune. He went inside, then returned. "There's no one in there. The Lion has escaped."

Sano cursed under his breath, then turned to Reiko. "Are you all right?"

Sudden shouts and pounding hoofbeats scattered the crowd.

"I'm fine." Coughing and retching, Reiko pointed. "Look!"

Up the street ran the man who'd entered the Good Fortune, no longer stooped and white-haired but upright and bald. The torn kimono flapped open, exposing muscular arms, chest, and legs blue with tattoos— the mark of a gangster. Mounted troops wearing the Tokugawa triple-hollyhock crest galloped after him. His face, with the broad nose and snarling mouth that had earned him his nickname, was wild with terror.

"It's the Lion!" Hirata exclaimed.

Sano stared as more soldiers charged from the opposite direction. "Where did they come from?"

The leader, clad in armor, slashed out with his lance. It knocked the

Lion flat, just a short distance from Sano. Instantly soldiers surrounded the Lion. Leaping off their horses, they seized him and tied his wrists.

"You're under arrest," the leader shouted.

Sano recognized his voice at once. Shock jolted him. "Chamberlain Yanagisawa!"

The chamberlain dismounted. Removing his helmet, he triumphantly surveyed the scene. Then his gaze fell upon Sano and Reiko. Dismay erased his smile. He stalked away, calling to his troops: "Take my prisoner to Edo Jail!"

In Sano's mansion in the Edo Castle Official Quarter, Sano, Reiko, and Hirata sat in the parlor, drinking medicinal tea to cleanse the poison from their systems. The sliding doors stood open to admit fresh air from the garden. Sano could still taste the acrid fumes on his breath. His head ached violently, and he knew they were lucky to be alive.

"This has gone on long enough," he said in a voice taut with fury. "Yanagisawa has been after me ever since I came to the castle." During the Bundori Murders case, Yanagisawa had sent a spy to give Sano false leads, and almost ruined a trap he'd set for the killer. "He's tried again and again to assassinate me." Sano had narrowly escaped death by attacks from Yanagisawa's henchmen. "When we were investigating the murder of Lady Harume last fall, his scheming almost destroyed me, but I'm the one he blames for Shichisaburō's death, which was his own fault. He's tried everything possible to get rid of me, including banishment." In Nagasaki, Sano had become embroiled in a politically sensitive case involving the murder of a Dutch trader and was almost convicted of treason.

"I've tolerated his evils for two years because I had no choice," Sano continued. According to Bushido—the Way of the Warrior—any criticism of the shogun's second-in-command implied criticism of Tokugawa Tsunayoshi himself. Any attack on Yanagisawa translated into an attack on the lord to whom Sano had sworn allegiance: blasphemy! Therefore, Sano had refrained from speaking out against Yanagisawa. "But he's gone too far by attacking Reiko."

"So you're sure the chamberlain is responsible for the bombing," Hirata said.

Sano nodded grimly. "His arrival on the scene was too coincidental, and he wasn't surprised to find us there—he was disappointed to see us alive. He must have somehow discovered our plans, then taken advantage of the situation."

A servant entered the room, knelt, and bowed. "Please excuse the interruption, master, but the shogun wants to see you right away."

"What does His Excellency want?" Sano asked.

"The messenger didn't say, except that it's urgent."

"At any rate, I have urgent business with him, too." Rising, Sano saw concern on the faces of his wife and retainer.

"You're planning to tell the shogun about Yanagisawa?" Hirata said.

"I can't fight off his plots forever; he'll get me eventually," Sano said. "It's time for open warfare."

"The chamberlain will deny everything you say," Reiko said. "He'll hate you even more for reporting him to the shogun. It might only make things worse."

"I'll just have to take that chance," Sano said, "because they won't get better by themselves."

He left the house and walked uphill through walled passages and security checkpoints to the shogun's palace. Inside, guards admitted him to the formal audience chamber, a long room lit by metal lanterns suspended from the ceiling. All the windows and doors were shut, the heat and smoky atmosphere stifling. On the dais sat the shogun, dressed in dark robes and cylindrical black cap. Attendants awaited orders. In the place of honor at the shogun's right, on the upper of two descending levels of the floor, knelt Chamberlain Yanagisawa. Both men silently watched Sano approach them. The shogun's mild, aristocratic face wore a pensive frown. Veiled hostility shimmered in Yanagisawa's dark, liquid gaze.

Frustration sharpened Sano's anger at the chamberlain. By airing his grievances with Yanagisawa there to oppose him, he risked immediate defeat in the opening round of battle, but if he waited until he could get Tokugawa Tsunayoshi alone, Yanagisawa's next attack might succeed first.

"Ahh, *Sōsakan* Sano." The shogun beckoned with his fan. His voice was distant, unfriendly. "Come. Join us."

"Thank you, Your Excellency." As Sano knelt in his customary spot on the upper level at the shogun's left and bowed to his lord, trepidation chilled him. Surely he was in trouble, and he thought he knew why. Bowing to Yanagisawa, he said, "Good evening, Honorable Chamberlain."

"Good evening," Yanagisawa said in a cold, polite tone.

"I've brought you here for two important reasons," the shogun said to Sano. "First, I regret to say that I am most, ahh, disappointed in your failure to capture the Lion of the Kantō. I have just been informed that you and your men were drinking and smoking in a tobacco shop tonight, and, ahh, accidentally set it on fire, while unbeknown to you, the Lion was right across the street! Your gross ineptitude forced Chamberlain Yanagisawa to step in and capture the Lion himself. He has displayed the, ahh, wits and initiative that you lack."

With horror, Sano saw his suspicions confirmed. Yanagisawa had twisted the truth to his own advantage, stealing credit for solving the case. The shogun, perhaps not the brightest dictator in the world, often misunderstood situations; he remained ignorant of the animosity between Sano and Yanagisawa. He was also too ready to believe whatever Yanagisawa told him. Although Bushido forbade Sano to contradict his lord, he had to amend this bizarre distortion of the facts.

"It wasn't exactly like that," he began cautiously.

Chamberlain Yanagisawa's suave voice cut in: "Are you saying that His Excellency has made a mistake and presuming to correct him?"

Sano was indeed, but when he saw displeasure darken the shogun's face, he said quickly, "No, of course not. I would just like to present my version of events."

Tokugawa Tsunayoshi silenced him with a raised hand. "There is no need. The, ahh, truth is evident. You failed in your duty. My faith in you has been, ahh, sadly misplaced."

The undeserved reproach wounded Sano. How unfair that one failure—which wasn't his fault—should negate everything he'd done right in the past! Although furious at Yanagisawa for thwarting his attempt to defend himself, he realized that persisting would only worsen Tsunayoshi's disapproval. He bowed his head. "My deepest apologies, Your Excellency."

Shame and dread sickened him as he suffered the blow to his honor and faced the likelihood of losing his post, and probably his life.

"However," the shogun said, "I have decided to give you a chance to ameliorate your, ahh, disgrace."

The prospect of a reprieve gladdened Sano, as did the sudden anxiety he sensed behind Yanagisawa's neutral expression. His defeat wasn't sealed, as the chamberlain had obviously hoped.

"This brings me to my second reason for summoning you," the shogun said.

He nodded to a servant, who left the room and immediately returned with a samurai clad in an armor tunic with red Tokugawa crests on the breastplate. The samurai knelt on the lower level and bowed.

"This is Captain Mori," the shogun said. "He is an envoy from the office of my, ahh, *shoshidai* in Miyako."

15

The old capital, unlike other cities, was governed not by a provincial daimyo—feudal lord—but by a special deputy. This *shoshidai* was always a Tokugawa relative whose rank and trustworthiness merited this important position.

After introducing Sano and Yanagisawa, the shogun continued, "The captain has just arrived with some disturbing news. Ahh . . ." Memory or words failed Tsunayoshi, and he gestured to the newcomer. "Repeat what you told me."

Captain Mori said, "Sixteen days ago, Konoe Bokuden, the imperial minister of the left, died suddenly. He was only forty-eight, and in good health. The court officials who reported his death were vague about how it occurred. Foul play seems a possibility. The *shoshidai* has begun an inquiry, but under the circumstances, he thought it best to seek advice from Edo."

Hope and apprehension rose in Sano as he realized that the shogun was going to send him to Miyako to investigate the death. A new case offered a welcome opportunity to reclaim his honor and reputation. Yet Sano didn't want to go away, leaving Chamberlain Yanagisawa free to menace Reiko and undermine his influence with Tokugawa Tsunayoshi.

"Even if Left Minister Konoe's death was murder, isn't the *shoshidai*'s police force in charge of handling all crimes in Miyako?" Sano said, stalling to delay the order he couldn't disobey. "May I ask why this matter concerns Your Excellency?"

Granted, the Imperial Court occupied a unique position in Japan. The emperor was revered by citizens as a descendant of the Shinto gods who had created the universe. He had the sole power to give official sanction to the nation's government.

Eighty-eight years ago, Emperor Go-Yozei had named Tokugawa Ieyasu shogun, conferring divine legitimacy upon the regime. However, the current emperor had no role in governing Japan, or authority over the *bakufu*. Other than mundane duties associated with running the palace compound, court nobles such as Left Minister Konoe performed a strictly ceremonial function. They were mere symbols of the real power their ancestors had once wielded from behind the throne. Konoe's death, however mysterious, should hold no personal interest for Tokugawa Tsunayoshi, who never went to Miyako, or the Edo *bakufu*, which delegated the administration of court affairs to its local representatives.

"There's more to the, ahh, situation than one might think, *Sōsakan* Sano." The shogun sighed unhappily. "Left Minister Konoe was a secret agent of the *metsuke*."

The *metsuke* was the Tokugawa intelligence network. It gathered information from all over Japan, monitoring citizens whose activities might pose a threat to Tokugawa supremacy. Sano, though startled to learn that an imperial noble had been a spy, couldn't miss the implications of this possible murder.

"Fifteen years ago, Left Minister Konoe killed a man," Captain Mori said. "He would have been tried, convicted, and executed, but we had a better use for him." Sano interpreted this to mean that the *bakufu* had hushed up the murder and recruited Konoe to inform on his associates. "Perhaps his death is related to that crime, or troubles within the Imperial Court."

"Or maybe it had to do with his secret life as a spy," Sano said, wondering how to protect his family and his interests during an absence from Edo. "Left Minister Konoe might have discovered something worth killing him to hide." History had shown that the Imperial Court, even when powerless, was a constant potential source of trouble, which the *bakufu* monitored for reasons inherent in the nature of Japanese government. "This is a serious matter. However, Your Excellency . . ."

"Yes, it is indeed serious," the shogun interrupted. "My regime may be in great danger. That is why I am sending you to uncover the, ahh, truth about Left Minister Konoe's death. You must solve the mystery and, ahh, neutralize any potential threats."

Sano glanced at Yanagisawa. The chamberlain's eyes had acquired a familiar opaque look that struck a chord of dread in Sano. Surely Yanagisawa was planning a new scheme against him.

"A thousand thanks for your generosity," Sano said to the shogun. "My only concern is about what might happen here while I'm gone."

While Sano sought words to explain his situation, the shogun said, "Much as I hate to see you go, I'm afraid I must make the, ahh, sacrifice. If a, ahh, problem arises while you're away, your chief retainer shall handle any necessary investigation."

Sano was ready to spill the whole story of his relationship with Chamberlain Yanagisawa and beg the shogun for mercy. Then Yanagisawa said, "Your Excellency, I commend the brilliance of your idea." He projected the whole force of his personality into his warm, sincere voice. "I predict that we shall all be glad you decided to send *Sōsakan* Sano to Miyako."

Tsunayoshi beamed, but when he turned back to Sano, distrust shaded his eyes. A smile hovered upon Yanagisawa's lips. Now Sano lost his meager hope of persuading the shogun to curb Yanagisawa's destructive machinations. Tonight's events had strengthened the bond between the shogun and Yanagisawa too much. The only way for Sano to regain the shogun's favor—or survive to defeat Yanagisawa—was to carry out the assignment with unstinting obedience and great success.

"I've already sent a messenger ahead to inform the Miyako authorities that you are coming," the shogun told Sano. "Now go and, ahh, prepare for a quick departure."

"Yes, Your Excellency," Sano said, bowing.

As he walked homeward down the castle's winding passages, ahead of him stretched the fifteen days to Miyako and fifteen back, plus however long the investigation took. How he would miss Reiko's company and advice! To leave her in Edo, at the mercy of Chamberlain Yanagisawa, was unthinkable, even though she would have the protection of Sano's troops and her powerful father. Then, as Sano entered the Official Quarter, a sudden idea elated him. It posed inherent difficulties, but it seemed a blessed solution.

In the bathchamber, Reiko scrubbed her body with rice-bran soap while two maids washed her hair. Then she sat in the deep, sunken tub, waiting for the warm water to rinse her clean, melt the tension from her muscles, and soothe her thoughts. But worry prevented relaxation. The smoke bomb had terrified her, and why had the shogun summoned Sano?

In working together on investigations, Reiko and her husband had become closer than traditional samurai couples in which the man handled business affairs and the woman tended the home. Even when apart, Reiko and Sano had a special sense of each other. Now this sense warned Reiko that something had gone wrong for Sano. She wished she could have accompanied him to his meeting with the shogun so she would know what had happened, but the flaw in their partnership was that she could never go everywhere Sano did, or fully exercise her talents. Sometimes she regretted the unusual upbringing that had destined her for discontent.

She was the beloved only child of the widowed Magistrate Ueda, who'd provided her the education usually accorded a son. She'd excelled at reading, calligraphy, mathematics, history, philosophy, law, political theory, the Chinese classics, and the martial arts. As a young girl, she'd dreamed of a future filled with adventure. She'd scorned the lot of women, who existed only to wed, serve their husbands, and raise children in homebound seclusion. Fortunately, she'd avoided this fate by marrying Sano. After some initial reluctance, he'd welcomed her help with his work. But too often, she ended up waiting at home, yearning for the freedom and authority granted to men.

Now Reiko was too restless to sit idle. She climbed out of the tub. As the maids dried her with towels, rubbed fragrant oil into her skin, and combed her hair, Reiko's thoughts moved to another matter that had occupied her mind recently.

Tradition decreed that a wife's most important duty was to provide her husband with an heir. Despite her unconventional nature, Reiko accepted her responsibility, and she wanted children born of her love for Sano. However, almost a year had passed since their wedding. Although Sano had never broached the subject, Reiko knew he yearned for a son, and she'd begun to worry. Surely conception should have occurred by now. Was she barren?

Then, last month, she'd missed her time of female bleeding. She hoped she was pregnant, but hadn't told Sano because she didn't want to risk disappointing him. If she missed her next bleeding, she would give him the good news.

She was sitting in the bedchamber, wrapped in a white silk dressing gown and drying her hair in the night breeze, when Sano returned. "What happened?" she cried.

Sano knelt beside her. As he described how Chamberlain Yanagisawa had stolen credit for capturing the Lion, and the shogun's rebuke, Reiko's heart sank. The blow to her husband's honor struck deep in her own spirit.

"However, I have a chance to set things right," Sano continued. He explained about the death of the Imperial Court noble, then said, "The shogun is sending me to Miyako to investigate."

Dismay stunned Reiko; she could hardly appreciate the reprieve from disaster. Miyako was so far away. They'd never been apart for more than a few days, and an extended separation seemed unbearable to contemplate. Tears stung her eyes. Still, she knew how much this investigation meant to Sano. She mustn't burden him with her unhappiness.

Averting her face, she rose, murmuring, "I'd better pack your things."

Sano caught her arm. "I want you to go with me."

"What?" Surprise jolted Reiko. Wives so rarely accompanied their husbands on trips that she hadn't even considered the possibility of going to Miyako. Confused, she stared at Sano.

He smiled and said, "Wouldn't you like to help me with the case?"

"Yes, oh yes!" Joyfully, Reiko hugged Sano, her earlier woe forgotten. She darted around the room, unable to contain her excitement. "I've always wanted to travel. What a wonderful adventure!"

"I still have to arrange a travel pass for you," Sano said. "That could be a problem."

The *bakufu* restricted the movements of women to prevent samurai clans from relocating their families to the countryside as preparation for revolt; hence, passes were hard to obtain. But this obstacle didn't faze Reiko, and neither did her possible pregnancy. Now she was glad she hadn't told Sano about it, because the news might change his mind about taking her, although she was strong and healthy and even if she was with child, a trip shouldn't hurt. "With all your influential friends, surely you can get me a pass," she said.

"I can't promise that there will be any work you can do on the investigation," Sano warned her. "The usual laws and customs apply in Miyako. In addition, the Imperial Court has its own special rules. You may end up with even less freedom there than here."

"I'm sure there will be something for me to do," Reiko said blithely, opening a wardrobe and sorting out kimonos to pack. "And I'll be with you."

"Yes."

A grim, decisive note in his voice stilled Reiko. Realization struck her. Turning, she said, "You're taking me so that Chamberlain Yanagisawa can't hurt me while you're gone."

"And because I want you," Sano said, rising and embracing her.

"We'll solve the case together," Reiko said, wanting to bolster his confidence in himself and their future. "We'll be free of Yanagisawa long enough for you to restore your honor and regain the shogun's favor."

2

A procession crowded the final stretch of the Tōkaidō, the east-west highway that linked Edo with Miyako. Mounted banner bearers, wearing flags emblazoned with the Tokugawa crest, led soldiers armed with swords and spears. Behind these, Sano rode alongside the palanquin that carried Reiko. Then came the two detectives Sano had brought in lieu of Hirata, whom he'd left at home to manage his detective corps. Servants carrying baggage followed, preceding the foot soldiers of the rear guard.

The journey had taken them through villages and woods, along the sea coast, across rivers and mountains. Now, in the late afternoon of the fifteenth day, they entered the plain where Miyako lay. Behind them rose the hills east of the city, the highest peaks lost in dense clouds. Mist hazed the forested slopes. The air, trapped by more hills to the north and west, had a moist, tropical warmth. Flies buzzed; mosquitoes swarmed. The segmented green poles and feathery foliage of bamboo bordered the road. Beyond stretched lush green rice fields, reeking of night soil. Peasants drove teams of black oxen; herons waded in ditches; flocks of wild geese winged across the sky. Reiko, enclosed in the palanquin, used a silk fan to supplement the meager flow of air through the sedan chair's open windows. She was perspiring and weary, and the hardships of the journey had dimmed the glamour of her adventure.

She now knew firsthand the difficulties experienced by women while traveling. Hot weather, crowded inns, and strange food were minor problems. To obtain Reiko's pass, Sano had spent a day bribing petty officials. However, neither the pass nor his high rank had guaranteed an easy passage through the checkpoints where the *bakufu* monitored activities along the Tōkaidō. There inspectors had interrogated Sano about his reasons for bringing his wife. Female assistants had searched Reiko's baggage and person for secret documents, smuggled weapons, or unusually large quantities of money. And highway laws prolonged the ordeal. Custom barred women from riding horses. To prevent the movement of troops and war supplies across Japan, the Tokugawa prohibited all wheeled traffic except for oxcarts owned by the *bakufu*. Hence, ladies traveled by palanquin—a slow, uncomfortable process. Reiko regretted the expense and delay she'd caused Sano.

Now she spoke through the window to him: "I'm sorry to be so much trouble."

He gazed affectionately down at her. "You're not. I'm glad you're here."

Yet he seemed distracted. He'd slept poorly during the trip, Reiko knew, even with his men standing watch. Chamberlain Yanagisawa's assassins had gotten past guards before, and what better time to attack than when Sano was on the road, where a murder could be blamed on bandits? And before leaving Edo, Sano had identified the spy in his house, a clerk who'd confessed to telling Yanagisawa about his plan to ambush the Lion. Reiko guessed that Sano feared more sabotage in Miyako.

Behind them, Detective Marume said, "Merciful gods, this heat is awful." Reiko liked Marume, who was powerfully built and an excellent fighter. "Oh, well, suffering is good for the spirit." Unfailing good cheer rang out in his hearty laugh. To his partner he said, "If I were as skinny as you, Fukida-*san*, the weather wouldn't bother me so much."

Reiko peered out the back window at Detective Fukida, who had brooding eyes beneath a brow creased by a seriousness far beyond his twenty-five years. Son of a minor Tokugawa vassal, the young samurai had a poetic bent. He recited:

> *"Though the summer day burns my skin,*
> *I shall cool myself by evening on the Sanjo Bridge."*

His allusion to a famous landmark over the Kamo River and the nearness of their destination revived Reiko's excitement. They would reach Miyako in less than an hour; a messenger had been dispatched to announce their arrival. When the investigation began, she would prove herself an asset to Sano instead of a hindrance.

In the near distance, the road ended at the Great Rampart, an earthen wall that surrounded Miyako, rising like a gray fortress from amid tall bamboo stalks. High rooftops and the framework structures of firewatch towers reached above the top. The Great Rampart had been built one hundred years ago, Reiko recalled, by Toyotomi Hideyoshi, who had fought under General Oda Nobunaga, risen through the ranks of Oda's army, and succeeded to power after his lord's death, reigning supreme over Japan. As governor of Miyako, he'd rebuilt the war-ravaged capital into the city that existed today. Now, as the procession drew closer, Reiko saw the Rashōmon Gate, main portal of the Great Rampart. Its red pillars supported gable roofs with gold dolphin finials; a flight of stone steps led into Miyako. Reiko had always wanted to see the site of so many historic events. A shiver of delight rippled through her.

"How wonderful," she murmured.

A quick smile from Sano told her he agreed.

Out the gate came a squadron of soldiers escorting two mounted samurai officials, one old, one young, wearing black ceremonial robes. This welcoming party crossed the arched stone bridge that spanned a wide moat. Sano's procession met the Miyako contingent on an expanse of paved ground at the foot of the bridge, the two sides facing each other in parallel lines.

The banner bearers introduced Sano by calling out his name and rank. Two Miyako guard captains chorused, "The Honorable Lord Matsudaira Moronobu, deputy and cousin of His Excellency the shogun!"

The older local official exchanged bows with Sano. "Greetings," he cried. "Welcome to the imperial capital!"

Shoshidai Matsudaira was an older version of the shogun, Reiko observed, with the same refined features and eager, subservient smile. He said to Sano, "I have heard much about you, and I regret that I've not had the honor of meeting you sooner, because I seldom leave Miyako. Why, it's been—" He turned to the official beside him. "Dear me, how long has it been since I was last in Edo?"

"A year, my lord," said the younger man. In his early thirties, he was tall and broad-shouldered, with an angular face that tapered from a square jaw to a sharply pointed chin. A wide, full mouth and heavy eyelids gave him a sensual masculine beauty. He had the confident poise of a good swordfighter and a competent man on his way up the *bakufu* hierarchy.

The *shoshidai* regarded him with affection. "This is *Yoriki* Hoshina, senior police commander of Miyako and my chief aide."

Reiko realized that *Shoshidai* Matsudaira resembled the shogun in more than just appearance: He, too, had a smarter, stronger second-in-command to think and act for him.

"Please allow me to introduce Detectives Marume and Fukida from my staff," Sano said. The two men bowed. Sano didn't introduce the rest of his party, and while Reiko understood that he was only following custom by relegating his wife to the anonymous ranks of his entourage, she hoped this exclusion wasn't a sign of things to come.

"Has there been any change in the status of affairs concerning Left Minister Konoe's death since your envoy delivered the news to Edo?" Sano asked the *shoshidai*.

"No, I'm afraid the mystery remains."

At least the case hadn't resolved itself already, Reiko thought gratefully.

"Then I should appreciate *Yoriki* Hoshina's assistance while investigating the matter," Sano said, and Reiko knew he'd guessed which local official would be most able to provide the help he needed.

"Of course, of course." *Shoshidai* Matsudaira bobbed his head, obviously glad that he wouldn't have to do anything himself. "And I shall host a banquet in your honor tomorrow night." Then, without moving, he faded into the background.

Yoriki Hoshina said, "Ordinarily, we would house an envoy from Edo in Nijō Castle." This was the *bakufu*'s stronghold in Miyako. "But I regret to say that the castle is undergoing major repairs at the moment. Therefore, the best accommodation we can offer is Nijō Manor, a private inn."

"That will be fine, thank you," Sano said.

"Would you like to settle in and rest now?" Hoshina asked.

"I'd rather start working right away," Sano said. "Please have your troops escort my entourage to Nijō Manor, then show me the scene of Left Minister Konoe's death."

To Reiko's dismay, Sano rode briskly through the Rashōmon Gate with Hoshina, Detectives Marume and Fukida, and a few guards, while she and everyone else lagged behind. She longed to accompany Sano, but she knew that for him to include his wife in his official business or pay her any attention now would seem peculiar to their hosts and undermine his authority. Cursing her uselessness, she sat trapped in her palanquin, praying that she would be able to make use of her talents later.

"Left Minister Konoe died in the Imperial Palace," *Yoriki* Hoshina told Sano as they entered Miyako. "Please come this way."

Beyond the Rashōmon Gate, another moat lined the Great Rampart, with another bridge leading into the old capital. Unlike Edo, a convoluted labyrinth, Miyako was laid out on a grid based on the ancient Chinese model of city design. A wide avenue extended as far as Sano could see. The procession moved down this, passing narrower streets set at perfect right angles, some edged by canals. Despite the buildings that occupied every plot of land, Miyako's layout gave an impression of spaciousness. This was a city of plastered wood houses, serene in its ordered uniformity. The low gray-tiled roofs peaked and fell like stylized waves. Over shop doorways hung blue curtains; bamboo blinds protected merchandise from dust, while arcades sheltered pedestrians from the weather. Rising up on north, east, and west, the hills held the city remote from the outside world, but the feature that especially reinforced the peaceful atmosphere was the dearth of samurai.

Of all the people who crowded the streets, most were merchants, peasants, or priests. Fewer men sported the shaven crown and two swords of Sano's class. Some were *bakufu* soldiers; others, accompanied by laden porters, were obviously travelers. Miyako was a civilian city whose business was commerce, religion, and hospitality. Inns, restaurants, and teahouses abounded. Sano glimpsed stores selling cloth and Buddhist prayer beads. In this place where fires, earthquakes, and floods necessitated frequent rebuilding, he saw nothing ancient and no trace of past wars.

However, his historian's eye superimposed another scene upon the tranquil cityscape. Ruined buildings hulked. Fleeing refugees carried bundles on their backs; orphan children wailed; beggars and marauding outlaws roved. Smoke rose from temples burning in the hills. Through streets lined with rotting corpses filed the ghosts of armies that had ravaged Miyako throughout history. This dark vision echoed Sano's troubled mood. Would he succeed at this investigation, or compound his disgrace with another failure? He thought of Reiko, who must surely be disappointed to miss a critical step of the case, but he couldn't afford to disrupt his concentration by worrying about her now.

Abruptly, the party halted at a marketplace that crowded the avenue. *Yoriki* Hoshina said, "I apologize for the inconvenience. You've arrived on the first day of Obon."

This was the Festival of the Dead, when people all over Japan welcomed the souls of the deceased back to the world of the living for a five-day visit. Vendors sold supplies for observing this important Buddhist holiday: incense and lotus flowers for tombs and altars, red earthenware dishes for serving the spirits of the dead during symbolic feasts, lanterns to guide the spirits home. Shoppers made way for the procession, which turned down another avenue, moving along a white plaster wall with vertical wooden beams, built on a stone foundation.

"This is the Imperial Palace," *Yoriki* Hoshina said, dismounting at a gate guarded by Tokugawa sentries. "The main portal is reserved for the emperor's use. We'll enter here."

Sano and his detectives dismounted. They and Hoshina entered a long passage inside the enclosure. From his study of palace maps, Sano guessed that the wall on his left hid the residence of abdicated emperors; only its trees and rooftops were visible. Opposite, fences bounded the estates of court nobles. A right turn led along another wall, through another gate, and Sano found himself transported to a time eight hundred years past.

An eerie calm lay over the Imperial Palace's famous Pond Garden. The lake spread like spilled quicksilver around islands, its surface overlaid with water lilies. Mandarin ducks roosted on a beach of black stones. Over beds of bright chrysanthemums, irises, and poppies, hummingbirds darted. Maple, cherry, and plum trees and bamboo stood resplendent in lush green leaf. The shrilling cicadas and tinkle of wind chimes, the scent of flowers and grass, the water and heat: all crystallized summer's timeless essence. In the distance, drooping willows screened villas built in ancient style—raised on low stilts, connected by covered corridors. Sano saw no one except a gardener raking leaves. From within the palace walls, the hills seemed closer, giving the illusion that the surrounding city didn't exist.

Awed to walk this sacred ground where the descendants of the Shinto gods lived, Sano trod respectfully; his men followed suit. *Yoriki* Hoshina marched down the gravel paths as if he belonged there: the *shoshidai*'s representatives had supreme authority over the palace. He led the way across a stone bridge to the pond's largest island. There, shaded by pines, stood a tiny cottage built of rough cypress planks. Bamboo mullions latticed the window.

"This is where Left Minister Konoe was found," Hoshina said, pointing at the foot of the cottage steps.

"How did he die?" Sano asked.

"The *shoshidai* wasn't notified until the body had been prepared for the funeral, so all my knowledge comes from the report issued by the Imperial Court several days later," Hoshina said. "That's a violation of the law—we're supposed to be informed immediately of all deaths in the palace. The court physician examined Konoe and said that he'd hemorrhaged almost all of his blood out his eyes, ears, nose, mouth, and anus. Apparently the internal organs had ruptured. And he was as limp as a rag because so many bones had been broken. But the doctor couldn't determine the cause of this condition. There were no bruises or any other wounds on the body."

26

Such a bizarre death couldn't have been natural, and the delayed notification implied a cover-up, with murder the likely reason. As a possible explanation for Left Minister Konoe's symptoms occurred to Sano, he felt a sudden apprehension. This could be a complex, dangerous case.

"Did anyone report a very loud, powerful scream at the time of Konoe's death?" Sano asked.

Hoshina regarded Sano with surprise. "How did you know? People all over Miyako heard it; I did myself, all the way from across town. It was . . . unearthly." A shiver passed over the *yoriki*. "Whatever happened to Konoe must have been extremely painful to produce such a scream from him."

Sano had a different interpretation for the scream, which confirmed his suspicions. "Left Minister Konoe must have been a victim of murder by *kiai*," he said. Combat without physical contact; the ultimate expression of the martial arts. "The scream was a 'spirit cry'—a burst of pure mental energy, concentrated in the voice of the killer."

Hoshina and the detectives stared at Sano in astonishment. That few samurai ever attained the ability to kill without weapons, by force of will alone, had made the practitioners of *kiaijutsu* the rarest, most fearsome and deadly warriors throughout history. The killer's presence, mighty and monstrous, seemed to darken the tranquil garden, and Sano knew his companions sensed it too.

Then *Yoriki* Hoshina chuckled. "I've never heard of anyone actually killed by a scream. That theory sounds like superstition to me," he said, expressing the modern skepticism that relegated amazing feats of martial arts to the realm of myth.

Sano had suspected that Hoshina might not be as compliant as he'd first seemed. Now he knew that Hoshina had a mind of his own; he wouldn't automatically accept the judgment of a superior. Sano wondered if the locals knew of the circumstances that had brought him here, and whether Hoshina might take advantage of Sano's shaky position in the *bakufu*. Many men rose to power by attacking vulnerable superiors, and while Sano had no particular reason to distrust Hoshina, he knew better than to think that Miyako politics were any different than Edo's. Aware that he must assert his authority, Sano rose to Hoshina's challenge.

"Toyotomi Hideyoshi's tea master, Sen-no-Rikyu, averted an attack from the great General Kato Kiyomasa with a single glance that took away his strength," Sano said. He himself had once thought *kiaijutsu* a lost art, but the murder of Left Minister Konoe had revived his belief that myths were based on fact. "Yagyu Matajuro, tutor of Tokugawa Ieyasu, could knock men unconscious with a shout."

"I've always thought those legends were invented by charlatans wishing to bolster their reputations." Hoshina's tone was deferential, but the fact that he dared to argue told Sano he liked to be right and wasn't afraid to take chances. "Certainly, there haven't been any recent, documented cases of death by *kiai*."

"The general level of combat skill has declined; there are fewer great martial arts masters today," Sano admitted. "But Miyako is a city with strong ties to the past. Someone here has apparently rediscovered the secret of *kiaijutsu*. The scream and the condition of the corpse indicate that Left Minister Konoe was indeed a victim of a spirit cry."

Pronounced by the shogun's highest representative, Sano's opinion became the official cause of death. Rather than pursue the discussion and risk censure, Hoshina nodded and said respectfully, "Yes, *Sōsakan-sama*." Sano observed that he knew when to yield for the sake of self-preservation.

"Who discovered the remains?" Sano said, moving on to the next important topic.

"When the palace residents heard the scream, they rushed to see what it was," Hoshina said. "Emperor Tomohito and his cousin Prince Momozono were first on the scene. They found Konoe alone, lying in a pool of blood."

So the case involved at least two important members of the Imperial Court, Sano thought. "What time did this happen?"

"Around midnight," said Hoshina.

"What was Left Minister Konoe doing out here so late?"

"No one admits to knowing."

"You've questioned the palace residents, then?"

"Yes, I conducted a preliminary investigation," Hoshina said, "to save you some trouble. The results are detailed in a report which I'll give you later, but I'll summarize them now. All the guards, servants, attendants, and courtiers were elsewhere at the time of Left Minister Konoe's death. He'd ordered everyone to stay out of the garden."

"Excellent work," Sano said, noting the raw edge of pride and ambition behind the *yoriki*'s modest demeanor: Hoshina enjoyed showing off, and he anticipated rewards for pleasing the shogun's *sōsakan-sama*. That their interests coincided inclined Sano to trust the helpful Hoshina.

"Were there any visitors or other outsiders present in the compound that night?" Sano asked.

"No," Hoshina said, "and there was no sign of forced entry, so it's unlikely that an intruder killed Left Minister Konoe."

Sano said, "Was everyone else in the court accounted for around the time of the murder?"

"I thought it best to wait until your arrival before questioning the imperial family," Hoshina said. "However, I've made discreet inquiries. There are some people whose whereabouts I haven't been able to establish. Emperor Tomohito and Prince Momozono weren't in their quarters as usual. Neither were the emperor's chief consort, Lady Asagao, or his mother, Lady Jokyōden."

Four potential murder suspects; all members of Japan's sacred imperial family. Sano contemplated the politically volatile nature of the case. By probing into palace affairs, he was bound to violate social and religious convention, thereby damaging relations between the *bakufu* and the institution that sanctioned its right to rule. Nevertheless, the killer must be caught, or others might die.

Looking upward, Sano saw the hills darkening in murky twilight. He couldn't call on the imperial family so late, on such short notice, without offending them. "I'll interview the emperor, his mother, cousin, and consort tomorrow morning."

"Of course," *Yoriki* Hoshina said. "I'll arrange appointments for you. Shall I take you to your lodgings at Nijō Manor now?"

The offer tempted Sano, who was hungry and tired, caked with sweat and grime; he needed food, a bath, and sleep. He also wanted to discuss the case with Reiko, but he hadn't finished the day's work at the palace. "Before we go, I'd like to inspect Left Minister Konoe's residence and question the household."

3

Sano, *Yoriki* Hoshina, Marume, and Fukida walked west along a passage that bisected the palace compound, through the district of the *kuge*, court nobles who were hereditary retainers to the imperial family. Fences bounded some hundred estates packed side by side, where buildings clustered with scarcely a gap between roofs. As the dinner hour approached, charcoal smoke billowed from many chimneys; the noise of activity and conversation made a constant, muted din. Through the passages strolled courtiers dressed in the old-fashioned short jackets and black hats of imperial tradition. Everyone bowed to Sano and his party.

At the Konoe estate, near the northern wall of the imperial enclosure, black mourning drapery decorated the lattice fence and double-roofed gate. Hoshina rang a bell that dangled from the portal. After a moment, the gate swung open to reveal a courtier, who looked startled by the unexpected arrival of four samurai, then bowed politely.

"Greetings, Honorable Masters. How may I serve you?"

Hoshina introduced Sano and said, "The *sōsakan-sama* is investigating the death of Left Minister Konoe. You shall assemble the family for questioning and show us the left minister's quarters."

The courtier led Sano's party along a flagstone path through a garden landscaped with pines. Within a gravel courtyard stood a mansion built in the same style as the palace. Wooden rain doors were raised to admit the mild evening breeze. Walking behind the courtier down hallways floored in polished cypress, Sano and his companions passed spacious parlors where cultured voices murmured and a samisen played behind paper partitions. In the reception hall, screens decorated with forest scenes formed an enclosure; lanterns cast a soft glow.

The courtier invited the four samurai to sit on the dais, then left. Presently he returned, announcing, "I present the honorable Konoe clan."

Sano watched in amazement as a long parade of people, young and old, filed into the room to kneel before the dais. The courtier introduced siblings, cousins, and other relatives of the dead man. Sano had known that court families were large but hadn't expected quite so many people living under the same roof. The men wore traditional court costume. The women were dressed in multilayered pastel robes with voluminous sleeves and narrow brocade sashes; long hair flowed down to their waists. Sano recalled that Tokugawa Ieyasu had established "Laws Pertaining to the Emperor's Retainers," which consigned the noble class to the practice of scholarship and arts rather than politics. Isolated from the world during the seventy-six years that had followed, these people fulfilled little purpose except to preserve their obsolete way of life. They were virtual prisoners of the *bakufu*, which financially supported them along with the imperial family. Now they comprised a huge pool of potential witnesses.

"My detectives will question the servants," Sano said to the courtier. "Is there a place where I can interview the family one at a time, in private?"

Evening immersed Miyako in tropical darkness. In the Market of the Dead, brightly lit stalls turned the streets into lines of multicolored fire where shoppers browsed among Obon supplies. Gongs rang, calling dead souls back to earth. On hillsides and along the Kamo River, bonfires burned, lighting the way for the spirits' journey. Pine torches blazed at the thresholds of houses; incense smoked on windowsills. Citizens bearing lanterns converged on the cemeteries to visit ancestors' graves. The air resounded with the clatter of wooden soles. On the boulevards fluttered the curtains of shops closed for the night, stirred by the wind . . . or passing ghosts.

In the city center stood the great bulk of Nijō Castle, built by Tokugawa Ieyasu eighty-nine years ago with funds levied from vanquished warlords. Its stone walls and five-storied keep loomed high above the surrounding houses. Gold Tokugawa crests crowned the curved roofs. No shogun had visited Miyako in more than five decades; since then, Nijō Castle had been occupied by a minimal staff of caretakers. A few sentries manned the gates and guard turrets above the wide moat. From the outside, the castle seemed an inert historical relic.

But deep inside its dark complex of barracks, gardens, and palace buildings, lights burned in the White Parlor, residence of visiting shoguns. There, in an austere room decorated with murals depicting winter landscapes, sat Chamberlain Yanagisawa and his chief retainer, Aisu.

Yanagisawa inhaled on his tobacco pipe, then expelled smoke in an impatient gust. Although circumstances required his present state of waiting, he hungered for action. Worry and anticipation consumed him.

"Are you sure Sano doesn't know I'm here?" he said.

"Oh, yes, master," said Aisu, who'd just returned from making covert inquiries on Yanagisawa's behalf. "No one in Miyako knows, except your local agents. They received your message from Edo in plenty of time to carry out your orders. They told *Shoshidai* Matsudaira that the shogun had issued orders to renovate Nijō Castle, then brought in laborers and supplies as if it were true, not just a ploy to keep Sano away. No one else suspects anything. My spies have been watching Sano since he left Edo, and he's completely oblivious. Oh, yes, the plan is working fine so far."

Aisu's nervous grin begged Yanagisawa to appreciate his efficiency, to see how much he deserved to keep his job despite the failed bombing. Yanagisawa had given him one more chance to prove his worth before dismissing him. Thus, Aisu's fate, as well as Yanagisawa's hopes, depended on the success of the plan.

"See that the operation proceeds along its present satisfactory course," Yanagisawa said, then murmured to himself: "The results had better justify the trouble this venture may cause me."

When the shogun had ordered Sano to investigate Left Minister Konoe's death, Yanagisawa had recognized a perfect opportunity to rid himself of his enemy and permanently secure his position in Tokugawa Tsunayoshi's graces. He'd decided that he, too, must go to Miyako. Hence, he'd waited until the meeting with Sano ended and he was alone with the shogun, then proposed that he should go to Omi Province—where Miyako happened to be located—on a top-secret mission to investigate corruption among local officials. The shogun had vacillated, demurred, and finally been persuaded.

Yanagisawa spent the rest of that night conferring with Aisu and his other top retainers, issuing orders, collating secret records, and drafting communications to be sent by express messenger to Miyako, while servants packed his baggage. Before dawn the next day, Yanagisawa rode out of the castle, accompanied only by Aisu and a few attendants and bodyguards instead of his usual huge entourage. They'd worn plain clothing without Tokugawa crests, and gained passage through highway checkpoints with documents that identified them by false names. Riding fast, stopping rarely, and sleeping a mere few hours each night, they'd reached Miyako two days ahead of Sano. Yanagisawa's agents had sneaked them into Nijō Castle disguised as carpenters. Yanagisawa and Aisu had made the necessary preliminary arrangements before Sano's arrival, yet the fact that everything had worked out so far didn't negate the inherent dangers of the plan.

Leaving the seat of power, even for a short time, was a perilous move for Yanagisawa. He'd impressed upon the shogun the confidential nature of his mission in Omi Province and the need for only the two of them to know about his absence from Edo, yet he didn't trust the dull-witted Tsunayoshi to keep a secret. He'd sworn his staff to secrecy, threatening them with death should they fail to cover his absence, but what if people discovered he was gone? Yanagisawa pictured subordinates robbing his treasury, his spies taking a holiday from gathering the information he needed, rivals usurping his authority and turning Tsunayoshi against him. And what if the shogun learned that Yanagisawa had lied to him about the reason for this trip? The shogun cherished a deluded belief in his officials' honesty; he wouldn't forgive being tricked. When Yanagisawa got back, he might find himself in utter disgrace, stripped of his rank and wealth, and sentenced to death.

Still, the potential advantages of the move justified the risks. In Miyako, Sano was in a vulnerable position, without his political allies or detective corps to assist and protect him. He wouldn't know to beware of sabotage by Yanagisawa. And operating in secret, away from the shogun and all the spies who scrutinized his every move in Edo, gave Yanagisawa the freedom he needed. Now he brooded, wishing he felt more comfortable with his choice. The smoke from his pipe hung in the stagnant air; ghostly moths flitted around the lanterns. Gongs rang in the distance; the incessant whine of insects came through the open doors. Yanagisawa shifted uncomfortably inside his sweat-drenched clothes. He hated Miyako and its awful heat. He longed to be back in Edo, secure in victory.

"Solving the mystery of Left Minister Konoe's death from behind the scenes won't be easy," he said. "The need to stay hidden until the critical moment presents complications."

However, secrecy wasn't the only problem. Reports from Yanagisawa's Miyako agents indicated that Konoe had been the victim of a bizarre murder. Yanagisawa had never investigated a crime, and he felt handicapped by his inexperience. But he'd set his scheme in motion, and he must follow it through to the end. He must apprehend the killer before Sano did, in a manner that created the impression that he'd happened along during the course of his inquiries in Omi Province, observed that Sano was making poor progress, and stepped in to solve the case. No one must guess that Yanagisawa had come here specifically to beat Sano at his own game, or think he'd won by underhanded means, because he didn't want it publicly known that he'd resorted to such desperate tactics. By the time he was finished, Sano's reputation as a great detective would be his.

"Let's drink a toast for good luck," Aisu said.

He clapped his hands. Female bodyguards—the only attendants allowed in this most private chamber—silently entered the room. On Aisu's orders, they served wine, then silently departed.

Aisu raised his cup and said, "Here's to your victory and the *sōsakan-sama*'s downfall."

Yanagisawa and Aisu drank. From the street drifted the laughter and shouts of the Obon crowds; more gongs clanged. The tart, refreshing liquor invigorated Yanagisawa; he smiled.

Refilling the cups, Aisu proposed another toast: "May you capture Left Minister Konoe's killer the way you did the Lion."

Malice hardened Yanagisawa's smile. "No," he said, "not quite like the Lion. Remember, this time, Sano won't get another chance to redeem himself."

Aisu's hooded eyes glistened; his sinuous body squirmed with anticipation. "How shall Sano die?"

"I don't know yet," Yanagisawa admitted reluctantly. "Nor can I predict the exact outcome of the investigation."

He leapt to his feet and paced the room in a fever of impatient energy. "Everything depends on the case itself. I must see what happens and use whatever opportunities arise. I don't have enough information to take the next step. However, that problem should be remedied very soon." Yanagisawa halted by the door and gazed out at the dark, lush garden, listening for sounds that would herald the arrival of the news he awaited.

"Then I'll decide what to do."

Several long, unproductive hours later, Sano finished interviewing the Konoe clan members. They'd been shocked to learn that the left minister had been murdered, instead of dying from a mysterious disease as they'd thought. They hadn't known he was a *metsuke* spy, and claimed no knowledge about which of the suspects might have killed him. All Sano managed to learn were two stray facts.

A cousin of Konoe's said he'd heard on several occasions a much less powerful version of the spirit cry. Afterward, dead birds had been found in the garden. This confirmed Sano's belief that someone in the palace did indeed have the power of *kiai*. Had he—or she—been practicing for the murder?

Fifteen years ago, Konoe's secretary, a young man named Ryōzen, had been stabbed to death. This was presumably the crime that the *bakufu* had covered up in order to force Konoe to spy for the *metsuke*, but Sano found no apparent connection between the incident and Konoe's murder. Nor did Detectives Marume and Fukida glean any clues from the servants.

Now Sano, Hoshina, and the detectives stood outside Konoe's private chambers, which occupied two adjoining rooms in an inner section of the house. Mullioned paper walls enclosed the space, affording greater privacy than the open plan of classic imperial architecture.

"Has anything in there been disturbed since Left Minister Konoe's death?" Sano asked the courtier who'd admitted him to the estate.

"The rooms have been cleaned, but his possessions are still there," the courtier said. "That's his office. This is his bedchamber." He opened the door, and a musty smell rushed out. After lighting a lantern in the room, he bowed and left.

Sano entered and swept his gaze around the room. The tatami floor was bare; sets of lacquered tables and silk cushions were neatly stacked. Sano saw no personal articles. Presumably, these were inside the built-in storage cabinet and wardrobe.

"Search this room," Sano told his detectives.

"What are we looking for?" Marume asked.

"Anything that can tell us about Konoe's life, what kind of person he was, or his relationships."

Marume began opening drawers in the cabinet. Fukida started on the closet. Sano and Hoshina moved through the connecting door to the office. There, an alcove contained a desk and built-in shelves of ledgers and books. Across the desk, open scrolls covered with calligraphy lay amid writing supplies. The doors of a cabinet stood ajar, revealing compartments full of clutter. A large wicker basket held paper scraps; fireproof iron chests stood three high.

While Hoshina watched, Sano scanned the scrolls on the desk. They concerned repairs to the palace walls. In the drawers Sano discovered Konoe's jade seal and a tobacco pipe and pouch, but no diary. Sano took a ledger off a shelf. It bore the title, "Proceedings of the Imperial Council, Teikyō Year 3." Although Sano doubted that the court archives contained what he was looking for, he examined each ledger for the sake of thoroughness. What a lot of words the imperial bureaucracy generated! Next, Sano went through the cabinet. He found official memoranda from the left minister's colleagues, pronouncements issued by emperors, and long documents describing imperial law and protocol. The trash basket contained scribbled notes about the palace budget.

"If Konoe left behind any records about whom he spied on and what he learned, I don't see them here," Sano said to Hoshina. "Nor is there any evidence of any activities except official business."

"Maybe your men are having better luck," Hoshina said.

But when they returned to the bedchamber, Detective Fukida said, "There's nothing here but clothes, bedding, toiletries, and the usual things that might belong to anybody. All we can tell about Konoe is that he dressed mostly in shades of brown."

"It's as though he lived and worked here without leaving any trace of himself, let alone the reason for his murder or the identity of his killer." Sano shook his head in bewildered disappointment. A murder victim's quarters were usually a source of valuable clues, but never had Sano seen any so devoid of personality. "Let's do a more thorough search."

While Marume cleared out the cabinet and probed the walls, seeking hidden objects or drawers, Fukida lifted the tatami to check for secret compartments in the floor. Sano and Hoshina went into the office. Hoshina sifted through official reports in search of stray personal papers. Sano pulled books off the shelf, shaking each one upside down in case Konoe had hidden something between the pages. Then, on a bared space of wall behind the shelf, Sano saw two horizontal cracks, a hand's span apart, crossing a vertical wooden wall panel. He inserted his fingernail into the top crack and pulled. Out popped a rectangular section of panel. From the shallow space behind it Sano withdrew a sheaf of papers.

"What's that?" Hoshina asked.

Sano examined the documents. "Letters," he replied with a thrill of gratification. "There are more than a hundred in all, with dates going back ten years." So carefully preserved and hidden, the letters might represent the key to the elusive Konoe's life, and murder. All bore the signature and seal of the left minister. All were addressed to the same person: Lady Kozeri, at Kodai Temple.

"Who is Lady Kozeri?" Sano asked Hoshina.

The *yoriki*'s eyes widened in recognition. "After Konoe died, I reviewed the *metsuke* dossier on him." The intelligence agency kept records on all prominent citizens, and Hoshina had again demonstrated his initiative. "Kozeri is his former wife. She left him to become a nun."

Sano scanned a few pages. "These are love letters." As he continued reading, he discovered that the one-sided correspondence consisted of endless variations on the same theme. He read sample passages aloud:

" 'How could you leave me? Without you, every day seems a meaningless eternity. My spirit is a fallen warrior. Anger corrupts my love for you like maggots seething in wounded flesh. I long to strangle the wayward life out of you. I shall have my revenge!'

" 'We are two souls distilled from the same cosmic essence. I knew as soon as I looked upon you. When I held your body close to mine, our union made us one spirit, one self. How can you not value my love and understand that I only did what was right?'

" 'Yesterday I came to you, but you refused to see me. Today another of my letters came back unread. But your attempts to sever our connection will ultimately fail. For I mean to have you, and someday I shall!' "

Hoshina grimaced. "Ten years of that?"

Sano marveled at the strength and longevity of this unrequited love. "Such obsessive passion can be dangerous. Might it have somehow led to Left Minister Konoe's death?"

Hoshina said, "Kozeri left the palace a long time ago. Nuns cease all contact with their worldly lives when they enter the convent, and it sounds as if that's what Kozeri did."

"There are no replies from her to Konoe," Sano admitted.

"Nor have we evidence of any relationship between Kozeri and the left minister besides the one that existed in his mind," Hoshina said. "And remember, there were no outsiders in the compound on the night Konoe died. I can't imagine that Kozeri is relevant to the murder."

Sano again sensed the potential for trouble between himself and the *yoriki*, even as he concurred with Hoshina's logic. Turning to the last page, he silently read more repetitive ramblings of love, lust, and rage that ended with a passionate declaration:

"Resist me, defy me, torture my heart all you wish, but we are destined for each other. Soon the forces of defense and desire will clash upon the lofty, sacred heights where spires pierce the sky, feathers drift, and clear water falls. Then you shall be mine again."

The letter's overblown sexual symbolism offered nothing new, but Sano said, "This is dated just seven days before Left Minister Konoe died. We can't ignore the possibility that Kozeri spoke with him during that critical period, or that she knows something important." He tucked the letters inside his kimono. "I'll call on her after I interview the suspects."

"Yes, *Sōsakan-sama*," Hoshina said, yielding once again. Sano checked the secret compartment for more clues, but it was empty. He and Hoshina systematically dismantled the rest of the office, examining walls, furniture, and ceiling, to no avail. Then Detectives Marume and Fukida joined them.

"We found these sewn inside the padded lining of a winter cloak," Marume said, holding out his open palm. Upon it lay three identical round copper coins. "There was nothing else."

Sano took a coin. Its face bore the crudely stamped design of two crossed fern leaves. The reverse side was blank.

"This isn't standard Tokugawa money," Fukida said, then turned to Hoshina. "Maybe they're local currency?"

Studying a coin, the *yoriki* shook his head. "I've never seen any like these before."

"Marume-*san*, Fukida-*san*: Each take a coin and show them around town tomorrow," Sano said. "I want to know what they are, where they came from, and why Left Minister Konoe had them."

Hoshina slipped the third coin into the leather drawstring pouch at his waist. "I'll make some inquiries, too."

Sano surveyed the shambles they'd made of Konoe's quarters. A sudden tide of fatigue swept over him. "We'd better restore some order here," he said. "Then we'll go to Nijō Manor for food and rest. We've got a long day ahead of us tomorrow."

4

"Is there anything you need, Honorable Lady Sano?" said the wife of Nijō Manor's innkeeper.

A middle-aged woman with bright, avid eyes, she hovered in the doorway of a suite inside the inn's complex of guest chambers. There, enclosed by walls decorated with painted scenes of Mount Mikasa, Reiko peered through the window at the torch-lit courtyard. Since her arrival at Nijō Manor, she'd bathed, changed into a yellow silk dressing gown, dined, and sent her maids to bed. Now she anxiously waited for Sano to come.

"No, thank you," Reiko told the innkeeper's wife, who had inundated her with offers of service all evening.

Still, the woman lingered. "You needn't fear for your safety here," she said, obviously seeking an excuse to stay and misinterpreting Reiko's interest in the view. "We have security guards, and the 'nightingale floors' in the corridors will squeak to let you know if someone's coming. And look!" She bustled across the room and opened a panel in the wall. "Here's a secret door, so you can escape during an attack."

Nijō Manor, a hybrid between a commoner's house and a fortified samurai estate, had been established to fill a need for this unique type of accommodation. Tokugawa law forbade the daimyo to have estates here, thus limiting their contact with the Imperial Court; but Nijō Manor gave the feudal lords a safe place to stay while in Miyako. Yet Reiko, who'd heard the history of the manor from the innkeeper's wife earlier, also craved privacy, which was in short supply.

She realized that she must be the most interesting guest ever to stay at

Nijō Manor, at least in the opinion of the women here. The innkeeper's wife had watched her constantly. The maids had helped unpack her baggage, whispering together as they examined her silk kimonos and exclaiming over the pair of swords she'd brought. Later, Reiko overheard them gossiping:

"I've never heard of a lady with swords!"

"What's she doing here?"

"Let's find out."

When Reiko went to the privy and the bathchamber, giggles and stealthy footsteps followed her. She heard furtive noises outside her window. The innkeeper's wife asked prying questions. Reiko had tried to discourage nosiness by explaining that she'd come to visit Miyako's famous temples—a dull, respectable reason to travel—but the news about the strange lady from Edo spread through the neighborhood. When Reiko peered out the gate to look for Sano, a crowd of curious peasant women stared back at her.

Now the innkeeper's wife continued extolling the virtues of Nijō Manor. Through the window Reiko saw the maids in the courtyard. They waved to her, tittering. Reiko fought annoyance as she waved back, then forced herself to smile at the innkeeper's wife. If there proved to be no part for her in Sano's investigation, she would be stuck here; she mustn't antagonize these women, because servants could take their revenge in small, aggravating ways.

The inn's floors and ceilings creaked as guests settled in for the night, their talk and laughter a continuous background noise. The night's humid warmth oppressed Reiko's spirits. Sano had warned her that she might have less freedom in Miyako than in Edo, where she had friends and relatives to visit, things to do, and a certain independence. In Edo, she also had her network to consult during investigations. Here she felt alone and helpless. She would go mad with boredom unless Sano found occupation for her.

At last she heard the voices of Sano and Detectives Marume and Fukida in the corridor. Quickly she said to the innkeeper's wife, "Please prepare my husband's bath and dinner."

The woman hurried off to obey. Sano entered the room, carrying a clothbound ledger. Fatigue shadowed his face, but he smiled at Reiko. Feeling the stir of desire and affection that his presence always evoked, she murmured, "Welcome."

Sano studied her anxiously. "I'm sorry I had to leave you. Is everything all right?"

That his immediate concern should be for her, even when he had serious business on his mind, filled Reiko with love for him. "Everything is fine," she said, forbearing to mention her own troubles. "I want to hear all about what happened, as soon as you've had time to relax."

After he'd bathed and dressed in a cool cotton robe, they sat together in their room. The maids brought Sano a meal tray containing clear broth, grilled river fish, pickled radish, and rice. While he ate, he told Reiko the circumstances of Left Minister Konoe's death.

"So it was murder," Reiko said, relishing the challenge of a hunt for a killer, "and an actual instance of death by *kiai*! This is going to be a very interesting case."

"And a difficult one," Sano said. He paused, using his chopsticks to pick bones out of the fish. "Hopefully, I'll soon have some clues, as well as statements from suspects, and we can discuss them. Your ideas will be very helpful."

A cautious note in his voice set off a warning signal in Reiko's head. Unhappy comprehension deflated her excitement. "Discussion and ideas— is that all you're going to allow me to contribute to the investigation?"

"Please don't get upset," Sano said, laying down his chopsticks as his troubled gaze met her appalled one. "Let me explain."

The disappointment was more than Reiko could bear. "But I should help search for clues and interview the suspects and witnesses. To develop any useful ideas about the murder, I need to see the people and places involved." Tradition forbade a wife to argue with her husband, but Reiko and Sano had a marriage that strained the bounds of convention. "Have I come all this way to sit idle while you toil alone?"

"I brought you here to protect you," Sano reminded her.

"From Chamberlain Yanagisawa, who is far away in Edo."

"From grave peril," Sano said. "And this investigation has great potential for that."

Yet Reiko preferred peril to boredom. "I've worked on murder cases before. This one is no different. I'm not afraid."

"You should be," Sano said somberly, "because this case is indeed different. The power of *kiai* makes this killer more dangerous than an ordinary criminal."

"The killer is no more dangerous to me than to you," Reiko said. Exasperation rose in her. With an eleven-year age difference between them, Sano often seemed like an overprotective father. "Your greater size and strength are no defense against a spirit cry."

"My many years of martial arts training are," Sano said. "I've practiced rituals for strengthening the will. A strong will is the foundation for the power of *kiai*, and the only weapon against it."

Reiko lifted her chin and squared her shoulders. "Do you think that just because I haven't lived long enough to study as much as you have, it means my will is weak?"

"Not at all," Sano said with a wry smile.

"Rituals you've never had a chance to test won't guarantee your safety if the killer attacks you," Reiko retorted. "Nor will your sex or rank. The killer's victim was male, and the highest official in the Imperial Court."

Sano picked up his soup bowl, then set it down. "There are also practical reasons I can't include you in the investigation. You couldn't go to the crime scene with me today. I can't take you along on my inquiries tomorrow. For a samurai's wife to follow him around, involving herself in official business—you know it just isn't done." His regretful expression told Reiko that he sympathized with her position, even as he defended his own. "I'm sorry."

"There must be something I can do," Reiko persisted. "Are there any witnesses to interview?"

"Not yet."

"What about suspects?"

"That ledger I brought contains *Yoriki* Hoshina's report on the investigation he did before we got here. He's cleared most of the palace residents of suspicion by confirming their alibis. But there are some people whose whereabouts at the time of the murder remain unknown. One is Emperor Tomohito, and another his cousin Prince Momozono." Sano explained that they'd discovered the body, then said, "I can't subject them to questioning by a woman. It would be a gross impropriety."

Reiko nodded, sadly conceding Sano's point. She saw the murder case moving farther and farther beyond her grasp. Nevertheless, something that he'd said gave her hope.

"If the emperor is one suspect and the prince is another," Reiko said, "then it sounds as though there are additional suspects. Who are they?"

"The emperor's mother, Lady Jokyōden, and his consort, Lady Asagao."

From the chagrin on his face, Reiko could tell that Sano hadn't wanted to tell her. "It wouldn't violate any customs for the wife of the shogun's representative to call on the women of the Imperial Court," she said, so delighted by this turn of events that she forgave Sano's attempt to conceal information. "I'll go tomorrow."

"Even though it's socially acceptable for you to visit Lady Jokyōden and Lady Asagao, there's still the threat of danger," Sano said. "I don't know of any historical incidences of a woman having the power of *kiai*, and it seems likely that the murderer is a man, but we can't yet rule out the possibility that the emperor's mother or consort killed Left Minister Konoe. For you to go prying into their business is too big a risk."

"The Imperial Court doesn't know that I help you with investigations," Reiko said. "When I visit the women, they'll think it's just a social courtesy."

"If they guess your real purpose, the consequences could be fatal," Sano said.

The room's cozy atmosphere chilled and darkened with the memory of a recent time when a killer had seen through Reiko's false pretenses while investigating the murder of the shogun's favorite concubine. Stifling a shiver, Reiko involuntarily placed a hand on her abdomen, where a new, fragile life might have just begun. She read in Sano's eyes his resolve to prevent another disaster.

"I've learned a lot since then," she said. "I won't let the emperor's mother and consort guess that I know they're suspects. Besides, women speak more frankly to one another than to men. Court ladies are probably unaccustomed to meeting samurai officials. I have a better chance of getting the information you need."

Sano nodded in reluctant agreement, then frowned, placing his chopsticks together across the center of his rice bowl and contemplating the equally divided contents.

Reiko sensed in him the struggle between love and duty, between caution and the need to employ every possible method to solve the case. Taking Sano's strong, hard hands in her small, slender ones, she said, "When we married, our lives and our honor were joined forever. I want to deliver the killer to justice as much as you do. For good or bad, I share your fate. Shouldn't I do everything in my power to bring us success?"

They shared a long look. Then Sano clasped Reiko's hands, expelled a breath, and nodded, his misgivings obvious. But triumph filled Reiko. She had enough faith in their partnership for both of them.

At Nijō Castle, a servant entered the White Parlor, bowed, and said to Chamberlain Yanagisawa, "Your visitor has arrived."

"Good. I'll receive him in the Grand Audience Hall." Yanagisawa turned to Aisu. "I'll handle this alone."

Disapproval flickered in Aisu's eyes. "But how can you be sure he's trustworthy?" Yanagisawa had been communicating with his chief Miyako agent via written messages; they'd never actually met. But now, with operations under way, face-to-face contact was necessary. "You need protection."

Aisu hated being excluded from important business, Yanagisawa knew; he feared that someone else would steal his master's favor. However, as a general precaution, Yanagisawa never shared all the details of a scheme with anyone, lest too much knowledge give other men power over him. Thus, he didn't want Aisu at this secret meeting between himself and the man through whom he would achieve his purpose.

"No one would dare attack me here," Yanagisawa said. "You're dismissed. I'll see you tomorrow."

"Yes, master." Aisu bowed resentfully.

In the Grand Audience Hall, a mural of gnarled pine trees on a gilt background decorated the wall behind the dais. Carved peacocks graced transoms; on the coffered ceiling, painted flowers glittered in the flames of many lanterns. Doors with ornate tassels marked rooms where guards stood watch. Exterior sliding walls were open to a garden landscaped entirely without trees, so that falling leaves could not evoke thoughts about the transience of life or political power. Indian lilac sent a smoky perfume into the castle.

Chamberlain Yanagisawa sat upon the dais. An attendant opened the door at the distant opposite end of the room and announced, "The Honorable Hoshina Sogoru, senior police commander of Miyako."

Toward Yanagisawa strode the tall samurai, clad in a dark cobalt kimono. As *Yoriki* Hoshina neared the dais, the sight of his powerful build and handsome, angular face caused a flash of sexual desire in Yanagisawa. Hoshina's heavy-lidded eyes regarded Yanagisawa with speculative interest. Then his full lips curved in a brief, bold smile. Yanagisawa instinctively recognized Hoshina as a man who liked men—and shared his attraction.

"Welcome," Yanagisawa said, marveling that written words conveyed so little of the writer's person. The *yoriki*'s businesslike letters describing the circumstances of Left Minister Konoe's death and the results of his preliminary inquiries hadn't prepared Yanagisawa for meeting Hoshina in the flesh.

Hoshina knelt before the dais and bowed. "Thank you, Honorable Chamberlain. It's a privilege to serve you."

"Did anyone see you enter the castle?"

Contemplating the *yoriki*, Yanagisawa admired the sculpted muscles of Hoshina's arms and chest. He'd spent the past nine months trying to forget his dead lover Shichisaburō, but although he'd gone through scores of partners, male and female, none had banished the memory of losing the only

44

person who had ever loved him. Now, however, Hoshina might prove to be a welcome diversion. Still, Yanagisawa sensed danger in their attraction.

"I don't think so," Hoshina said. "I came alone, through the back gate, as you ordered." A glimmer of mischief brightened his somber gaze, as if he'd read Yanagisawa's thoughts.

He had a good opinion of himself, Yanagisawa thought, but not unjusti- fiably. Hoshina had first come to Yanagisawa's attention three years ago. Local *metsuke* spies had recommended the *yoriki* as a man of talent whose job put him in a good position to monitor the activities of Miyako's citi- zens. Since then, Hoshina had reported on these in regular dispatches to Edo. Yanagisawa had been impressed with the quality of the information Hoshina sent; routine double checks always proved it reliable. Hoshina was also a competent detective, but it remained to be seen whether he was capable of more difficult, complex work.

"Tell me what happened with Sano today," Yanagisawa said.

"I took him and his detectives to the Imperial Palace to see where Left Minister Konoe died."

Hoshina lowered his eyes respectfully, but Yanagisawa could feel the *yoriki* taking measure of him. No doubt Hoshina knew all about the enmity between himself and Sano. Yanagisawa guessed that the *yoriki* had also done some research on him. He noted Hoshina's immaculately knotted and oiled hair, and the elegant silk kimono patterned with silver trees and rivers: Hoshina had groomed himself for this occasion.

"Did you win Sano's trust?" Even as Yanagisawa recognized Hoshina's ploy as one he himself had used on the shogun, he admired the *yoriki*'s daring.

"As much as possible," said Hoshina. A note of pride, veiled with mod- esty, echoed in his voice. "He clearly knows better than to trust a man he's just met, but he requested my particular assistance. He didn't seem to sus- pect that I'm anything besides a policeman who wants to advance his career."

"Excellent. I need someone to keep me informed on Sano's progress." Yanagisawa also needed the benefit of Sano's expertise to help him solve the case. "What did Sano deduce from the crime scene?"

"He decided that the sound heard on the night of Left Minister Konoe's death was a spirit cry," Hoshina said. A faint, derisive smile twisted his lips. "But I don't believe that a spirit cry killed Konoe, because *kiai* is just super- stition, and I told Sano as much."

The idea of *kiai* seemed like superstition to Yanagisawa, too. Still, nothing else could explain the condition of the corpse, and he couldn't encourage Hoshina's disturbing tendency to take the initiative and assert himself. "You shouldn't have disagreed with Sano," he said. "I don't want you to antagonize him. From now on, keep your opinions to yourself."

Bowing his head, Hoshina said, "Yes, Honorable Chamberlain. Please forgive me."

"Very well," Yanagisawa said, mollified. He mused, "I'm sure there will be some circumstance of the case that I can use as a weapon against Sano. What did you tell him about the murder?"

"I said I'd done a preliminary investigation and identified Emperor Tomohito, Prince Momozono, Lady Jokyōden, and Lady Asagao as suspects," Hoshina said, "just as your message ordered. He knows there was a cover-up by the Imperial Court, and that Konoe banned everyone from the Pond Garden that night."

Yanagisawa nodded his approval. "Much as I dislike making things easy for Sano, you had to convince him that you're competent and honest by giving him useful information that will stand up to any checking he may do. But you didn't tell him about your other findings, did you?"

"No, and I'm sure he doesn't even suspect that there are any."

Yanagisawa smiled. The withheld information, which he deemed more valuable than what Hoshina had revealed to Sano, gave him an advantage over his enemy. "What else happened?"

"Sano interviewed the Konoe household," Hoshina said.

"And?" Although Hoshina had made discreet inquiries among the victim's associates before Sano arrived in Miyako, it was possible that Sano had turned up clues that Yanagisawa wouldn't want him to have.

"It was a waste of time."

"I suppose Sano inspected Konoe's chambers." Yanagisawa had sent Aisu to search Konoe's house and remove everything of potential interest prior to Sano's visit. Several chests of papers were now in Yanagisawa's possession. "He didn't find anything important, did he?"

Hoshina hesitated, then said, "Actually, he may have." Seeing Yanagisawa's frown, the *yoriki* hastened to add, "There were things hidden in places that would have been overlooked, had Sano not searched as thoroughly as he did. It's understandable that your man missed them."

The news of yet another mistake by the formerly reliable Aisu infuriated Yanagisawa. He couldn't afford to tolerate errors, and he must find a new chief retainer soon.

"Sano found some letters in a secret compartment," Hoshina said. "They were written by Left Minister Konoe to his former wife, Kozeri."

"Kozeri. Ah. Yes." Yanagisawa recognized the name from Konoe's *metsuke* dossier. "What did the letters say?"

Hoshina described the passages that Sano had read aloud. "Unfortunately, Sano took the letters, and I was afraid he would get suspicious if I objected."

Perceiving a possible connection between Kozeri and the murder, Yanagisawa fumed at the thought of such valuable information in Sano's hands.

"I pointed out reasons he should consider Kozeri irrelevant to the case," Hoshina said. "He won't ignore her, but I managed to convince him to put off following up on her until after he interviews the suspects."

"Good," Yanagisawa said. Perhaps Hoshina's initiative was an asset rather than a liability; his quick thinking had bought Yanagisawa time to send someone to investigate Kozeri before Sano could. Admiration for Hoshina increased Yanagisawa's desire, although another man's wits had never attracted him before. His past lovers had been young maidens, adolescent boys, or frail, older men like the shogun—all physically smaller and weaker than himself, and intellectually inferior. The unexpected departure from habit troubled Yanagisawa.

"What else did Sano find?" he asked Hoshina.

The *yoriki* reached into the pouch at his waist and removed a small object. Yanagisawa extended his open palm; Hoshina reached up and placed a coin in it. Their hands touched. The warm contact of flesh against flesh startled Yanagisawa; he stifled a gasp. For an instant, their gazes held. Hoshina smiled uncertainly, his boldness vanished. Something incomprehensible passed between them. To hide his confusion, Yanagisawa examined the fern-leaf design on the coin.

Hoshina sat back on his heels. "There were three of those hidden in Konoe's cloak." Rapid, audible breaths punctuated his speech. "Sano's detectives have the others. When Sano told them to find out what the coins are and whether they have any relevance to the murder, I said I would make some inquiries too. My contacts in the city should give me an advantage over Marume and Fukida."

"Whatever you learn, report it to me, not Sano." Recovering his composure, Yanagisawa said, "What are Sano's plans for tomorrow?"

"I'm taking him to the palace to interview Emperor Tomohito, Prince Momozono, Lady Jokyōden, and Lady Asagao," Hoshina said, his voice steady now. They regarded each other coolly, master and servant again—at least on the surface. "In the evening, we'll attend the *shoshidai*'s banquet."

Yanagisawa mentally arranged his plans around these events, then said, "Have you located a site that meets the criteria I specified in my message to you yesterday?"

"Yes, Honorable Chamberlain." Hoshina described a certain house and its location.

"That sounds just right," said Yanagisawa. They finalized plans for Yanagisawa to pursue the major lead in the case, while Sano investigated the minor ones for him, with Hoshina as his eyes and ears. "Be ready to report everything to me tomorrow night. I'll let you know the time and place."

Then a thought occurred to Yanagisawa. "What has Lady Reiko been doing?"

"Staying in Nijō Manor. The innkeeper's wife is my informer, and I've ordered her to watch Lady Reiko. So far, she hasn't done anything of interest."

However, Yanagisawa knew enough about Reiko to doubt that Sano had brought her all this way just to keep him company. "I want to know where she goes, whom she sees, and what she does."

"Yes, Honorable Chamberlain."

Their business was finished, but Yanagisawa didn't utter the command to dismiss Hoshina. Outside, a distant temple bell tolled the hour of the boar. Hoshina waited, watching Yanagisawa. Neither moved nor spoke, but their silence clamored with questions, expectancy, and the inaudible, accelerating pulse of blood.

Then Hoshina said, "Honorable Chamberlain. . . . If there's anything else you wish of me . . ." His voice was quiet, his expression somber yet highly charged. "I would be more than happy to provide it."

The sexual innuendo inflamed Yanagisawa, but Hoshina's nerve affronted him. How dare Hoshina make the first move toward a personal relationship? That was Yanagisawa's prerogative.

"Would you?" Yanagisawa said sharply. "And what do you expect in return? Wealth? Property? A position on my staff?"

Though he guessed that Hoshina wanted all those things, the *yoriki* spread his hands and said nonchalantly, "Just a chance to prove I'm worthy to serve you." Then he leaned forward, staring at Yanagisawa with unmistakable intent. "And the honor of your company."

In the past, Yanagisawa had shunned ambitious lovers who sought to use him for personal gain, but Hoshina's bold proposition tempted him strongly. He rose, stepped down from the dais, and stood over Hoshina.

The *yoriki*, still kneeling, gazed up at him, muscles tense, eyes feverish with need and ambition.

"I'll see you tomorrow," Yanagisawa said abruptly, then strode toward the door without a backward glance. But he felt Hoshina's gaze on him, and the ache of frustrated desire. Despite the fear of treachery, he looked forward to their next meeting.

5

Above the Imperial Palace rose a sky of pale, bleached blue; glaring white sunlight bathed the crowds that thronged Teramachi Avenue. A small procession drew up to palace gate reserved for *bakufu* officials. At the front rode Sano and *Yoriki* Hoshina. Behind them marched a few guards; then came Reiko in her palanquin.

Earlier, when Hoshina had arrived at Nijō Manor to escort him to the palace, Sano had said, "My wife is coming along to call upon the emperor's mother and consort."

To his relief, Hoshina had accepted without question this explanation for Reiko's presence. Hoshina merely said, "I'll send a messenger ahead to tell the imperial women to expect a guest."

Now Sano and Hoshina dismounted; palace sentries opened the gate. Inside the walls, the procession divided as Sano and Hoshina headed toward the imperial enclosure for an audience with the emperor, while a courtier led Reiko's palanquin down another passage. The odors of sewage, charcoal smoke, and tropical flowers saturated the air in the passageways of the *kuge* district like warm, fetid breath; stormclouds layered the hills visible beyond the city. But in spite of the hot weather, Sano felt refreshed and energetic. A good night's sleep had renewed his confidence. Surely, his investigation would be successful, and he'd made the right decision by agreeing that Reiko should assist him.

In the southern sector of the imperial enclosure stood the Purple Dragon Hall, site of important court events. The austere half-timbered building faced a courtyard bounded with covered corridors supported by vermilion posts. The ground was covered with white sand to reflect the light of the sun and moon onto the hall. A cherry tree and a citrus tree flanked the entrance, representing the guardian archers and horsemen of ancient tradition. Leading up to the door, eighteen steps, framed by red balustrades, symbolized the number of noble ranks in the court hierarchy. Sano and Hoshina approached the bottom of the steps, where a line of courtiers waited. One, a man in his sixties with short, sleek gray hair, stepped forward and bowed.

"Greetings, *Sōsakan-sama*," he said in a strong, resonant voice. He wore a black cap with a vertical flap at the back, a moss green silk court robe, and baggy white trousers. Deep lines creased his forehead and bracketed his mouth, giving character to a long, elegant face. He had shrewd, intelligent eyes, and teeth dyed black in the ancient court style. "It is a singular honor to receive such a great personage as yourself."

Yoriki Hoshina introduced the courtier to Sano: "Allow me to present the honorable Right Minister Ichijo."

"Many thanks for consenting to act as intermediary in my dealings with the Imperial Court," Sano said, although the right minister had no choice but to serve his needs. Ichijo's aura of refinement commanded respect and disconcerted Sano. From studying history, he knew that the man's noble lineage went back a millennium, to a time when his own ancestors were peasants and the samurai class hadn't yet emerged from the ranks of primitive tribal chieftains. Ichijo was a member of the famous Fujiwara clan that had once dominated the Imperial Court. Their era had produced masterpieces of painting and poetry; their name was still synonymous with culture and prestige.

"His Majesty the Emperor awaits you," Ichijo said.

As Sano mounted the steps, flanked by Ichijo and Hoshina, he experienced a vast sense of awe. He, like all Japanese, revered the emperor as a direct descendant of the Shinto sun goddess Amaterasu. The emperor could invoke her power on behalf of human affairs; he had a special ability to perceive the moral order of the universe and impose it upon society. In the cosmic scheme of Confucian tradition, Japan's military dictatorship was just an instrument through which the emperor ruled.

They paused in the entranceway to remove their shoes, then proceeded to the audience hall. Sunlight streamed in through latticed windows. A long white mat bridged the polished cypress floor. Ichijo led Sano up this, between rows of kneeling courtiers. More attendants knelt by the imperial throne. This was an elaborate, cushioned lacquer seat inside an octagonal pavilion canopied with silk curtains and elevated upon a railed platform. A huge gold phoenix surmounted the throne's roof; paintings of Chinese sages decorated the wall behind it. The air smelled of incense.

Right Minister Ichijo knelt before the throne and bowed; Sano and *Yoriki* Hoshina followed suit. "Your Majesty, I present Sano Ichirō, Most Honorable Investigator to His Excellency the Shogun," Ichijo said, then turned to Sano. "I am privileged to introduce to you Supreme Emperor Tomohito, One Hundred and Thirteenth Imperial Sovereign of Japan."

As he and his first murder suspect faced each other, Sano hid his surprise. He'd known the emperor was only sixteen and had ascended the throne upon his father's abdication four years ago; therefore, Tomohito's extreme youth didn't shock Sano. However, the emperor seated within the pavilion looked nothing like his elegant formal portraits. Big for his age, Tomohito wore a purple robe stamped with gold imperial chrysanthemum crests and a tall black cap. He had a solid, muscular build, but his face was childishly round, with full, rosy cheeks and mouth, smooth brow, and bright eyes. He regarded Sano with the insolence of a misbehaving youngster who is too big for anyone to punish.

Right Minister Ichijo said, "*Sōsakan* Sano is investigating the death of Left Minister Konoe, and he would like to ask you some questions, Your Majesty."

"Oh?" Tomohito asked truculently. "Well, that's too bad, because it is *I* who shall ask questions of *him*."

Sano was shocked by this rudeness, even though he'd been prepared for it. During the ride to the palace, he'd asked *Yoriki* Hoshina to brief him on the suspects. Regarding the emperor, Hoshina had said, "He's been overindulged his whole life. A crown prince's training usually teaches manners and discipline, but it didn't work on Tomohito. He thinks he can do whatever he likes. Hardly anyone in the palace dares to criticize him because of his temper; he threatens to bring down the wrath of the heavens on the country when he's in a bad mood."

Now an uncomfortable silence hung over the Purple Dragon Hall as everyone waited to see how Sano reacted to the emperor's contrariness. Although Sano feared offending the emperor and straining relations between the *bakufu* and the Imperial Court, he needed to establish control over the interview.

"I'll answer your questions on one condition," Sano said. "You have to answer mine."

Tomohito scowled, as if ready to refuse. "Oh, all right," he said grudgingly. Then, with a naughty gleam in his eye, he said, "Is it true that there are places where girls sit in window cages and men can buy them for the night?"

So the great emperor had the same prurient interests as ordinary boys. "Yes," said Sano, "in the licensed pleasure quarters."

"Have you ever been there?" An insinuating grin quirked Tomohito's mouth.

"Your Majesty, I advise you to confine your questions to subjects of a less personal nature," Right Minister Ichijo said. "You don't want to insult the *sōsakan-sama*." *Or the shogun by implication,* said the warning note in his voice.

"He has to answer," Tomohito said. "That was the deal."

"But it's my turn to question you now," Sano told him. "What was your opinion of Left Minister Konoe?"

Tomohito's eyes widened in surprise. Sano deduced that few people ever held him to his word or changed the subject of a conversation without his permission. Then he frowned. "I heard Konoe was murdered. Do you think I had something to do with it?"

Holding up a hand, Sano shook his head. "Remember our agreement."

The emperor gaped. He looked around for help, but when no one intervened, he said sullenly, "The left minister was my adviser since I was a little boy. He taught me how to perform sacred rituals and court cere-monies. He listened to me recite my lessons and made sure I understood everything." Tomohito shrugged. "He was a good teacher."

Sano considered what he knew of the emperor. "There's only a few people he'll listen to," *Yoriki* Hoshina had said. "His mother, Lady Asagao, and Ichijo. Left Minister Konoe also had influence over him, but now that Konoe is dead, Tomohito is worse than ever—acting as if he owns the world, always trying to see what he can get away with." Had the emperor resented Konoe for checking his unruly behavior?

"Now it's my turn to ask something," Tomohito said. "Is it true that there is a very long road from Miyako to Edo that passes through many cities?"

"There are fifty-three village post stations," Sano said, "and the trip takes about fifteen days."

"Fifty-three villages? Fifteen days?" Obviously disconcerted, Tomohito said, "I didn't know Edo was so far. How long would it take to travel across the whole country?"

"Around three months, depending on the weather."

Chewing his lip, the emperor brooded on this fact, then said in a chas-tened voice, "I didn't know that."

Tomohito's ignorance about his nation was understandable, because emperors ventured outside the palace only when natural disasters necessitated the court's evacuation. Tomohito saw few people from outside his court and remained cloistered for good reasons.

First came physical safety. Japan's sacred sovereign must be protected from accidents, attacks, and diseases. Second, his spiritual well-being required isolation from impure things, places, people, or ideas that might pollute his soul. Therefore his education was limited to court tradition and the arts. However, the most important reason was political. The *bakufu* feared that dangerous elements of society might persuade an impressionable sovereign to act against the shogun's regime by establishing a rival government, raising armies, commandeering the loyalty of the populace, and weakening Tokugawa rule. Young Emperor Tomohito was a storm center around which the winds of insurrection could coalesce. Better that he remained secluded and ignorant than be free to realize his inherent power.

"You had lessons and practiced rituals and ceremonies with Left Minister Konoe, and received his advice," Sano reiterated. "He would have criticized your performance, corrected your mistakes. Perhaps he sometimes shamed you?"

Jolted out of his preoccupation with the size of Japan, Tomohito shook his head. "It was for my own good. The left minister wanted me to be the best possible ruler and fulfill my great destiny. I was thankful for his attention."

"Weren't there ever times when you would rather have been amusing yourself than working?" Sano suggested gently. "Did you ever get angry at him for disciplining you, when he was a mere subordinate and you his lord?"

The emperor's face flushed; his eyes turned stormy. "The left minister never made me do anything I didn't want to do," he said defiantly. "He never chastised me. He couldn't even touch me. I obeyed him because I chose to."

"I see."

However, Sano knew that cutting remarks from an older man could wound a tender young ego, and Tomohito's unbidden reference to chastisement suggested that his relationship with Left Minister Konoe had included this element.

"If you think I killed him, you're crazy!" Emperor Tomohito burst out. He leapt off his seat and stood. Fists clenched, he glared at Sano. His eyes darted, as if looking for something to throw. "How dare you accuse me?"

"Is it really necessary to provoke him, *Sōsakan-sama?*" murmured Right Minister Ichijo.

"The forces of the cosmos are mine to command. Insult me, and you'll be sorry!" the emperor shouted.

"Please accept my apologies," Sano said hastily, shocked by this sudden fit of temper, which offered disturbing proof of the emperor's volatile nature. Perhaps Tomohito had argued with Left Minister Konoe in the garden. Did he really have deadly mystical powers, as his threat implied?

"Do you regret the loss of the left minister?" Sano asked Tomohito.

The emperor flung himself stomach-down inside his pavilion, his temper spent and his expression merely sullen now. "I miss him. But I don't need him anymore."

"What do you mean?" Sano said, intrigued by this odd remark.

"Nothing."

Setting his jaw, Emperor Tomohito stared at the floor. Sano waited, but when the emperor didn't elaborate, Sano changed the subject. "I understand that you discovered the left minister's body."

"Yes, that's right," Tomohito said, giving Sano a furtive, wary glance. "My cousin was with me." Then a sly smile brightened his face. "I suppose you want to talk to him, too."

"Yes, Your Majesty." Sano needed to verify the emperor's story, and the cousin might be more cooperative than Tomohito.

Turning to his attendants, the emperor said, "Summon Prince Momozono."

As her palanquin carried her through the labyrinth of the imperial compound, Reiko experienced an odd sense of moving far away from
everyday life, into a place that existed outside time. The archaic costumes
of the people who passed her in the narrow lanes, and the old-fashioned
houses glimpsed through open gates, evoked ancient legends of emperors
and empresses, princes and princesses, nobles and ladies. But the dark
reality of murder overshadowed the romantic past.

Now the old, white-haired courtier led her into a separate compound
within the palace, to a large hall that presided over a quadrangle of connected buildings. The bearers set down the palanquin. Stepping out, Reiko
saw curved eaves shading wide verandas and ornately latticed windows.
Birds winged over trees visible beyond the horizontal ridge of the roofs.

"What is this place?" Reiko asked the courtier.

"It is the Palace of the Abdicated Emperor."

Reiko knew that emperors surrendered the throne for various reasons.
Some did so because of old age or poor health; some preferred to let a successor take over the wearisome rituals while they managed court affairs
from behind the scenes. Others entered monasteries. However, many
were forced off the throne. Strife within the imperial family could depose
weak emperors; bad omens unseated others. When the reign of Emperor
Go-Sai had been plagued by natural disasters, the court had deemed these
evidence of his unfitness as a ruler and ordered his abdication. The grand-
father of the present emperor had clashed with the *bakufu* over the establishment of laws that limited his power; he'd resigned in protest. Reiko

couldn't recall why Abdicated Emperor Reigen, father of Tomohito, had retired.

"Lady Jokyōden spends most days here," said the courtier. "She awaits your arrival."

Mounting the steps, Reiko pictured the emperor's mother as a frail, shy old woman who was hardly likely to possess the power of *kiai*. Reiko smiled to herself, recalling Sano's warnings about danger. At best, she hoped to clear up the mystery of Lady Jokyōden's whereabouts on the night of the murder and cross one suspect off the list.

In the hall's spacious, bare audience chamber, raised wall panels framed a view of a park outside, where maple and cherry trees created cool oases around a miniature mountain from which the former emperor could view the city. Brightly dressed figures strolled; their laughter blended with the tinkle of wind chimes. On the veranda overlooking the park, a man and woman knelt side by side, their backs to the room. A line of seated nobles faced them; servants waited to one side.

"As you will note from these figures, the imperial budget for this year exceeds the funds provided by the *bakufu*," said a noble. "Since we can't reduce expenses without degrading the emperor's manner of living, we recommend selling some more of his poems to the public. Do you approve, Your Highness?"

"He approves," said the woman. "Draft an order for all court poets to write verses for the emperor to copy and sign."

A secretary wrote busily. The courtier led Reiko over to the group and said, "Honorable Abdicated Emperor and Imperial High Council, please excuse the interruption." Conversation ceased as Reiko knelt on the veranda and bowed. "The wife of the shogun's *sōsakan-sama* has come to see Lady Jokyōden."

Abdicated Emperor Reigen gave a weary sigh. In his late thirties, he had a pudgy, placid face; his stout body sagged against cushions that propped him up. He regarded Reiko with calm indifference. "Greetings," he said in a lethargic voice.

Reiko murmured a polite reply, her attention riveted upon the woman.

"How good of you to come, Honorable Lady Sano." In sharp contrast to her husband, Lady Jokyōden sat upright and alert; her cultured voice was brisk. Some years older than the abdicated emperor, she had a smooth, youthful complexion and long, blue-black hair upswept with combs. She was a classic Miyako beauty: slender, long-limbed, with thin, delicate nose and mouth, her eyes narrow ovals beneath high, painted brows. But Reiko detected strength in the body beneath the ivory and mauve silk layers of

Jokyōden's garments. There was intelligence in those lovely eyes, and confident self-possession in the way her pale, tapered hands rested, fingertips together, on top of the ebony desk before her. "Your attention is an undeserved honor for this humble woman."

Reiko's preconceptions about the emperor's mother shattered like the reflection in a pond when a stone drops on the surface. Flustered, she said, "Many thanks for receiving me."

"Please allow me a moment to conclude my business," said Lady Jokyōden. It was less a request than an order, given by a woman accustomed to commanding obedience. Lady Jokyōden turned to the abdicated emperor. "My lord, you will please sign the directive to the court poets?"

Reigen sighed again. "Well, if I must, I must."

The secretary handed over a scroll. Jokyōden inked Reigen's jade seal. Lifting his hand, she molded it around the seal, stamped the document, and gave it back to the secretary. Then she dismissed the nobles, who bowed and departed; servants hoisted Reigen onto a litter and bore him away.

Reiko stared in awe. She'd thought herself daring and clever for helping Sano with his work, but here was a woman who did her husband's thinking for him and gave the orders.

Lady Jokyōden performed the customary welcoming ritual of serving tea. In her curiosity about her hostess, Reiko forgot manners. "How is it that you can conduct business that is usually the province of men?" she blurted.

Filling Reiko's tea bowl, Jokyōden looked momentarily startled. Then she eyed Reiko with heightened interest. The atmosphere between them altered subtly, lifting the social constraints that allowed only superficial talk during formal visits. Jokyōden answered with equal frankness: "My husband has always been disinclined toward physical and mental exertion. He married me because he knew I could act in his stead. Abdicating relieved him of certain duties, but I continue to manage the household for him until our son is ready to do so. The court accepts the situation out of respect for my husband."

"Forgive my impertinence in asking," Reiko said, noting the parallel between Lady Jokyōden's situation and her own: Marriage had brought both of them the chance to exercise their particular talents. "It's just so rare to see a woman in charge."

"It is also rare for the wife of an Edo official to travel to Miyako," said Jokyōden. "May I ask how that came about?"

Reiko experienced a stab of trepidation. Surely Jokyōden knew that Sano was investigating the death of Left Minister Konoe. Would she guess that Reiko was here on Sano's business? Now his warning didn't seem so groundless.

"My husband thought I would enjoy seeing the old capital," Reiko said.

"Indeed." Jokyōden sounded skeptical. "And what is your impression of Miyako?"

"I haven't seen much yet, but it's very different from Edo," Reiko said, glad that Jokyōden hadn't challenged her explanation. "I'm particularly fascinated by the Imperial Palace."

A wry smile touched Jokyōden's lips. "You would find it less fascinating if you had spent your entire life here."

"You've never been outside?" Reiko said.

"On four occasions during my lifetime, when the court was evacuated from the palace because of fires. But I've not left the compound in sixteen years."

Reiko believed that she herself would go mad under such circumstances. "Do you mind very much?"

Her expression serene, Jokyōden shrugged. "Although I sometimes crave different scenery and a wider acquaintance, there's no lack of stimulation here. The palace is the world in miniature, with all the excitement of human drama."

"And crime," Reiko said, seizing the opportunity to turn the conversation to the subject of her interest.

"Then you know something about the murder that your husband is investigating?" Jokyōden asked coolly.

Aware of a sudden tension, Reiko said, "All I know is that the imperial left minister was killed by a spirit cry, in the Pond Garden. My husband prefers that I have nothing to do with his business here, but I can't help being curious. Did you know the left minister?"

"Yes, of course." Abruptly, Jokyōden set down her tea bowl and rose. "Shall we walk in the park?"

They descended the steps from the veranda. Jokyōden was taller than Reiko, her stride quick yet fluid. While they strolled together along a path that wound between trees, Reiko conjectured that Jokyōden had disrupted their conversation because she needed time to think about what Reiko's interest in the murder meant and how to respond. Surely, Jokyōden was wondering if everything she said would be reported to Sano.

Feigning chagrin, Reiko said, "I'm sorry. I shouldn't have brought up the murder." She must convince Jokyōden that she wouldn't tell Sano about their conversation. "My husband would be very angry if he found out I distressed you by prying into matters that are none of my business."

Lady Jokyōden walked in silence, contemplating a group of courtiers who had gathered for a picnic on the miniature mountain. "There's no need for apology," she said at last. Perhaps she'd decided there was no harm in discussing the murder with Reiko, because she explained, "I've suffered no personal loss. I frequently saw Left Minister Konoe when he was advising my son, and I often spoke with him about the administration of the palace, but our relationship was not close."

Reiko could detect no falseness in Jokyōden's neutral tone or manner, yet she understood that the sudden rapport between the two of them didn't preclude dishonesty. Just as Reiko was deceiving Jokyōden, so might Jokyōden be deceiving her.

"What kind of person was the left minister?" In case her interest seemed too avid, Reiko said, "I never knew anyone who was murdered. I'm interested to learn why someone could hate a man enough to kill him."

After a moment's hesitation, Jokyōden replied, "He was more respected than liked. Underneath his handsome looks and charm, he had a selfish, ambitious spirit and a great need for power over other people. He couldn't tolerate anyone defying him, or admit he was wrong."

Those qualities could have easily provoked violence. "How did you get along with him?" Reiko asked.

"We had no quarrels." As they passed under a vine-covered arbor, the sudden dimness obscured Jokyōden's face. "I didn't always approve of the way he managed the palace finances or handled my son, but it wasn't my place to question his judgment. It was my duty to obey his orders."

Yet Reiko observed that Jokyōden's description of Konoe might very well fit Jokyōden herself. Had they clashed over control of the court? If so, Konoe would have won by grace of his rank and sex. Had Jokyōden then taken revenge by killing him?

"Didn't the left minister mind having a woman in a position of influence?" Reiko asked.

"He tolerated the situation," Jokyōden said, "because he knew it was temporary. When the emperor is mature enough to rule the court himself, my efforts will no longer be necessary."

Reiko recalled Jokyōden presiding over the meeting of the Imperial High Council. Maybe Konoe had viewed her as a threat to his own domination of the court. Had she sought to protect her position for however short a time that remained? How much had she gained by Konoe's death?

They emerged from the arbor into the open space around a pond. Jokyōden bent her shrewd gaze upon Reiko, who felt exposed and transparent in the hot sunlight. Surely, Jokyōden could guess what bearing her relationship with Konoe might have upon the murder case.

"Imperial politics can be brutal even though times have changed and courtiers fight over rank and privileges instead of control of the nation," Jokyōden said firmly. "Left Minister Konoe had numerous enemies, including certain high-ranking nobles."

But they, along with almost everyone else in the court, had alibis for the night of Konoe's murder, according to *Yoriki* Hoshina's report, which Reiko had read yesterday evening. "Who do you think killed him?" Reiko asked.

"It's hard to envision any of one's associates as a murderer."

Reiko believed that Jokyōden must have some ideas about potential culprits—if she hadn't killed Konoe herself. As if in idle thought, Reiko said, "The killer must be an expert martial artist, to have mastered the power of *kiai*."

"Indeed he must," Jokyōden said, ignoring Reiko's unspoken invitation to speculate.

"You said 'he,' " Reiko observed. "You believe the killer was a man."

"Only because men have the freedom to move about at will," said Jokyōden, "whereas the imperial women are confined under strict supervision."

Although Reiko saw the logic of this reasoning, she also realized that it benefited Jokyōden, as well as Lady Asagao, by eliminating them as suspects. And the lack of freedom also applied to the emperor, who would be constantly surrounded by attendants and seldom left the palace. That left the emperor's cousin as the killer. Of course Jokyōden would prefer to see Prince Momozono convicted of murder than herself, her son, or his consort.

"Who might have been in the Pond Garden with the left minister that night?" Reiko said, hoping that her interest would pass for natural curiosity.

"Left Minister Konoe had ordered everyone to stay away from the garden. There are very few people who dared disobey him and risk punishment."

Reiko noted Jokyōden's repeated evasion of questions. She realized that Konoe's orders had informed all the suspects that he would be alone in the garden. Had one of them taken advantage of the circumstances? She voiced another possibility: "Perhaps the killer had arranged to meet the left minister for a private rendezvous."

"As far as I know, Left Minister Konoe never told anyone why he wanted the garden to himself," Jokyōden said, gazing at the circular green lotus leaves that covered the pond. She added, "I didn't see him at all that night. The weather was very hot; I couldn't sleep. So I took a walk around the summer pavilion, which is north of the Pond Garden. I was sitting outside, watching the moon, when I heard the scream."

"Did you see anyone else around?" Though aware that these questions might give away her ploy, Reiko needed the answers.

"No. The area around the pavilion was deserted. And I didn't take any attendants with me or tell them I was going out because I desired solitude."

This story explained why Jokyōden hadn't been in her chambers and had no witness to give her an alibi. Still, Reiko found herself pleased that Jokyōden had no apparent motive for the murder. Meeting Jokyōden, she realized with concern, had altered her hopes for the investigation.

She'd come to the palace bent upon pursuing a killer, wanting it to be one of the suspects she interviewed. Now she didn't want Jokyōden to be guilty of murder because she felt a sense of kinship with her. But she couldn't let her feelings toward a suspect compromise her judgment.

Lady Jokyōden's cool voice penetrated her thoughts: "Such a thorough discussion of murder is quite unusual during a social call. Perhaps I'm not the only wife who performs her husband's duties. And perhaps the *sōsakan-sama* need not bother interviewing me, because you've obtained from me the answers that I presume he would ask of me himself."

Alarmed, Reiko was quick to protest. "Oh, but I would never even try to do a man's work." Her earnestness sounded unconvincing even to her own ears. "Whatever information my husband needs, he'll ask for himself. I don't know anything about detection. I just wanted the pleasure of meeting you."

Jokyōden watched Reiko's discomfiture with the amused air of an older sister observing the antics of a clumsy younger sister. "Dare I suggest that you are still hiding behind the false pretenses under which you came here, Honorable Lady Sano?" She laughed, a low, melodic sound. "But perhaps you're not the only one whose motives are ambiguous."

Too flustered to think of a reply, Reiko wondered who'd been manipulating whom. Maybe Jokyōden had sinister reasons for welcoming Reiko and speaking so freely. Had Jokyōden intended for their conversation to be communicated to Sano, so she could plant in his mind the idea that she was innocent? Maybe she meant to prejudice him in her favor by befriending his wife.

Certainly Jokyōden possessed a strong will, the foundation for the power of *kiai*. That she must have known all along that she would be investigated by Sano cast doubt upon everything she'd said.

The crunch of footsteps on the gravel path broke the silence between Reiko and Jokyōden. A maid came up to them, bowed, and said to Jokyōden, "Please excuse me, but His Highness the Abdicated Emperor wishes you to come to him."

Grateful for the chance to escape, Reiko said quickly, "I mustn't impose on your hospitality or interrupt your business any longer. I'll go and pay my respects to His Majesty's honorable consort now."

A ripple of mirth crossed Jokyōden's face, as if she knew what Reiko was thinking. After they exchanged bows, Jokyōden said, "Thank you for a most interesting chat. Will you please visit me again before you leave Miyako? I should welcome the chance to improve our acquaintance."

"So would I. Yes, I'll come back."

While glad of an opportunity to learn more about Lady Jokyōden's possible role in the murder, Reiko glimpsed new dangers ahead. If Jokyōden was the killer, might she perceive Reiko as an enemy to destroy?

7

A series of hoots and yelps sounded outside the Purple Dragon Hall, where Sano, *Yoriki* Hoshina, and Right Minister Ichijo waited with Emperor Tomohito.

"Momo-*chan*!" the emperor called from his throne. "Come in here."

The side door opened. A small, skinny young man, perhaps a few years older than Tomohito, entered. He approached the emperor with a jerky stride. The strange noises issued from his mouth; his head tossed like a horse's. As he knelt near the throne, courtiers looked away from him; their mouths tightened with the disgust usually accorded cripples. Sano stared, unable to hide his shock.

"My cousin, Prince Momozono," the emperor announced.

Right Minister Ichijo whispered to Sano: "The prince is a hopeless idiot who can't control himself."

But Momozono was clearly trying. His jaws clenched in an effort to silence the sounds; his mournful eyes rolled. Sweat beaded his thin, pallid face. When he bowed to the emperor, his left arm suddenly shot up into the air. He forced it down with his right hand.

Tomohito said, "Momo-*chan*, this is *Sōsakan* Sano," with an impudent glance at Ichijo and the attendants, as though he enjoyed subjecting them to his cousin's loathsome presence; he didn't seem to share their disgust. "He wants to find out who killed Left Minister Konoe."

"I b-beg to be of assistance," said Prince Momozono. He let out more hoots, then cried, "A thousand apologies!"

On the way to the palace, when Sano had asked Hoshina about the prince, Hoshina had said, "Momozono is the emperor's pet." However, the *yoriki*'s description of the prince had failed to prepare Sano for the appalling spectacle of him.

"The two of you discovered Left Minister Konoe's body together?" Sano addressed the emperor, too startled to think of communicating with his cousin.

Right Minister Ichijo said, "Really, Your Majesty, I don't think it's necessary for Prince Momozono to be present." Distaste curdled his polite tone. "You can answer the *sōsakan-sama*'s questions by yourself."

"Momo-*chan* can stay if he wants," the emperor said. Turning to his cousin, he said, "Do you?"

"Yes, p-please!" Prince Momozono's hands flapped.

Sano observed the devotion in his eyes and the entreaty in his voice: The "pet" adored its master. Pity alleviated Sano's initial repugnance. Sano also perceived shame in Momozono's blinking eyes: He had the wits to know how repulsive he was.

Folding his arms, Tomohito glared down at his subjects. "If any of you don't like it, *you* can leave."

No one did. In a low aside, Ichijo said to Sano, "Please pardon the inconvenience."

"That's quite all right." Sano understood the embarrassment that having an idiot in their midst must cause the Imperial Court, even while he regretted their cruel attitude toward Momozono. He said to the boys, "Tell me how you happened to find Left Minister Konoe's body."

While Momozono hooted and tossed his head, Tomohito said, "We heard a scream in the garden, so we went to see what it was. We saw the left minister lying by the cottage."

"Did you see anyone else there?" Sano asked.

"Everyone c-came right after us," Momozono said.

"Not then, but when you first arrived," Sano said, noting the boy's surprisingly clear, cultured speech. Upon closer examination, Sano saw that Momozono had a well-proportioned body; the spasms gave the false impression of physical deformity. His fine features might have been handsome, if not for the strain of trying to control himself. "Was there anyone in the garden already?"

"I don't think so," Tomohito said. "But it was dark, and we hardly had time to look around."

"Did you hear anything?" Sano asked.

"People r-running and shouting," Prince Momozono said. His mouth twitched violently.

The prince wasn't an idiot after all, Sano realized. Momozono's attempts to direct the conversation away from the time he and Tomohito had spent in the garden before the others arrived suggested that he understood the implications of their finding Left Minister Konoe. For the moment, Sano allowed the diversion. "So the whole court gathered in the garden. Was your mother there, Your Majesty?"

"Yes," Tomohito said impatiently.

"And your consort?"

"As Momo-*chan* said, everyone came."

Sano hoped that Reiko would learn more about Lady Jokyōden's and Lady Asagao's movements that night. Perhaps one of the women had murdered Konoe, then joined the crowd in the garden. Yet the same possibility applied to Tomohito and Momozono, with stronger justification. They'd been first to reach Konoe; therefore, they must not have been far away when he died. They could have pretended to discover the body together, after one of them had killed Konoe.

"Where were you before you went to the garden?" Sano said.

"In the study hall," Emperor Tomohito said.

Sano watched his hands begin to fidget. "Doing what?"

"Playing darts," Tomohito said, picking at his fingernails.

"At midnight? Why so late?"

Though Tomohito unflinchingly held Sano's gaze, his fingers picked faster. "I just felt like it."

"Your cousin played, too?" Sano said in disbelief. He imagined Prince Momozono wildly flinging missiles in all directions. He caught himself committing the same error of judgment as the court by presuming that Momozono's affliction rendered him a complete mental and physical cripple. Yet surely Momozono lacked the self-control necessary to master the power of *kiai*. Of the two boys, Tomohito was far and away the better suspect.

"Yes. Well, I mean, Momo-*chan* watched me play. I scored three perfect shots."

"Was anyone else with you?"

"No. But we were there." Tomohito's belligerent tone dared Sano to doubt him. "Both of us. Together."

"I see." Sano appraised Tomohito's nervousness and observed that Momozono had remained perfectly quiet during the exchange. It was obvious that they were lying. Sano considered pressuring them into telling the truth, but he saw the danger of doing so.

Understanding Japan's political climate, he could predict what would happen if he discovered evidence against Emperor Tomohito and charged him with murder. Tomohito would deny the allegation and accuse Sano of framing him. The Imperial Court would support his claim, while the *bakufu* sided with Sano, causing a rift between the nation's military and spiritual institutions. Emperor Tomohito would denounce the shogun's regime, withdrawing the divine sanction that only he had the power to confer. With the legitimacy of the government destroyed, upheaval would result. Discontented citizens would rebel. The daimyo, eager to take advantage of the situation, would mount a war to overthrow the government.

Whether they succeeded in establishing a new regime, or the Tokugawa managed to maintain control, Sano would be blamed for bringing disaster upon Japan.

"I'm bored with all these questions," Tomohito said peevishly, gnawing at his fingernails while Prince Momozono yelped and jerked. "Are you finished yet?"

Nor could Sano avoid trouble by focusing his efforts on Prince Momozono. While Sano doubted that the Imperial Court or the *bakufu* would care what happened to Momozono, he shared Tomohito's alibi; breaking it would cast aspersion upon the emperor. Sano's honor depended upon solving this case, but he dreaded the prospect of arresting Tomohito. He fervently wished the emperor's mother or consort would turn out to be the killer.

"I'm finished for now, Your Majesty," Sano said.

After leaving the emperor, Sano, *Yoriki* Hoshina, and Right Minister Ichijo gathered outside the Purple Dragon Hall.

"I understand that you wish to see Lady Jokyōden and Lady Asagao," said Ichijo. "Shall I take you to them?"

"Not yet," Sano said, preferring to wait until he'd heard what Reiko had learned from the women. "I'd like to see the study hall and speak with His Majesty's personal attendants." Perhaps he would find witnesses to prove that Emperor Tomohito and Prince Momozono hadn't been in the study hall. If so, he must then challenge their alibi, whatever the consequences. "*Yoriki* Hoshina can take me."

Ichijo hesitated, then said, "Is there anyone else with whom you would like to speak?"

"Perhaps later. Many thanks for your assistance," Sano said, politely releasing Ichijo.

An opaque expression veiled the right minister's features; he bowed in farewell. As Sano walked away with Hoshina, he had a vague, inexplicable sense of hidden dimensions to the case. In his mind floated the disturbing thought that he'd overlooked something important.

A garden of pines, willows, red maple, and flowering shrubs decorated the walled compound where the emperor's consorts lived. As the old courtier walked Reiko through the compound, music and laughter floated in the warm, still air.

"Her Highness the Chief Imperial Consort is amusing herself with her attendants," the courtier said. "She has invited you to join them."

In a courtyard shaded by the wings of buildings, wisteria vines, bright with purple blossoms, climbed lattice frames. A painted mural depicting moonlit woods formed a backdrop for a canopied wooden platform. On this stood a young woman and man. She wore a lavish kimono of crimson silk; floral ornaments adorned her elaborate upswept hairstyle. He was dressed as a peasant in cotton robe and straw sandals. Nearby, three musicians played flute, samisen, and the wooden clappers used in Kabuki theater. Gentlemen and ladies in traditional court garb knelt on cushions in front of the makeshift stage, watching the drama unfolding there.

"The time has come for us to die!" the actor proclaimed with exaggerated passion, seizing his partner's hands.

Sobbing, the woman lamented, "Though in this life we could not be together, in the next world we shall be husband and wife."

The pair stumbled through the imaginary dark forest, clinging together toward a ceramic urn that contained an immense, leafy bamboo plant.

Reiko recognized the play as *Love Suicides at Kamakura*, popular in Edo's theater district some time ago, based on the true story of a prostitute and a potter, forbidden lovers. Standing behind the audience, Reiko watched with amazement while the amateurish attempt at Kabuki—cheap, low-class entertainment—compromised the decorum of the Imperial Court.

"That is the Honorable Lady Asagao," the courtier murmured to Reiko, indicating the woman acting the role of the prostitute.

Reiko's amazement increased as she beheld the emperor's consort. In her early twenties, Lady Asagao had a round face with rouged cheeks, a snub nose, and round eyes accentuated by painted lids. A generous bosom and curvy hips filled out her kimono. That a woman of her exalted status would stoop to such vulgarity!

The actor playing her lover was handsome, with delicate features and a slender build. He led Lady Asagao to the bamboo plant and cried, "Let us make our end, in the shadow of this bamboo thicket!"

He knelt by the urn. Lady Asagao began to sing:

"Never have we known
A single day of peace—
Instead, the torment of an ill-starred romance."

She minced about the stage, fluttering her eyelids at the actor. Her voice was sweet, but she couldn't carry the tune.

"You must kill me with your hands,
Release me from this torture,
Then follow me into death!"

Falling to her knees beside her lover, she wept, begging, "Please, hold me one last time before I die."

They embraced; a sigh rose from the audience. The actor's hands fondled Lady Asagao, who eagerly returned the caresses. They seemed to be enjoying themselves a little too much, and their ardor embarrassed Reiko.

The actor pulled a wooden dagger out of his sash. "Here's our guarantee that our souls will never part!"

"I'm ready. Be quick!" Lady Asagao closed her eyes and sat up straight.

Weeping, the actor pretended to stab Lady Asagao's chest. She screamed, collapsed, and writhed in simulated death throes. He held her until her moans subsided and she lay still. Then he exclaimed, "My beloved, I shall join you now!" and plunged the dagger into his own breast.

The audience cheered and applauded. The doomed couple lay immobile for a moment, then stood and bowed, laughing. Now Lady Asagao caught sight of the newcomers. Her eyes lit. She hopped down from the platform and sashayed over to Reiko.

"Honorable Lady Sano! I'm so happy to meet you," she gushed. To Reiko's escort, she said, "You're dismissed." He obediently departed. Lady Asagao giggled, while her eyes appraised Reiko with the calculating expression of a woman always on the lookout for admirers or rivals. "How marvelous that you've arrived in time for our play. What did you think of my performance?"

"I've never seen anything like it before," Reiko said, striving for a compromise between honesty and flattery.

The dubious compliment provoked delighted laughter from Asagao. "My humble talent hardly deserves such praise! And from you, who have surely been entertained by Japan's best actors. Oh, how I wish I could see them too!" Her full, red lips pouted prettily. "We're so secluded here in the palace, and we must make do with our own little amusements, but we try to be authentic. The stage scenery was made by one of the best court artists. He also designed my costume." She pirouetted in front of Reiko. "Does it become me?"

"Yes, you look beautiful," Reiko said. The kimono was a work of art, although Asagao would benefit from a darker color and simpler pattern to make her look slimmer.

"Oh, thank you! You're so kind." Asagao preened. Beckoning to her audience, she called, "Come meet our guest from Edo." Courtiers and ladies-in-waiting flocked around Reiko, smiling, bowing, and murmuring greetings while Asagao performed introductions. Asagao laid a proprietary hand upon the arm of the actor who'd played her lover onstage. "This is Lord Gojo. He's one of the emperor's secretaries."

The two exchanged a smiling, intimate glance. Then Asagao widened her eyes and exclaimed, "I've just had the most marvelous idea. Lady Sano must take a part in our play!"

"Oh, I couldn't." Horrified, Reiko backed away.

The group greeted Asagao's idea with enthusiasm. Lord Gojo said, "She can be the heroine's best friend."

"But I don't know the lines," Reiko protested, desperate to avoid making a spectacle of herself.

"That doesn't matter," Asagao said. "You can read them from the script for now, and memorize them later." She thrust out her lower lip, her expression reproachful. "You won't disappoint us, will you?"

The petulant whine in Asagao's voice warned Reiko that Asagao was quick to take offense at anyone who denied her wishes. Reiko understood that if she refused to act, the emperor's consort would cut short their visit and she would lose her chance to ask questions about the murder.

"Of course I couldn't disappoint you," Reiko said with forced sincerity. "I'd be honored to act in your play."

"Wonderful!" Asagao laughed and clapped her hands, her good humor restored. Everyone else cheered. Asagao critically surveyed Reiko's simple, knotted hairdo and sea-blue silk kimono printed with pale green ivy leaves. "We'll have to find a costume for you later, but let's give your face and hair some glamour. Come along!"

Asagao and her ladies-in-waiting took Reiko to a corner of the courtyard, where a large parasol shaded a table that held a mirror, brushes, combs, hair ornaments, and jars of makeup.

"Bring us some wine, Gojo-*san*," called Lady Asagao, "then go and prepare the stage for the first scene."

The young man complied. Two ladies-in-waiting began restyling Reiko's hair, while the others drank wine and offered suggestions. Reiko sipped the sweet plum liquor, hoping it would ease her embarrassment. Asagao smeared a mixture of grease and white rice powder on Reiko's face.

"You must think we're frivolous to spend our time this way," Asagao said, pausing to gulp wine from her cup, "but there's so little else to do here, and life gets terribly dull."

Reiko tried not to wince as the warm, thick makeup coated her skin, or recoil from the too-intimate contact with her new acquaintances. "I would have thought that the shocking incident in the Pond Garden offered some diversion."

Asagao looked perplexed; then her face cleared. "Oh, you mean the death of Left Minister Konoe." She dismissed the murder with a flick of her fingers. "That was ages ago. The excitement is past. You probably think I'm callous for having fun during the mourning period, but I refuse to suffer months of gloom and boredom, even though my father says I should."

She added, "My father is Right Minister Ichijo."

Reiko remembered that Ichijo was the man serving as intermediary in Sano's relations with the Imperial Court, and that he'd become its chief official after the death of Konoe. Apparently, he had followed the ancient practice by which nobles achieved dominance over the throne: intermarriage with the imperial family.

"I see no reason to grieve for the left minister," Asagao said, picking up a brush and applying pink tint around Reiko's eyelids, "especially since I'm glad he's dead."

Her blunt admission hung in the air like a bad smell. The ladies-in-waiting suddenly became very busy refilling the wine cups and applying camellia oil to Reiko's hair. Reiko was too startled to speak, but Asagao continued as if unaware of how her words might reflect upon her: "That horrible old tyrant! Do you know what he did to me?"

"No, what did he do?" Reiko said, hiding her eagerness.

"He decided I was spending too much money," Asagao said, puffed up with indignation. "So he reduced my allowance. I was to have no new clothes or amusements for the rest of the year. I, the emperor's consort, was to live like a pauper!"

"It must have been very unpleasant for you." Reiko marveled at her luck in having a suspect so ready to volunteer information. She hinted, "I wouldn't blame you if you had decided to take revenge against the left minister."

"And that's just what I did," Asagao declared, swallowing another drink.

Her words had begun to slur, and her eyes had a glassy shine. Perhaps intoxication had loosened her tongue, Reiko thought, but Asagao seemed the kind of person who often neglected to think before she spoke. What a contrast between the emperor's mother and his consort! The ladies-in-waiting were pulling Reiko's hair upward and jabbing in pins, but Reiko, intent on Asagao, hardly noticed the pain in her scalp.

"First I went to my father, but he said there was nothing he could do; Left Minister Konoe outranked him." Asagao applied rouge to Reiko's cheeks with a sponge. "Then I complained to Tomohito. But Tomohito said I should go along with the left minister and stop wasting money.

"I begged. I cried. I was so angry! Why should he listen to a mere *kuge* official instead of me? Oh, how I hated the left minister for coming between us!" Asagao's voice rose to a querulous pitch.

Reiko nodded and murmured sympathetically. "What did you do next?" she said, her heartbeat quickening with anticipation.

A moment passed in silence as Asagao dipped a small brush into red pigment, moved closer, and began painting Reiko's lips, frowning in concentration. Her features, magnified by proximity, seemed stronger, rendering her less giddily feminine. Reiko stifled an urge to flinch. In Asagao's veins ran the blood of ancestors who had ruled Japan from behind the emperor's throne. To satisfy her appetite for power, might she have studied the martial arts in secret, exercising the spiritual energy that existed in every human, until she acquired the force of *kiai*?

Could the spirit cry have issued from that soft, sensuous mouth?

Asagao drew back, set down the brush, and drained her wine cup again. "I didn't do anything," she said, her expression sulky. "There was no way to get back at the old miser. When he died, I thanked the gods, because now my father is in charge, and he lets me have everything I want."

Disappointment flooded Reiko. She chastised herself for expecting a confession. Lady Asagao might lack Lady Jokyōden's intelligence; yet her vanity indicated an instinct for self-preservation. However, Reiko couldn't quite picture Asagao as the killer. Despite her obvious antipathy toward the victim, Asagao appeared basically weak and flighty. It was easier to believe she had benefited from someone else's crime. But Reiko couldn't eliminate her as a suspect without establishing the important missing fact about Asagao.

"Did you see anything on the night of the murder that might reveal who killed the left minister?" Reiko asked.

"How could I have?" Asagao looked puzzled. "I was nowhere near the Pond Garden."

"Oh? Where were you?" Reiko said casually.

Alarm leapt in Asagao's eyes. Reiko heard a simultaneous intake of breath from the ladies-in-waiting. They sat frozen and stoic, heads bowed.

"I don't remember. It was such a long time ago." Asagao's gaze skittered away from Reiko, then back again, bright with the need to convince. "Wait!" she cried. "I was in the summer pavilion, with my ladies-in-waiting. We were drinking wine and playing the samisen." She looked to the other women, her expression demanding confirmation. "Weren't we?"

With uncertain smiles, the women nodded; yet Reiko didn't need to see their guilty reactions to know they were lying. *Yoriki* Hoshina's report had placed the ladies-in-waiting in their quarters together just before the murder, not with Lady Asagao. And if Lady Jokyōden had been walking around the pavilion as she claimed, she would have noticed the lights and noise of a party. The evidence supported Jokyōden's story and refuted Asagao's.

The consort huffed, "All this talk about murder upsets me terribly. Let's have no more of it." She inspected Reiko, and a pleased smile banished her nervousness. "I think you're ready for the stage." She held up the mirror so Reiko could see herself. "How do you like it?"

Reiko stared at her reflection, aghast. Her hair was sculpted into mounds and coils studded with gaudy floral ornaments. Exaggerated brows arched on her forehead; pink half-moons colored her eyelids. A circle of rouge dotted each cheek, and large, curving red lips masked her own. She looked the exact picture of a low-class courtesan.

"I don't know what to say," she murmured, cringing in shame. Asagao's handiwork disgraced her rank, samurai heritage, and natural modesty. Reiko knew that many men admired the style of prostitutes, but Sano would be horrified to see her this way.

Asagao laughed in delight. "You look beautiful!" The ladies-in-waiting chorused their agreement. "Come along!"

The women ushered Reiko to the stage, which now sported a new backdrop showing a street in the pleasure quarter where the play's doomed lovers had met. Lord Gojo and the other courtiers positioned a large wooden cage that represented the window of a brothel. Asagao, Reiko, and the ladies-in-waiting sat inside this. Someone handed Reiko a silk-covered book.

"We're ready. Let's begin!" Asagao cried.

Courtiers strolled back and forth in front of the window cage, cracking lewd jokes and ogling the women.

"Oh, how this sordid life saddens my spirit," Asagao recited in a tragic voice. "I wish my darling Jihei could buy my freedom and marry me!" She opened Reiko's playbook, whispered, "Your character's name is Snowdrop. Start reading here," and pointed to the correct line.

"How unfortunate that you've fallen in love with a poor potter who already has a wife," Reiko read in a barely audible voice. As a leering courtier approached her, she continued, "Ah, master—the cherry blossoms are in full bloom tonight. Would you partake of their sweetness?"

Flirtatious banter followed. Ready to die of humiliation, Reiko blushed under her makeup. The daughter of a magistrate and wife of the shogun's *sōsakan-sama*, behaving thus! She longed to rush off the stage, yet determination held her captive. Lady Asagao had reason and probable opportunity to commit murder, and still no alibi. If Reiko wanted to find evidence against Asagao, she must stay in the good graces of the emperor's consort.

The play progressed. Between lines, Asagao nudged Reiko and whispered happily, "Isn't this fun?"

9

The merciless afternoon sun illuminated the tile roof and half-timbered walls of the imperial study hall, a small structure within the conglomerate of buildings that comprised Emperor Tomohito's residence. While Sano interviewed the emperor's attendants inside the hall, Right Minister Ichijo stood on the shaded veranda, eavesdropping through the open window. Watching several of Sano's troops pacing through the landscaped grounds between the study hall and the Pond Garden, he was secretly anxious because the *sōsakan-sama* hadn't questioned him regarding Left Minister Konoe's murder.

Was Sano unaware of his relationship with Konoe? Ichijo had no doubt the *metsuke* records described it in detail, and couldn't believe that Sano hadn't targeted him as a suspect. Sano had learned that Emperor Tomohito, Prince Momozono, Lady Jokyōden, and Lady Asagao had been away from their quarters, their whereabouts unknown, at the time of the murder; why didn't he also know that the same incriminating circumstance applied to Ichijo?

Still, Sano's ignorance was a stroke of good fortune, because Ichijo knew that if Sano found out about him and accused him of murder, he would be convicted; virtually all trials ended in a guilty verdict. Ichijo envisioned his distinguished career ending at the public execution ground, amid uproarious scandal. All morning he'd hovered around Sano, listening to the interviews in constant fear that someone would tell Sano what many in the court knew and might reveal if asked the right questions. Although

Sano didn't need his services at present, Ichijo was too anxious to keep track of the investigation to force himself to leave.

Yet he realized that his behavior might provoke Sano's suspicion. Now he forced himself to walk away, out the gate, and down the passage through the *kuge* district toward his residence.

Suddenly, a Tokugawa soldier stepped from around a corner. Solid and grim-faced, he blocked Ichijo's path. "Honorable Right Minister, please come with me," he said.

"Where?" Ichijo said, startled. "Why?"

The soldier merely repeated, "Come with me," in a tone that discouraged refusal.

Alarm seized Ichijo. Every instinct warned him not to go, but disobeying a *bakufu* order would bring harsh punishment. Longing for the days when his ancestors ruled Japan and the power of the Imperial Court was supreme, Ichijo let the soldier escort him out the northern palace gate.

In the street outside waited more soldiers, and a black palanquin manned by four bearers. "Sit inside," the soldier ordered Ichijo.

Ichijo reluctantly complied. When the soldier closed the slatted blinds over the windows of the sedan chair and barred the doors shut, Ichijo's alarm turned to fear. "What's going on?" he called. "Am I under arrest?"

No answer came. The palanquin rose as the bearers shouldered the poles, then began moving at a brisk pace. Ichijo didn't dare try to break out or call for help. He desperately sought a reason for his abduction. Perhaps the *bakufu* did suspect him of killing Left Minister Konoe; perhaps he was on his way to trial. But if so, then why this secretive capture? The Tokugawa usually made a spectacle of criminals as a warning to the public, and *Sōsakan* Sano, officially in charge of the murder investigation, didn't appear to be involved in this. Fighting panic, Ichijo tried to determine where his captors were taking him.

He heard the noise of the crowds on Imadegawa Avenue. Then the palanquin turned right, heading north. Familiar smells of fish and lacquer emanated from some shops, and the noise of saws on wood from others; gongs rang in a shrine. Ichijo deduced that he was traveling along Karasuma Avenue. The motion nauseated him; nervous sweat drenched his body. Soon the traffic noises diminished. The palanquin tilted upward at a gradually increasing angle as it wound into the hills. Birds sang above the bearers' labored breaths and the steady tramp of their feet. Inside the dim, hot compartment, every breath Ichijo drew reeked of his own terror.

Abruptly, the ground leveled. Ichijo heard the creak of a gate swinging on rusty hinges. The bearers set down the palanquin. The door opened, but before Ichijo could glimpse his surroundings, a soldier leaned in and dropped a black cloth sack over his head. Strong hands dragged him from the palanquin.

Gasping in the smothering darkness, Ichijo tried to pull off the sack and struggle free, but the soldiers pinned his arms behind him and marched him across grassy earth. He felt wind whipping his garments, and the heat of sunlight. Then a door slid open. The wind and heat abated as the atmosphere around him condensed into the vacuum of an interior space. The soldiers kicked off his shoes; his feet stumbled along a wooden floor. Ichijo wanted to protest, but in his terror, he feared he would vomit if he tried to speak.

The floor beneath his feet changed to firm, cushioned tatami. The soldiers pushed him down on his knees and let go of him. Their footsteps retreated; a door closed. Ichijo sensed a human presence in the room with him. His panic mounted. He couldn't breathe. Desperately, he tore the sack off his head.

Bright light blinded him. As his vision focused, he saw that he was in a bare, spacious room. Sliding walls stood open to a vista of blue-white sky and hazy green hills bathed with sunshine. Murals depicting similar scenery gave the illusion that the room was an extension of the landscape outside. Then a man moved into Ichijo's view. He was a tall, slender samurai, clad in dark silk robes, swords at his waist. He stood proudly erect; his face had a striking, sinister beauty.

"Who are you?" Ichijo demanded, grasping at a semblance of his usual authority.

The samurai smiled; his intense gaze scrutinized Ichijo. "My apologies for any discomfort or inconvenience you've suffered. Be assured that I wouldn't have employed such an unusual method of conveying you here unless it was absolutely necessary. I am Chamberlain Yanagisawa Yoshiyasu."

Now Ichijo noticed the gold Tokugawa crests on the man's surcoat. "The shogun's second-in-command?" he asked in bewilderment. Fresh terror followed. The chamberlain was the most powerful man in Japan, with a reputation for cruelty. This secretive encounter—in a mysterious location and where no one knew Ichijo had gone—held the possibility for evil beyond imagination. "But . . . I did not know you were in Miyako."

"Very few people do know," the chamberlain said, "and for now, I intend to keep it that way."

"Why?" When important *bakufu* officials came to town, they invariably did so with great fanfare.

"My reasons are none of your concern."

The chamberlain's suave arrogance outraged Ichijo. After he'd been coerced out of the palace, carted away like a piece of baggage, and frightened almost to death, his pride rebelled against further disrespect. Anger gave him daring.

Rising, he said haughtily, "Whatever business you have with me, I prefer to discuss it in my office, under civilized conditions. Therefore, I shall go now."

He turned and started toward the door, but the chamberlain's quiet voice halted him: "I wouldn't advise that. The soldiers who brought you are waiting outside. They'll use force to stop you. You'll suffer much pain and accomplish nothing. So you'd best resign yourself to staying awhile."

Defeated, Ichijo faced his adversary's scornful smile. "What do you want from me?" he said, hating his impotence, hating the whole Tokugawa regime.

"Information," the chamberlain said. He paced a swift circle around Ichijo; his steps wove an invisible snare. "Information regarding the murder of Left Minister Konoe."

With keen interest, Chamberlain Yanagisawa studied his prisoner. Right Minister Ichijo's face was red and sweaty, his gray hair disordered, and his garments wrinkled, but his stance was confident; his noble breeding gave him an unshakable dignity, despite the terror that Yanagisawa's sharp instincts detected in him. Admiration and misgivings stirred in Yanagisawa. Here was an opponent whose defeat would bring him great satisfaction, but he couldn't expect an easy victory. Nor did he know exactly what he would do with whatever information he got from Ichijo.

"Tell me about your relationship with Konoe," he said.

Ichijo's features assumed an impassive expression that didn't quite mask how much he longed to avoid the subject of his dead colleague. He said, "That seems more a matter of concern to *Sōsakan* Sano, who is investigating Konoe's affairs, than to yourself. Why are you treating me this way?"

"Let's just say that I have a personal interest in the case." Yanagisawa recognized a ploy to divert the conversation away from the left minister. He'd thought himself the master of verbal warfare, but Ichijo equaled him. The knowledge rankled, and he found satisfaction in remembering the decline of Ichijo's clan, the Fujiwara.

They'd once controlled huge areas of land by giving protection to the owners in exchange for revenues and loyalty, but as decades passed, they'd squandered their energy on frivolous amusements. Their hold on the provinces relaxed. Revolts broke out in the countryside. The Fujiwara were forced to rely upon the Taira and Minamoto warrior clans to maintain order. Eventually those clans clashed during the Gempei Wars two centuries ago. The Minamoto won the right to rule in the name of the emperor, marking the end of the Fujiwara era and the triumph of the samurai. Right Minister Ichijo and his kind were artifacts of a dead regime.

"Does *Sōsakan* Sano know you're doing this?" Ichijo asked.

His impertinence vexed Yanagisawa. "You're here to answer questions, not ask them," he said. "Stop stalling. Kneel!"

With a look that disdained Yanagisawa and the entire samurai class as crude louts, Ichijo knelt.

"Now tell me about Left Minister Konoe," Yanagisawa said.

A brief pause conveyed Ichijo's opinion that the matter was none of Yanagisawa's business and he would comply only because of the threat of punishment. "Konoe-*san* was wise, diligent, and respectable. A brilliant administrator."

Chamberlain Yanagisawa perceived an artificial note in Ichijo's voice. "You didn't like him, then."

"We were colleagues, and cousins." A faint twitch of the right minister's aristocratic mouth rebuked Yanagisawa for questioning his family affection—the Konoe, too, belonged to the Fujiwara clan. The Imperial Court was a world united against outsiders, but Yanagisawa had a special weapon with which to penetrate it: the *metsuke* reports he'd hidden from Sano and studied during the journey to Miyako.

"I understand that the post of imperial prime minister is vacant," he said.

"Yes, that is correct." A subtle stiffening of Ichijo's posture indicated that he guessed where this was leading. "The last incumbent of that office died this spring."

The prime minister was the highest court official. He acted as chief adviser to the emperor, controlled communications between the sovereign and the five thousand palace residents, and governed the noble class. Power over such a tiny kingdom seemed trivial to Yanagisawa, but he knew it mattered to the nobles, who had nothing else to aspire to because they were barred from engaging in trade or holding real government posts.

"When did the emperor plan to name a new prime minister?" Yanagisawa asked, though he already knew the answer.

"At the end of this month."

"Who were the leading candidates?"

Ichijo hesitated, then said, "Really, Honorable Chamberlain, I fail to see why court appointments should concern you."

"Answer the question."

"Left Minister Konoe and myself were in line to be the next prime minister," Ichijo conceded.

"And which of you was more likely to win the honor?" Yanagisawa said.

"As left minister and head of the senior branch of our clan, my cousin Konoe-*san* outranked me." Ichijo's features had gone rigid. "His Majesty the Emperor would have taken that into consideration, naturally."

"Naturally," Yanagisawa agreed, "but you minded, nonetheless?"

Ichijo glared at him.

Yanagisawa pressed on: "You were superior to Konoe in age, experience, and character." Ichijo's reputation was free of scandal, his career a dull testament to duty. "You deserved to be prime minister, and Konoe considered you a rival. I daresay you didn't appreciate the methods he used against you."

"Whatever are you talking about?"

The sharp, black edges of Ichijo's teeth flashed between lips that barely moved; both menace and fear laced his quiet monotone. An enthusiast of the No theater, Yanagisawa pictured himself and Ichijo as two actors on stage, moving toward a dramatic climax. Beyond the balcony overlooking the hillside, Obon gongs and birds' cries mimicked the music and chorus of No drama. As afternoon slipped into evening, a shaft of coppery sunlight angled through the window, illuminating Ichijo's kneeling figure.

"Konoe circulated rumors among the most influential members of the court," Yanagisawa said. "He claimed that you were getting senile; you'd lost control of your bladder and bowels, and he'd seen you wandering about the city, unable to find your way home. According to Konoe, you were in no shape to be prime minister, regardless of your excellent record."

Indignation burned red slashes across Ichijo's high cheekbones. "I suppose your spies told you what Konoe said. His accusations were nothing but vicious, self-serving slander."

The papers Yanagisawa had taken from Konoe's office had included plans to discredit Ichijo, and copies of reports sent to high court nobles. "Now that Konoe is dead, who will be the next prime minister?"

"The selection process has begun over again, and the outcome is uncertain." Ichijo had regained his composure, and he spoke with chill asperity.

"But who is now the highest court official? Who's in the best position to ingratiate himself with the emperor?"

Ichijo greeted the accusing questions with a thin smile. "In the ancient art of statesmanship, it is unnecessary to belabor the obvious." His tone implied that only a samurai would commit such a sin. "However, I shall answer you. Yes, I shall probably be appointed prime minister."

"Did you murder Konoe to win the promotion?" Yanagisawa demanded, bristling at Ichijo's unspoken insult.

"Your accusation is ridiculous and unfounded," Ichijo said disdainfully, "and since you already think you know so much, you don't need me to answer your questions. It is obvious that nothing I say will change your twisted interpretation of the facts, so why stage this farce?"

While Yanagisawa had considered Ichijo the prime murder suspect from the start, he'd needed to confirm his judgment by meeting Ichijo. He hadn't really expected a confession, although it would have helped. Ichijo's intelligence and forceful character reaffirmed his decision to hide from Sano the facts about the right minister. Yanagisawa could believe that Ichijo's talents included the power of *kiai*. Ichijo and Konoe had been political enemies, and Konoe's death had benefited Ichijo, but other circumstances also implied his guilt.

Yanagisawa said, "The Imperial Court allowed days to pass before notifying the *shoshidai* of Left Minister Konoe's death. I understand that it was your decision to delay news of the murder."

"It was my decision for the court to conduct an inquiry and document the incident before reporting the death."

"Fancy language for attempted deception," Yanagisawa remarked. "Where were you when Left Minister Konoe died?"

"I was in the tea ceremony cottage, where I often go in the evenings," Ichijo said, his manner calm. "My daughter Lady Asagao was with me." He added, "She is the emperor's consort."

Chamberlain Yanagisawa hid his glee at catching Ichijo in an outright lie. According to *Yoriki* Hoshina's report, a young noble and a lady-in-waiting had used the tiny, one-room cottage for a lover's tryst that night. Ichijo and his daughter couldn't have been there at the same time. The right minister knew Lady Asagao was a suspect, and he clearly intended to secure an alibi from someone he could trust to lie for him, and to protect his connection with the emperor.

"If you were in the tea cottage, then you must have heard the scream, and the uproar after Left Minister Konoe's death," Yanagisawa said, "but you didn't go to the Pond Garden to see what was happening, although

Lady Asagao did. When the palace guards went to report the death to you, they couldn't find you anywhere." These were more facts that *Yoriki* Hoshina had withheld from Sano. "Why didn't you appear and take charge?"

"I admit I was negligent." Ichijo sidestepped the question with commendable agility, then said, "If you are so sure I am a murderer, why do you risk antagonizing me?" Black teeth gleamed in his smile. "Are you not afraid I will kill you before you can summon your guards?"

Chuckling, Yanagisawa paced in a narrowing spiral around Ichijo. "Risks are an essential part of life." He refused to betray that he did indeed fear Ichijo. "Besides, you surely realize that my associates know where I am and with whom, as well as all the facts about you. You couldn't get away with killing me."

"Well, then," Ichijo said, rising stiffly and staring down Yanagisawa, "I suppose you will arrest me for the murder."

"Oh, no. You're quite free to go." Yanagisawa clapped his hands; two guards entered the room. He ordered, "Take the right minister back to the palace."

Ichijo stared in astonishment. "But . . . if you're not arresting me, then why abduct me?" Distrust and incredulity mingled in his voice. "Why accuse me, then release me?"

Chamberlain Yanagisawa merely smiled, bowed, and said, "A thousand thanks for your company, Honorable Right Minister." He'd gotten what he needed from Ichijo: the chance to assess the prime suspect, and an idea for the next step in his scheme to solve the case, trap the killer, and destroy Sano.

He sensed Ichijo's desire to escape, but the right minister remained immobile, his calculating gaze fixed on Yanagisawa. "I presume the *sōsakan-sama* isn't aware you're in Miyako because you don't want him to know, and you're the reason he hasn't identified me as a suspect. What if I were to tell him about our talk?"

"That would be a mistake," Yanagisawa said, "because then Sano would focus his investigation on you. If he doesn't discover by himself what I know about you, I'll tell him. Either way, he'll arrest you. So I trust you will keep our meeting a secret?"

Ichijo conceded with a grudging nod. The slight tension of anxiety relaxed in Yanagisawa, because if things progressed according to plan, he needn't interview anyone else, and he'd silenced the only person who might expose him.

10

"I'm troubled about this case," Sano said to Reiko.

Having finished the day's work at the Imperial Palace, they were back in their room at Nijō Manor. While twilight darkened the windows and gongs heralded the start of the evening's Obon rituals, Sano dressed for the *shoshidai*'s banquet, which was for men only. Reiko sat nearby.

"It's only been one day," she said. "You can't expect to solve the mystery so soon."

"I know." As he put on a maroon silk kimono over wide trousers, Sano tried to define his feelings. One of the things he cherished most about his marriage to Reiko was the way their two minds often came up with answers that eluded his lone efforts. At first he'd had a hard time accepting a woman's help, but now it seemed natural to discuss his ideas with Reiko.

"Between us, we've interviewed all the suspects," Sano said, "and they all seem equal in terms of opportunity to commit the murder. Emperor Tomohito and Prince Momozono have only each other for an alibi. Attendants in the imperial residence saw them both before the household retired for the night, but not between then and Left Minister Konoe's death. They might have been in the study hall together, as they claimed—or not.

"Lady Jokyōden says she was alone and heard the spirit cry from outside the summer pavilion. I checked with everyone in the abdicated emperor's household on the chance that someone might have seen or followed her without her knowledge, but no one did. Lady Asagao lied about her alibi, and I haven't been able to find out where she was during the murder, which puts her in the same situation as the other suspects."

"Not quite," Reiko said. "Lady Asagao is the only one with a clear motive—by her own admission, she hated the left minister for cutting her allowance and influencing the emperor against her."

Sano tied a brocade sash around his waist. "But do you really think Lady Asagao is capable of a spirit cry? From your description of her, I don't." Now Sano pinpointed one problem: "In fact, I can't imagine any of these people as the killer."

"Even if Lady Asagao is mentally incapable of mastering the force of *kiai* and Prince Momozono is physically incapable," Reiko said, "the emperor is still a possibility, and so is Lady Jokyōden. Besides, we can't eliminate all the suspects on the basis of a hunch."

"Yes, you're right. . . ." Sano sat and pulled white cotton socks onto his feet. "Still, there's more to my concern than the fact that I'm not satisfied with the suspects. The whole case feels wrong."

"Wrong, how?" Reiko said, her expression puzzled.

Sano stood. "I keep thinking I'm missing something."

"But why? What could it be?"

"I wish I knew." Sano's feeling was like an itch whose location shifted when he tried to scratch it.

Reiko's face reflected his worry. "What shall we do?"

"I still have the letters I found in Left Minister Konoe's house," Sano said. "Maybe his former wife, Kozeri, is the missing element. I'll visit her tomorrow. Then there are the fern-leaf coins. Marume and Fukida canvassed the city today with no luck, but they'll keep trying. *Yoriki* Hoshina was also supposed to investigate the coins, and I asked him to question the *metsuke* palace spies and gather information on the suspects, so maybe when I see him at the banquet, he'll have something to report."

Now Sano realized that Hoshina was a factor in his misgivings about the case. He said, "I wonder if the results of Hoshina's preliminary investigation are accurate."

"You think he might be less competent or honest than he seemed at first?" Reiko said.

"Not necessarily. Maybe people lied to him about where they were during the murder, or what they know." Fastening his swords at his waist, Sano shook his head in distress. "I may have to restart the investigation from the beginning. Left Minister Konoe may have enemies who've managed to conceal their involvement in his death. One of them could be the killer."

A flash of inspiration came to Sano. "Maybe the killer removed incriminating evidence from Konoe's room before I searched it, and that's why I found so few clues."

Rising, Reiko smoothed Sano's robes and said, "I can try to find out who other suspects might be when I go back to the palace."

"But you've already spoken with the emperor's mother and chief consort," said Sano. He'd been reluctant to risk Reiko's safety even when he'd thought he'd known who all the suspects were; now, with the possibility of many unknown potential killers at the palace, he really didn't want Reiko there.

"Both Lady Jokyōden and Lady Asagao have invited me to visit again," Reiko said. The determination in her voice told Sano how much she wanted to remain a part of the investigation. "Lady Jokyōden mentioned that the left minister had enemies among the other nobles. I could find out who they are."

"She also knows you're my spy," Sano said. "It's improbable that she'll reveal any compromising facts about members of the court, and likely that she might try to mislead you. Besides, Jokyōden seems the best out of the four suspects we have. If she's the killer, it's too dangerous for you to associate with her." Placing his hands on Reiko's shoulders, Sano said, "Promise me you'll stay away from Lady Jokyōden."

Reiko nodded reluctantly. "If that's what you really want." Then she said, "Lady Asagao has no idea why I called on her. Neither of us thinks she's the murderer, but we can't drop her from the list of suspects until we know where she was at the time of the murder. Besides, she's close to Emperor Tomohito, Lady Jokyōden, and probably other high-ranking palace residents. She wants me to act in her play, and that's a perfect opportunity to learn what she knows about the court."

Sano couldn't disagree; nor could he resist the entreaty in Reiko's voice. "All right," he said. "Visit Lady Asagao tomorrow, while I interview Lady Kozeri at Kodai Temple."

Her smile brimming with gladness and affection, Reiko said, "Don't worry about me, or the case. Everything will be fine."

They embraced, and desire kindled between them. Finally Sano said, "Well, I'd better go, or I'll be late for the *shoshidai*'s banquet. I'll come back as soon as I can."

In Pontochō, an entertainment quarter on the west bank of the Kamo River, star-shaped lanterns adorned the eaves of teahouses and restaurants full of noisy revelers. Music drifted from windows; crowds filled the streets. On this second night of Obon, temple gongs rang continuously. People lowered pine boughs down wells so the spirits could climb up from the netherworld.

Sano and Detectives Marume and Fukida arrived at a large teahouse guarded by Tokugawa troops. Attendants ushered Sano and his men to an outdoor platform built above the river. Lanterns hung on stands, their colored streamers rustling in the cool breeze. The black water shimmered with reflections of the fading sunset, lights at other teahouses along the embankment, and bonfires lit on the shore to guide the spirits. Laughter rose from the river's wide stone flanks, where pedestrians strolled. Moving lights traced the arch of the Sanjo Bridge as citizens headed to the hillside cemeteries. The night was redolent with the odors of fish, cooking, and the citrus oil burned to repel mosquitoes.

A few guests had already assembled for the banquet. When *Yoriki* Hoshina came over to greet Sano's party, Sano drew him aside for a quick consultation and asked, "What did you discover this afternoon?"

"I talked to all the palace spies. No one seems to have paid any attention to Prince Momozono, but Emperor Tomohito's relationship with Left Minister Konoe was a stormy one," Hoshina said. "Konoe dominated the emperor with a firm hand. Sometimes the emperor would get furious and throw tantrums; other times, he was docile and virtually worshipped Konoe. As for Lady Jokyōden, she and Konoe had an ongoing feud about how to manage the court, and over control of her son. And Konoe made an enemy of Lady Asagao."

"That corroborates what I suspected about the emperor, and other evidence besides." Sano related what Reiko had learned from Asagao and Jokyōden. Still, Hoshina's information offered no new leads. "What about the fern-leaf coin?"

Hoshina shook his head. "I showed it around the police department, but no one there has ever seen a coin like that before. I'll start making inquiries in the city tomorrow."

"Fine." Sano tried to sound positive, but disappointment added to the weight of his troubles.

"May I ask what your plans are for tomorrow?" Hoshina said.

"I'm going to see Kozeri, while my wife visits Lady Asagao again."

Nearby, servants arranged meal trays and cushions on the floor while musicians began playing a cheerful tune on samisen, drum, and flute. On the riverbank below, a bonfire crackled brightly. More guests arrived, and *Shoshidai* Matsudaira came up to Sano.

"Ah, *sōsakan-sama*. Welcome!" Smiling, he introduced Sano's party to various local officials, then said, "Come, the banquet is due to begin."

. . .

The thirty samurai at the *shoshidai*'s banquet consumed grilled quail garnished with feathers, sliced lily root, turtle soup, sashimi, broiled sea bream, rice, and sweet pickled melon. Afterward, the men performed the ritual of pouring sake for their companions and accepting drinks in return. Toward midnight, when the local officials were very drunk and regaling Sano with hilarious stories, *Yoriki* Hoshina slipped away and descended a flight of stairs leading to the river. The crowds had vanished. Hoshina hurried along the stone path beside the water, past bonfires that had burned down to ash, glowing embers, and thin smoke, leaving the entertainment quarter.

Standing with two bodyguards on the balcony of a villa on the river, Chamberlain Yanagisawa saw Hoshina emerge from the darkness and move toward him. His pulse raced with anticipation; the desire he'd suppressed last night stirred anew.

Hoshina drew near, looked up, and bowed in greeting. "I left the banquet as soon as I could. My apologies if I've kept you waiting," he called.

"Not at all. Come up."

Hoshina climbed the stairs to the balcony. They left the guards outside and entered the house, which was a holiday home borrowed from one of Yanagisawa's local agents. The cool river breeze filtered through bamboo blinds that covered the windows of a summer parlor bathed in the light of a round lantern. Yanagisawa and Hoshina knelt opposite each other. Yanagisawa could smell Hoshina's masculine scent of wintergreen hair oil, tobacco smoke, liquor, and sweat. The atmosphere between them felt simultaneously intimate and threatening. As he poured sake from a decanter on a table beside him, Yanagisawa's hands trembled. He passed Hoshina a cup, careful not to touch the *yoriki* this time.

"Well?" he said, meeting Hoshina's predatory gaze with forced control. "What have you to report?"

Hoshina described what Sano had done and said that day.

Nodding in satisfaction, Yanagisawa said, "Sano has saved me the tedious work of investigating the minor suspects. That he hasn't built a strong case against any of them supports their innocence. What else have you got?"

"While I was making inquiries around the palace today, I learned a few interesting things."

"Such as?"

"Lady Jokyōden has a caller who comes every day at the hour of the sheep. It's a young man, probably of the merchant class, from the description of his hairstyle and clothes. He brings letters and waits at the palace gate while they're conveyed to her, then takes her replies away with him."

"Who is he?" Yanagisawa asked.

"He identifies himself as Hiro," said Hoshina. "No one seems to know who he is. The guards have tried to follow him a few times, but he got away."

"What's in these letters?"

"No one knows that, either. Jokyōden's chief lady-in-waiting always carries the messages. She's very loyal to her mistress. If she knows what's going on, she's not saying."

"Whatever Jokyōden is doing may or may not have any relevance to Left Minister Konoe's murder," Yanagisawa said thoughtfully. "Assign spies to find out who Hiro is and what those messages say."

"Yes, Honorable Chamberlain," Hoshina said. "What I discovered about Right Minister Ichijo may be more helpful, however. Ichijo leaves the palace about once a month, after dark, alone. Sometimes he stays away for a day or two; sometimes he comes back the same night."

"Where does he go?"

"Again, no one knows."

Although Yanagisawa could think of innocuous reasons for a noble to sneak out of the palace at night, Hoshina's discovery might have serious ramifications for the murder case. "If Ichijo was away at the time of the murder, then he couldn't have killed Konoe," Yanagisawa said.

"I couldn't find any witnesses who can swear he was in the palace that night," Hoshina said, "so he may indeed have been gone, but the fact that no one saw him doesn't necessarily mean he wasn't there. Even if he did leave, he could have killed Konoe first."

"True," Yanagisawa said. "Ichijo is still the prime suspect, with the strongest motive and a personality that fits the crime."

Hoshina mused, "I wonder what Ichijo does that's so secret he doesn't want anyone to know?"

"It might be worth looking into," Yanagisawa said, "but what interests me most about Ichijo is that he lied to give his daughter an alibi. My guess is that he would go much further to protect her. We can use his motives to trap him and destroy Sano at the same time."

"How?" asked Hoshina.

Yanagisawa described the plan he'd devised.

"That's good." Hoshina gazed at him in frank admiration. "Really brilliant."

The spontaneous praise pleased Yanagisawa more than all Aisu's lavish compliments ever had, and Hoshina was proving to be more competent than Aisu had been lately. It occurred to Yanagisawa that Hoshina might be the new chief retainer he needed.

"Timing is critical," Yanagisawa said, refocusing his thoughts on his plan. "What's Sano's schedule for tomorrow?"

"He's going to see Kozeri in the morning," Hoshina said.

"I have agents checking on her, but they haven't reported in yet. Hopefully, she won't matter to the case." Yanagisawa added, "It's good that Sano won't be at the Imperial Palace."

"However, his wife is going to visit Lady Asagao."

"You'll have to act fast, then."

"I'll start tonight," Hoshina said. "On my way home, I'll get what I need, then stop at the police stables."

"This has to look just right," Yanagisawa warned.

"A little heat should do the trick." Hoshina smiled, proud of his own ingenuity.

"The problem is getting inside," Yanagisawa said. "You shouldn't attempt it yourself."

Hoshina nodded. "I have someone who can do it for me."

"But the next step requires your personal attention as well as secrecy," Yanagisawa said.

"I'll use the *bakufu* chambers in the palace, and send a trusted messenger with the summons. No one else will know I'm there, or what I'm doing."

"What Sano will do is predictable," Yanagisawa said, "but the question is when he'll do it. Send hourly status reports to me at Nijō Castle. We'll have to be ready to act immediately, or wait indefinitely. However, my guess is that we'll have results within a day or so. Then we can set up the final phase of the plan."

"Yes, Honorable Chamberlain," said Hoshina.

"Until tomorrow, then," Yanagisawa said, rising.

Hoshina also rose, but instead of taking his cue to leave, he said, "Unless there's something more I can do for you tonight?"

His tone was husky with sexual invitation, his full mouth not quite smiling. That he should attempt seduction again, after last night's rejection! His nerve both offended and excited Yanagisawa. Of equal height, they stood face to face; Yanagisawa met Hoshina's stare without looking down. Their mutual desire was like a third presence in the room, charging the air. Yet Yanagisawa also sensed that this was different from the sexual dalliances of the past, and not only because Hoshina differed from his former partners.

He wanted more from Hoshina than sex, though he couldn't have said exactly what. A need greater than lust deepened the void he'd carried inside him since the death of Shichisaburō. And the need frightened him, because need represented weakness; it gave other men power over him. Now Yanagisawa's fear turned to anger at Hoshina.

"Do you think of me as a rung in your ladder to power?" he demanded. "Would you use me the way you did *Shoshidai* Matsudaira?" From Hoshina's dossier, Yanagisawa knew that Hoshina had achieved his position by seducing the *shoshidai* and taking advantage of the malleable older man. Yanagisawa also knew that Hoshina's career, forged on looks, wits, and sex, had begun some twenty-five years ago. "Or do you confuse me with Arima Nagisa, Miyako inspector of buildings?"

Hoshina flinched, as if Yanagisawa had struck him. "So you know all about me," he said with a forced laugh. "Well, mine is a common story, isn't it?"

But something had broken in his gaze. In it, Yanagisawa saw the misery of the eight-year-old Hoshina, apprenticed to Inspector Arima, who'd used him sexually and then passed him around to other men. At age sixteen, Hoshina had become the paramour of the Miyako chief police commissioner and worked his way up to the rank of *yoriki* before attracting the *shoshidai*'s attention. But as Yanagisawa saw through Hoshina, his own eyes must have revealed something inside himself, because Hoshina's expression turned to one of wonder.

"Yes, it is a common story." Hoshina answered his own question in a voice hushed with dawning comprehension.

Yanagisawa had never revealed his own past to anyone; he'd suppressed the history of his apprenticeship to the daimyo his clan had once served, threatening death to anyone who gossiped about him. Therefore, his boyhood of forced sex and cruel discipline at the mercy of Lord Takei weren't common knowledge. He could tell that Hoshina hadn't known, until now. In samurai culture, where stoicism was the rule, men didn't talk of personal matters. Now Yanagisawa felt naked before Hoshina.

"Don't look at me like that!" he ordered. "Keep your distance. Show some respect!"

"A thousand pardons." Hoshina stepped backward, but his gaze held Yanagisawa's.

As on the previous night, something passed between them—a strange, piercing current that gave Yanagisawa pleasure and pain in equal measures.

He heard Hoshina's quick intake of breath at the sensation, and instinctively knew what else he and Hoshina had in common.

While many men had similar experiences in this world that exalted manly love and exploited the weak, Yanagisawa had never imagined that anyone ever suffered as he had. Now he understood that Hoshina also knew the pain, shame, and rage. The same emotions had shaped both their lives.

Hoshina said, "When I found out you were coming to Miyako, I did plan to do what you accused me of doing." He sounded younger, abashed. "But now . . ." Dropping his gaze, he shrugged. "If you want me to go, I will." He started toward the door.

"Wait." The command slipped involuntarily out of Yanagisawa. Hoshina paused, and Yanagisawa sensed how much he was torn between wanting to flee and wanting to stay. Hoshina stood to gain vast rewards for pleasing the most powerful man in Japan; but if he failed to please, he could lose his life. He'd excelled at the game of sex and exploitation in the past, but the rules had changed; he was uncertain how to act.

The same uncertainty and contrary impulses tormented Yanagisawa, because of what he himself stood to lose. He and Hoshina shared more besides carnal attraction and childhood traumas. They were both users of men, dedicated to self-interest. He'd lied, cheated, schemed, ruined lives, and killed to get to the top of the *bakufu*. Was Hoshina capable of the same?

But these realities crumbled under the pressure of the undefined yearning. Yanagisawa held out his hand to Hoshina. "Come here," he said.

Yanagisawa saw his own hope, fear, and desires mirrored in Hoshina's eyes. Their hands clasped. In the shock of the warm press of skin against skin, a rush of arousal swept through Yanagisawa. None of his impersonal couplings with other partners had prepared him for whatever this was, but instinct guided him. He lifted his free hand and gently touched Hoshina's cheek. Hoshina cautiously laid his hand on Yanagisawa's shoulder. They stood frozen in position, their gazes riveted upon each other's faces, for a short eternity.

Then they were caught up in a brutal embrace, hands caressing smooth skin over hard muscle, bodies thrusting and straining. Their gasps drowned the clang of distant Obon gongs. Yanagisawa smelled the smoke from bonfires; he felt an overwhelming physical rapture. As he and Hoshina sank to the floor together, he had the perilous sense of launching into an adventure that would change both their lives forever.

11

The next morning brought dense clouds that relieved Miyako's sweltering heat but increased the moisture in the air. Pagoda spires grew hazy where they met the low sky; mist rendered far hills invisible. While the ancient capital awoke to life, a damp wind blew ash and torn paper flowers from last night's Obon festivities past the gate of Kodai Temple, where Sano had come to see Left Minister Konoe's former wife.

Founded in ancient times, Kodai Temple had gained prominence after Toyotomi Hideyoshi's death almost a century ago. His successor, Tokugawa Ieyasu, had granted it to Hideyoshi's widow, who had become a nun, taking the religious name Kodai-in and retiring to the temple convent. Later, bent on eliminating potential challengers, Ieyasu had besieged the Toyotomi stronghold at Osaka Castle. Kodai-in, who had gone there to join her son, had been annihilated along with the last remnants of the Toyotomi clan. Now the Widow's Temple memorialized her.

Sano walked along the Reclining Dragon Corridor, an undulating covered bridge with roof tiles shaped like scales. Around him spread ponds, gardens, ceremonial halls, and residences. To the east, Higashi Cemetery ascended a hillside in tiers of gravestones. Sano entered the sanctuary. Carved gold lacquerwork on the walls and altar reflected the flames of thousands of oil lamps. Incense smoked before a golden statue of Kannon, the Buddhist goddess of mercy; shrines held wooden images of Hideyoshi and Kodai-in. Heat shimmered like currents under water. An elderly nun, small and stooped with a shaven head, bowed to Sano as he approached her.

"I am the abbess of Kodai Temple Convent," she said. "May I assist you?"

After introducing himself, Sano said, "I'm here to see a nun named Kozeri."

The abbess's wrinkled face hardened into unfriendly lines. "If you've come on behalf of Kozeri's former husband, you've wasted your time. She has nothing to communicate to the left minister, and she sees no one from outside the temple. To visit repeatedly and send letters or envoys is futile. Perhaps if you relay that message to the left minister, he will accept the situation and leave Kozeri alone."

"I'm not the left minister's envoy," Sano explained quickly. "I'm investigating his murder."

"Murder?" Shock rounded the abbess's blurry eyes. "I'm sorry; I did not know." She shook her head. "Here, we shun news from the outside world. . . . Forgive me for mistaking your purpose."

"I need to speak with Kozeri as part of my inquiry," Sano said. "It won't take long."

The abbess hesitated, then said, "I will fetch Kozeri."

"Please don't tell her who I am or why I'm here," Sano said. "I'll do that myself."

"Very well."

After the abbess left, Sano dropped a coin in the offertory box, lit a candle, and placed it on the altar. He silently prayed for the success of his mission, and for the safety of Reiko, who was at the Imperial Palace now.

"Lady Asagao has been called away, but she told me to have you try on your new costume for the play," said the lady-in-waiting who greeted Reiko outside the imperial consorts' residence.

A gust of wind ruffled the trees and wisteria vines in the courtyard where they stood. Thunder shuddered the overcast sky, and raindrops hissed onto the gravel-covered ground. The lady-in-waiting said, "It's going to storm. Let's hurry inside."

She ushered Reiko into the low building. Here, Reiko knew, no men except the emperor were allowed. As she and her escort walked through the corridors, maids lowered the wooden rain doors along the exterior wall. Mullioned paper partitions defined a series of chambers. Through their open doors Reiko saw young women sipping tea and grooming themselves. They smiled at her and bowed. The emperor apparently had many consorts besides Lady Asagao, with many attendants to serve them. Chatter and laughter filled the air.

Lady Asagao had a suite at the center of the residence. Entering this, Reiko saw rain doors and sliding paper panels standing open to a garden landscaped with willows and lawn. Painted landscapes decorated folding screens that divided the suite into three sections, each crammed with furniture and personal articles. In the dressing area, an alcove held built-in cabinets whose drawers and shelves spilled colorful clothing. Lamps burned on a low table littered with combs, brushes, jars, and a mirror. Shoes lay scattered on the floor. The lady-in-waiting pointed to a wooden stand that displayed a lavish emerald silk kimono embroidered with pink lilies.

"This is your costume," she said to Reiko. "May I help you change?"

"Oh, no, thank you, that's not necessary," Reiko said. "Don't trouble yourself."

"It's no trouble," the lady-in-waiting said with a smile. "I'm honored to serve you."

"Oh, but I'm sure you're very busy. And really, I can manage alone."

The young woman hesitated.

"It's all right," Reiko said. "I won't disturb Her Highness's things, and I'll call you if I need help."

After the woman left, Reiko waited a moment to make sure she was gone, then hastily closed the doors to the corridor and the exterior wall panels. Her heart raced in panic because she didn't know how much time she had to search the chamber before Lady Asagao returned. Nor did she know exactly what she hoped to find, except proof that Asagao was someone other than who she seemed.

Reason told her to look for letters or other personal papers. Reiko sped around the folding screen into the central area of the suite, which appeared to be a parlor. A samisen, musical scores, and playing cards lay on the tatami. Furnishings consisted of low tables, lanterns, floor cushions, an iron chest, and a writing desk. The desk was a flat, square red lacquer box. On the slanted lid lay four small, clothbound books. Reiko opened one. She scanned the pages and recognized lines from the play she'd performed in yesterday. She tossed the scripts aside and lifted the desk's lid. Inside, empty jars, frayed writing brushes, and an inkstone covered with dried, flaking pigment lay amid piles of crumpled papers. Reiko snatched up the papers and riffled through them. Some were theater programs. Others were copies of classic poems—probably childhood calligraphy lessons. If Asagao had written anything later or more revealing, Reiko didn't find it.

Rain clattered on the tile roof; the wind rustled through the garden. Reiko flung up the lid of the iron chest. Inside were dolls and other toys apparently saved from Asagao's youth. Hearing female voices nearby, Reiko froze, holding her breath. Then came a series of thumps as maids lowered the rain doors outside the suite. Darkness shadowed the parlor. The maids moved on. Reiko exhaled in relief. Closing the chest, she hurried around the folding screen into a sleeping area.

There a futon and light summer blanket lay beside discarded night robes. Reiko yanked open drawers and doors in the wall cabinet and found bedding, charcoal braziers, lamps, and candles. Chests contained winter quilts. The only unusual discovery was a stash of wine jars in a cupboard.

Reiko rushed back to the dressing area. She rummaged through the clothes in the cabinets. The scent of lily perfume issued from silk robes and sashes. Touching these personal things made Reiko guiltily aware that detective work often violated courtesy. As she examined drawers of fans and hair ornaments, she wondered whether she'd breached Asagao's privacy for no good reason, because she found nothing she wouldn't expect of a rich, pleasure-loving, and harmless young woman. But then she pulled open the door of a compartment level with her face. . . .

A sour metallic smell billowed out, familiar and disturbing. Reiko's breath caught. As her heart began pounding, she peered into the compartment. Its contents lay far back in the shadowy recesses. Slowly she reached inside. Her fingers touched fabric that had an odd texture—smooth and soft, with stiff patches. She drew out a bundle of heavy mauve silk and thinner white cloth, both blotched with reddish-brown stains.

Dried blood.

Shocked, Reiko separated the bundle into two garments—a noble-woman's court robe and an under-robe. The blood had darkened the front hems of the garments. Into Reiko's mind came a picture of Asagao, wearing the robes, standing in the midnight Pond Garden. At her feet lay Konoe's corpse, oozing blood. Reiko envisioned the blood spreading across the ground, seeping into Asagao's long robes. Asagao panted, recovering the breath expended in the spirit cry, a look of evil triumph on her pretty face. . . .

Reiko shook her head in confusion. Wind lashed torrents of rain against the building; water dripped and splattered outside; a crack of thunder provoked excited cries from the palace women. The air in the room was hot and still, the atmosphere suffocating.

"Merciful gods," Reiko whispered.

Here was a clue that implicated Lady Asagao in the crime. Yet the discovery was less gratifying than disturbing, because Reiko couldn't believe

Asagao was the killer. Holding the robes at arm's length, she gazed at the bloodstains and sought another explanation for them.

Maybe they weren't Left Minister Konoe's blood. Maybe Lady Asagao had accidentally soiled her clothes during her monthly bleeding. However, this looked like too much blood for that, and why only on the hems? Maybe Asagao or someone else had gotten injured and bled on the floor, then Asagao had stepped in the blood. But why hide the garments instead of cleaning them? Then again, if she was guilty of murder, why hadn't she destroyed the evidence?

The quiet sound of a door sliding open jolted Reiko out of her contemplation. With a gasp of surprise, she clutched the robes against her chest, turned, and saw Asagao entering the room. Guilty shame leapt in Reiko.

"Oh, hello, Your Highness," she said brightly. "I was, uh, just about to try on my costume for the play."

Asagao made no reply. All her vivacity had vanished; she seemed a forlorn ghost of her usual self, and her bright makeup a mask painted onto her expressionless face. She looked at Reiko, and confusion wrinkled her brow, as if she couldn't quite remember who Reiko was.

"Your Highness?" Reiko said, puzzled.

Asagao's gaze shifted to the robes that Reiko held, then moved downward to the bloodstained hems. A strange mixture of disbelief, terror, and resignation filled her eyes. With a tiny whimper, she sank to the floor, burying her face in her hands.

The summer storm enmeshed Kodai Temple in veils of wind-blown rain. As Sano listened to the thunder and watched a draft elongate the flame of the candle he'd lit on the altar in the sanctuary, he felt someone beside him. He turned and saw a nun, who'd entered the room so quietly he hadn't heard her.

The nun smiled. She was of average height and perhaps in her mid-thirties, and wore a loose gray robe. "I am Kozeri," she said. Her soft voice echoed in the shadowy hall. "You wish to speak with me?"

"Yes," Sano said, then took a closer look at the nun. Her high brow and cheekbones and the skull beneath her bare scalp were exquisitely molded. Her ivory complexion gleamed in the lamplight. Her eyes were long crescents beneath heavy, slumberous lids, her smiling lips full and sensuous. Admiration leapt in Sano; his heartbeat and breath quickened. This sudden, physical response to Kozeri caused him considerable surprise. He'd thought that age and marriage had put him beyond the point where a stranger's beauty could captivate him.

Hiding his discomfort, Sano introduced himself and said, "Unfortunately I have some bad news for you. Your former husband, Left Minister Konoe, is dead."

Kozeri stiffened; her smile faded, and she turned away to face the altar. "How did it happen?" she asked.

"He was murdered." As Sano gave details and explained why he'd come, he thought Kozeri's shock seemed genuine and her question logical. But was she disturbed by Konoe's death, or by the arrival of the shogun's detective? Sano said, "I must talk to you about some things that may have a bearing on the crime."

She swallowed hard. "All right."

"How did you happen to marry Left Minister Konoe?" Sano asked, moving over to stand beside Kozeri.

"I'm from the Nakanoin clan." This was a minor *kuge* family. "When I was fifteen, I married a cousin, but he died." The lamps illuminated Kozeri's profile. "Left Minister Konoe was a widower. He arranged our match with my family."

"Were you willing at the time?" Sano asked, trying to shake the uneasiness that Kozeri's presence engendered, and disturbed to recognize the onset of sexual attraction. Kozeri was a nun and a potential witness in the murder case. He had a wife he loved dearly; since their marriage, he hadn't even noticed other women. What was happening to him?

Kozeri stared into the flames as if trying to see across the years. "It was so long ago." She folded her hands across her bosom, absently stroking the tops of her breasts. "I put the past behind me when I entered the nunnery."

Watching her, Sano couldn't help imagining the softness of her skin, the warm pliancy of her body. Lamp flames guttered in the draft; outside, the rain battered the roof and cascaded off the eaves. With difficulty Sano banished the troubling thoughts from his mind.

"Did you love the left minister?" he asked.

"No." A faint smile lifted the corner of Kozeri's mouth. "I was seventeen when we married. He was thirty-two." She glanced sideways at Sano. "We were never close. I suppose we just weren't suited to each other."

"You never had any children?" Sano asked.

A blush warmed her ivory complexion. "Left Minister Konoe has grown daughters." Sano had interviewed these women along with the rest of Konoe's family; they had firm alibis and no apparent reason to wish their father dead. "But he and I were married only a year." Again Kozeri glanced at Sano. "I suppose there wasn't enough time for us to have a child together."

"You ended the marriage." When Kozeri nodded, Sano said, "Why?"

"I decided that I wanted to devote my life to my spiritual calling."

"Did you have any other reasons for leaving the left minister?"

"No," Kozeri said. "He was a good man who gave me everything a wife could wish for."

Evidently the passion in the marriage had been one-sided, and the spiritual connection a figment of Konoe's imagination. Taking from under his kimono the letters he'd found in Konoe's house, Sano said, "Let me read you something:

" 'How could you leave me? Without you, every day seems a meaningless eternity. My spirit is a fallen warrior. Anger corrupts my love for you like maggots seething in wounded flesh. I long to strangle the wayward life out of you. I shall have my revenge!' "

Kozeri shuddered. The heavy lids veiled her eyes. She raised her hand at Sano, as if fending off the ugly words.

"That was written by the left minister, to you," Sano said. "Hadn't you read it?"

". . . I stopped reading his letters years ago. When I was a novice, I wrote back, trying to make him understand that I meant to stay here. Then, after I took my vows, the temple returned all the letters unopened." Kozeri pressed her hands against her face. "I'd forgotten what they were like."

"I've read through these," Sano said, riffling the letters. "He sounds violent and spiteful. Didn't he act that way toward you when you were married?"

Kozeri shook her head, absently running shaky fingers down her neck. "He changed after we separated."

Though Sano knew that a broken marriage could compel people to extreme behavior, he didn't believe that a man's basic nature could change so radically. But he also saw how a man could become obsessed with Kozeri. Her enigmatic allure explained Konoe's determination to possess her, and his enraged frustration when thwarted. Sano found himself extremely curious about Kozeri.

Who are you? he wanted to ask Kozeri. *What secret thoughts do you banish with meditation and prayer?*

Instead Sano said, "Konoe never mistreated you in any way?"

"Never." She turned away from the altar to face Sano. In her eyes he saw a growing awareness of him as not just a *bakufu* official, but a man. Unspoken questions punctuated her reply, as though she wanted to know about him too.

"What did you think about the left minister's persistent attentions?" Sano was too disconcerted by Kozeri's interest to know whether he should believe her.

"I didn't understand why my husband acted the way he did," Kozeri said. "I felt as though I must have driven him to it, although I gave him no encouragement. At first I was resentful, but after years passed, I came to see the left minister as a man with a flaw in his spirit. He thought he could have whatever he wanted, and he was too stubborn to accept defeat. I pitied him."

An extraordinarily forgiving attitude, Sano noted. "Still, you must be glad Konoe is dead, because now you're free of the nuisance."

Kozeri gave him an uncertain smile. "Perhaps his spirit now enjoys a peace he never knew in life. But I wouldn't wish murder upon anyone. And I've not had time to absorb the fact that he's truly gone. I suppose I shall rest easier, but I can't help blaming myself for the pain we caused each other."

Sano wondered whether her guilt arose from a different source. Had she played a role in Konoe's death? The room seemed to have grown hotter, and the effort of thinking in Kozeri's presence strangely difficult. "The left minister visited you," Sano said, trying to will away confusion. "When did you last see him?"

She frowned, remembering. "At the beginning of summer, I think. He forced his way into the convent, as he had many times before. The guards escorted him out, as always."

If Kozeri was telling the truth, then she had no motive for killing Konoe. Yet Sano would have to check the story of their relationship with people who'd known them both, because Kozeri was still a suspect. Fifteen years in a Buddhist convent offered a possible connection between her and the method used to murder Konoe.

"Do the nuns practice *shugendo* here?" Sano asked.

Shugendo, the Way of Supernatural Powers, had been pioneered by Buddhist priests. The legendary hero En-no-Gyoja, who'd lived sixteen hundred years earlier, could command armies from far away, walk on water, fly through the air, and appear in different places simultaneously. His followers were renowned for their knowledge of the occult. Ancient magistrates hired them to read men's minds and divine facts through magic trances. Throughout history, samurai had studied with Zen monks who taught the esoteric techniques of mental control . . . including the art of *kiai*.

"We practice some methods related to *shugendo*," Kozeri said, "but only those that involve developing inner harmony." She added, "This is a peaceful religious order. We shun violence and have no need of supernatural combat skills."

This had been far from true in the past, however, when Buddhist monasteries had participated actively in warfare. Finally the samurai had razed enough temples and slaughtered enough priests to subjugate the clergy. The Tokugawa kept them under strict surveillance. But here at Kodai Temple, a haven of Buddhist tradition, had ancient practices survived? Maybe *Yoriki* Hoshina was mistaken in believing there'd been no outsiders in the Imperial Palace on the night of the murder. Was it possible that Kozeri could have acquired the ability to kill with her voice? Maybe she was the enemy who had failed to turn up in the preliminary investigation.

Contemplating her, Sano grew ever more aware of Kozeri's attractions. Her unconscious habit of touching herself suggested a delight in the senses despite her choice of a religious life. Sano pictured the lush body concealed beneath her robe. Sexual desire assailed him in a hot, turbulent rush.

He asked his next question while hardly conscious of the words he spoke: "A clerk from Left Minister Konoe's staff was murdered soon before you married Konoe. Can you tell me anything about it?"

Kozeri's veiled eyes and parted lips gleamed wetly in the smoky light. "I vaguely recall the incident." Hearing her breath catch, Sano knew she felt desire, too. The thought thrilled him. "But I was quite ill at the time, and not much aware of anything except my own troubles. I'm sorry I can't help you."

Now horror and guilt overwhelmed Sano; he barely heard Kozeri's words. How could he want another woman when he had Reiko?

There was something important that he'd forgotten to ask Kozeri, but he couldn't think what it was. He must get out of here, now. "Excuse me," he said abruptly.

Leaving Kozeri standing alone, he fled the sanctuary. The rain had slackened to a drizzle; puddles in the temple grounds reflected the leaden sky. Sano breathed the moist, fragrant air and wondered what had come over him. Then he heard someone call out his title. He saw one of his soldiers hurrying toward him.

"I have an urgent message for you," the soldier said, "from your wife."

12

Sano said to Lady Asagao, "I've summoned you here to discuss the murder of Left Minister Konoe."

He was seated in the reception hall of the *bakufu* office that had been built in the imperial enclosure for ceremonial visits from shoguns, and to accommodate local officials on business at the palace. Opposite him sat Lady Asagao, Right Minister Ichijo, Lady Jokyōden, and a group of court nobles. Emperor Tomohito occupied a canopied dais nearby. Asagao's expression was vacant and Tomohito's bewildered, while caution hooded the faces of their companions. Tokugawa troops stood guard around the room.

"My wife found these in your room, Your Highness," Sano said, pointing to a clothes stand that held the bloodstained robes. "Please explain them."

The message Reiko had sent to Kodai Temple had asked Sano to meet her at Nijō Manor immediately. When he got there, she'd given him the garments and told how she'd discovered them. Sano had left Reiko there and ridden to the palace. His order for Asagao to report to the *bakufu* office had also brought the emperor and his mother, chief official, and top advisers.

Right Minister Ichijo said coldly, "For your wife to search Lady Asagao's rooms without her permission was a grave insult to the Imperial Court."

"Lady Asagao and I offered your wife friendship, and she took advantage of our trust by spying on us." Lady Jokyōden spoke with stern reproach. Beautiful and authoritative, she was exactly as Reiko had described her to Sano. "Such underhanded tactics are deplorable."

The emperor glared at Sano. "Lady Asagao is my sacred consort. It's against the rules for anyone to order her around as if she were a commoner. She doesn't have to talk to you."

Asagao sat mute and immobile. She was pretty, as Reiko had said, but her bright clothing ill suited her lifeless manner. Sano couldn't imagine her performing in amateur Kabuki or spilling drunken confidences to Reiko.

"She had nothing to do with Left Minister Konoe," Emperor Tomohito said. "You've no right to treat her this way!"

Sano saw his earlier fears realized: Through his investigation, he'd seriously offended these people. By worsening the age-old tension between the Imperial Court and the *bakufu*, he risked upsetting Japan's balance of power. He—and Reiko, who'd precipitated the crisis—could expect punishment from the shogun if he continued this way. Yet he saw no alternative.

"I'm sorry, Your Majesty," he said politely, "but justice takes precedence over court rules. I have orders to investigate Left Minister Konoe's death, and I must find out the truth about it. I'm not accusing Lady Asagao of any wrongdoing. I just want to know how the blood got on her clothes." Sano turned to Asagao. "Your Highness?"

She looked at him as though he'd spoken in a language she didn't understand.

"You've frightened her so badly that she can't talk," the emperor said.

"*Sōsakan-sama*, there's obviously been a mistake. You seem to be suggesting that Lady Asagao soiled her clothes while killing the left minister. Yet we don't even know if those are in fact her clothes." Ichijo attempted to defend his daughter in a controlled, reasonable voice. "The stains may not even be the left minister's blood."

"Someone else could have put the stained robes in Lady Asagao's room," said Lady Jokyōden.

Sano had considered these possibilities. Now he noted that the three people trying to protect Lady Asagao had reason to do as Jokyōden suggested, to divert suspicion toward Asagao and away from them. But although he sympathized with the confused young woman, he needed to hear her story.

"Are they not your clothes, Your Highness?" Sano said gently.

Instead of answering, Asagao gazed at a point somewhere beyond him.

"Did someone hide them in your cabinet?"

No reply came. The emperor muttered angrily; the nobles watched

Sano, their faces and postures rigid. Weak sunlight cast the wind-stirred shadows of trees against the paper walls, but in the reception hall, no one moved.

Then Asagao bowed her head and spoke in a trembling, barely audible voice: "They're mine. I wore them the night Left Minister Konoe died. I killed him."

The frozen vacuum of silence filled the room. Emperor Tomohito's mouth dropped; shock blanched the elegant features of Right Minister Ichijo and Lady Jokyōden; the nobles stared. Then everyone spoke at once.

"No! You couldn't!" Scrambling to the edge of his dais, the emperor grabbed his consort by the shoulders and shook her. "Why do you say such a thing? Take it back before you get in trouble!"

The nobles murmured anxiously among themselves. Ichijo said, "Speak no more, daughter." Panic shone through his controlled manner as he turned to Sano. "She's not in her right mind. Don't believe what she says."

"You've intimidated her into saying what you want to hear," Jokyōden said. "Now she's distraught and ill. We must take her to her room and call a physician."

The group rose, except for Asagao, who knelt with eyes downcast and arms clasped around her stomach.

"Sit down!" Sano ordered. He hated to antagonize the Imperial Court any further, but he had to reestablish control over the situation. "No one leaves this room."

Soldiers blocked the doors. The emperor, Jokyōden, Ichijo, and the rest reluctantly resumed their places. Sano perceived fear beneath their infuriated expressions. In the uneasy quiet that ensued, he focused his attention on Lady Asagao.

Cowering on the floor, she appeared steeped in guilt. But although Sano had hoped for a quick solution to the murder case, Asagao's confession had come too easily, before he could even ask her if she'd killed Konoe. He still couldn't believe he'd explored the full scope of the case, and he wouldn't act on the confession until he made sure it was valid.

"Your Highness," he said, "you stated that you killed Left Minister Konoe. Is that correct?"

Asagao nodded.

"This is a very serious claim," Sano said. "Do you understand that it means you could be sentenced to death?"

Emperor Tomohito opened his mouth to speak, but Lady Jokyōden quelled him with a glance.

"I understand," Asagao whispered.

"In case you weren't telling the truth before," Sano said, "I'm giving you a chance to do so now. Did you kill Left Minister Konoe?"

Ichijo leaned toward Asagao, his gaze intense, as if willing her to speak the words that would save her. A strangled sound of protest came from the emperor. Jokyōden and the nobles waited and watched, motionless.

"It was the truth." Asagao spoke louder, but in a dull voice barren of conviction. "I killed him."

Sano inhaled a deep breath, held it a moment, then let the air ease from him. He'd shown more consideration toward Lady Asagao than the law required, yet he still wasn't satisfied.

"Why did you kill the left minister?" he said.

"I was angry at him."

"Look at me, Your Highness."

Asagao raised her face to Sano. Her mouth trembled.

"Why were you angry?" Sano said patiently.

"He had been paying attention to me since last spring. He gave me gifts and compliments. He was so handsome and charming, I fell in love with him." Asagao continued in the same dull monotone; her eyes kept darting sideways. "A few months ago, when he wanted to make love to me, I let him."

"No!" Emperor Tomohito stared at his consort in wounded fury. "You're mine. You aren't supposed to have anybody else. And the left minister was my teacher—my friend. You both deceived me!"

With a howl, he struck out at Asagao. His palm smote her head. She rocked sideways. Tomohito retreated to the back of his dais, where he knelt, his back to everyone. His shoulders quaked with angry, muffled sobs.

Ichijo shook his head, dazed. The nobles exchanged horrified glances. Belatedly, Sano looked to see Jokyōden's reaction. Her expression was calm.

As if no interruption had occurred, Asagao continued, "The left minister and I met whenever we could." She gave Sano a strained, pleading smile. "But then I found out he seduced me because he wanted to separate me from the emperor. He was going to say that I was the one who seduced *him*, so Tomo-*chan* would get jealous and drop me. The left minister's youngest daughter is Tomo-*chan*'s second favorite lady. She would have been promoted to chief consort. The left minister was Tomo-*chan*'s idol; Tomo-*chan* would have forgiven him for making love to me. He would have ended up with even more power over the court. But I didn't want to give up my position. I couldn't let the left minister tell anyone about us. So I killed him."

This scenario gave Asagao a stronger motive for murder than the quarrel over money that she'd mentioned to Reiko. But Sano realized that an affair between Asagao and Konoe also cast stronger suspicion in other directions.

"Who knew about this affair?" Sano asked.

"Only the left minister's personal attendants. They carried messages between us and arranged our meetings."

The nobles whispered among themselves. Sano eyed Emperor Tomohito, who'd stopped weeping and sat with his head half-turned, listening to the conversation. Maybe his shock at the news of his consort's infidelity was just an act. What if he'd already known that Konoe had seduced Asagao? Jealous temper could have spurred him to murder. Yet Sano could think of someone else besides Asagao who would have suffered if Konoe made the affair public. Someone besides Emperor Tomohito who might have lashed out at Konoe.

Sano contemplated Right Minister Ichijo. Before Konoe died, Ichijo had been the second highest imperial official. Had the two men been rivals? If Konoe had intended to attack Ichijo by ousting Asagao, then his death would have preserved Ichijo's status. And after the murder, Ichijo had become the top court official. The affair and resulting scandal would have hurt him more than Lady Jokyōden, whose position in the court didn't depend on her son's choice of consort, or Prince Momozono, who had no part in imperial politics.

The right minister met Sano's gaze. Sudden wariness sharpened his aspect, as if he sensed a threat. Sano knew that Ichijo wasn't a suspect; *Yoriki* Hoshina's report had placed him at home, in the presence of his family and attendants, at the time of the murder. Just the same, Sano wondered whether Ichijo merited investigation.

"How did you know that Left Minister Konoe meant to betray you?" Sano asked Asagao.

"I overheard his attendants talking," she said. "They praised him for the cleverness of his plan and laughed at me for being stupid enough to fall for it."

Sano heard a rising inflection at the end of her sentences, as though she wanted him to verify their accuracy. "Tell me what happened the night Left Minister Konoe died," he said.

"It was soon after I found out what the left minister was doing to me. I got a message from him, asking me to go to the Pond Garden at midnight. I saw my chance to get rid of him before he could ruin me. So I went to the garden early and waited for him. When he came, I followed him to the cottage." Asagao had begun speaking faster and faster as she went along; now she ended in a rush: "Then I killed him. I heard people coming, and I was in such a hurry to get away that I accidentally stepped in his blood."

Her story had a convincing logic that established Asagao's motive for the crime and opportunity to kill Konoe; it explained the bloodstained clothes, her lack of an alibi, and why Konoe had gone to the garden after ordering the palace residents to stay away. However, questions remained in Sano's mind.

"If you didn't want the emperor to find out about your affair with Left Minister Konoe, then why are you admitting to it now?" Sano said. "Why are you so eager to confess to murder, when the penalty is death?"

"Because murder is wrong. I'm sorry for what I did. To purify my spirit, I must pay for my crime." Again, that tentative, questioning note inflected Asagao's voice.

"Yesterday you told my wife you were glad the left minister died," Sano reminded her.

Asagao shifted uncomfortably. "I changed my mind."

"I see." Sano paused, thinking that if her story was a lie, it was a better one than he could imagine Asagao inventing by herself. "Was it your idea to confess?"

"Yes. Of course." The emperor's consort nodded vigorously, while everyone watched, alert and tense.

"Then no one told you what to say?"

"No. Nobody did," Asagao said, looking away from Sano, then back again.

"You're not trying to protect someone by taking the blame for the murder?" Sano looked around the room at Ichijo, Jokyōden, and Tomohito.

"I resent your implication that I would have my daughter sacrifice herself to protect me," Ichijo said with haughty indignation. "I am not a murderer. Neither is she. That she says these things can only mean she has gone mad."

"I haven't gone mad!" Turning on her father with a vehemence that made him draw back from her, Asagao insisted, "I'm telling the truth. I killed the left minister."

"There's one way to settle the matter," Sano said. "Lady Asagao, I order you to demonstrate the spirit cry for me."

There was a moment of stunned quiet. Sano heard silk garments rustle with small, involuntary movements, and saw consternation on the faces around him.

Then Ichijo said scornfully, "This is ridiculous. My daughter isn't capable of any such thing."

"Since you obviously doubt that she killed the left minister, it is unnecessary and cruel to encourage her sick fantasies," Lady Jokyōden reproached Sano.

But expectancy charged the atmosphere in the room. Emperor Tomohito fixed his consort with a curious, fearful gaze. Interest animated the guards' usually stoic faces. Under everyone's scrutiny, Lady Asagao shrank into herself.

"Well, Your Highness?" Sano said. "I'm waiting."

"But I might hurt someone," Asagao protested weakly.

Sano rose, walked across the room, and slid open a wall panel. Outside, in the lush green garden, blackbirds perched on a fence. "You needn't use the full force of *kiai*. Just knock those birds unconscious."

Asagao squirmed, looking frightened. "It won't work. Not with everyone watching."

"You can't utter a spirit cry, can you?" Sano said, closing the wall panel. "Not now; not ever. And you didn't on the night Left Minister Konoe died."

"Of course she didn't," Ichijo said, his voice sharpened by desperation. "Tell the truth, daughter, before it's too late!"

She said defiantly, "I admit I killed the left minister. Isn't that enough?"

It was enough to convict her, because a confession was legal proof of guilt, and Sano was duty-bound to observe the law whether or not he believed she'd committed any crime. With great reluctance, he said, "If you stand by your confession, then I must arrest you."

He nodded to the soldiers, who advanced on Lady Asagao.

"No!" The harsh objection burst from Ichijo, while Jokyōden and the nobles stared, aghast.

Emperor Tomohito leapt to his feet and off the dais. He stood, arms spread, between the soldiers and Lady Asagao. "You stay away from her!" Though he'd repudiated his consort, he apparently didn't want to give her up.

"Please stand aside, Your Majesty," Sano said, dreading a scene.

"I won't. You can't have her. You'll have to kill me first!" Childish rage contorted Tomohito's face.

The soldiers looked to Sano for guidance. He walked over and reached out a hand to the emperor.

"It's the law, Your Majesty. She chose to confess. Now she must go."

He hadn't touched Emperor Tomohito, but the young man sprang away as if Sano had struck him, yelling, "How dare you try to lay hands on me?" He stumbled backward and fell on his buttocks.

The nobles exclaimed in outrage: "Blasphemy!" "Sacrilege!" Tradition prohibited the emperor's body from touching the ground where ordinary people walked. Horror assailed Sano. He was responsible for Reiko's search of Lady Asagao's room, and now this worse insult to the Imperial Court. Instead of regaining the shogun's favor, he would be reviled for his poor handling of the investigation. Yet his orders compelled him to proceed.

"Take her," he told the troops.

When they grasped Lady Asagao by the arms, a look of sheer terror came over her face, as though she finally understood the consequences of her actions. Kicking and thrashing, she screamed in high-pitched bursts. The soldiers hauled her toward the door. Jokyōden, Ichijo, and the nobles surrounded Sano.

"You shall not commit this atrocity," Jokyōden said.

Ichijo commanded, "Release my daughter at once!"

Did their efforts to help Lady Asagao hide a desire to see her blamed for the murder and themselves exonerated? Sano wondered.

"Father!" shrilled Asagao. "Don't let them take me!"

The emperor set upon the troops, trying to pry their hands off Asagao. "Somebody help me!"

Loud hoots signaled the arrival of Prince Momozono, who must have been listening outside. He lurched into the room and hurled himself at Sano, crying. "Y-you can't h-have His M-majesty's consort!"

Sano flung up his hands to repel the prince's wild blows. The nobles hurried to their sovereign's aid. A melee of pushing, shouting, and grabbing erupted, with the shrieking Lady Asagao at the center. Fearing that a riot might spread throughout the palace, Sano drew his sword. The crowd fell back amid cries of fear. Lady Asagao and the emperor broke into hysterical tears. With many doubts and no sense of victory, Sano led his men and their prisoner out of the room.

"Where are you taking her?" Right Minister Ichijo demanded, following them down the corridor. "A woman of her position doesn't belong in the city jail."

"Lady Asagao will be kept in a safe, comfortable place for a while," Sano said. He needed time to investigate her story.

"And then?"

"I'll take her to Edo for her trial."

Unless he found justification for his misgivings about Lady Asagao's confession.

13

It was evening by the time Sano rode his horse up to the gate of
Nijō Manor. Above the plaster walls and spreading tile roof of the inn, an
ocher residue of daylight stained the western rim of the soot-colored sky.
Lanterns burned in the windows of surrounding houses. Noisy crowds
streamed toward the shrines, temples, cemeteries, and pleasure quarter
for Obon celebrations. When Sano entered the courtyard of Nijō Manor,
he found it filled with newly arrived travelers. He got a stableboy to take
charge of his horse. As he walked down the corridor to his rooms, he
looked forward to Reiko's company, yet he also felt a strong desire for
solitude.

A long day of inquiries hadn't resolved his problems with Lady
Asagao's confession. Mentally and physically exhausted, Sano needed to
relax for a while. Reiko would be waiting to hear about everything, but
Sano wasn't ready to face her questions, her youthful energy, her eager-
ness for debate. Besides, he had another reason for not wanting to see
Reiko.

The subject of Left Minister Konoe's former wife hadn't yet come up
between them, but eventually Reiko would remember that Sano had gone
to Kodai Temple. She would ask about Kozeri. Usually Sano enjoyed the
intuitive understanding between him and his wife, but he didn't want
Reiko to guess how Kozeri had affected him.

Servants hauling baggage down the corridor momentarily blocked the
door to Sano's suite. He welcomed the chance to compose himself. Then
he entered the room.

110

Reiko was there, fresh and pretty in her yellow dressing gown. When she saw him, she leapt up from her seat by the window, eyes bright with anticipation. "What happened?" she cried.

Sano experienced the usual gladness and affection at the sight of Reiko, followed by guilt. "We have a solution to the case," he said, "but I'm not exactly happy about it."

He placed his swords in a wall rack, then lay down on the floor, resting his head on a cushion. Relief permeated his muscles, but his nerves remained on edge.

"You're tired. I should let you rest instead of bombarding you with questions," Reiko said contritely.

Kneeling beside him, she spread a damp, cool cloth on his forehead. She poured a cup of water for him. Her solicitude increased Sano's guilt. "That's all right," he said, and described Lady Asagao's confession and arrest.

Reiko exclaimed in amazement. "I can't believe she confessed. Nor can I believe she's guilty. Have you checked her story?"

"Yes, I have." For some reason, Sano resented her implication that he would accept Asagao's statement at face value. He said, "After the arrest, I went back to Left Minister Konoe's mansion and interviewed his personal attendants. They admitted to knowing about his affair with Lady Asagao. They also delivered the message asking Asagao to meet Konoe in the Pond Garden on the night he died. When I asked why they hadn't mentioned this when I questioned them the first time, they said they'd kept quiet to prevent a scandal, but since Asagao had confessed, they could tell the truth. So there was an affair, and a strong motive for Asagao to want Konoe dead."

"But what about the means and opportunity to kill?" Reiko asked.

"As I've said, Asagao wouldn't—or couldn't—demonstrate a spirit cry. But she apparently did have the opportunity to murder Konoe." Sano drank water from his cup, swallowing his irritation at Reiko. Did she think he'd forgotten the basics of detective work? "I questioned the ladies-in-waiting you met yesterday. They admitted they'd lied to you when they said Asagao was with them during the murder. She'd left her chambers shortly before midnight—to meet someone. The women didn't know who it was, or where she was going, but she'd been sneaking out often for the past few months. Their story is indirect confirmation of the affair, and it breaks Asagao's alibi."

Reiko sat mulling over the information, innocently oblivious to Sano's mood. "Granted, Asagao isn't very smart, but she must have known the danger involved in taking a lover. How could she risk losing her position? And for a man old enough to be her father!"

Though the age difference between himself and Reiko was less than a generation, Sano thought she should understand that love wasn't confined to couples similar in age. "Some women like older men, who often have a sophistication that young men lack," he said with controlled impatience. "And didn't Asagao complain to you that life in the palace is dull? Perhaps she couldn't resist the excitement of an illicit romance."

Reiko must have perceived antagonism in Sano's voice, because a puzzled frown marred her smooth brow. "But you might not have learned about the affair if she hadn't told you. It would have been better for her just to keep quiet." Then Reiko's eyes lit with inspiration. "What if the emperor found out about the affair, but he loves Asagao too much to hurt her? Instead, he kills Konoe, pretends to discover the body, and thinks that's the end of his problems. But then you come to investigate the murder.

"The emperor panics, because if he's charged with a serious crime, at the very least, he'll lose his throne, and at worst, his life. He asks Prince Momozono to give him an alibi, but he's afraid that's not enough. So he tells Right Minister Ichijo and Lady Jokyōden what he's done and begs them to help him. They decide that Lady Asagao should sacrifice herself to save the emperor."

"And that happens between yesterday, when you left her after the Kabuki play, and this morning, when she walked in on you searching her room," Sano said.

Reiko nodded. "It would explain why she was so frightened and unhappy, and why her confession sounded so unconvincing. She lied—all the while knowing what would happen to her."

"What about the bloodstained robes?" Sano asked.

After some thought, Reiko said, "Left Minister Konoe thought he was meeting Asagao in the Pond Garden, but what if the emperor intercepted the message? His Majesty went to the rendezvous. It was dark, and he wore Asagao's clothes, so that if anyone saw him, they would think he was Asagao. It was he who stepped in Konoe's blood. He took off the clothes and hid them; later, he or Lady Jokyōden put them in Asagao's room."

"That's pretty far-fetched," Sano said. "However, I did consider the possibility that Asagao was forced into confessing." Sano thought Reiko should have given him credit for that much intelligence. "I went to see her. She's at police headquarters, in a special cell." Samurai charged with crimes usually awaited trial under house arrest, and peasants in public jails, but because of the number of travelers who visited Miyako, other accommodations for high-ranking citizens were available. "I thought that if I spoke to Asagao alone, she might be more likely to tell the truth, but we've gone over and over her story, and it never changed. I tried to persuade her that if she's innocent, she shouldn't take the blame for the murder. Asagao still swears by her confession."

"But you don't believe she's guilty any more than I do," Reiko said.

"No," Sano admitted. "I've felt there was something wrong about this case all along, and the feeling is even stronger now. This is a false confession. I know it."

"Yet you arrested Lady Asagao anyway," Reiko said.

"Because I had to," Sano said defensively. "She's guilty by law. For me to let a confessed murderer go free would be to forsake my duty to the shogun and the public. I would be subject to official censure for failing to uphold the power of the *bakufu*—as if I don't have enough troubles already."

"What about Lady Asagao's troubles?" Reiko said. "Would you let her die for a crime she didn't commit, and have the real killer go free? Don't you want to discover the truth anymore?"

"Of course I do!" Now Sano's temper snapped. That Reiko should accuse him of compromising his personal principles for the sake of a quick solution to the case! He sat up and turned on his wife. "You just don't understand the stakes involved. One more mishap after the fiasco over the Lion, and I'll be expelled from my post, or even put to death. Shall I make you a widow who shares my disgrace? Is that what you want?"

"Of course not." Anger and bewilderment clouded Reiko's eyes. "And I do understand what's at stake. What I don't understand is why you're so angry with me."

"I'm not. Why must you take every disagreement so personally?"

"If you're not angry, then why are you shouting?"

As they glared at each other, Sano realized that he was angry at himself for desiring Kozeri, and taking it out on Reiko. He had a frightening premonition that this case would destroy his marriage along with everything else that mattered to him. Forcing a smile, he took Reiko's hand. "I'm sorry. It's been a long day, and I'm irritable. Forgive me."

Reiko sat wary and unrelenting for a moment; then she smiled back, and her hand clasped Sano's. "I do know why you arrested Lady Asagao, and I shouldn't have spoken so strongly. You were right to be angry. I'm sorry, too."

Her honest apology only fed Sano's guilt.

"It's just that I feel responsible for what happens to Lady Asagao," Reiko continued in a worried voice. "I was the one who searched her room. I found the clothes and gave them to you."

"You didn't make her confess," Sano said. "It was my decision to have you investigate the palace women, and your duty to turn whatever you found over to me."

"I know," Reiko said unhappily, "but still . . ."

Sano couldn't offer any absolution, because he shared her sense of responsibility for Lady Asagao. They sat for a moment, holding hands, joined in dread of the future.

"What shall we do?" Reiko asked. "Find the real killer?"

"Or try to," Sano said. "There's not much time. Delaying Asagao's trial will give me a bad reputation that could spread to Edo and have me thrown out of the *bakufu* before I can solve the case. Someone else will take over my job, and Asagao will die."

"But we won't give up yet," Reiko declared.

"No, we won't," Sano said, heartened by his wife's determination. "Tomorrow I'll restart the investigation. If there are any clues or suspects *Yoriki* Hoshina missed, I'll find them."

"Speaking of other suspects," Reiko said, "I forgot to ask if you saw the left minister's former wife."

Suddenly the space around Sano seemed a landscape of quicksand, deep holes, and sharp-edged rocks. He withdrew his hand from Reiko's, lest she feel his nervousness, and said, "Yes, I did." Then, in as neutral a voice as he could manage, he recited the dry facts from his interview with Kozeri.

"So Konoe was a constant problem for his wife since she left him," Reiko mused. To Sano's relief, she didn't seem to suspect anything amiss. "Kozeri belongs to a peaceful Buddhist order that shuns violence and doesn't practice the martial arts. Still, I find it hard to believe she bore no ill will toward Konoe. I wonder if she told you the whole story. She might be more frank with another woman. Maybe I should go see her."

"No!" The word burst from Sano. Reiko looked at him, obviously perplexed by his vehemence. "I mean, I think Kozeri is a less likely suspect or witness than the members of the Imperial Court."

He had to keep Reiko and Kozeri apart. If Reiko saw Kozeri, she might guess how he'd felt toward the beautiful nun. Also, if the investigation required another interview with Kozeri, he wanted to be the one who went, because he wanted to see her again. The knowledge filled Sano with fresh guilt.

"But she's the only lead I can follow," Reiko said, disappointed. "Now that the Imperial Court knows I spied for you, there's no use in my going back to the palace; the women won't tell me anything. It would be better for me to talk to Kozeri than just sit here and do nothing while time runs out for you—and Lady Asagao."

A knock at the door spared Sano the necessity of answering. "Come in," he called, grateful for the reprieve.

Detectives Marume and Fukida entered the room. They bowed to Sano and Reiko. Marume said, "Please excuse the interruption, *Sōsakan-sama*, but just as we arrived at the inn, an imperial messenger came asking for you."

"He brought you this," Fukida said, holding out a cylindrical black lacquer scroll case decorated with gold chrysanthemums.

Sano opened the case and unrolled the document inside. He scanned the message written in bold, black calligraphy and inspected the signature seal. "It's from the emperor," he said. "His Majesty demands that I come to see him immediately."

"What for?" Reiko said.

"He doesn't say, but I'm guessing that he wants to persuade me to free Lady Asagao." Sano's heart sank at the prospect of another clash with the Imperial Court. "Still, I can't ignore an order from the emperor. I have to go."

With a sense of leaving one dangerous situation for another, Sano rose and donned his swords. "Marume-*san*, Fukida-*san*, come with me." To Reiko, he said, "We will finish our conversation later."

14

Sano, Marume, and Fukida rode up to the Imperial Palace just as the temple bells signaled half past the hour of the dog. Outside the palace gate, two sentries—one a Tokugawa soldier, the other an imperial watchman—stood guard.

Dismounting, Sano introduced himself and said, "I'm here to see the emperor, at his request."

"Yes, *Sōsakan-sama*." The Tokugawa soldier bowed, then turned to the watchman. "Go and fetch the imperial escort."

The watchman went inside the palace. Sano and his detectives waited in the quiet, empty street. Beneath a deep violet sky full of stars, a dark mass of leafy treetops rose above the palace walls. Time passed. The moon's irregular white orb floated over the hills. Sano grew restless as hunger, thirst, and weariness of body and spirit strained his patience. Looking at the tired faces of his men, he knew they felt no better than he. They'd spent all day investigating the fern-leaf coins, to no avail. On the way to the palace he'd told them about Lady Asagao's confession and arrest. They shared his doubts, and had loyally seconded his decision to seek out the truth before taking Asagao to Edo for trial. They, too, would suffer if he got in trouble, because their livelihood and honor were tied to his.

Finally the watchman returned with two guards bearing lanterns. They led Sano and his men into the imperial compound.

The palace was a different world at night, enfolded in a darkness more dense than in the city outside. The guards' lanterns spilled weak light against fences and cast long shadows as they preceded Sano,

Marume, and Fukida through the *kuge* quarter. They met no one. Their footsteps echoed forlornly; the only other sounds were the trickle of water in drains and the ever-present insect songs. The warm, humid air breathed a scent of earth, ashes, and the decay of centuries past.

"This place is eerie," said Marume. His jovial voice sounded hollow in the gloom. "Give me the noise and lights and bustle of Edo Castle any day."

Fukida looked around nervously. The same uneasiness infected Sano, who imagined hidden watchers peering at him. In his tired, tense state, the notion of three armed samurai afraid of the dark didn't seem as laughable as it should have. He wished the guards would hurry, but they maintained a slow, decorous pace.

Entering the imperial enclosure, they crossed a lane and passed through an inner gate to a compound of interconnected buildings. They walked a circuitous route around halls, then through a passage and into an open courtyard surrounded by dark buildings and roofed walkways.

Suddenly the guards divided and fled in opposite directions, taking the lights with them, and vanished.

"Hey, what is this?" Marume demanded, his voice raised in surprised protest.

The compound, plunged into darkness, became a labyrinth of shadows. The white gravel and walls shone faintly in the moonlight, but black gloom filled the walkways and surrounded the buildings.

"Wait. Come back!" Sano called to the guards.

The echo of their rapid footsteps faded into the distance.

"Something strange is going on here." Suspicion disturbed Sano. "This feels like a trap."

He and his detectives started across the courtyard, swords drawn, treading quietly. Sano experienced a peculiar sensation, like a silent, windless air current vibrating around him. His skin prickled; his heartbeat accelerated; his breath quickened involuntarily with the physical urgency of fear. His muscles tightened in reaction to an evil presence.

Halting, he said, "What is it?"

Marume and Fukida had also stopped, apparently arrested by the same inexplicable feeling. Sano felt his heart beating harder, and the blood pulsating in his head.

"Where are you?" Fukida muttered, waving his sword as if under attack by a ghost.

"Show yourself!" Marume lunged at shadows.

In the near distance beyond the courtyard, through a walkway and the lacy black foliage of trees, a strange, pale haze tinged the air. The vibrations issued from this eerie brightness, muting noises that sounded like frightened cries. Sano pointed and said, "Whatever it is, it's over there."

Marume and Fukida hurried to stand between him and the unknown threat. "*Sōsakan-sama*, we're taking you out of here," Fukida said.

"Come on, let's go," Marume said.

But now, Sano's sense of danger was overpowering. Ignoring his men's attempt to protect him, he ran across the courtyard, bounded over the walkway, and through a garden toward the light.

The detectives chased after him, calling, "No! Stop!"

Sano came upon a wall that stood between him and the eerie glow. He could still feel the ominous presence, like an invisible net. Then he heard the loud, raspy breathing of some monstrous creature. Battling an instinctive urge to flee, he sheathed his sword. He crouched, arms raised, then jumped. His hands grasped the top of the wall; his feet scraped the plaster as he pulled himself up.

Suddenly the night exploded in a scream of thunderous intensity, as though a million voices had combined into a single horrific sound. Its force knocked Sano off the wall. He landed hard on his back, but he hardly noticed the pain. Rolling facedown, he clasped his arms over his head, trying to block out the dreadful noise that blasted through him. Involuntary sobs wracked him as he felt his muscles tremble uncontrollably, his tendons contract, and his ears throb in pain. Every nerve vibrated; his stomach and chest shuddered. Sano realized that this terrible scream was the spirit cry heard across Miyako the night of Left Minister Konoe's murder.

He cried out in terror, but he couldn't even hear himself over the noise. He feared for the safety of his detectives as the killer unleashed the deadly power of *kiai*.

Who was it?

Despite his agony, Sano experienced a sense of awe. Witnessing this ultimate expression of the martial arts affirmed not only his belief in *kiai*, but his faith in the Way of the Warrior.

The scream abruptly stopped. A huge void of silence spread across the night. Sano gasped in relief. His ears rang from the blast. He ached all over; his head throbbed; his heart still pounded. Pushing himself to his knees, he inhaled deep breaths of air and looked around. The strange brightness was gone. In the moonlight Sano saw two inert bodies sprawled on the grass nearby.

"Marume-*san*!" he cried. "Fukida-*san*?"

To his relief, the men stirred and sat up. "Merciful gods, am I alive or dead?" Marume groaned.

"I'll never again think of *kiai* as just an ancient superstition," Fukida said, gasping.

Sano realized that they'd all survived because they'd been far enough away from the source of the spirit cry to feel only minor secondary effects. He said, "Now we know for sure that Lady Asagao didn't murder Left Minister Konoe, because she's locked up in police headquarters. The killer is still out there."

From beyond the wall came the rapid, irregular rhythm of retreating footsteps.

"Quickly!" Sano said.

He and the detectives helped one another scramble over the wall, into another compound. Out of the darkness before them rose long buildings with piles of wood stacked against the walls and huge stone hearths outside. A hush pervaded the palace, as though everyone knew that the scream heralded death and chose to hide until the danger passed.

"These must be the kitchens," Sano said in a low, hurried voice. "We'll spread out. If you see the strange light or feel the vibrations again, make a lot of noise and disrupt the killer's concentration to prevent another spirit cry."

Marume and Fukida disappeared into the shadows. Sano crept around the hearths, alert for any movement or other hint of the killer's presence. He remembered the horrendous noise and power of the spirit cry, and icy fear seeped through him while he searched the kitchen compound. Then he spied a dark shape on the ground outside a building. He approached cautiously and recognized the shape as a prone human figure, lying motionless on its stomach, arms and legs splayed, a sword clutched in its hand.

Blackness surrounded the body like a viscous shadow. Sano touched the shadow, and hot liquid smeared his fingers. The raw, metallic odor of fresh blood and the reek of feces assailed him. He listened for the sound of breaths, but heard nothing. Sano rolled the corpse over. It had a weird pliancy, as if the bones had dissolved, and felt oddly warm. Despite the meager light, Sano saw that the dead man's face was awash in blood that had poured from his nose, mouth, eyes, and ears, drenching his clothes. He recalled *Yoriki* Hoshina describing Left Minister Konoe's death: ". . . *hemorrahaged almost all his blood . . . internal organs ruptured . . . many bones broken . . .*"

Nausea and horror churned Sano's stomach. Because he hadn't solved the case, someone else had died.

Hurrying footsteps pounded toward him. Was the murderer returning to attack again? He looked up, saw Marume and Fukida coming, and exhaled in relief.

"We couldn't find the killer," Marume said. "Whoever it is could be anywhere in the palace, or out in the city by now." Then he saw the corpse beside Sano. "Merciful gods!"

"Who is it?" Fukida said.

Sano took a cloth from under his sash. He wiped the blood off the corpse's face, revealing familiar heavy-lidded eyes, flat nose, and thin mouth. "It's Aisu," he said, startled. "Chamberlain Yanagisawa's chief retainer."

Marume said, "He was a piece of scum. I'm certain he threw that bomb at us in Tobacco Lane. He deserved to die."

"What was he doing here?" Fukida said.

"I don't know, but his presence must mean that Yanagisawa is in Miyako, because they're never far apart." Sano experienced the disturbing shock of discovering that reality had a far different shape than he'd perceived. Rising, he cursed under his breath. He'd thought himself safe from Yanagisawa, free to restore his honor and regain the shogun's favor in peace. But his enemy must have secretly followed him here. Why had Sano imagined that Yanagisawa would let him off so easily?

"But why would the chamberlain risk leaving Edo?" Marume said, his voice skeptical. "Where is he now, and what's he up to?"

As Sano stood contemplating Aisu's corpse, he realized that Yanagisawa must be the hidden element in the murder case. Yanagisawa was working another plot against him. Its exact details weren't clear, but Sano glimpsed its intent, with mounting dismay.

"This whole investigation was rigged as a trap for me at the start," he said. "Yanagisawa has been working behind the scenes, directing my every move—Aisu wasn't clever enough to manage such a tricky operation alone. Events were supposed to culminate in my death from the spirit cry tonight. But the murderer killed Aisu instead of me."

Marume and Fukida looked at him as if concerned for his sanity. "How do you know?" Marume said. "And how could Yanagisawa manipulate you? Even if he sent the message summoning you here and ordered the guards to abandon us inside the palace, how could he cause the killer to attack? And why was Aisu here?"

Sano had ideas, but no definite answers yet. A plan began forming in his mind. Whatever stroke of luck had saved his life, plus the knowledge he'd gained, gave him a chance to turn Yanagisawa's scheme to his own advantage. But he needed to act fast. Instead of replying to Marume's questions, he raised his head, listening to the night. He heard distant voices. The glow of lanterns hazed the air above surrounding areas of the palace, and he knew that soon people would flock to see what new destruction the spirit cry had wrought.

"There's no time to talk," Sano said. "Just listen, then do as I say. Fukida-*san*, give me your surcoat."

The detective frowned in confusion, but obeyed. Sano spread the garment over Aisu's face. "You stay with the corpse. Tell the Imperial Court that it's me, that I was the killer's victim." Ignoring his men's shocked exclamations, Sano rushed on: "Aisu was taller and thinner than I am, but the blood and filth will discourage anyone from taking a close look. You'll have to remove the corpse as quickly as possible and figure out a way to hide it. Then issue an official report of my death. Keep the real events of tonight a secret."

"Yes, *sōsakan-sama*." Although Fukida sounded dazed, Sano knew he would carry out the orders.

"Marume-*san*, you come with me now," Sano said. "We have to get out of the palace before anyone sees me."

"Wait, please, *sōsakan-sama*," Fukida said. "What shall I tell your wife?"

The question almost shattered Sano's resolve. While the voices grew louder, moving lights shone up through trees outside the kitchen compound, and precious time sped away, he imagined how the news of his murder would affect Reiko. To let her think him dead was much worse than his lust for another woman. When Reiko found out the truth, she might never forgive his deceit. But if he didn't use this chance to combat Yanagisawa's machinations, he might never solve the case or win his battle against the chamberlain. Failure would doom Reiko along with him. He had to save them both.

"Break the news to my wife as gently as possible," Sano said at last. "Not even she can know I survived, until I finish what I have to do." Any lapse in secrecy could ruin everything. The fewer people who knew about his ploy, the better. Sano added, "With luck, I won't have to deceive her for long." Then he and Marume left quickly.

15

As Sano and Marume raced past buildings in the imperial enclosure, dark windows brightened. Glowing lanterns moved within corridors. All around them, Sano heard voices and movement. He and Marume changed directions repeatedly in order to avoid the notice of the people converging on the murder scene. In a garden, they ducked behind a pavilion to hide from a horde of palace watchmen. They dashed through courtyards and passages until they reached the wall that separated the enclosure from the northern sector of the *kuge* quarter. They scaled the wall and leapt down to the lane below.

"Which way?" Marume asked, panting.

Sano didn't know a direct route out of the palace, and he couldn't risk getting lost or being seen in the *kuge* quarter. He said, "We'll take the overhead shortcut."

He and Marume climbed the fence opposite the imperial enclosure and pulled themselves onto the low eaves of a villa. Rooftops spread around them like an eerie gray landscape of tiled peaks. They sped across this, and Sano hoped that if the residents heard them, they would be far away before anyone got a good look at them. They jumped from house to house and over narrow lanes. At last they surmounted the main palace wall and halted in the darkness of Imadegawa Avenue.

"What now?" Marume said.

"Go to the gate we went in by and get our horses," Sano said. "Ride away, then double around and meet me in the alley across Teramachi

Avenue and two blocks north from the gate. Don't let the palace guards see you come back."

Marume hurried off to obey. Sano's own path took him through the deserted city streets around the palace, past dark houses and closed shops. By the time he reached the rendezvous spot, Marume was already there, waiting for him beneath a balcony with the horses.

"Care to let me in on what's next?" Marume said.

Sano quickly outlined his plan. Then they stood in the alley, watching the avenue. After a brief wait, Marume said, "Look, here he comes."

Just as Sano had predicted, *Yoriki* Hoshina rode up to the gate, accompanied by a group of other policemen. The group dismounted and went inside the palace.

"Let's go," Sano said.

They mounted their horses and rode to Miyako police headquarters, which was in the city's administrative district, near the mansions of local officials. A stone wall enclosed stables, barracks, and a main building that housed offices. Torchlight flared within the compound. Sano had interviewed Lady Asagao here in her prison cell earlier. He'd also met with Hoshina to discuss the arrest, so he knew where Hoshina's private quarters were. Now he and Marume left their horses in a side street. Marume went to the gate to tell the guards he wanted to talk to Hoshina about the murder at the palace. Sano crept around to the rear of the complex.

Pairs of idle, bored-looking sentries manned gates at intervals along the wall; clearly, they didn't expect anyone to break into police headquarters. Sano climbed over the wall, dropped into the deserted compound, and located the barracks, four long, single-story buildings with narrow verandas in front and privy sheds behind, arranged around a courtyard. Hoshina had a corner suite in the east unit. Just as Sano reached the rear door, he heard voices at the front of the building: Marume, talking with the guard who had escorted him into headquarters to wait for Hoshina. Presently Sano heard a door open and noises inside; the windows of Hoshina's quarters lit up. The broad silhouette of Marume appeared on the paper panes and moved toward Sano. Then the door slid open.

Marume looked out, saw Sano, and nodded. Sano entered silently, following Marume into a bedchamber where Hoshina's futon lay on the floor, through paper partitions to an office furnished with a desk and cabinets, then a parlor where a lantern burned above floor cushions and a low table. Marume knelt in the parlor and Sano on the other side of the partition in the shadow of a cabinet to wait for Hoshina.

Reiko heard the spirit cry from her room in Nijō Manor.

After Sano had left for the Imperial Palace, she'd lain down on the futon while waiting for him to come back, and had fallen asleep. The chilling scream jarred her into alertness. Around her, floors creaked as the inn's other guests stirred; voices clamored.

"Did you hear that noise?"

"What was it?"

But Reiko knew instinctively what it was. She also knew for certain now that Lady Asagao wasn't the killer, because the spirit cry had come from the direction of the palace. In the moonlight that shone through the windows, she saw that she was alone; Sano hadn't returned. A rush of panic agitated Reiko. The spirit cry had heralded death once before. Not much time could have passed since Sano left; he could still be inside the palace. She had to make sure he was safe.

She dressed hurriedly, then ran out to the corridor. The innkeeper's wife appeared, clad in a night robe.

"That was the same noise we heard the night the imperial left minister died," said the woman. "Everyone knows he was killed by a ghost with magical powers." This, then, was how the superstitious townspeople explained the scream and the murder. "You must stay in your room where you'll be safe."

"I have to see if my husband is all right." Reiko started toward the door.

The innkeeper's wife held her back. "But you can't go out alone at night. Outlaws will attack you."

"I'll take my husband's guards with me," Reiko said, eager to reach Sano.

"You must stay." Concern gave the woman's manner authority. "Let me send a manservant to the palace to see what happened."

Reiko reluctantly consented, less because of fear for herself than the thought that Sano was probably busy investigating another murder and would be upset if she interrupted him. The innkeeper's wife dispatched the servant. Reiko lit a lamp in her room and sat drinking tea, wondering who had uttered the spirit cry and why the killer would strike again.

After an hour, the innkeeper's wife reappeared and said, "The servant just came back. He spoke to the guards at the palace gate. All they told him was that there had been another death. They wouldn't say who it was."

Reiko felt a sudden stab of fear. "Thank you," she said.

Alone in her room, she told herself it couldn't be Sano who had died; she would have sensed if anything had happened to him. But wouldn't he know she would hear the spirit cry? Wouldn't he send a message to reassure her? Dread mounted in Reiko. The inn quieted as the other guests settled down to sleep, and in the stillness, the thudding of her heart echoed in her ears. The room was hot, but Reiko's hands turned cold from an inner chill. She thought of sending one of Sano's guards into the palace for news, then reconsidered. She wanted to know, yet she did not want to know.

Time dragged on. Then Reiko heard footsteps approaching her room. She threw open the door. There stood Detective Fukida. One look at his haggard face told her what she'd been dreading. She had a sensation of a black void absorbing all the light and warmth and joy in the world.

"No," she whispered.

"We were on our way to see the emperor." The young samurai's voice trembled. "The killer ambushed us inside the palace, and—"

"No, it's impossible. When he left, he said he would see me later." Reiko heard herself forestalling the inevitable truth. She backed away from Fukida, glancing wildly around the room. "His things are still here. He can't be—" She could not make herself say it.

Fukida came to her and grasped her hands. Because he would never touch his master's wife under ordinary circumstances, the gesture convinced Reiko and pierced her heart. She pulled her hands out of Fukida's and hunched low, arms clasped around herself.

"Honorable Lady Reiko, I'm sorry," Fukida said, looking ready to weep. "Your husband is dead."

"Where is he?" Now Reiko experienced a consuming need to be with Sano. Although she remained outwardly calm, emotion began building inside her, as if her spirit stood in the path of a violent storm. "Take me there."

Fukida shook his head. "I can't," he said wretchedly. "There was such great injury to him . . ." The young detective gulped, then continued: "Before he died, he used his last breath to order me to spare you the sight of him. I'm sorry."

"But I'm his wife. You can't keep me away." The storm inside Reiko gathered power; she could hear the gusting winds of grief and the thunder of outrage coming closer, and see the turbulent black clouds of despair lowering upon her. "Where is he? I demand that you take me to my husband immediately!"

Now the storm overpowered Reiko. Falling to her knees, she howled, "No. No. No!" Raised in samurai tradition, she'd been trained to value stoicism and practice self-control, but this terrible moment taught her that training was inadequate preparation for tragedy. She didn't care if she compromised her dignity. With her beloved husband dead, what did social standards of behavior matter anymore?

Through the tears that streamed from her eyes, she saw Fukida standing by, helpless and shamefaced. He said, "I'll get help," then fled. Soon Reiko's maids came. They hugged her, murmuring words of comfort that she barely heard above her own sobs and moans. They held her still while a local physician poured a bitter liquid down her throat. It must have been a sleeping potion, because the world grew hazy, and Reiko drifted into unconsciousness.

Temple bells tolled the next hour, and the next, while Sano and Marume waited for *Yoriki* Hoshina. At last Sano heard brisk footsteps cross the courtyard and mount the wooden stairs to the veranda. He stood in the shadow of the cabinet, braced for action. The front door opened. Now the shadow of a second figure appeared opposite Marume's on the paper partition.

"Ah, Marume-*san*," said Hoshina's voice. "The sentries just told me you were here. I'm sorry you had such a long wait, but after I finished at the palace, I had to go to the *shoshidai*'s mansion to report what had happened."

Both shadows bowed; Hoshina's knelt. Marume said, "It's I who should apologize for coming here without notice."

"Under the circumstances, formality is unnecessary," Hoshina said in a kind, forgiving tone. He obviously had no idea that he and Marume weren't alone. "My condolences on the murder of your master."

"Thank you," Marume said sadly. "That's why I'm here."

"If you wish to take over the investigation, I'll do everything in my power to help you identify the killer and obtain justice for the *sōsakan-sama*." Hoshina's sincerity grated on Sano's nerves. The *yoriki* acted the part of the sympathetic, dutiful subordinate with perfection, no doubt rejoicing all the while.

"Well, I'm glad you're so willing to help," Marume said, his voice cheerful now, "because here's your big chance."

Sano stepped around the partition, into the parlor. "Good evening, Hoshina-*san*."

Shock widened the *yoriki*'s eyes. "*Sōsakan-sama*," he said. "But I thought—"

Aware of Hoshina's part in the plot against him, Sano was gratified by his reaction. He permitted himself a sardonic smile. "You thought I was dead? Of course you did, after coming from the scene of my murder."

Hoshina rose, staring at Sano. Marume stood, too, surreptitiously moving between Hoshina and the door. Hoshina shook his head in disbelief. "But I saw your body, and your blood on the ground, and Detective Fukida grieving over you."

"Obviously, you and your men didn't see any need to look at the face of the corpse," Sano said, glad that his prediction of the police's behavior had proved accurate. "That was a stupid mistake for someone as smart as you think you are."

The insult brought a scowl to Hoshina's face. His breathing quickened and his mouth worked as he struggled to get his emotions under control and understand what had happened. "If you didn't die at the palace, then who did?" he asked.

"It was Aisu," Sano said.

He saw instant recognition of the name in the *yoriki*'s gaze, then fear. But Hoshina quickly masked his response with a bewildered expression. "Who on earth is Aisu?"

"He was a high-ranking *bakufu* retainer from Edo. You may have met him during the past few days."

". . . No, I don't believe so." Hoshina frowned in a studied attempt at remembering, then said, "I'm sorry; I've never even heard of the man." But the energy of racing thoughts and mounting distress radiated from him. "What was this Aisu doing in Miyako?"

"You tell me," Sano said.

Hoshina gave a nervous chuckle. "How can I, when I didn't know him?" Then he spread his arms as if to embrace Sano, and said earnestly, "Look, I'm overjoyed to see you alive and well. But why have you let everyone think you dead?"

Sano's plan required the element of surprise, which had already unbalanced *Yoriki* Hoshina, and which he hoped to employ to even greater advantage soon.

"Why did you sneak into my quarters?" Hoshina added.

Ignoring the questions, Sano said, "Where is he?"

"Where is who?" Hoshina spoke in a tone of puzzled innocence, but his gaze shifted furtively.

"Chamberlain Yanagisawa," said Sano.

"The shogun's second-in-command? In Edo, I suppose. How would I know?"

Marume laughed in derisive amusement. "You're a pretty good actor. Maybe you should have chosen a career in the Kabuki theater instead of with the police force, because then you wouldn't be in as much trouble as you are now. Answer the *sōsakan-sama*'s question."

"I assure you that I would if I could," Hoshina said. Anger and panic shone through the transparent veil of his courtesy; his tongue flicked out to wet his lips. "If you're threatening me, I don't understand why. Maybe I could be of more help if someone explained what's going on."

Sano was growing impatient with Hoshina's false innocence, but he found a certain satisfaction in laying out what he'd deduced. "Yanagisawa wants to solve the mystery of Left Minister Konoe's death and destroy my reputation as a detective and my standing with the shogun by beating me at my own game. He won't risk a public defeat, so he came to Miyako secretly. But he can't identify the killer without information about the victim, the crime scene, and the suspects that he couldn't get for himself while staying hidden. He also intends to benefit from whatever leads I find.

"Therefore, he needs someone to feed him facts and inform him on my progress. Someone inside the local *bakufu*, with expertise in investigating crimes, upon whose assistance I would rely. Someone he could trust to sabotage me by withholding information about the case." Sano stared at *Yoriki* Hoshina. "Someone like you."

"With all due respect, you've got the wrong idea about me." Now Hoshina arranged his face in the confident, ingratiating smile of a man accustomed to using looks and charm to ease his way through life. Yet the air in the room was sour with the reek of his anxious sweat. "I've done everything in my power to help you. I haven't withheld anything from you. If Chamberlain Yanagisawa is in Miyako, it's news to me. And there's not one reason why I should sabotage your investigation."

"There's exactly one reason," Sano said, eyeing Hoshina with a contempt that extended to himself for thinking this man merely untrustworthy and no real threat. "Ambition."

"All right; I am ambitious. That I want to advance in the world is no secret. Therefore, it was in my interest to do my best for you so you would think well of me and recommend me for a promotion in Edo." Hoshina was all reasonableness and affability. "I've nothing to gain by making you look bad."

"You have much to gain by serving a man who can do more for you than I can."

"I'm sorry you've taken such a dislike to me," Hoshina said contritely, but his eyes had the wary look of someone humoring a madman. "At least tell me what it is you think I've done against you, so I can defend myself and set things right."

"You knew I needed to make further inquiries about Lady Asagao after she revealed her quarrel with Konoe and lied about her alibi to my wife. You guessed that I would search her rooms or send someone to do it. You planted the bloodstained robes in her cabinet."

Sano watched Hoshina for a reaction, but the *yoriki*'s face showed only consternation that might indicate either guilty or innocent surprise.

"One of your palace spies must have stolen her clothes for you," Sano continued. "If I look in the police stables, will I find a horse with a recent cut? Did you dip the robes in the horse blood and heat them over a fire to dry them and make the stains look a month old? You and Chamberlain Yanagisawa arranged a false arrest so he could show up later, catch the real killer, and take all the credit."

Hoshina burst out laughing; he slapped his knee. "Pardon my amusement, *sōsakan-sama*, but that's the most far-fetched story I've heard in a long time. Surely, the real killer planted the fake evidence to frame Lady Asagao. That seems to me a more logical explanation."

He might be right, Sano realized, and even if not, Hoshina wasn't going to admit to anything. Now that he'd recovered from the shock of seeing Sano, he'd regained his bluffing skills. The longer the interrogation went on, the less Hoshina would give away, and the greater the chance that someone might come and see that Sano was alive.

Sano said, "You didn't stop at withholding information and misguiding me. You and Chamberlain Yanagisawa set me up to be murdered tonight."

The *yoriki*'s face froze in its amiable, concerned expression. His body tensed, and Sano knew what he was thinking. Hoshina could get away with sabotaging the investigation because Yanagisawa had ordered him to do so; he wouldn't suffer any punishment as long as he had Yanagisawa's protection. But conspiracy to murder the shogun's *sōsakan-sama* was a graver charge. Even without proof of the plot, or of Hoshina's involvement in it, Sano could ruin his career just by accusing him publicly. If Sano put him on trial for the crime in a judicial system where most trials ended in a guilty verdict, he would be condemned to death. Yanagisawa would let Hoshina take the whole blame, sacrificing the *yoriki* to save himself.

This awareness flashed in Hoshina's eyes in an instant. His smile became a grimace; he relaxed his muscles with slow, deliberate effort, but held himself cautiously still, as if he stood at the brink of a deep gorge. "I don't know what you're talking about," he said.

Without warning, he bolted toward the door. Sano lunged after him, but Marume moved faster. The burly detective locked his arms around Hoshina's thighs and brought down the *yoriki* with a crash. Hoshina kicked and flailed, trying to break free. Marume hung on. Sano wasn't surprised that Hoshina had decided to run. His best hope of avoiding ruin was to find a way to warn Yanagisawa that Sano was alive and knew about the plot.

Hoshina tore loose from Marume's grasp. As he scrambled across the floor, Sano jumped on him. Marume grabbed his ankles. Hoshina had formidable strength, muscles like flexible steel, and fast reflexes. He fought savagely, bludgeoning Sano and Marume with his fists, knees, elbows, and head, but he didn't try to use the swords at his waist: Only escape would save him; killing two *bakufu* officials would get him in deeper trouble. Sano caught a stunning blow to the jaw, and Marume a kick in the stomach, but they both held on to Hoshina. They stifled cries of pain and exertion, because noise might bring people who would see Sano. Hoshina didn't call for help, probably because he didn't want to explain why he was fighting with his two superiors. The only sounds in the room were harsh gasps, the thump of blows to flesh and bone, scabbards clattering, and the crash of bodies against floor and walls.

Then Marume and Sano pinned Hoshina facedown under them. He heaved and bucked, but when Sano twisted his arm sharply, he went stiff. Marume stripped off his own sash and cut it in half with his sword. He and Sano used the lengths of fabric to bind Hoshina's ankles together and wrists behind him, then knotted the loose ends of the restraints so that Hoshina's knees doubled backward. The *yoriki* writhed on the floor, muscles straining to break his bonds. Sweat gleamed on his face; blood trickled from his nose. With his hair in wild disarray and his teeth bared, he looked more animal than human.

Sano stood, mopping his own perspiring face on his sleeve. Sore spots on his chest and limbs marked the places where bruises would soon appear. Marume leaned against the wall, his left eye red and swelling.

"You have two choices," Sano told the *yoriki*. "One: You can stick to your lies. I don't recommend this, because if you do it, I'll destroy you."

Hoshina struggled harder and spat curses at Sano.

"Two: You can cooperate with me, and I'll let you off," Sano continued. "All you have to do is tell me everything you know that relates to the murder of Left Minister Konoe, what Yanagisawa is planning, and where he is. I'll place you under protection so he can't punish you for betraying him."

Hoshina gave Sano a look of contempt. "That's not two choices, but one: certain death!" A strangled laugh burst from him.

Sano knew that a promise of protection against the most powerful man in Japan was of questionable value, and that he might be exacting cooperation at the cost of Hoshina's life, but he couldn't relent. "Choose now," he ordered.

The *yoriki* heaved sideways, gasping and grunting, in a futile effort to escape. His head tossed; the tendons of his neck bulged. Then, with a shuddering moan, he went limp. He closed his eyes and nodded in defeat, just as Sano had anticipated he would. Hoshina was no noble samurai who would sacrifice himself out of loyalty to Yanagisawa.

"Thank you." Sano exchanged a satisfied glance with Marume. "Now, what information did you withhold from me? What lies did you tell?"

His expression sullen, Hoshina spoke in a quiet monotone, confirming notions Sano had already entertained.

"Tell me about Chamberlain Yanagisawa's plot against me."

Hoshina revealed disturbing details of the plot, but Sano sensed major gaps in his knowledge. "Where is Yanagisawa?" Sano asked.

"I don't know where he is right now; he didn't tell me all his plans for tonight. But I'm supposed to meet him at a villa in the hills in the morning." At Sano's request, Hoshina gave directions.

Sano stood, beckoned Marume to follow him to the back door, and said quietly, "Lock Hoshina up and guard him so he can't run to Yanagisawa or spread the news that I'm not dead. You can send Lady Asagao home and put Hoshina in the special cell here in police headquarters. Order his colleagues not to tell anyone he's there." Sano added, "Tell Fukida-*san* to look after Reiko."

The thought of his wife awakened guilt and longing in Sano. She must have heard the news of his murder by now. He wished he could go to her so that she wouldn't have to suffer needlessly, but the most critical part of his task still lay ahead of him. "I'll be back as soon as possible."

"You're going after Yanagisawa alone?" Marume said, frowning in concern.

"I'll have to risk it," Sano said. "Gathering our troops will take too much time and increase the chances that the Miyako spies will see me and report my resurrection to Yanagisawa."

Sano and Marume bowed to each other, their glances conveying wishes for mutual good luck. Then Sano opened the door and stole away into the night.

After an empty, timeless interval, Reiko stirred awake. The windows framed pale squares of dawn light; her maids lay asleep on a futon beside hers. At first she didn't know where she was. Heavy lassitude filled her body; her head throbbed; her eyes burned. She had a vague sense that something awful had happened. Then she remembered. She was in Miyako and Sano was dead. Reiko closed her eyes; more tears leaked through the swollen lids. She wanted to go back to sleep. She wanted to die.

Yet something deep within Reiko would not let her give up so easily.

Her husband had been murdered. This was an intolerable outrage. Now fury cut through Reiko's pain like a blade lancing a wound. She must avenge Sano's death. Until she did, she would neither rest nor succumb to grief. She hoped more than ever that she was pregnant, because then a part of Sano would survive him. And she could not let their child grow up knowing that its father's murderer had gone free.

Determination gave Reiko strength, and she sat up. Vertigo spun the room around her. Breathing deeply, she waited for the after-effects of the sleeping potion to pass. She began planning what to do. Before she could avenge Sano's death, she had to solve the murder case in order to learn who had killed him. But serious obstacles loomed ahead of her.

She had no authority to investigate crimes; hence, the Imperial Palace was off-limits to her. She couldn't expect help from Marume and Fukida because they were under no obligation to obey her orders. They'd accepted her participation in Sano's work out of duty to him, but they didn't really approve of her. In fact, they might decide to take the responsibility of solving the case and avenging Sano's death upon themselves and send her home.

Then a plan sprang into Reiko's mind. It involved great potential danger and depended on the cooperation of someone with little reason to cooperate, but there seemed no other way.

Reiko rose on shaky legs. One of the maids awakened, saw her, and said, "Mistress, what are you doing?"

"I'm going out," Reiko said.

"But you need rest. You must come back to bed. Please——"

Reiko silenced the maid with a glance that threatened unspeakable punishment to anyone who tried to stop her. "I'm going out," she repeated. "Help me wash and dress."

16

Sano crouched in the underbrush beneath tall cedars, gazing up a steep dirt road at a mansion that stood behind a plank fence in the hills north of Miyako. Dew drenched his trousers. Early morning mist drifted over the woods, diffused the daylight spreading across the sky, and obscured his view of the city. A shrill chorus of birds rose in the treetops.

From a distance, the house appeared unoccupied. The second-story windows visible above the fence were shuttered, and during the hour since Sano had arrived, he'd observed the property from all angles without seeing any sign of activity. However, the gate bore the spiral crest that *Yoriki* Hoshina had described while giving directions to the mansion, and Sano could feel Chamberlain Yanagisawa's nearness like a warning tingle in his spirit. Now he moved cautiously uphill through the woods.

The closest other houses lay far above and below on the hillside, and the main road passed to the east; Sano knew because he'd already scouted the area and discovered that Yanagisawa had chosen an isolated place for his secret activities. Sano paused at the edge of the level clearing where the mansion stood. The fence was some fifteen paces away. Through the cracks between the planks Sano saw a human shape move past: a patrolling guard. After a short interval a larger figure passed. Sano timed the guards' routine by counting silently as he watched them circle around again. Feeling the strain of an eventful, sleepless night and the long ride from the city, he mustered his flagging energy.

He waited for the right moment, then sped over to the fence. He climbed it and balanced on top. With a quick glance, he took in the scene below: a garden of shrubs, boulders, and grass outside a rustic house with latticed windows and half-timbered walls. He heard footsteps on the gravel path that bordered the garden. Here came a samurai whom he recognized as one of Yanagisawa's bodyguards. Sano jumped down in front of him. The guard grunted in surprise. When he reached for his sword, Sano struck him hard in the face. The guard reeled backward, crashed to the ground, and lay still.

More footsteps signaled the approach of the second guard. Sano ducked behind a boulder. He watched the man come upon his comrade's body and squat to examine it. Sano sprang out and kicked the second guard on the chin, knocking him unconscious. He used the guards' sashes to bind their hands and feet, then crammed their socks into their mouths as gags. His pulse racing, he checked the grounds for more guards. He prayed that he wouldn't have to kill anyone. Although violence was a samurai's natural domain and an inevitable part of Sano's work, every death he caused haunted him.

There were no other guards outside the house. Sano slipped quietly in the back door. Tiptoeing along dim corridors, he peered into the kitchen, reception room, and study, all furnished with the simple elegance of a wealthy samurai's summer home, all unoccupied. In the front entryway he found a third guard seated against the wall, asleep. Sano stole up to the guard, grasped his neck, and pressed on the main blood vessels. With a jerk and a whimper, the guard passed from sleep to unconsciousness. Sano quickly tied and gagged the guard. He crept up the stairs.

On the second floor, he found another corridor. Near the end was an open door from which light spilled. Sano drew his sword. As he moved closer, he heard violent coughing. He stood to one side of the door and peered through it into a bedchamber. The light of a hanging lantern glowed on gilt murals and lacquered furniture. On a futon in the center, Chamberlain Yanagisawa crouched on knees and elbows, retching into a basin. He wore a white silk under-kimono. His complexion was a ghastly shade of gray, his expression agonized. Again and again he retched, producing merely a thin drool that ran down his chin. At last he fell back on the bed, gasping.

Sano entered the room, nonplussed because he'd never seen Yanagisawa in less than perfect health and had expected to find the chamberlain either asleep or celebrating the downfall of his rival. What was wrong with him?

At the sound of Sano's footsteps, Yanagisawa turned his head. He saw

Sano. "You," he said in a tone of terrified disbelief. Pushing himself upright, he shouted, "Guards!"

To Sano's relief, no one came. "All your men are incapacitated at the moment," he said, advancing on Yanagisawa. For once, the balance of power was weighted on his side. The knowledge elated Sano. "It's just you and me."

The chamberlain gulped as if he might get sick again, but he lurched to his feet and faced Sano with courage rooted in arrogance. "What are you doing here?" he demanded.

"I've come to talk about your sabotage of my investigation into Left Minister Konoe's murder," Sano said. "You thought you could solve the case yourself, impress the shogun, and destroy me at the same time, didn't you?"

Yanagisawa ignored the question; he seemed not to have heard it. He said, "How did you find me?"

"*Yoriki* Hoshina gave me directions," Sano said.

"Hoshina? He told you I was in Miyako?" The disbelief in Yanagisawa's voice was even more pronounced than when Sano had appeared before him. "He sent you here?" The chamberlain shook his head in vehement denial. "No. He couldn't have."

"He did." Confusion halted Sano a few steps away from Yanagisawa. Something was wrong with this conversation. Why was Yanagisawa more disconcerted to learn how he'd been discovered than surprised to see Sano alive? "Didn't you receive a report of my murder at the Imperial Palace?"

Yanagisawa took a step toward Sano, moving carefully, as if in pain, his expression unfathomable. "Where is Hoshina?"

"In a safe place," Sano said, increasingly perplexed. Yanagisawa must have been waiting for the news. Surely one of his agents would have rushed it to him. "I put Hoshina under protection after I convinced him to tell me about your plot against me."

A ragged laugh issued from Yanagisawa. Again he shook his head, but this time at some private, bitter joke. He didn't even try to deny the existence of a plot. As Sano tried to make sense of the chamberlain's reaction, various aspects of the situation that hadn't seemed directly related came together for him. Aisu's presence in the palace, Yanagisawa's illness, and the scheme his enemy had previously used added up to a startling picture.

"You were there with Aisu, weren't you?" Sano said, dazzled by enlightenment. "You forged the message from the emperor that brought me to the palace. You and Aisu lay in wait, planning to arrest the killer and take credit for solving the murder case after I was dead—the same trick you tried when I ambushed the Lion. But something went wrong. The killer attacked you and Aisu instead of me. It was you two that I heard crying out right before the spirit cry. Somehow you escaped, and the only harm you suffered is sickness from the after-effects of exposure to the force of *kiai*."

Clutching his stomach, the chamberlain winced. He dropped to his knees on the futon. His eyes, with their dark, liquid irises and blood-veined whites, watched Sano intently. Sano was disturbed to realize how close his own scheme had come to failing. Yanagisawa might have sent someone to track him down and stop him before he got this far. "You weren't surprised to see me alive," Sano said, "because even though you heard about my death, you knew the truth—that Aisu was the killer's victim, not I. You must have been waiting for Hoshina to come so you could plan what to do next." Yet an important question remained. "How did you set up my murder?"

Yanagisawa suddenly lunged toward the head of the bed beneath him. He thrust his hand under the futon. Sano leapt forward and jabbed the point of his sword against Yanagisawa's throat. The chamberlain cried out in alarm. His hand jerked up, holding a dagger that he'd obviously meant to hurl at Sano. He fell on his side, straining away from the sword.

"Drop the dagger," Sano ordered, his heart hammering in delayed panic. "Drop it, or I'll kill you!"

Fear shone in Yanagisawa's eyes. He lay rigid, knees drawn up, awkwardly supporting his body on his left hand, the dagger extended in his right hand. But his mouth twisted in an insolent smile.

"You won't kill me," he said in a breathy, corrosive voice. "You hate to kill, and you think it's because you're so noble, so benevolent, that taking a life is beneath you." He uttered a derisive snort of laughter. "But I know the truth. You're not only an incompetent detective who fell into the trap I set for you, you're a coward. You're afraid of what will happen if you kill the shogun's second-in-command. You're incapable of looking me in the eye and cutting my throat!"

Indeed, Sano had spoken his threat merely to frighten Yanagisawa into obedience; he'd had no real intention of killing. But a sudden fury swept over him. That Yanagisawa should insult his professional ability and his honor! For more than two years, Sano had endured the chamberlain's physical and verbal attacks. He'd stifled the urge to retaliate because of his duty to respect the shogun's second-in-command, and because Yanagisawa had the power to destroy his family. Yet now, in the heat of rage that had built to a critical point, he knew he could kill Yanagisawa and not care about the consequences. What he thought about Yanagisawa, but had never spoken before, exploded from him.

"You call *me* incompetent?" he shouted. "You, who couldn't find the Lion by yourself, and certainly wouldn't have accomplished anything on this investigation without help from *Yoriki* Hoshina and me!"

Yanagisawa gaped in amazement at Sano's outburst. "How dare you speak to me this way?" Anger flushed his pale complexion. "Have you forgotten who I am?"

"You've forgotten that you're at my mercy," Sano retorted, jabbing his sword fiercely at Yanagisawa, who gasped and scuttled backward, still gripping the dagger. Sano advanced until he had Yanagisawa pinned against the wall. "If you think I'm a coward, there's no bigger coward in the world than you! You send flunkies to assassinate me because you're afraid to do it yourself. You stab your enemies in the back because you haven't the courage to challenge them face to face!"

"Shut up!" Yanagisawa commanded.

Sano was shaking with righteous anger, exhilarated by the release of pent-up fury. "Your way is to stab and hide, but I can make sure you won't live to do so ever again. Now drop the dagger, you corrupt, evil, backstabbing, and cowardly disgrace to Bushido!"

Bloodlust obliterated prudence. Sano's vision narrowed until all he could see was the hateful face of his enemy. His muscles tensed, ready to drive the sword deep into Yanagisawa's throat. Yanagisawa must have felt the increased pressure on the blade and realized what a state Sano was in, because horror replaced the insolence in his gaze. As they stared at each other, the moment stretched into a deadly space in time where the worst could happen.

Yanagisawa opened his hand and let the dagger fall.

The clatter it made hitting the floor was like a chunk of ice dropped into a hot porcelain bowl. The cold impact of reason shattered the murderous rage in Sano. The savage pleasure of holding Yanagisawa's life in his hands vanished. He kicked away the dagger and eased his grip on his sword. What if he had killed the chamberlain?

Across his mind flashed images of himself standing over the bloody corpse of his enemy; his trial for murder; himself, Reiko, their entire families, and all their close associates marching to the public execution ground to die for his crime of high treason against the Tokugawa regime. Sano was horrified to know himself capable of an insanity where even honor mattered less than satisfying his anger.

He saw the same knowledge, and new respect, mirrored on Yanagisawa's face. Sano realized that Yanagisawa had never really feared him before, had always relied on the self-discipline that had kept him from striking back. But this incident had destroyed Yanagisawa's belief that he could attack Sano without serious consequences.

"That's better," Sano said. His voice had returned to its normal calm pitch, but in the wake of his rage, a heady sense of power remained. "Now tell me how you set up my murder."

Yanagisawa glanced down at the blade that still impinged on his throat. "Would you mind if I sat up first?" His tone had a courteous entreaty with which he'd never before addressed Sano.

When Sano withdrew the sword just far enough so it was no longer touching him, Yanagisawa expelled a long, tremulous breath and gingerly eased himself upright. Sweat trickled in rivulets down his face. He said, "The night of the *shoshidai*'s banquet, Hoshina told me that Lady Asagao had admitted hating Left Minister Konoe and lied about where she was during his murder. I anticipated that you would search her chambers for evidence, so I had Hoshina get some robes of the type she wears, stain them with horse blood, and plant them there.

"The next morning, Hoshina held a secret interview with Lady Asagao. He informed her that you would be coming to talk to her, and he conveyed my orders that when you did, she should confess to the murder. He told her the story she should tell, and said she must convince you that she was guilty. She didn't want to do it, but Hoshina gave her my promise that if she cooperated, she would be pardoned later. If not—or if she told anyone what he'd said—she would be executed."

Now Sano understood why Asagao had behaved so oddly, produced such a logical yet dubious confession, and seemed as terrified as determined to persuade him that she'd killed Konoe. Asagao had lied not to protect Emperor Tomohito and the Imperial Court, but to protect herself from the punishment with which Hoshina had threatened her.

"You manipulated me into making a false arrest," Sano said with a grudging admiration for Yanagisawa's cleverness. "Hoshina pressured Left Minister Konoe's attendants into confirming the affair and the ladies-in-waiting into retracting Asagao's alibi. You planned to make your official appearance in Miyako after I was dead, take over the investigation, and catch the real killer. You picked Asagao for bait because she's so unlikely a suspect that I would look stupid for arresting her, although the law gave me no choice. You couldn't be satisfied with my death; you wanted to destroy my reputation, too."

"Yes," the chamberlain conceded reluctantly, "Lady Asagao suited my purpose. But I didn't choose her for herself alone. I had to give the real murderer a reason to kill you."

The connection between Lady Asagao's arrest and the killer's attack now became apparent to Sano. "Hoshina didn't tell me that Right Minister Ichijo is a suspect because you believe he's the killer and you wanted to keep him to yourself. Lady Asagao is his daughter; her position as the emperor's chief consort gives Ichijo special influence over the Imperial Court, which he would lose if anything happened to her. You thought the arrest would make Ichijo desperate enough to try to save Asagao from execution by killing me, which would spare you the trouble."

The chamberlain said, "When Hoshina sent you the forged message, he also sent anonymous ones to Right Minister Ichijo, Emperor Tomohito, Lady Jokyōden, and Prince Momozono, telling them you were coming to the palace."

Of course, the devious Yanagisawa wouldn't stake his success on a gamble that Ichijo was indeed the killer, Sano thought; he'd hedged his bet by alerting the other suspects. Sano could think of reasons some of them might wish to eliminate the man in charge of the murder investigation.

"Those messages also specified the route that the palace guards would follow while escorting you through the imperial enclosure," Yanagisawa continued. "I went there early with Aisu and my bodyguards to catch Ichijo in the act of murder and arrest him. When we were heading toward the spot where the guards were supposed to abandon you, I felt a strange vibration in the air. We saw an eerie light and heard loud breathing. I felt someone following us, and I was suddenly terrified. So were my men. I ordered everyone to stay together, but my bodyguards ran off. I followed Aisu to the imperial kitchens. And then . . ."

The muscles of Yanagisawa's throat contracted; he shuddered. "Merciful gods, that scream. It knocked me flat. I couldn't move, couldn't do anything except lie there howling in pain while the terrible noise went on and on." The chamberlain took a deep breath, then said, "Finally it stopped. My ears were ringing; I was trembling and sore and nauseated. I got up and found Aisu lying nearby. He was dead. Then the vibration started again. It was very faint, coming from between the buildings. The killer was there; I could feel him. He was getting ready to scream again and kill me."

Sano hadn't felt any vibration after the spirit cry, probably because he'd been too far away. Suddenly Yanagisawa began to laugh. Hysteria tinged his merriment.

"What's so funny?" Sano said, wondering if the spirit cry had demented Yanagisawa's mind.

"It's ironic. Do you know what saved me?"

Mystified, Sano shook his head.

"You." Yanagisawa pointed at Sano. "I heard you and your detectives talking. The vibration suddenly stopped. I saw a movement in the shadows, and I couldn't feel the killer anymore. You scared him away." Now Yanagisawa's humor faded into the glumness of defeat. "You, of all people, saved my life."

Pity diluted Sano's animosity toward the chamberlain. To be rescued by the foe whose death he'd plotted—what a blow to his pride! "Did you see the killer?"

"No," Yanagisawa said. All the resistance had left him. He looked pale, sick, and broken. Perhaps he mourned the loss of Aisu. Or was something else bothering him?

"You referred to the killer as 'him,' " Sano continued. "Does that mean you think it was a man?"

Yanagisawa shook his head. "At the time, I thought of him—or her—as 'it.' " He added, "I caught up with my bodyguards outside the palace gate. We rode straight here. I asked them if they'd gotten a look at the killer. They said no."

"Unfortunately, the only other witness is dead," Sano said. "But it's unlikely that more than one person has the power of *kiai*, so it was probably the same killer as in Left Minister Konoe's murder. The attack on you has cleared Lady Asagao and narrowed the field to four suspects. I can determine where each of them was last night."

"How wonderful that my terrible experience was so helpful to your investigation," Yanagisawa said with a touch of his old sarcasm. Then an aggrieved expression came over his features. "Why would the murderer want to kill me?"

"That's a good question. The answer might provide a clue to the murderer's identity."

"I suppose you're going to place me under guard in some secret place until your work in Miyako is finished," Yanagisawa said. "Then you'll take me back to Edo and tell the shogun what I've done. His Excellency will be so furious that I deceived him and tried to ruin the investigation he ordered that he'll believe whatever you say about me. No doubt *Yoriki* Hoshina will be glad to corroborate your story in exchange for a pardon." A grim, desolate note inflected Yanagisawa's voice. "I'll lose my post, and probably my life."

Sano had come here intending to do exactly as Yanagisawa had described. It was what Yanagisawa deserved, and would rid him of the chamberlain's interference. But a strange, fleeting sensation came over him, like the invisible touch of ancestral spirits returning for Obon. Sano found himself thinking that fate had brought him and Yanagisawa together for some important purpose, that there was a reason for the way things had turned out, and he would regret following his planned course of action. Sano frowned, puzzling over the bizarre omen. Had his own mind been affected by the spirit cry? Yet an instinct stronger than common sense urged him to obey intuition.

He said to Chamberlain Yanagisawa, "Yes, I could destroy you, but instead, I'm going to offer you a deal."

Yanagisawa's brows rose in astonishment; then he narrowed his eyes suspiciously.

"If you'll agree to a truce between us and help me solve the case," Sano said, "then I won't report your sabotage to the shogun."

Yanagisawa gave an incredulous laugh. "You're not serious."

"Indeed I am," Sano said. "I want information you have. You want to be a detective. If we work together, I can fulfill the shogun's orders, and you can share the credit."

From the opaque look in the chamberlain's eyes, Sano knew Yanagisawa was calculating the benefits of the deal, the price of staying out of trouble, and how he could come out ahead.

"All right. We'll work together. But surely you understand what I can do to you if you allow me my freedom." Yanagisawa regarded Sano with resentment and scorn.

"And you understand what I'll do to you if you cross me," Sano said. The gaze he fixed upon Yanagisawa reminded the chamberlain how close he'd come to death tonight. It promised that next time Sano wouldn't control his temper. *No matter where you hide or how many guards you have, I will get to you,* Sano thought, *and I will show no mercy.*

Yanagisawa stared, appalled, then nodded in resignation. "Very well, *Sōsakan* Sano. A truce it is."

17

Reiko took a bath that rinsed away tears and restored strength; heavy makeup covered her puffy eyelids and mottled complexion. She pinned up her hair, which she would later cut off and put in Sano's coffin as a token of her fidelity, and dressed in a pale gray silk kimono with a pattern of summer grasses because she hadn't had time to buy drab mourning robes. Then she ordered her palanquin bearers to take her to the Imperial Palace.

Out in the city, however, sorrow nearly defeated Reiko. As she rode through Miyako in her palanquin, the bright sunshine, colorful shops, and busy crowds seemed unreal. It was as if the death of the man she loved had left no mark upon the world. Worse, Reiko couldn't shake the feeling that Sano was still alive. Whenever she spied a samurai of his age and build, her heart leapt. Then, after she saw it wasn't Sano, fresh despair crushed her. Tears stung her eyes; she dabbed them dry to avoid ruining her makeup, and closed the palanquin's windows.

At last Reiko arrived in the quadrangle of the Palace of the Abdicated Emperor. As she disembarked from her palanquin, Lady Jokyōden came to meet her.

"Greetings, Lady Sano," Jokyōden said. Her face was impassive, her posture regal. She bowed in a cool, formal manner. "Please accept my sincere condolences on your loss."

"A thousand thanks." Reiko fought to steady her trembling voice, because a display of emotion would shame her and offend this woman who obviously didn't want her here.

"I did not expect to see you again," Jokyōden said.

"You asked me to come," Reiko reminded her.

Mild surprise lifted Jokyōden's painted brows. "So I did. But that was before yesterday's events proved that you were no friend to me and a danger to the Imperial Court. When we talked before, I guessed that you wanted to help your husband by questioning me about Left Minister Konoe's murder. I was intrigued by you, and decided that it wouldn't hurt to further our acquaintance because you seemed capable of little harm.

"But you had the gall to search for evidence in private quarters. Your discovery led to the arrest of the emperor's consort by your husband, who chose to make a quick end to his work by persecuting an innocent woman." Jokyōden's tone was hard, unforgiving. "How you can presume to come here now is beyond my comprehension."

"I want to apologize," Reiko said humbly. "I did take advantage of Lady Asagao's trust. It turned out to be a terrible mistake." Yet Reiko also wanted to counter Jokyōden's criticism. "But a murder investigation often requires devious means to serve justice. My husband arrested Lady Asagao instead of immediately looking elsewhere for the killer because it was his duty to charge her with murder after she confessed." Reiko couldn't keep the bitterness out of her voice. "He paid for my mistake and his actions with his life."

Pity softened Jokyōden's expression, though she remained aloof. "I regret that you've suffered," she said. "However, I presume you have some other purpose for coming here besides discussing past events. What do you want from me?"

"I want you to help me find out who killed my husband," Reiko said.

"I see." The noncommittal reply carried a strange inflection, as though Jokyōden had half expected Reiko's request, but couldn't quite believe she'd actually heard it. Then she brought her hands together in front of her, fingertips pointed outward and touching. "Don't you think the bakufu will assign someone to investigate the matter?"

"Yes. But I want to finish my husband's work and learn the truth about his death." Reiko forbore to mention that she intended to execute Sano's killer with her own hands.

"While I sympathize with your wishes," Jokyōden said, "investigating crimes is hardly within your purview anymore. Your husband's status gave you freedom and power that you no longer have." She said gently, "May I offer my advice? You are young; time will heal your pain. Your family will eventually arrange another marriage for you; with luck, you'll find love and happiness again. Accept reality, go on with your life, and let the authorities handle official business."

Wild desperation filled Reiko as she realized Jokyōden wasn't going to help her. The suggestion that she would forget Sano and should abandon her quest for justice infuriated her. She retorted, "I doubt that you've ever accepted fate or left any business you care about to others. Shall I do as you say, not as you do?"

Jokyōden stared, affronted by Reiko's blunt speech. Then she shook her head and smiled in self-mockery. Her rueful gaze conveyed a new respect for Reiko. "I see that hypocrisy cannot persuade you," she said.

Reiko took this response as a sign that Jokyōden might relent. She pressed on: "I realize I'm powerless without my husband. But you command much authority in the Imperial Court. You can take me where I need to go in the palace. You can introduce me to witnesses and ask them to cooperate with me. You can provide information I need." Belatedly, Reiko feared that she sounded too presumptuous. "If you choose to grant my request," she added.

Frowning, Jokyōden interlaced her fingers and looked down at them for a moment. "What you do not seem to realize is that my interests run opposite to yours. You are asking me to open the palace to you, for your purpose of incriminating someone here. Since Lady Asagao has been proven innocent, the array of suspects has narrowed to those who were in the palace last night. That includes the emperor. Do you expect me to betray my own son for your sake?" Incredulity edged Jokyōden's calm voice. "And I am still a suspect. Would you expect me to lead you to evidence of my own guilt?"

Reiko had known that Jokyōden was still a suspect. She also knew the danger of involving a suspect in her investigation, especially one as intelligent as Jokyōden. To protect herself, her son, and the court, Jokyōden could destroy clues, plant false evidence, and order witnesses to lie. Reiko would never be sure whether she was helping or sabotaging. And there was a possibility of more extreme treachery if Reiko enlisted Jokyōden's aid. Maybe the killer had feared that Sano wouldn't believe Asagao was guilty and had halted his investigation by slaying him. If Jokyōden was the killer, she might do the same to Reiko. Working with Reiko would give her plenty of opportunity.

However, Reiko had no choice except to take the risk. "Before my husband died, he said he had a feeling there was more to the murder case than was obvious. He thought there might be other suspects nobody knew about, and that one of them was more likely the killer than His Majesty the Emperor, Prince Momozono, or you. By helping me discover the truth, you could clear yourself and your son."

Jokyōden regarded her skeptically. She unlaced her hands and folded her arms.

"I have no one else to turn to," Reiko said, abandoning logic in favor of an emotional appeal. She knelt before Jokyōden. "If you won't help me, I'll have to go back to Edo without knowing who killed my husband, and depend on the *bakufu* to obtain justice for him. And I—I can't bear—"

An upheaval of suppressed grief shattered Reiko's artificial poise. She thought of Sano, his voice, his smile, the scent and feel of him. She imagined the long years ahead without him. Desolation swept over her. She pressed a hand against her mouth to stifle a sob and tried to compose herself by focusing on her surroundings: the morning sunlight casting the shadows of buildings across the quadrangle; the bearers standing by her palanquin; the floral pattern woven into Jokyōden's azure silk robe.

Jokyōden watched her in silent speculation. Was she weighing sympathy for a bereaved widow against her loyalty to the Imperial Court? Was she thinking of what she and Reiko shared as women unique in society and how she could honor their comradeship while protecting her kin? Or was she a murderess considering how to exploit the situation to her own advantage?

Then Jokyōden said, "My authority does not entitle me to let you roam around the palace or interrogate members of the court, but perhaps there is another way I can be of assistance, if you will accompany me on a short trip."

She spoke as though leery of committing herself, and her shrewd gaze held no warmth, but Reiko was too overjoyed to mind her manner.

"A million thanks," Reiko exclaimed, fighting tears of gratitude. "You won't regret your decision."

Jokyōden gave her an enigmatic smile. "I sincerely hope that neither of us will," she said.

Reiko chose to ignore the implicit warning in the words. She didn't know what had finally swayed Jokyōden in her favor. She could not afford to care.

Miyako's textile industry was centered in a district known as Nishijin—"Western Camp"—named for the army encampment located there during the civil wars. The main avenues of Kuramaguchi and Imadegawa on north and south, and Horikawa and Senbon on east and west, bounded a grid of narrower lanes that ran through Nishijin. Down these flowed stinking open sewers. Workers carried bolts of cloth and baskets containing silk cocoons. Women sprinkled water on thresholds to keep down the dust. Outside shops, hawkers invited customers to view shelves of bright fabrics. The rattle-clack of many looms resounded.

A procession of imperial guards and Tokugawa troops escorting two palanquins halted in the middle of a block. Reiko stepped out of her palanquin and Lady Jokyōden from the other. Together they walked to a shop. Unlike the establishments on either side, whose open storefronts were filled with customers, this one stood deserted, its tall wooden doors closed.

"What are we doing here?" Reiko asked.

Jokyōden said, "This shop belonged to Left Minister Konoe. He purchased it some years ago."

"What for?" Reiko said, baffled. The noble class didn't engage in trade, and she couldn't imagine Konoe wanting quarters in the noisy, dirty, and bustling textile district.

"He wanted privacy that he couldn't get at home." Jokyōden unlocked the shop's doors, and Reiko followed her inside.

Hot, musty darkness engulfed them. Jokyōden picked up a long wooden pole that stood near the entrance, pushed open the trap door of a skylight, then closed the doors. In the dust-flecked light from above, Reiko saw a room that had once been the display area of a textile business. It was empty, the floor littered with dead insects. She smelled mildew; sweat trickled down her temples. The ache of grief swelled in her. Would that she were here working with Sano instead of investigating his murder! She kept her misery at bay by speculating on why Left Minister Konoe had needed the privacy afforded by this shop.

Konoe had been a *metsuke* spy. Had he bought the shop because he needed a place from which to conduct espionage? If so, he'd found the perfect location to live a secret life: conveniently near the palace, but on the other side of the class boundary, where he could be anonymous. And maybe this secret life was related to his murder.

With the purposeful stride of someone who knew where she was going, Jokyōden walked through an open doorway at the back of the room. Reiko joined her in a second room, where an abandoned loom stood, festooned with spiderwebs, faded threads clinging to its broken beams.

"How do you know about this place?" Reiko asked.

Another door, this one closed, led to the rear of the shop. Jokyōden halted with her back against it and said, "If I am to tell you, I must first have your promise that what I say will be kept in strict confidence."

Reiko hesitated, because although instinct told her that Jokyōden's answer might be important to her investigation, she didn't know whether she could honor such a bargain. Avenging Sano's death took priority over Jokyōden's wishes. If revealing later what Jokyōden told her would benefit her cause, then she must do it. Still, perhaps she could somehow manage to keep Jokyōden's secrets without jeopardizing her own mission.

"I promise," she said.

For a long interval, Jokyōden regarded her in silence. The room was dim and Jokyōden's face in shadow, so Reiko couldn't see her expression. The incessant clatter of looms from the adjacent shops echoed through the walls. Then Jokyōden said in a tone devoid of emotion, "Left Minister Konoe and I were lovers at one time. We used to meet here, where no one who mattered would see us together."

Surprise stunned Reiko. When she and Jokyōden had talked about the left minister two days ago, Jokyōden had betrayed no personal feelings toward him. Now Reiko felt a stab of apprehension as she wondered what else Jokyōden had concealed.

"When was this affair?" she asked.

"Before Left Minister Konoe's death, obviously." With her sarcastic reply and forbidding tone, Jokyōden proclaimed that she didn't intend to elaborate on the subject. She turned to open the door, then let Reiko into the shop's last room, which had once been the proprietor's living quarters.

When Jokyōden opened the skylight and windows, Reiko saw a kitchen on one side, where a kettle sat on the hearth; shelves held a few pieces of crockery, parcels of tea, and dried fruit. On the other side, a charcoal brazier stood beside a dingy futon on the frayed tatami; a pine table held a lamp; an umbrella leaned against the whitewashed plank wall. The only item that reflected Konoe's noble rank was a desk made of dark teak with gold geometric inlays. The windows overlooked an alley whose privy sheds and garbage bins sent foul odors into the room. Reiko couldn't imagine the elegant Jokyōden lying on that bed, in this dismal place.

"This is the one place I can show you that might contain clues about what the left minister did during the days just before he died, who he saw, or why someone wanted to kill him," Jokyōden said. Her dignified poise hid any shame she felt at bringing Reiko to the scene of her illicit romance. "He sometimes kept personal papers here."

He'd kept very few things here, Reiko thought; hardly enough even for a quick tryst once in awhile. Then she noticed indented, rectangular shadows on the tatami where furniture had once stood, and hooks on the walls that might have held paintings or drapery. And she understood. The room had been comfortably furnished when Jokyōden and Konoe had come here together. Konoe must have removed unneeded furnishings because the affair had ended even before his death.

"We always traveled here separately," Jokyōden said. "Sometimes he would be writing when I arrived, and he always put the papers away in the desk. Perhaps they're still there."

Even as Reiko knelt at the desk, questions burgeoned in her mind. Why had the affair ended, and when? Reiko remembered asking Jokyōden how she got along with Konoe, and Jokyōden's answer: "We had no quarrels." But what if there *had* been a quarrel, one that had caused a breakup between Konoe and Jokyōden shortly before his death? Reiko thought about Lady Asagao's story of seduction by Konoe. If it was true, then perhaps his infidelity had angered Jokyōden. Earlier, Reiko had conjectured that the pair had clashed over imperial politics, but love gone bad was also a strong motive for murder.

She looked up at Jokyōden, who stood by the window, looking outside. Sunlight slanted across her profile, glittering in her eye; a cold serenity masked her thoughts. Fear turned the sweat on Reiko's skin into a film of ice water as she remembered Jokyōden closing the front doors and sealing them both in the shop. Was it Jokyōden who had killed Konoe—and Sano? Had she arranged this trip for the purpose of eliminating a woman who sought to expose her guilt?

Then Reiko dismissed her fear as ludicrous. She didn't really believe Jokyōden was a murderer, but even if she was, she wouldn't kill again here. There were people outside, including Reiko's guards; she couldn't get away with murdering Reiko. Still, Reiko's heart thudded as she examined the desk. A uniform coating of dust dulled the inlaid surface, and she hoped that this place had remained undisturbed since Konoe last came here. Her hands shook as she lifted the lid of the desk.

Inside, amid writing brushes, inkstones, and ribbons for binding scrolls, she found stacked papers, all blank. Disappointment crushed Reiko. She pulled everything out of the desk, searched for scraps she'd missed, or hidden compartments, without success. Konoe had apparently not left any writings here. As a *metsuke* spy, he would have taken care to conceal documents related to espionage for fear that his secret life would be exposed. Or had someone else removed things, careful not to leave signs of the disturbance?

148

Reiko looked up to see Jokyōden watching her. She said, "Who else besides you and the left minister knew about this place?"

"No one, as far as I know."

"When was the last time you came here?"

"If you are asking if I have been here since the left minister died, the answer is no." Jokyōden turned back to the window.

Yet maybe she'd come back after the murder, to take away personal items she'd left behind or anything else that revealed her relationship with the left minister. Reiko knew that the Imperial Court viewed adultery in much the same way as did society in general: Married men enjoyed the freedom to have affairs, but women paid dearly for sexual dalliance. If Jokyōden's affair with Konoe had become public, the abdicated emperor would probably have divorced her; she'd have lost her authority over the court amid humiliating scandal.

However, Reiko saw another reason for Jokyōden to remove papers from the desk, if they could implicate her in Konoe's murder. Such an intelligent woman would recognize the need to destroy evidence against her. Reiko wondered whether Jokyōden had brought her here while knowing she would find nothing. Had she pretended to help with the investigation so Reiko would think her innocent?

Plagued by doubts, Reiko looked around the room for somewhere else to search. Her gaze lit on the charcoal brazier. Excitement quickened her pulse. She hardly dared to hope . . .

She hurried to the brazier, a square wooden box with multiple slots in the top and three sides. Kneeling, she peered through the grate on the fourth side. Inside sat a metal pan containing ash, sooty coals, and a wad of partially burned paper. Reiko's heart leapt. Opening the grate, she lifted out the paper, heedless of the ash that smudged her fingers. She peeled away delicate black layers. Only the innermost had survived the fire. Darkened at the edges, it was a fragment from a page of scribbled notes. An inked circle surrounded the name Ibe Masanobu. This, Reiko knew, was the daimyo of Echizen Province. Other notations read: "Site surveillance? Watch night movements." "Arrived Month 3, Day 17." "Eleven more inside yesterday." "No outsiders allowed." "Infiltrators?"

Reiko sat perfectly still, nurturing a hope as thin and fragile as the paper she cradled in her hands. This could be notes on a *metsuke* job that Left Minister Konoe had been working on just before he died. Lord Ibe and whomever else Konoe had spied on could be connected to his murder. Among them might be his killer—and Sano's. Reiko allowed herself to believe this, because with the Imperial Palace closed to her and Lady Jokyōden unable to help her further, she had no other leads by which she might solve the case and avenge Sano's death.

"Have you found what you were looking for?" Jokyōden asked.

"Yes," Reiko said firmly.

18

"Well, *Sōakan-sama*, I am most surprised and glad to see you alive," said *Shoshidai* Matsudaira. "And Honorable Chamberlain Yanagisawa, it is certainly a privilege to welcome you to Miyako."

After their confrontation in Yanagisawa's hideout in the hills, Sano had told the chamberlain how they would make their deal official. While Yanagisawa dressed, Sano had untied the three guards; then the five of them had ridden into Miyako together. Now they were seated in the reception room of the *shoshidai*'s mansion. Mastsudaira, kneeling on the dais, looked confused by the simultaneous appearance of Sano, whom he'd believed dead, and Yanagisawa, his cousin the shogun's exalted second-in-command.

"In the confusion of last night's events at the Imperial Palace, mistakes were made." Sano spoke from his place below the dais to the *shoshidai*'s left. "It was actually one of my retainers who died, not myself." This was the story that Sano had concocted to explain the murder of Aisu. "I shall now do everything possible to resolve any problems created by the erroneous report of my death."

"Very well." The *shoshidai* sounded unconvinced, but as Sano had anticipated, he was too timid to raise questions.

Yanagisawa sat at the *shoshidai*'s right, with his three bodyguards behind him. Clad in rich silk robes, he looked his usual self, although his complexion still had a sickly gray pallor. "I've been traveling through Omi Province on business for the shogun. Since that business is finished, I have decided to lend my assistance to the *sōsakan-sama*'s investigation into the murders at the Imperial Palace."

"That is very generous of you." The *shoshidai* smiled, obviously deceived by Yanagisawa's genial manner.

But Sano had perceived the resentful undertone in Yanagisawa's voice, and knew how humiliating it was for the chamberlain to bow to blackmail. "Yes, his help will constitute a major improvement." *Over his sabotage,* Sano thought, glancing at Yanagisawa, who shot him a covert, venomous look.

"My troops, clerks, and other staff are at your service," said the *shoshidai*.

"Since I'm traveling with a very small retinue," Yanagisawa said, "that is much appreciated."

Sano knew he would have to keep a close watch in case Yanagisawa recruited new henchmen to work against him.

"I wish that *Yoriki* Hoshina, my senior police commander, were here," the *shoshidai* said. "He's a most capable detective who has been assisting the *sōsakan-sama*. But Hoshina-san seems to have disappeared."

"A pity," said Yanagisawa.

Subtle menace shaded the chamberlain's voice. Sano hoped he could keep Hoshina hidden long enough to finish the case. However, that would still leave the problem of what to do with Hoshina afterward. He couldn't protect the *yoriki* from Yanagisawa's wrath indefinitely.

"Of course you'll be needing a place to live while in Miyako," the *shoshidai* said to Yanagisawa. "I regret that Nijō Castle is undergoing a major renovation at the moment, but you can stay at Nijō Manor with the *sōsakan-sama*."

"The renovation is suspended as of now," Yanagisawa said, and Sano knew how much he wanted to avoid sharing the same roof. "I'll move into Nijō Castle at once."

"Well, all right." The *shoshidai* sounded doubtful, but not even the shogun's cousin dared challenge the most powerful man in Japan.

"We'll be going now," Sano said. "We have much work to do, and I must brief the Honorable Chamberlain on the status of the investigation."

Outside, they mounted their horses in the narrow lane crowded with the strolling dignitaries of Miyako's administrative district. Low clouds hid the distant hills, but the sun had burned the morning mist from the sky; heat shimmered in the air. Sano felt sweaty, rank, and in dire need of a bath.

Yanagisawa said in a surly voice, "I suppose you found that farce of cooperation and friendly camaraderie amusing."

"Not so much amusing as necessary." Sano hoped that making their partnership public would force Yanagisawa to behave honorably, although he had his doubts.

"As for briefing me," Yanagisawa said, "that's unnecessary because I already know everything you know. And I've told you everything Hoshina withheld from you."

They'd talked during the ride to town, but Sano didn't believe Yanagisawa had really made a full disclosure. "I want your *metsuke* dossiers on the Imperial Court," Sano said, having guessed that Yanagisawa had plundered the records in Edo before he'd read them. "I also want the material you took from Left Minister Konoe's office."

"Fine. I'll send it to Nijō Manor." Yanagisawa sat astride his horse, with his bodyguards flanking him. "That's all I'm willing to do for today. I still feel very unwell, and I need to rest. Farewell until tomorrow."

The chamberlain and his guards rode away. Sano set off toward Nijō Manor. The first thing he needed to do was to see Reiko. Second, he must assign men to spy on Yanagisawa.

When Reiko rode up to Nijō Manor in her palanquin, Detective Fukida was waiting for her outside the gate. "Where have you been?" he cried.

"I've been investigating my husband's murder," Reiko said, climbing out of the palanquin. Afire with excitement, she explained how she and Lady Jokyōden had gone to Left Minister Konoe's secret house in the textile district, then showed Fukida the scrap of notes she'd found in the charcoal brazier. "Look. I'm sure this means the left minister was spying on Lord Ibe, who might be connected to the murders."

Fukida frowned. "You went to the palace?" he said. "On your own?"

"Yes. Lady Jokyōden told me that Lord Ibe has a house in the cloth dyers' district where he stays when he visits Miyako. We must go there right now!"

"I don't think that's such a good idea," Fukida said. "Perhaps we should wait."

"For what?" Reiko said, perplexed, then incredulous. "Do you intend to sit idle while your master's killer goes free?"

Instead of meeting Reiko's eyes, Fukida gazed around the bright, bustling street. "The *sōsakan-sama* told me to watch over you. I must obey his orders. I can't take you to Lord Ibe's house or anywhere else that might be dangerous."

"Then go yourself," Reiko said.

"I can't leave you."

"Where is Detective Marume? He could go."

Fukida looked so miserable that Reiko pitied him, but she was angry at his refusal to help her avenge Sano's death. "All right," she said. "If you won't take me, then I'll go alone."

"I'm sorry, but I can't allow that." Fukida turned to Reiko's palanquin bearers and guards and said, "You're not to take her on any more trips without my permission."

The bearers and guards bowed, chorusing, "Yes, Fukida-*san*."

"You can't do this!" Reiko cried, infuriated.

"Please go inside, Honorable Lady Reiko," said Fukida.

She glared at him in helpless rage. Tears rushed to her eyes as the grief she'd suppressed all morning resurfaced. Head high, she entered the inn, walked into her room, and shut the door so hard that the frame rattled. Alone, she fought the impulse to lie down and weep. She changed her silk kimono for a simple blue cotton one, and her high-soled shoes for comfortable straw sandals. She strapped a dagger to her arm under her sleeve. Then she peered out the windows and door to look for Fukida. He was nowhere in sight; he'd underestimated her determination. Reiko slipped out of Nijō Manor and began walking.

The hot sun beat down on her. Soon she was drenched in sweat and longing for a cool drink, but ladies didn't carry money, and as a stranger in town, Reiko had no credit with Miyako vendors. Samurai on horseback and peasants carrying loads of supplies jostled past her through narrow streets lined with shops. Dust, horse manure, and filthy water from open drains soiled her shoes and hem. She avoided looking other pedestrians in the eye, praying that no one would accost her. Something in her expression must have warned off predators, because although some men leered, they left her alone. Perhaps they thought she was a madwoman. Exhausted and footsore, she finally reached the cloth dyers' district northeast of Sanjo Bridge.

In workshops, craftsmen stirred steaming dye vats and painted designs on silk. Reiko followed a path beside the Kamo River, seeking Lord Ibe's house. She knew that while the feudal lords occupied grand estates in Edo and their provinces, Tokugawa law forbade them to maintain residences in Miyako. Therefore, a daimyo who desired a home here would avoid the authorities' notice by keeping a modest, discreet establishment. Reiko hadn't asked how Lady Jokyōden knew where Lord Ibe's illegal residence was. She would not allow herself to consider the possibility that the notes she'd pinned her hopes on were irrelevant to the murders and she'd come all this way for nothing.

Along the path on Reiko's right, textile shops crowned the embankment; drying cloth flapped on roofs and balconies. On her left, dyers rinsed long, brilliantly colored fabrics in the river, turning clear water into a sea of painted flowers, landscapes, and geometric designs. Reiko followed Jokyōden's directions up a path leading inland to a neighborhood of narrow, two-story houses behind high fences. Maids and porters hurried down the streets; bearers carried passengers in palanquins. Lord Ibe's house was the second to last on its block, behind a double gate suspended between two square pillars capped with a gabled roof.

Reiko circled the block, covertly inspecting the area. Other houses showed signs of life—maids shaking brooms out windows, children playing in front—but bamboo blinds covered the balconies of Lord Ibe's place. During an hour of watching, Reiko didn't see anyone enter or leave. Nervously, she walked up to the gates and knocked on the wooden planks.

No answer came. Reiko knocked again, louder. She heard the rasp of a sliding door, and footsteps. Then came the metallic scrape of a bar drawing back; the gates parted to reveal a man dressed in a short brown cotton kimono. He had the thick build and close-cropped hair of a laborer. Suspicion darkened his pockmarked features as he looked Reiko up and down.

"Yes?" he growled.

His unfriendly manner and disreputable appearance intimidated Reiko. "I—I'm looking for Lord Ibe," she said.

"Nobody by that name here."

The man started to close the gates. "Wait," Reiko said, pushing against them. "I know this house belongs to Lord Ibe. I must speak to him."

A lascivious smile came over the man's face. "You're wrong," he said, "but maybe you should come in anyway. We could have fun with a pretty girl like you." He reached over and chucked Reiko under the chin.

She recoiled at the liberty. "Who are you?" she asked, trying to sound stern.

"None of your business. Who do you think you are?" The man scowled, obviously displeased that a woman should dare to question him.

"Who's in there?" Reiko persisted. "What's going on?"

"Get lost, girl."

The man slammed the gates shut. Reiko heard the bar slide into place. She looked up at the house in desperation. The man had acted as if he had something to hide. She had to know what Left Minister Konoe had discovered here, because this represented her only chance to solve Sano's murder. But how could she, a woman alone, find out the secrets of the house?

Reiko hurried to the gate of the house behind Lord Ibe's and knocked. A maid answered. "Yes, madam?"

"Excuse me," Reiko said, arranging her face in an apologetic smile, "but I wonder if I could use your place of relief?" This was the polite term for the privy. "I'm sorry to bother you, but it's an emergency. . . ."

"Yes, of course." The maid smiled back, eager to help a lady in need. "Come this way."

She led Reiko around the house, into a narrow backyard that contained a fireproof storehouse and a privy shed.

"Thank you, you're so kind." Feigning casual interest, Reiko pointed at the daimyo's house and said, "Who lives over there?"

"Some men. . . . I don't know who they are."

"How many?"

Puzzled, the maid shook her head. "They keep to themselves." She opened the privy door. "If you need anything, just call."

"Many thanks." Reiko went into the privy, waited until the maid was gone, then came out again. She surveyed the yard. Along the fence lay rakes, baskets, urns, a wooden barrel. Quietly Reiko overturned the barrel, stood on it, and peered over the fence. She saw a yard similar to the one she was in, with a storehouse and privy. Wooden bars shielded the back windows of Lord Ibe's house. As Reiko watched, the door opened, and a muscular man dressed in a loincloth emerged. His body was covered with tattoos, a mark of the gangster class. Leaving the door ajar, he went into the privy.

That open door exerted a powerful, tempting pull on Reiko. Spurning caution, she started to climb the fence. When her long, full robe hindered her, she impatiently tied the skirts around her hips. She eased herself down on the other side, then tiptoed across Lord Ibe's yard. The presence of a gangster and a peasant ruffian in a daimyo's house signaled trouble, and Reiko had no doubt that the left minister's notes referred to their activities. Peeking in the back door, she saw a dim, vacant corridor with rooms opening off it. She glanced toward the privy. Grunts issued from the man inside. Reiko slipped through the door of the house and stood with her back pressed against the wall. Hearing male voices, she tensed.

Footsteps creaked above the ceiling: The men were upstairs. Even armed with a dagger, Reiko had no desire to confront them alone. She'd thought that grief had put her beyond caring what happened to her, but now she regretted her impulsiveness; it was all too clear what men would do to a young female trespasser. She wanted to leave, but then she heard footsteps behind her, outside: The gangster was coming.

Reiko darted down the corridor and through the nearest door, into a storeroom crammed with boxes. Holding her breath, she waited until the man walked past. Planks squeaked as the gangster mounted the stairs. A bitter odor caught Reiko's attention. She looked around, and when her eyes adjusted to the dimness, she saw wall racks full of spears, swords, and bows. Stacked wooden chests almost covered the floor. Curious now, Reiko lifted a lid. She found a suit of armor.

Uneasiness stirred within her. The odor grew stronger as she moved toward the door leading into the adjacent room. It held more chests. Reiko opened one, and her heart lurched. Inside lay a cache of arquebuses—long, tubular steel guns. Barrels, round wooden boxes, and square wicker baskets stood nearby. When Reiko pried the lid off a barrel, the smell billowed up into her face, smoky and acrid. She dipped a finger into fine black granules. Though she'd never seen gunpowder before, she knew this must be it. In the boxes she found spherical iron bullets. The baskets contained arrows. Reiko wouldn't have been surprised to find swords and spears in a daimyo's house, though not in such huge quantity. And guns were reserved for the sole use of the Tokugawa, but she'd just discovered enough weapons and ammunition to equip a small army.

The implications of the discovery stunned and enlightened Reiko. Left Minister Konoe must have watched men gathering at the house, bringing the arsenal. Surely this activity was the object of the surveillance mentioned in his notes. If Reiko was correct about the purpose of the weapons, then here was a secret that constituted the true motive for Konoe's murder.

Reiko hastened to the door, looked cautiously, and saw no one. Even though the temptation to flee was overpowering, she forced herself to move down the corridor, toward a flight of stairs that led to the second story. The voices sounded louder; Reiko discerned at least three different men speaking. Slowly she ascended the stairs, easing her weight down on the creaky planks. Fear nauseated her, and the sweat on her skin turned cold; she held herself rigid, fighting the sickness. Telling herself she must be strong for Sano, she climbed higher and saw another empty corridor that extended past more doors. The voices came from the second room on the right. Tiptoeing up the last steps, Reiko emerged into hot, stuffy air thick with tobacco smoke. Muddy daylight filtered through the balcony blinds and the paper walls of the corridor. Reiko crept to the doorway of the second room and listened.

"You shouldn't have been so rude," said a young man's worried voice. "You made her suspicious."

There were murmurs of agreement. Then another man spoke with defensive belligerence: "Who cares what some stupid woman thinks?"

Reiko recognized the voice of the fellow at the gate. "She's probably just some whore that Lord Ibe uses when he's in town, and that's how she knows this is his house. Anyway, she's gone."

"You should never open the gate without looking to see who's there, Gorobei-*san*," another man said in cultured Miyako speech.

"I thought it was Ikeda, with another load of weapons," Gorobei said sullenly. "I already said I was sorry."

"I am afraid that this matter is far from done. You know how whores gossip. What if that one has clients in the *bakufu* and tells them there's something funny going on here? They could send troops to raid us."

"They won't bother," said a different voice. "Even if they believe her, those *bakufu* bureaucrats are lazy."

"It was a mistake to use our master's place, even though he won't be back until winter," fretted the first man.

"Well, where else could we go that's big enough, private enough, and right in town?"

These two must be Lord Ibe's retainers, assigned to guard the property, Reiko realized. Instead, they'd taken advantage of his absence by turning the house into an armed fort.

"We shouldn't be doing this, it's too dangerous."

"I'm sick of your whining. Shut up!"

The man with the cultured voice said, "We've no more time for argument. We must figure out what to do so that Gorobei's carelessness won't jeopardize our mission."

The nature of that mission seemed obvious to Reiko. The conspirators were planning a military assault. She didn't think it involved feuding peasant gangs; that wouldn't have required illegal weapons, or interested the *metsuke*. The mission could be nothing less than a revolt against the Tokugawa. This threat was the reason for the law that prevented daimyo from gathering troops and arms in Miyako—so they couldn't seize the old capital as the first step toward taking over Japan. Horror and elation filled Reiko as she realized that the conspiracy must include many people besides the ones here, at least one of whom was likely to be involved in Sano's murder.

A sudden, ominous silence in the room alerted her. Then the man with the cultured voice said, "There is someone else in the house."

Reiko froze, aghast.

"How do you know?" Gorobei asked.

"I can feel it."

"You're just nervous," said one of the guards. "It's all in your imagination."

"After the unfortunate incident that just occurred, I refuse to take any chances. Come. We shall check downstairs."

Reiko darted into the adjacent room, hid behind a cabinet, and watched the men file past the door. First came a priest with a shaved head and athletic build, dressed in a saffron robe and carrying a spear. Then came three samurai, swords drawn, wearing the square Ibe crest on their robes: the guards. Gorobei, the gangster, and three more tough-looking peasants, all bearing stout clubs, and two shabbily attired samurai who appeared to be *rōnin*, followed. Their grim expressions told Reiko that they would kill her if they caught her. Heart pounding in panic, she rushed onto the balcony. She pushed aside the bamboo blinds and looked outside.

The balcony overhung the side fence. Directly opposite stretched the balcony of the house next door. As Reiko climbed onto the rail, she heard the men moving about downstairs. She perched for a moment, then sprang with all her strength. She sailed through the air like a large, awkward bird and landed on the other balcony, taking the impact on her knees and forearms to protect her womb. Huddling there for a moment, she sobbed in relief. Then she rose and lowered herself over the rail to the ground and hurried in the direction of Nijō Manor.

She must tell Marume and Fukida what she'd seen in Lord Ibe's house and convince them to do something about it.

19

Twilight had dissipated the worst heat of the day and dimmed the sky to misty gray when Reiko got back to Nijō Manor. She went to look for Detective Fukida, but neither he nor Sano's other men were in their quarters. Her maids had vanished, too. Covered with sweat and grime, hair disheveled, and weary to the bone, Reiko shut herself in her room to wait for Fukida because she couldn't go to the authorities by herself; they probably wouldn't even give a woman an audience. She drank water and wiped her face with a damp cloth and thought about taking a bath, but it seemed like too much work. She lay down to rest, letting the mild breeze from the windows waft over her.

But sleep wouldn't come, despite her exhaustion. In desolation, she realized she'd almost convinced herself that if she worked hard enough, Sano would return to her. She'd still believed he was out in the world somewhere, and if she demonstrated enough strength and courage, they would be reunited. But of course, avenging his murder wouldn't bring him back. Grief wracked her body, and she wept.

The door opened. Through her tears, Reiko saw a man silhouetted in the light from the corridor. He had a samurai's shaved crown and swords, and Sano's dimensions. Reiko felt a spring of hope, then crushing disappointment as she recognized another illusion created by the same wishful thinking that had populated Miyako with men who resembled Sano. It was probably just a nosy guest.

"Go away," Reiko called, sobbing harder.

The man said in Sano's voice, "Reiko-*san*, it's me."

Shocked, she sat up, rubbing her eyes. "No. It can't be." Then, as he knelt beside her, the light from the windows illuminated Sano's worried face. Reiko laughed hysterically as disbelief and joy collided in her.

Sano gathered her in his arms. She wept and moaned, stroking his face and his chest, reveling in the miracle of his resurrection. Her efforts must have worked after all; she'd brought him back.

"I'm sorry," Sano murmured into her hair. "I'm so sorry." Then he said, "I was worried about you. Where have you been?"

Confusion halted Reiko's catharsis. She drew back to look at Sano. "Where have *I* been?"

"I came back this afternoon and found everyone gone," Sano said. "I've been out looking for you. Where were you?"

Now Reiko understood that there must be a rational explanation for Sano's return. She wanted so badly to know what it was that her own activities seemed beside the point. "If you weren't murdered, what really happened? Where have *you* been?"

"Before I tell you," Sano said, "let me first say that I never meant to hurt you." His expression somber, he explained that Aisu had been the killer's victim, and he'd faked his own death to force Chamberlain Yanagisawa into the open.

That Sano had been around all along explained why Reiko had felt as if he were still alive, and Yanagisawa's presence in Miyako clarified many things about the murder case. But Reiko's joy turned to puzzlement. "Why did you let me believe you were dead?"

"I had to keep hidden, even from you, because there are so many spies, and I was afraid that the news might reach Yanagisawa. As things turned out, he knew already, but my plan still worked." Sano described how he'd confronted the chamberlain and secured his cooperation.

Reiko knew she should be glad of the plan's success, but she was too deeply hurt. "You let me suffer because you didn't think I could keep a secret. How could you trust me so little?"

"It's not that I don't trust you." Sano clasped Reiko to him, a pleading note in his voice. "But I couldn't take the chance that someone might guess the truth from your behavior."

"I could have acted the part of a grieving widow well enough," Reiko retorted, furious now. "Have you any idea what you've put me through?"

"I can guess," Sano said contritely, "and I beg you to forgive me."

His touch suddenly seemed repugnant to Reiko, his apology spurious. She pounded him with her fists, shouting, "Forgive you? Never! What you did was terrible and cruel."

Sano looked stricken, then sad. "I deserve every bit of your anger. Please believe that I am truly sorry."

"That's not good enough!"

Reiko jumped to her feet and bolted away. Sano chased her. He locked her in an unrelenting embrace. She struggled to break free, screaming, "Go away! Leave me alone!" Then her anger dissolved into weeping; he held her tight.

"Shh," he said, stroking her hair. "It's all right."

He eased her onto the floor, lying beside her. The warm pressure of his body ignited fierce desire in Reiko. She moaned, arching against him, and felt the hardness in his groin. Then they were tearing away garments, entwining in the dim bands of light from the windows. After the wild coupling that overwhelmed them both with pleasure, they lay still in a sweaty tangle of limbs and clothing. Bars of waning light striped their bodies; incense smoke drifted in on the cooling breeze.

Sano touched Reiko's cheek. "Can you possibly forgive me?" he said softly.

Her body had already forgiven him; eventually, her heart would too. Basking in physical and spiritual well-being, Reiko murmured, "I never thought that love with a dead husband would be so good."

They laughed at her joke, and she saw relief in Sano's eyes. The joy of having him back was almost worth her ordeal.

There was a commotion outside, then a knock at the door. "Honorable Lady Reiko, are you in there?" called Fukida's voice.

Rising, Sano donned his kimono and went to the door. He opened it a crack.

"Oh, good, you're back, *Sōsakan-sama*." Despite the relief in his voice, Fukida looked frantic with worry. The guards and Reiko's maids stood in an anxious group behind him. "I regret to say that I've failed in my duty to protect your wife. She left the inn without telling anyone. We've all been out searching for her, but we couldn't find her."

"She's here," Sano said. "It's all right." He dismissed his staff, shut the door, and turned to Reiko. She was sitting up, wrapped in her white under-robe, uneasily watching him.

"Maybe now you'll tell me where you've been," Sano said.

"I went to the palace to ask Lady Jokyōden to help me solve the murder case," Reiko said.

"What?" Sano exclaimed in alarm. "You saw Jokyōden, after you promised me you would stay away from her?"

"Yes, because I didn't know you were still around to care about promises," Reiko said defensively. "It seemed more important to find your killer and avenge your death."

Sano realized that he should have expected Reiko to behave this way; not even his death would quell her determined spirit. Now he was disturbed to learn that his short absence had been too long to leave Reiko on her own.

"Are you mad?" he said, standing over her. "Didn't you see that the second murder reduced the number of suspects and made Jokyōden even more likely to be the killer? Didn't you recognize the danger of associating with her?"

"Of course I did. But the risk was worth it." Rising, Reiko walked to the table, picked up her embroidered silk purse, and removed a fragment of paper, which she handed to Sano. "I found this in a house that Left Minister Konoe owned in the textile district."

As she described the house, how she'd gotten there, and her idea that Konoe had used it for espionage, Sano barely glanced at the words on the paper. He said, "Lady Jokyōden took you to this place?"

Vexation crossed Reiko's features. "We weren't alone. I brought my guards with us. Please give me credit for some intelligence."

"You believed what Lady Jokyōden told you about Left Minister Konoe purchasing the house? How did she know, anyway?"

"She didn't say."

An evasive note in Reiko's voice signaled a lie. For the sake of peace, Sano chose to overlook it for the moment. "Look, I know you were upset and not thinking clearly, but even so, you should have known better than to trust a murder suspect. So far, there's no evidence except Jokyōden's word that the house belonged to Konoe, or that this paper is his. Jokyōden might have been misleading you to divert suspicion away from herself."

"Well, yes, I was upset. Whose fault was that?" Reiko said sarcastically. "I did consider the problems you mentioned, but there must be a way to verify that Konoe owned the house and wrote the note. Besides, what I discovered next proves that it doesn't matter whether or not I was thinking clearly, or what Jokyōden's motives were for taking me to the house. I thought the note referred to spying that Konoe did on Lord Ibe. So I went there, and—"

"Wait." Sano held up his hands. He had an ominous feeling that he was going to hear something else he wouldn't like. "Slow down. You went where?"

"To the daimyo's house in the cloth dyers' district," Reiko said patiently. "Lady Jokyōden gave me directions."

"She did, did she?" When Sano had met Jokyōden, he'd thought her arrogant and contrary; now he liked her even less for abetting his wife's misadventures.

"I asked Fukida-*san* to go with me," Reiko said, "but he wouldn't. He even took away my palanquin and guards. I realize now that he wanted to wait for you to come back before doing anything, but at the time I thought he was ignoring an important clue. So I went alone."

Horror filled Sano. "You walked across town by yourself?" If he'd known what she would do, he would have risked letting her know the truth about his faked death. "Didn't you think of what might have happened to you?"

"Nothing did, so there's no need to worry now." Reiko hesitated, then said, "I met a rough-looking man at Lord Ibe's house. He wouldn't answer my questions, and I was suspicious, so I sneaked through the back door for a look inside."

She spoke as if she'd done the most reasonable thing in the world. Sano stared, dumbstruck.

"And guess what I found!" Animated with excitement, Reiko described an arsenal of weapons and a gang of samurai, gangsters, peasant ruffians, and an armed priest.

Sano was too upset by her daring to think about the implications of her discovery. He shouted, "I can't believe you did that! You could have been killed! That was the most stupid, reckless, thoughtless, dangerous, foolhardy—"

"And the most important piece of evidence yet," Reiko said.

"You shouldn't have done it!"

"What's done is done. Now please stop yelling and consider what this means to the case."

"First I want you to promise you'll never do such a thing again," Sano said.

"Only if you'll promise never again to trick me into thinking you're dead."

This was one of those times when Sano longed for a traditional marriage where the husband set the rules and the wife obeyed them, instead of this constant negotiation. "All right, I promise," he said. "Do you?"

"Yes," Reiko said, then hurried on: "I believe the gang is plotting to overthrow the Tokugawa regime, and that someone in the Imperial Court is behind the plot. One of the murder suspects must be arming troops in preparation to restore power to the emperor. Left Minister Konoe must have found out, and the murderer killed him to prevent him from telling the authorities."

Sano saw the logic of her reasoning, and the new political element in the case disturbed him, but he strove for objectivity. "That's quite a leap to make from a few scribbled notes, a few troublemakers, and a few guns."

"There were more than just a few guns," Reiko said, "and the size of the arsenal means there must be hundreds, even thousands of troublemakers involved in the plot. They could launch a full-scale siege of Miyako at any moment." She grasped Sano's hands. "You must do something immediately."

"Of course I'll investigate the situation," Sano said. "Any potential threat against the regime must be taken seriously. But let's not jump to conclusions. You were in the house for only a short time, while you were under severe emotional stress. Maybe there weren't as many weapons as you thought; maybe you misinterpreted what the men said."

"I know what I saw and heard," Reiko said stubbornly. "If you don't arrest those men and seize the arsenal, there could be a revolt that turns into nationwide civil war. Entire provinces could fall under rebel control before the *bakufu* has time to mount an effective defense. Eventually, war could reach Edo."

"That's a distinct possibility." While Sano could think of arguments against the theory, he hesitated to raise them lest he reawaken Reiko's hurt and resentment over his deception. "Therefore, I have to proceed with caution. A revolt goes beyond the scope of the murder investigation. I must inform the *shoshidai* and Chamberlain Yanagisawa."

"Soon, I hope?" Reiko said.

"Tonight." Instead of the evening of rest that he'd wanted, Sano anticipated hours of secret meetings. "And tomorrow I'll begin looking for the instigator of the plot at the Imperial Palace."

20

At dawn, a brisk wind rattled the window blinds, awakening Sano in his room at Nijō Manor. He smelled smoke, heard bells clanging, and bolted up in bed, heart pounding as he recalled a fire that had almost claimed his life. But the inn was quiet except for the ordinary noises of guests rising. Sano washed and dressed. Leaving Reiko asleep, he took his morning meal with his detectives in their rooms and gave them their orders for the day. Then he rode to the Imperial Palace.

Smoke hovered over Miyako, adding an acrid pall to the hazy, oppressive heat. From newssellers who hawked broadsheets, Sano learned that the wind had blown down some Obon lanterns and started a fire that had spread across the southern part of town. Nervous citizens kept watch for more fires. Sano's own mood was troubled as he recalled his meeting with *Shoshidai* Matsudaira and Chamberlain Yanagisawa at Nijō Castle last night, when he'd told them about the outlaws and guns at Lord Ibe's house.

At first, Yanagisawa had scoffed at the possibility of an imperial restoration attempt. "The court is powerless. How could they dare to attack the *bakufu*?"

"It's happened before," Sano said, prepared to counter the objections that had occurred to him when Reiko had broached the idea. "Four hundred and seventy years ago, Emperor Go-Toba tried to overthrow the Kamakura dictatorship with the help of militant monks and rebellious samurai clans."

"I'm familiar with history," Yanagisawa said. "Go-Toba's coup failed. So did the one led by Emperor Go-Daigo two hundred years later. Although he managed to seize control, his reign lasted only a short time. I doubt that the Tokugawa regime is in any danger from his descendants now."

"Indeed," the *shoshidai* murmured.

"I agree that those attempts were futile," Sano said. "My point is that someone did try. And Emperor Go-Daigo's coup eventually resulted in a shift of power to a new regime. This could happen again, if the revolt spreads and the daimyo unite against the Tokugawa. Miyako is a good starting place for civil war. It's far from the shogun's forces in Edo, and the emperor is a natural rallying point for malcontents seeking a new leader. Left Minister Konoe must have realized all this. An armed insurrection against the *bakufu* is high treason—punishable by death for everyone involved, plus their families and associates. Therefore, Konoe had to be eliminated before he could report his discovery."

Yanagisawa frowned, and Sano knew he wanted to disagree for the sake of disagreeing. He must hate having Sano inform him about a development that he hadn't managed to discover himself. Nevertheless, Yanagisawa couldn't ignore any threat against the regime he controlled, no matter how little he liked acting on Sano's recommendation.

"I'll handle the situation at Lord Ibe's house," Yanagisawa said.

"My troops are at your service," said the *shoshidai,* clearly glad that he wouldn't have to take charge himself.

Sano hoped that the task would keep Yanagisawa too busy to cause new troubles for him, but he doubted it. He feared that he would live to regret his strange partnership with the chamberlain.

Now a party of nobles conveyed Sano into the palace. Courtiers huddled along the passages of the *kuge* quarter, conversing in whispers. They fell silent and bowed as Sano passed. Seeing the animosity in their eyes, he presumed they were discussing the murder, the false report of his death, and the arrest of Lady Asagao. Obviously no one wanted him here. Yet anticipation lifted Sano's mood. The discovery of the arsenal and outlaw gang gave him a new chance to solve the case.

At Right Minister Ichijo's estate, attendants had gathered in the court-yard. Down the stairs of the mansion came Ichijo, dressed in a formal black cap and robes and leaning on an ebony cane. When he saw Sano, he halted on the bottom step.

"Congratulations on your miraculous return to the world of the living, *Sōsakan-sama*," he said, bowing with stiff dignity that bespoke his displeasure at Sano's arrival. "Forgive me if I haven't time to receive you, but I must go to my daughter. She is home now, but quite upset from her ordeal."

Sano braced himself for a dangerous, difficult interview. The murderer had already killed one Tokugawa retainer, and antagonizing a suspect might provoke another attack. In addition, Sano had unintentionally created bad blood between the *bakufu* and the Imperial Court.

"I beg your pardon for my treatment of the honorable Lady Asagao," Sano said, forced to grovel for the mistake connived by Chamberlain Yanagisawa. "Please accept my sincere apologies."

Ichijo looked slightly mollified. "Thank you for freeing my daughter." With a trace of waspishness, he added, "Of course, freedom is no more than Lady Asagao's due. Certainly she has been exonerated."

"Yes, she has," Sano said, "and I won't delay you long, but I must ask you some questions."

"Such as?"

"Where were you during the murder the night before last?"

Shaking his head in annoyance, Ichijo walked past Sano. "My activities are none of your concern, since I was never under suspicion for Left Minister Konoe's murder, and therefore not for this one, which was obviously committed by the same person."

"I've spoken with Chamberlain Yanagisawa. He supplied information that changes your situation."

Sano watched Ichijo halt, and saw the wary look on his face as he reluctantly turned. Ichijo had seemed surprised not to be questioned about Konoe's murder, Sano recalled, and loitered around during the inquiries in the palace. He must have wondered why he hadn't been targeted as a suspect. After his interrogation by Yanagisawa, he'd probably lived in fear for his life. Now Sano could see the crafty old politician marshaling his defense.

"I was here at home, asleep, when the scream woke me," Ichijo said. "Soon afterward a servant came to tell me there had been another death. My household can verify that."

Observing the closed faces of Ichijo's staff, Sano knew these men would lie to protect Ichijo from the despised *bakufu*.

"Before the second murder, you received a message that I would be in the palace that night," Sano said.

"Yes." Ichijo tapped his cane on a paving stone. He scrutinized Sano with shrewd calculation.

"But you did nothing about it?"

Ichijo gave Sano a sour smile. "I disdain anonymous communications and therefore ignored this one. I've been informed that similar messages were delivered to Lady Jokyōden, Prince Momozono, and the emperor. I spoke with them this morning and learned that they, too, ignored the messages."

"I see." Sano felt vexed at Ichijo, who had surely advised the other suspects to claim they'd disregarded the opportunity to attack him, thereby protecting themselves and obstructing his investigation.

"If you've finished, I shall be going," Ichijo said.

"Not just yet." Hastened into blunt speech, Sano said, "Your daughter has been exonerated, but you're still a suspect. You and Left Minister Konoe were rivals for the post of prime minister. My arresting Lady Asagao gave you reason to want me dead, and killing me while she was imprisoned would clear her."

Anger bared Ichijo's blackened teeth; his thin hand gripped the gold handle of his cane. In a cutting voice he said, "Even if you disregard my alibi, do you really think I have the power to kill with a scream?"

"Perhaps we should talk about that in private," Sano said, "along with some other matters that you might not care to discuss out here."

He saw a flash of apprehension in Ichijo's eyes: Whether guilty of murder or not, Ichijo had something to hide. Then, with a martyred expression, the right minister led Sano into the mansion and to his office.

"Now that we're alone," he said, "what did you wish to discuss with me?"

Sano reminded himself that Yanagisawa had picked Ichijo as his prime suspect. With all Sano's fighting skill, he was defenseless against the power of *kiai*. If Ichijo had that ability, Sano courted death during every moment spent with the right minister. A current of fear ran through Sano as he circled the room, examining the paintings on the walls. The first panel showed a garden where wisteria vines draped an arbor, under which stood two men, both wearing the costumes of a thousand years ago.

"Nakatomi Kamatari," Sano said, pointing to the older man in the painting. "Your ancestor. And the young man is Naka-no-Oye, an imperial prince and disgruntled member of the Soga clan, which once dominated the court. The two plotted to oust the Soga and seize power. When they succeeded, the prince became emperor. Kamatari took the new name Fujiwara—wisteria—in memory of the garden where they conspired. As the emperor's mentor, he won great power for his clan. For some five hundred years afterward, the Fujiwara ruled Japan from behind the throne."

"I am impressed by your knowledge of my heritage," Ichijo said with chill asperity, "but surely it cannot be the reason for your interest in me."

"On the contrary." Sano moved to the next panel. It showed the Purple Dragon Hall of the Imperial Palace. On the veranda, a courtier stood beside a boy dressed in the tall black hat and elaborate robes of the emperor. Pointing to the courtier, Sano said, "This must be Fujiwara Yoshi-fusa, regent for the young Emperor Seiwa, who reigned seven centuries ago. Yoshifusa established the tradition of marrying Fujiwara daughters to emperors. A father-in-law can exert much influence over a young sovereign, yes?"

Ichijo compressed his mouth in annoyance at this allusion to his relationship with Emperor Tomohito.

"But the zenith of Fujiwara glory was the great Michinaga," Sano said. "His daughters were consorts to four emperors; two other emperors were his nephews, and three his grandsons. He ruled supreme for thirty-two years." Sano contemplated the last painting, a view of a temple at night. In the sky floated a huge, round moon. "Michinaga founded this monastery at Hojo Temple. He wrote a poem boasting that he was a master of his world, 'like the flawless full moon riding the skies.' "

"That is true," Ichijo said impatiently, "but I fail to see what relevance it has to your investigation."

"After Michinaga's death, the Fujiwara fortunes declined. Power shifted to the samurai class." Sano faced Ichijo. "Don't you regret the passing of those glorious days?"

Disdain shaded Ichijo's face. "Even if I did, that gives me no reason for wanting Left Minister Konoe dead. The post of prime minister confers no power outside the Imperial Palace. Killing my rival would not have reestablished Fujiwara control over Japan."

But perhaps Konoe had discovered that Ichijo was planning to restore imperial rule and Fujiwara supremacy by mounting a revolt against the Tokugawa, Sano speculated. Ichijo was in a unique position to influence Emperor Tomohito, both as chief adviser and as father of the imperial consort. If a coup succeeded, Ichijo would dominate the throne—and the nation—as his ancestors had. Therefore, Ichijo was a prime candidate for instigator of the rebel conspiracy.

"Do you know Lord Ibe Masanobu?" Sano asked.

Ichijo raised his eyebrows, although Sano couldn't tell whether he was surprised by the apparent non sequitur or if the name had significance to him. "The daimyo of Echizen Province? We have never met."

"Have you ever been to his house in the cloth dyers' district?"

"It is my understanding that the daimyo are forbidden to have estates in Miyako, and since I'm not acquainted with Lord Ibe, there would be no reason for me to visit him. Really, I do not see the point of these questions."

"Have you any contact with priests at the local monasteries?"

"Of course. They perform ceremonies here at the palace." Folding his arms, Ichijo said, "I get the impression that you are accusing me of something besides the murders. At least be specific so that I may defend myself."

If Ichijo knew about the activities at Lord Ibe's estate, he was doing an excellent job of pretending he didn't. However, this veteran of court politics would have mastered the art of dissembling, and Ichijo's clan had masterminded secret plots for centuries. But Sano wasn't ready to make an open accusation yet.

"Even if you aren't acquainted with Lord Ibe, I believe your family has close ties with other daimyo clans," he said. "The Kuroda and the Mitsu, in particular."

"Many of us have married into those families," Ichijo said stiffly. This was a common practice by which the samurai gained prestige via connections with the Imperial Court, while the nobles shared in the daimyo families' wealth.

"Then you've had the opportunity to study the martial arts with them?"

"The opportunity, yes; the desire, no," Ichijo said with a moue of distaste. "We in the court are glad to give the benefit of our learning to the samurai class. But with all due respect, we prefer to maintain the integrity of our culture by not absorbing yours."

However, Sano knew that cultural influence flowed both ways. As men of the daimyo clans studied art and music with their imperial in-laws, so might nobles practice Bushido under the direction of samurai relatives. Sano perceived the strong will hidden behind Ichijo's refined countenance, and will was the foundation for the power of *kiai*, the perfect weapon for a courtier who wanted a means of self-defense—or murder.

"Unless you have something else to discuss," said Ichijo, "I really must go. My daughter needs me."

"Just one more thing," Sano said.

The right minister's look of aggrieved impatience did not change, but alarm radiated from Ichijo. Sano wondered what he was hiding. He also wondered whether there was something that Yanagisawa had neglected to tell him about Ichijo.

"I need to speak with His Majesty the Emperor, Lady Jokyōden, and Prince Momozono," Sano said. "I would prefer to see them alone, without giving them advance notice."

"That is against court protocol, but I suppose an exception can be made." Through Ichijo's grudging consent, Sano saw relief. Whatever he was hiding must be serious, for him to readily grant an objectionable request just to avoid more questions. "I shall escort you to the imperial enclosure now."

"Thank you," Sano said.

Ichijo started toward the door. Sano lagged behind. Then he lunged forward and grabbed the right minister, locking his right arm around Ichijo's shoulders, his left across Ichijo's throat. For an instant, Ichijo stiffened. Sano was startled to feel tough, wiry muscles: Despite his age, Ichijo kept himself fit. Sano recalled the unearthly scream, and Aisu's bloody corpse. What if Ichijo did indeed possess the power of *kiai*? At this close range, he could kill Sano by barely raising his voice. Sano knew the risk he took by provoking Ichijo, but what better way to expose the truth?

Then Ichijo went limp. He struggled feebly in Sano's grasp, bleating, "Help, help!"

Sano let go. Relief and disappointment filled him. The door opened and two servants appeared. They hurried to the aid of their master, who sagged against the wall, coughing. Ichijo's cheeks were red, his eyes watery. He glared at Sano.

"I know why you did that," he said, "and I hope you are satisfied. You almost killed me."

"If that's the case, then I apologize," Sano said, unconvinced. Might a man who could master *kiaijutsu* also be quick enough to hide his skill by feigning weakness? "I'll see the imperial family now."

21

The procession of fifty mounted samurai, resplendent in full armor, halted outside the walled compound of police headquarters. Chamberlain Yanagisawa swung down off his horse. "Wait here," he told his troops.

Detective Marume said, "Why are we stopping?"

Detective Fukida said, "Shouldn't we proceed directly to Lord Ibe's house?"

Hanging his helmet on his saddle, Yanagisawa barely controlled his anger. His own retainers would never dare question anything he did, but Sano's exhibited the same annoying outspokenness as their master. That Yanagisawa needed their help only worsened his bad mood. First he'd had to agree to cooperate with Sano. Now he must confront the worst humiliation of all.

"I have business here," he told Marume and Fukida.

He strode through the gate, into the main building. There, two *doshin* and their civilian assistants loitered around a high platform where a clerk presided over a desk piled with ledgers. Yanagisawa stalked past the platform, through a doorway, and into a labyrinth of offices and corridors.

"Hoshina!" he shouted.

Marume and Fukida hurried after him. "Hoshina's not here," Marume said. "Let's just go, please."

"If he's not here, then why are you so eager to stop me?" Yanagisawa kept going. "You thought I wouldn't find your master's hostage, but I did."

Yesterday, Yanagisawa had set his Miyako spies to the task of locating the *yoriki*. It hadn't been easy, because Hoshina had loyal friends on the police force who'd tried to protect him. Not until late last night had Yanagisawa learned where Sano had hidden Hoshina. Now fury at Hoshina's betrayal rose within him like hot, poisonous steam.

The betrayal was made all the more painful by Yanagisawa's memories of the night of the *shoshidai's* banquet, when he and Hoshina had spent hours in the house by the river, alternating bouts of urgent sex with talk about politics, their experiences, current events, and mutual interests in art and theater. They'd shared an intimacy that Yanagisawa had never enjoyed with anyone else. For once he had felt exuberantly alive, yet at peace.

Just before Hoshina left, they had toasted each other. "To a successful venture," Hoshina had said.

They drank, then Yanagisawa said, "To Miyako's best police commander, a fine comrade, and a valuable addition to my staff."

Pleasure and consternation mingled on Hoshina's face. Frowning down at the cup in his hands, he said, "But I'm only your comrade and a member of your staff for as long as you're in Miyako."

"Ah. Well."

"I understand the difficulty that traveling so far from Edo causes you," Hoshina said. "I know I can't expect you to come to Miyako again, and I can't abandon my duties here to visit you. So . . ." He shrugged with unconvincing nonchalance. "After you leave, I probably won't see you again."

"That's true." Stalling for time to sort out his thoughts, Yanagisawa imagined his return to Edo Castle, where his only close companions were the ghosts of his father, Lord Takei, and Shichisaburō. The prospect filled him with desolation.

Hoshina drew a deep breath, then said, "If I were to go to Edo with you . . ." He paused, cautiously gauging Yanagisawa's response.

It was a tempting idea. If Hoshina came with him, Yanagisawa wouldn't be alone, and who better than Hoshina to help build his personal empire within the *bakufu?* Hoshina was strong, intelligent, and more capable than anyone else in Yanagisawa's retinue. . . .

And there lay the danger of promoting the *yoriki*. Hoshina had already taken over the *shoshidai's* office, proving his desire to usurp authority. Loyalty wasn't his strongest virtue: He had no qualms about deserting the *shoshidai* for a better patron. What if he got tired of the affair with Yanagisawa and sought new amorous adventures? Worse, Hoshina might win the shogun's favor, form alliances within the *bakufu*, and eventually seize power.

"A matter like this cannot be decided in haste," Yanagisawa hedged.

Yet he'd almost made up his mind to take Hoshina to Edo as his new chief retainer and risk everything for a chance at happiness. Now he couldn't believe he'd been so foolish.

He found the prison cell in the rear corner of the building. Two soldiers stood guard outside the iron-banded door. "Open it," Yanagisawa ordered.

The guards hesitated. Yanagisawa spoke in a quiet, steely voice: "If you don't let me in, you will be executed."

Hastily, the guards unbolted and opened the door. Yanagisawa stood on the threshold of the cell. Inside, barred windows illuminated a tatami floor with a bed on one side and a chamber pot on the other. *Yoriki* Hoshina stood in the center. His clothes were rumpled; his hair hung loose. Dismay filled his eyes as he stared at Yanagisawa.

"Traitor," Yanagisawa said softly.

Hoshina extended his hands in a gesture of entreaty. "Please let me explain."

Yanagisawa strode over to the *yoriki* and struck him on the mouth. Hoshina gave a startled cry, touched his lip, and frowned at the blood on his fingers.

"What is there to explain?" Yanagisawa said contemptuously. "You told Sano everything you knew. You told him where I was. You betrayed me!"

He kicked Hoshina in the stomach. Hoshina went reeling across the cell, hit the wall, and slid to the floor. "Sano offered you the promotion you wanted in exchange for delivering me into his hands," Yanagisawa said. "You accepted his bribe and shifted your allegiance to him."

Hoshina clambered to his feet. "No!" he protested. "I would never deliberately harm you after—" He broke off.

"Shut up!" That the *yoriki* dared to mention the night they had spent together infuriated Yanagisawa even more.

"Sano didn't bribe me," Hoshina said, raising his hands to ward off more blows. "He would have destroyed me if I refused to cooperate. I'm not a traitor, just a coward." He knelt, his expression strained with desperation and woe. "Please allow me to apologize. Please forgive me."

With a harsh, scornful laugh Yanagisawa said, "A million apologies won't buy my forgiveness or excuse you for trying to murder me."

"Murder you? What are you talking about?" Hoshina gazed at him in confusion.

Yanagisawa bitterly regretted trusting the *yoriki*, because he'd figured out why Hoshina must have been planning to betray him all along. He spoke in a fierce whisper so no one else in the building would hear: "Sano wasn't the only person you withheld information from and tricked with a false report about Left Minister Konoe's murder. Your position gives you access to the imperial compound. You were there the night Konoe died, weren't you? He went to the Pond Garden because you ordered him to meet you there. And you killed him with the power of *kiai*. Then you protected yourself by manipulating me to suit your schemes."

This humiliated Yanagisawa even more than having to work with Sano. "Right Minister Ichijo, Emperor Tomohito, Lady Jokyōden, and Prince Momozono knew Sano was going to be at the palace last night, but you were the only person besides Aisu and my guards who knew *I* would be there too. You followed us. You killed Aisu, but Sano came before you could get to me. Then you came back to investigate the murder you'd committed."

"I didn't kill Konoe or Aisu." Indignation flared in the *yoriki*'s voice. "Why would I?"

"Keep your voice down!"

"And why attack you?" Hoshina whispered furiously.

"To safeguard yourself from treason charges," Yanagisawa said. "You're too ambitious to be content with running the *shoshidai*'s office or being my personal retainer. You're part of the conspiracy that Sano discovered. Konoe found out about it, and you had to kill him before he turned you in to the *metsuke*."

"What conspiracy?" An incredulous look came over Hoshina's face. "Turned me in for what?"

"Don't play stupid with me. You've been gathering troops and weapons at Lord Ibe's house, and you couldn't take the chance that I might discover the plot to overthrow the Tokugawa. My death would cause a great upheaval in the *bakufu*. It would be a while before anyone reopened the investigation into Konoe's murder, and in the meantime, you could launch your coup. So you came after me. You killed Aisu because you couldn't tell which of us was which in the dark." Yanagisawa slammed Hoshina against the wall. "Murderer! Traitor!"

Now Hoshina's eyes blazed with anger. "Those are fine insults, coming from you. I've never murdered anyone, but everybody knows you have. I'm not plotting to overthrow the government, but you've already stolen the shogun's authority. If you want to see a real murderer and traitor, look in the mirror!"

176

The *yoriki* shoved Yanagisawa away from him. Rage erupted within the chamberlain. "How dare you lay hands on me?"

"You were perfectly content to have my hands on you the other night," Hoshina retorted.

"Don't mock me!" Yanagisawa kicked at Hoshina's knees and crotch, flung blows at his head and chest, all the while yelling curses.

At first Hoshina only ducked the strikes. "How can you treat me like this, after what I've done for you?" he cried. "I put myself in jeopardy by sabotaging Sano. Would I have risked conspiring against the shogun's *sōsakan* if not to help you?"

"Stop trying to justify what you did!" Yanagisawa grabbed Hoshina, then punched his chin so hard that his head jerked back. "You wanted the power and wealth that I could give you. You wanted Sano gone so he couldn't interfere with your plans."

The *yoriki* shot out a forearm and bludgeoned Yanagisawa's face. Pain exploded in Yanagisawa's head. Then they were caught up in the whirlwind of earnest combat. Yanagisawa's armor protected his body, but he took more blows to his face. He pummeled Hoshina. They crashed to the floor together. As they grappled for each other's throats, desire inflamed Yanagisawa. He wanted Hoshina as badly as he wanted to kill the man with his bare hands.

Then the cell was full of men. They dragged Hoshina off Yanagisawa, begging, "Stop, Hoshina-*san*!"

Yanagisawa sat up and saw two *yoriki* holding Hoshina. Fury contorted Hoshina's face as he struggled against them. Marume helped Yanagisawa stand. His left eye had begun to swell and his entire body was sore, but as far as he could tell, nothing was broken. As he stalked out of the cell, his spirit ached with an agony that had nothing to do with physical pain.

"Yanagisawa-*san*."

Hoshina's voice, filled with pleading, stabbed Yanagisawa like a jagged metal blade. Against his will, he turned.

Now Hoshina stood meekly while the police held him. "I swear upon my honor that I never wanted to hurt you, and I'm truly sorry I did." Sincerity shone in his eyes, which gazed out at Yanagisawa from a bloody, bruised face.

"More lies and apologies won't save you from paying for your crimes. I sentence you to death." Even as he condemned Hoshina, Yanagisawa suffered an onslaught of desire and grief. He acknowledged a devastating truth.

He was in love with Hoshina. Love was the cause of the yearning he'd felt for the *yoriki*, the source and substance of the comradeship that had grown between them. He should have known. And he should have known better.

"If you'll give me another chance, I'll make it up to you," Hoshina said. "I'll help you solve the murder case, devote my life to your service— anything you want. I'll prove that I'm innocent of any crimes. Just please . . ." Emotion cracked his voice. "Have mercy."

Yanagisawa turned his back on Hoshina. Even if the *yoriki* wasn't guilty of murder or treason, he deserved to die. He must die so that Yanagisawa could thwart Sano's blackmail. And Yanagisawa would never again make the mistake of falling in love.

"You'll be executed tomorrow morning," he said.

The battering ram struck the gate of Lord Ibe's house with a thunderous crash, splintering wood and breaking hinges. Soldiers rushed through the portals. More troops climbed the fences around the house and swarmed the property. Brandishing swords and spears, they shouted, "In the name of the shogun, come out and surrender!"

Chamberlain Yanagisawa charged into the front yard after his men. He welcomed action that would take his mind off the pain of Hoshina's betrayal. He wanted to forget that he still loved Hoshina and mourned the *yoriki*'s impending death, even though he'd ordered it himself. He must avert the possible threat to the regime, and the capture of the outlaws represented a new chance to solve the murders.

The troops were inside the house now. As Yanagisawa entered, they stormed the corridor and rooms. Above him pounded the footsteps of the men who'd invaded the second story. Shouts echoed in the dim, musty space. Yanagisawa gripped his sword. His desire to be a great detective persisted; he discovered in himself a need to prove he was capable of more than just sabotaging Sano. The thrill of the raid stirred the place deep inside him where his samurai spirit lay dormant. With a strange, heady anticipation, Yanagisawa hungered for battle.

Then Detective Marume came running from the back of the house. "Nobody in here, Honorable Chamberlain," he said.

Detective Fukida clattered down the stairs. "Second floor's empty, too. They've all cleared out."

Yanagisawa's spirits plunged. "What about the weapons?"

Fukida shook his head. Marume said, "We didn't find any."

The soldiers gathered in the corridor, sheathing their swords. Yanagi-

178

sawa cursed, using temper to hide the despair that filled him as his suspicions about Hoshina grew. Had the *yoriki* somehow managed to send orders for the outlaws to move the arsenal after Sano imprisoned him? Yanagisawa didn't wish to acknowledge the worst sins of his lover, or admit defeat. He wanted to torture Hoshina into revealing the outlaws' whereabouts; he wanted to vent his fury while slaking his desire.

"Search the place again," he said. "Look for anything that might tell us where the outlaws are or what they're planning."

While the men obeyed, Yanagisawa inspected the storerooms. They were empty, although the air still reeked of gunpowder. A single round bullet lay under the window. Yanagisawa picked up the bullet and cupped it despondently in his palm. His mood grew bleaker when the troops came to report an unsuccessful search.

"Ask the neighbors if they know where the occupants went," Yanagisawa said. "If not, I want the city and surrounding areas searched for the arsenal. The outlaws may have gone to join their confederates. Find them before we have a war on our hands."

He lingered in the empty arsenal. Tracing the outlaws would probably require a long, tedious search that would keep him in Miyako for ages. Yanagisawa hated the thought of reporting the bad news to his *bakufu* subordinates, who would spread the tale of his unsuccessful raid, setting him up to take the blame if a revolt did materialize. He dreaded spending the night alone at Nijō Castle, knowing that Hoshina would soon be dead. Crouching on the floor, he laid his head on his knees and succumbed to misery.

22

An incongruous sight greeted Sano and Right Minister Ichijo at the emperor's residence. Two armies of banner bearers, archers, gunners, spearmen, and mounted swordsmen faced off across the courtyard. The troops wore armor in the style of four centuries before, featuring huge arm flaps, long tunics, and intricate lacing. Sunlight glinted off polished helmets; a war drum boomed across a battle scene straight out of history.

Then, as Sano drew nearer, the illusion dissolved. The weapons were wooden; the horses were painted papier-mâché heads mounted on sticks. None of the soldiers was more than sixteen years old. Most wore only bits of tattered armor, as though the imperial treasure-house hadn't supplied enough equipment for everyone. These were young courtiers at play, not samurai at war. Waiting for a signal to begin fighting, they giggled and pushed one another.

Suddenly a loud whoop rang out. At the rear of one army, Emperor Tomohito, clad in a complete, splendid suit of armor, raised a war fan bearing the gold imperial chrysanthemum crest. Straddling his toy horse, he ran up the side of the battlefield. So much for the rule forbidding the emperor's feet to touch the ground, Sano thought.

"His Majesty enjoys war games," Ichijo said, then bowed and departed.

The archers let blunt-tipped arrows fly. Gunners aimed toy arquebuses, shouting, "Bang! Bang!" Wooden swords and spears made a racket as foot soldiers and horsemen clashed. Some boys on the emperor's side wore the insignia of northern and western samurai clans; others sported the white cowls of warrior priests. The other side wore armor with the red lacing associated with the Minamoto regime that had once ruled Japan. Recognizing the battle, Sano wondered why Emperor Tomohito had chosen to reenact it.

Then he heard hoots coming from the sidelines. Near a collection of spare weapons stood Prince Momozono. He wore a plain cotton kimono and a helmet much too big for him. His arms and head jerked.

Approaching, Sano greeted the prince.

Momozono's hoots turned to squeals of alarm. As he lurched around to face Sano, his leg buckled, and he fell. Fear glazed his rolling eyes as he struggled to rise.

"I'm sorry I startled you," Sano said, again feeling instinctive disgust. He warned himself that the prince was still a suspect, and one he hadn't had a chance to investigate thoroughly. He couldn't assume that Momozono was harmless. Hiding his distaste, Sano reached out to the fallen prince. "Let me help you up."

"N-no, thank you, that's all right." *Hoot, puff, gasp.* Twitching all over, Momozono somehow managed to stand.

Pity moved Sano. He spoke gently, as if to a child: "Well, this is certainly an exciting battle. Are you the captain of the arsenal?"

"I'm not much good at anything, but H-his Majesty is kind enough to give me a p-part in his games."

More noises accompanied Momozono's answer, but Sano couldn't mistake the emphasis on the last word. Momozono was no childlike cripple, but a mature man who understood the difference between make-believe and the terrible reality of his own existence.

"You're fond of the emperor, then?" Sano asked, watching Tomohito gallop across the battlefield.

"Yes." Momozono made barking sounds, like a dog.

"I understand that His Majesty treated you kindly and gave you a place at court when no one else wanted you around."

"He did m-more than that." Momozono gripped his arms, forcing them to hold still. "If not for him, I would be dead." Unpleasant memory clouded his straining face.

"Tell me what happened," Sano said.

Prince Momozono hesitated: He obviously knew the danger a murder suspect courted by confiding in the shogun's *sōsakan*. Yet Sano sensed in him an impulse that opposed caution. How often did anyone bother talking to him? How much he must yearn for communication! Finally, Momozono spoke.

"W-when I was young, I lived in the imperial children's palace with the other p-princes and princesses. Then, in the s-spring when I was eight, my affliction started. I w-was scolded and beaten, but I couldn't control myself. The d-doctors couldn't discover what was wrong with me. They forced m-medicines down my throat and gave me purges and enemas." Through the grunts that punctuated the words echoed the anguish of a child who didn't understand what was happening to him. "Priests s-said I was possessed by a demon. They lit fires around me and ch-chanted spells to drive it out.

"B-but nothing worked. I got worse. Finally I was l-locked in a store-house. Every day a s-servant opened the door and put food inside. I was allowed to come out only wh-when the storehouse was c-cleaned. The s-servant would throw b-buckets of water inside and sweep out the filth. Then he stripped me and threw water on m-me. There was only one w-window in the storehouse. All I could s-see was the sky through the b-branches of a cherry tree. For a whole y-year I lived there."

Sano imagined the young Momozono hooting and convulsing in his prison, watching the cherry blossoms bloom then drift to the ground, the leaves unfurl then drop, until snow covered the boughs. Empathy had no place in a murder investigation, but the prince's story affected Sano deeply.

"Then one night, s-some men came. They wrapped me up in qu-quilts so I couldn't m-move, and tied a gag over my mouth. They c-carried me away in a palanquin. They didn't t-tell me where they were taking me, but I h-heard them talking about how I was going to live in exile. I was glad because I thought Exile was the n-name of a place where children like m-me could be happy. I didn't know any better."

His voice broke on a sob; his eyes teared. Grimacing and puffing, he said, "We traveled for a l-long time. At last we stopped at a m-mountain village. It was d-dark and snowing and very c-cold. The men set me down outside the v-village and untied my gag. Then they picked up the palanquin and left." Momozono sniffled; he tried to wipe his nose, but his hand flew upward, and he used the other to pull it down. "I was terrified. I didn't know what to do, so I sat and w-waited.

"F-finally it began getting light. The v-villagers came. They d-didn't want me any more than the Imperial Court did." The prince gulped and blinked. "I sat alone for t-two days, freezing and h-hungry and scared." Ragged sobs choked him. "P-please excuse me."

Filled with pity, Sano imagined what had happened when the villagers found Momozono. Probably they'd taunted him and stoned him before leaving him to die.

"Then I b-began to feel sleepy and warm," Momozono said. "I stopped caring what h-happened to me. I was on the verge of d-death. But then the m-men returned. They took me back to the palace. I was washed and fed and given a r-room in the emperor's residence. His M-majesty came in. He s-said he'd dreamed about a demon who threatened to cause a terrible p-plague unless h-he rescued me and made me his c-companion. L-later I heard people saying he'd invented the whole story and b-brought me back to spite everyone. But I was too g-grateful to care why he'd saved me."

His face twisted with tics and emotion, Momozono gazed at Emperor Tomohito, who was beating his sword on the helmet of another soldier. Boyish cries arose as the battle raged on. "Because of His M-majesty, I'm allowed to live here." He added softly, "I've done my b-best to repay His Majesty."

By giving him a false alibi? Sano wondered. Whatever the emperor's motive for saving Momozono, he'd won the devotion of his cousin. Sano caught himself falling into the assumption that Momozono's affliction rendered him incapable of any worse crime than lying to protect the emperor. Momozono had revealed himself as a man of intelligence. To have survived his ordeals, he must be stronger than he looked.

"Your loyalty must be of valuable help to His Majesty," Sano said. Momozono humbly shook his head, but his eyes brightened with pleasure. "Now perhaps you can help me. How well did you know Left Minister Konoe?"

The prince hopped up and down, hooting and growling, striking out with his fists.

Startled, Sano dodged the blows. "You didn't care for the left minister, then?"

Rolling his eyes, Momozono reeled backward. "Forgive me, I can't h-help myself."

"I think it's more than that," Sano said. "What did Konoe do to you?"

"I suppose you'll find out from someone else if I don't tell you. L-left M-minister Konoe was the one who had me locked up in the storehouse. H-he gave the order to exile me." Momozono looked Sano straight in the eye, and Sano fought the impulse to avert his gaze from the prince's twitching face. "Yes, I-I hated him," Momozono said defiantly. "When His Majesty and I found him dead, I rejoiced. But I didn't do it. If I'd wanted to kill him, why would I have waited t-ten years?"

Hatred could fester over time, Sano knew. Momozono and the emperor shared an alibi. Which of them was it really meant to protect? Tomohito had rescued his cousin once already.

With a self-deprecating laugh, Momozono said, "How can you think I could k-kill anybody?"

Just then, Emperor Tomohito waved to him from across the battlefield, calling, "Bring me another sword!"

Momozono picked up a sword from the pile of toy weapons. He dropped it twice as he lurched toward the emperor. Watching, Sano tried and failed to imagine him as the killer. If Momozono fumbled the simplest tasks, how could he master the art of *kiai*? Where would he have learned it? Perhaps he exaggerated his symptoms, but Sano still believed that the conspiracy and the murder of Left Minister Konoe were related. How could a despised outcast mount an insurrection?

The emperor spied Sano. Ignoring the sword Momozono offered him, he dropped his toy horse and swaggered over. "What do you want?" he demanded.

Kneeling, Sano bowed, honoring the churlish youth as the descendant of the gods. Had they granted his bloodline the power to manipulate cosmic forces? Had his imperial ancestors bequeathed to him the secret of *kiai*?

"I've come to ask you some questions," Sano said.

"Stand up," Tomohito ordered.

Obeying, Sano returned the emperor's scrutiny. The armor added bulk to Tomohito's large build, and menace to his petulant, childish face. He said, "You've got nerve coming here, after what you did. You arrested my consort! You knocked me down!"

Sano noted these offenses as motives for Tomohito to want him dead.

"May lighting strike down all you Tokugawa bullies!" the emperor shouted.

While Momozono emitted anxious yelps, Sano experienced a stab of alarm, accompanied by the urge to laugh. The emperor had the power to invoke the wrath of the heavens, yet Tomohito's curse sounded like a child's extravagant threat. If he also commanded the power of *kiai*, his unbridled temper would make him all the more dangerous.

Sano hastened to appease the emperor: "I regret what I did. Lady Asagao has been freed."

But Tomohito, with the short attention span of youth, had lost interest in the subject. "You're a real fighter, aren't you?" he said, studying Sano with grudging admiration. Pointing at Sano's long sword, he ordered, "Let me see that."

Sano couldn't refuse an order from the emperor. He unsheathed his sword and handed it over.

"This is really nice." Tomohito ran a grubby finger along the blade. Suddenly he leapt backward and slashed at Sano, yelling, "Hah!"

Sano ducked just in time to escape a cut to the head. "Careful! That's not a toy."

"N-no, Your Majesty," Momozono wailed.

He grabbed the emperor's arm, but Tomohito pulled away. His eyes shone with the thrill of wielding a real blade. He circled, feinted, and sliced at the air. Sano noted Tomohito's skill. The emperor outshone many samurai of his age. His footwork was quick, each strike gracefully executed.

"You're pretty good, Your Majesty," Sano said. "How long have you studied *kenjutsu*?"

"All my life!"

"Who taught you?"

The emperor aimed a swipe at Sano's legs; when Sano jumped to avoid it, he laughed. "The best swordsmen in Miyako."

"What other martial arts did they teach you?"

"You ask too many questions!"

The emperor's impressive swordsmanship meant he could discipline his energies when it suited him, and discipline was crucial to the power of *kiai*.

"The battle your soldiers are fighting," Sano said. "It's the Jokyu War, isn't it?"

That was the war by which Emperor Go-Toba had tried to overthrow the military dictatorship. He'd summoned the Minamoto to a festival in Miyako where his army had attacked them.

"So what if it is?" Tomohito whirled and slashed around Sano.

"Then you're not being true to history," Sano said, flinching as the blade came dangerously close. "Your imperial faction is beating the Minamoto." On the battlefield, boys in red-laced armor played dead. "But in real life, the Minamoto defeated your ancestor. Instead of seizing power, he died in exile."

"If I'd been in his place, I would have won!"

"Is it a game, or are you rehearsing for a real revolt?"

The sword flew out of Tomohito's grasp. He exclaimed in annoyance. Sano retrieved his sword and sheathed it. "Please answer my question, Your Majesty."

Prince Momozono had an attack of spasms. The emperor scowled. "I just got clumsy for a moment. Of course the battle is a game, to pass the time. There's not much to do here; I get bored."

Observing Tomohito's refusal to meet his gaze, Sano said, "Has anyone encouraged you to think about restoring power to the Imperial Court and ruling Japan yourself?"

"Nobody tells me what to think. And I'm tired of talking. I've got better things to do."

The emperor and Momozono started toward the battlefield. Sano blocked their way. "Do you know of a house in the cloth dyers' district owned by Lord Ibe of Echizen Province?"

"I don't know any people or places anywhere but here," Tomohito said sullenly. "I can't go outside."

But an accomplice could, and there was one other promising candidate for that role besides Right Minister Ichijo.

"Where were you during the second murder?" Sano asked.

Jutting his chin belligerently, Tomohito said, "I was praying in the worship hall when I heard the scream. My cousin was there, too."

Sano looked at Prince Momozono, whose face went into a terrible frenzy of tics. The emperor must have sensed Sano's disbelief, because he looked uneasy and muttered, "We have to go now. Come on, Momo-*chan*."

"W-wait," said the prince. "I just remembered s-something about the n-night the left minister d-died. After the s-scream, when we were h-hurrying through the P-pond Garden, I saw a light in the c-cottage. It went out b-before we got there."

If this was true, then there'd been someone else at the scene of the murder. Sano looked at the emperor.

"Yes, there was a light," he said eagerly. "I remember now. I saw it too."

Sano discounted the story as a lie designed to pin the crime on a mysterious unknown culprit. Watching the emperor resume his battle and Prince Momozono his station beside the arsenal, Sano tallied the results of the interview. He had Momozono's motive for the first murder, Tomohito's for the second, and a new joint alibi as flimsy as their previous one. Even if the prince didn't have the power of *kiai*, the emperor might, and Sano was sure that the conspiracy involved Tomohito's participation. But he understood the consequences of incriminating the emperor. He envisioned Tomohito denouncing the Tokugawa regime, and the ensuing civil war. Hopefully, he could prove the guilt of a lesser person.

Perhaps Lady Jokyōden was the murderer and traitor. Sano had planned to visit her next, but a disturbing alternative suddenly occurred to him. He left the palace, knowing that he was risking trouble as well as seeking information.

23

The Jokyu War was over. The troops had dispersed, and the emperor had retired to his bathchamber. There a big, round wooden tub held cool water. Sunlight shone through latticed paper windows; white curtains decorated with the imperial crest hung over open transoms. Emperor Tomohito lay naked and motionless on a platform while attendants washed his body and hair. His eyes were closed. Ritual decreed that an emperor could be groomed only while asleep, so that touching him wouldn't compromise his sacred dignity.

In a corner of the chamber sat Prince Momozono, quivering and jerking as he watched the ablutions. The attendants ignored his presence. Tomohito seemed oblivious to everything. However, Momozono could tell that he wasn't really asleep; he flinched and frowned when the attendants scrubbed too vigorously, but he knew that if he protested, his servants would immediately withdraw their attentions. Momozono waited, stifling grunts with a hand over his mouth. For months he'd tried to work up the courage to speak frankly to his cousin. He could keep quiet no longer, even though he risked offending Tomohito, because his silence could doom them both.

At last the attendants finished washing the emperor, bowed to his inert figure, and departed. Tomohito opened his eyes and sat up. "I thought they'd never finish," he complained. He got off the platform and climbed into the tub, immersing himself with a sigh of contentment. "Someday I won't have to put up with people washing me like a baby."

Someday . . . It was a refrain that Momozono had heard often. He recalled an eight-year-old Tomohito trying to sneak out the palace gate, getting caught by the watchmen, and yelling, "Someday I'll be able to go outside if I feel like it!" Tomohito had also rebelled against studying and performing ceremonies: "Someday no one will be able to make me do this!"

Prince Momozono heard in the words a new, serious conviction. Tomohito was no longer a young crown prince indulging in childish fantasies. He was a grown emperor, bent on making fantasy a reality. Momozono must bring him to his senses.

"Y-your Majesty . . . there's s-something I must say," he ventured timidly.

Tomohito sank in the water up to his chin; his long hair floated around him like a black fan. "Go ahead."

More than anyone else in the court, Momozono depended upon the emperor's favor for his survival. Stalling, he said, "Wh-what do you think of the *sōsakan-sama?*"

"He's supposed to be a great swordsman, but I bet I could beat him."

Momozono's heart sank as he perceived the extent of his cousin's delusion. For all his skill, Tomohito was no match for a real samurai fighter. If Tomohito failed to recognize this, how could Momozono make him see the dangers he faced? Prince Momozono knew all too well who had fostered Tomohito's false sense of grandeur. Anger sent spasms through his limbs; he fought to still them.

"Doesn't it w-worry you that the *sōsakan-sama* is alive and still asking questions?" Momozono asked anxiously.

Tomohito laughed. "He doesn't scare me."

Unable to restrain himself, Momozono burst out, "Y-your Majesty, perhaps you *should* be afraid!"

The emperor sat up in the tub, scowling. "Are you presuming to tell me what to do?"

"No, no!" Momozono scuttled over to the tub, knelt, and bowed, trembling in his haste to appease his cousin. "I-I'm only trying to p-protect you, Your Majesty."

He had done so before. When Tomohito had reached the age of thirteen, his unhappiness with his sheltered existence had grown unbearable. More than ever he had yearned to experience life outside the palace, and so had befriended three roguish courtiers a few years his senior. Momozono had watched the emperor listen to their talk of drinking in teahouses, romancing girls, and skirmishing with Miyako's ruffians, his eyes aglow with vicarious excitement. Soon he craved more active participation in the trio's fun. He began planning adventures for them. At first these were mere pranks, such as stealing fruit from the market and putting an ox calf in a firewatch tower. When the courtiers came back to the palace, Tomohito reveled in their descriptions of the stir they'd created.

Then one day the emperor decided that his friends must break into the *shoshidai*'s house and bring back some token as proof of their success. Prince Momozono happened to be walking through the *kuge* quarter when the three courtiers returned from their escapade. Hidden by the darkness, he'd heard them arguing and realized that the fun had gone dreadfully wrong.

"We should never have done it!"

"Everything would have been fine if we'd left right after getting inside and taking the *shoshidai*'s personal seal. But no, you got greedy. You had to break open that chest and steal the gold coins."

"How was I supposed to know that the daughter would hear the noise and find us there?"

"Well, you shouldn't have forced yourself on her!"

"I was so drunk I didn't know what I was doing."

"What do we tell His Majesty?"

"Nothing. We'll say that it went perfectly. I'll hide the gold." The latter speaker was Lord Koremitsu, the trio's leader, the one who'd stolen the gold and raped the *shoshidai*'s daughter. Prince Momozono was terribly jealous of Lord Koremitsu, and hated him for his bad influence on Tomohito. "No one will ever know what we did."

The next day, however, police came to the palace. They reported the theft and rape to the chief court nobles, explaining that the *shoshidai*'s guards had chased the criminals to the imperial compound. They meant to identify and punish the culprits. Upon hearing the news, Prince Momozono was filled with dread. What if the *bakufu* traced the crimes to Tomohito? They wouldn't arrest him, but with this evidence of his bad character, they might force him to abdicate.

Momozono couldn't let his beloved cousin risk such a calamity. If Tomohito abdicated, the next emperor might throw Momozono out of the palace. Momozono had to make sure the *bakufu* found the culprit and the investigation stopped there. But he couldn't tell what he knew; the *bakufu* would never believe an idiot. He had to find another way.

Hurrying to his chambers, Momozono wrote on a sheet of paper: *Lord Koremitsu is the man you're looking for.* He rolled the message inside a scroll case. Then he went to the *kuge* quarter, where the police were going to every estate, looking for the criminals. He hid around a corner and waited until they came down the passageway. Subduing his noises and spasms by sheer act of will, he threw the scroll case in the police officers' path, then fled.

The police went to Lord Koremitsu's home. When they found the gold hidden there, he confessed and revealed the names of his accomplices. To protect their families' positions at court, the young men didn't incriminate the emperor. They were exiled, and the *bakufu* never learned of Tomohito's role in the crimes. The emperor was safe, and so was Prince Momozono.

But soon new trouble arose. Left Minister Konoe had posed a worse threat to the emperor than had Lord Koremitsu. The emperor's new venture was no harmless prank, and carried a much heavier penalty than theft or assault. Konoe's death hadn't averted the danger. The second murder had focused the *sōsakan-sama*'s investigation more strongly on the emperor. Anonymous letters wouldn't help in this situation. Momozono's only chance of preventing disaster lay in convincing the emperor to cooperate.

Now Momozono said, "Please, y-your Majesty, I beg you to see r-reason. These are dangerous times. *Sōsakan* Sano will keep searching for the k-killer until he's exposed every s-secret in the palace. You must be very careful and n-not give him cause for suspicion."

"Momo-*chan*, you worry too much," Tomohito said irritably. "The *sōsakan-sama* doesn't know anything." With a regal lift of his head, Tomohito added, "He can't hurt me. No one can. I have the divine protection of the gods."

Still, Momozono could tell from Sano's questions that even if he didn't know the truth, he suspected plenty. "D-divine protection won't shield you from the Tokugawa."

"All we have to do is stick to our story," Tomohito said, "and everything will be fine. We were playing darts together when Left Minister Konoe died. The other night I was praying in the worship hall. You were with me."

"B-but *Sōsakan* Sano thinks we're l-lying."

"Who cares what he thinks, when he doesn't have proof?" The emperor laughed. "And he'll never get any, because we were together those nights." He fixed a meaningful stare on Momozono. "*Weren't we?*"

Momozono had no choice but to nod, agreeing to maintain their precarious claim of innocence. Yet he couldn't give up without one last attempt to sway his cousin. "Th-this thing that you're d-doing . . ." He could hardly bear to think of it, let alone call it by name. "You can't p-possibly succeed. If you go through with it, you'll d-destroy yourself and the whole Imperial Court!"

"Don't be an idiot," Tomohito huffed. "Of course I'll succeed. It's my destiny to rule Japan. And someday . . ." He lay back in the tub, closed his eyes, and smiled. "Someday soon, I'll be able to do whatever I want."

24

At Nijō Manor, Reiko awakened alone in bed. The room was bright with sunlight. The nightmares of believing Sano dead and her adventures while seeking his killer seemed far away, but they'd exhausted her, and she'd slept past noon. As she sat up, a maid entered the room, carrying her breakfast tray.

"Where is my husband?" Reiko asked.

"He and his men have already gone out," said the maid.

"What about my guards and palanquin bearers?"

"They went, too."

Reiko felt annoyed at Sano for leaving her with no means of transport. How odd that yesterday she would have given anything, endured any hardships, just to have him back, but now the minor irritations of their life together could fret her once again! Drinking tea and eating pickled vegetables on rice, she pondered how to spend the day. She feared that she'd compromised the investigation by involving Lady Jokyōden, and wished to make up for whatever harm she'd done, but there seemed little she could do.

A glint of light caught her eye. On the table lay one of the coins that Sano had found among Left Minister Konoe's possessions. Reiko picked up the coin and studied the fern design thoughtfully. Detectives Marume and Fukida hadn't yet managed to discover the coins' significance, but maybe she would have better luck.

Reiko washed, dressed, and left the inn, taking two maids for company. They walked up and down the hot, crowded streets, visiting shops and teahouses, food stalls and marketplaces. Everyone Reiko questioned denied having seen such a coin before. Merchants who welcomed her into their establishments turned grim and reticent when shown the coin; clerks, customers, and roving peddlers seemed afraid to look at it. After hours of futile inquiries, Reiko was baffled and frustrated.

"Everyone's lying," she said to her maids. "There's something strange going on."

They stopped at a restaurant that sold tea and cold noodles. A teenaged servant girl with a plain, friendly face brought their food. While they ate, Reiko noticed her watching them. When she knelt to refill Reiko's tea bowl, she whispered, "May I please speak to you?"

Curious, Reiko nodded.

The girl cast a furtive look toward the kitchen, where an elderly couple tended pots boiling on the stove. "I heard that you were asking about coins with a fern leaf on them," she said, still whispering. "Please excuse me if I seem rude, but you must be a newcomer, so I have to warn you that no one here talks of such things, and you shouldn't, either."

"Why not?" Reiko asked.

"Because it's dangerous." The girl leaned closer and said, "The fern leaf is the crest of the Dazai clan. They're very bad men—thieves, hoodlums, murderers. They come to businesses like this and demand money, and they beat up shopkeepers who won't pay. They kidnap girls to work in their unlicensed brothels. They run gambling dens, and if you don't pay your debts, they torture you.

"They're very powerful, very much feared. It's no use reporting them to the police, because they bribe the police to leave them alone. They kill anyone who makes trouble for them. Even to speak of the Dazai is bad luck."

"Mayumi-*chan*!" called the man in the kitchen. "Stop bothering the customers. Get back to work!"

"Excuse me, I must go." The girl bowed. Before hurrying away, she whispered, "Please heed my warning, for your own good."

Reiko sat mulling over what she'd just heard. Why did the Dazai clan mint coins bearing their crest? How had Left Minister Konoe come to possess the coins? Perhaps he'd been spying on the Dazai. Reiko recalled the thugs she'd seen at Lord Ibe's house. Were they members of the Dazai and a link between Konoe's murder and the plot against the Tokugawa? Reiko shared Sano's belief that the coins were a critical element in the mystery, but how would she discover their meaning if everyone in Miyako refused to talk about them or the Dazai?

• • •

The five-hundred-year-old temple of Sanjūsangendō was located in Miyako's southern sector, near the east bank of the Kamo River. Worshippers and priests thronged the precinct around its halls, shrines, and pagoda. Gongs clanged; children romped. Sano stood alone inside the vermilion east gate, watching the activity while he questioned the wisdom of coming.

He needed information that Left Minister Konoe had probably concealed from the Imperial Court but might have confided to someone outside the palace, however little she'd welcomed his confidences. Hence, Sano had gone to Kodai Temple in search of Kozeri, but his rising agitation forced him to recognize that he wanted more than just answers from her. He told himself that his pursuit of the truth required him to withstand his attraction to Kozeri.

Upon reaching the convent, he learned that she'd gone out begging for alms at Sanjūsangendō. Her absence was a good excuse to avoid her, yet he needed evidence to connect the rebel conspiracy with the murder case. Now he walked through the precinct to the main hall. This was brightly painted, with red pillars, white walls, green window gratings, blue and yellow trim. Inside stretched a room like a cavernous tunnel, broken only by huge wooden pillars. Sano followed worshippers whose murmurs echoed to a high, beamed ceiling, alongside an altar that extended the length of the room. Candles and incense sticks burned on stands. Behind these loomed statues of wind and thunder gods. Above them, rising in eleven tiers like a golden army, stood the famous thousand and one statues of the goddess Kannon.

The flickering candlelight animated the figures and their serene faces crowned by spiked haloes. Their many hands, which held flowers, knives, skulls, and prayer wheels, seemed to flex and gesture. When Sano emerged into the searing sunlight of the courtyard, he saw three nuns in hemp robes and wicker hats, carrying wooden begging bowls. Kozeri stood in the middle. Surprise and pleasure lit her lovely eyes.

"Good afternoon, *Sōsakan-sama*," she said.

Her presence kindled a dark excitement in Sano. She was a witness with information he wanted, but he mustn't let her inspire dangerous thoughts.

With a shy smile, Kozeri said, "What brings you to Sanjūsangendō?"

"I was looking for you." Seeing a blush color Kozeri's cheeks, Sano understood that she'd craved another meeting as much as he; she welcomed his words as a sign of his interest in her. Flattered, Sano condemned himself as a vain, selfish boor. That he should forsake his wife to enjoy a nun's affections! "Actually, I have more questions to ask you," he said, trying to sound businesslike. "About Left Minister Konoe."

"Oh. I see." Although Kozeri kept smiling, disappointment and caution extinguished the light in her face. She inclined her head. "All right."

"Is there someplace we can talk?" Sano asked, surveying the busy temple grounds.

Without meeting his gaze, Kozeri nodded. She said to her companions, "Please excuse me."

"Perhaps we should stay with you," said the older of the two nuns, eyeing Sano shrewdly.

Perhaps you should, thought Sano as his heart jumped at the chance to be alone with Kozeri. But when she told the nuns, "It's all right, I'll be back soon," he let them go. He and Kozeri left the temple and strolled down an avenue bordered by the villas of imperial nobles who could afford second homes outside the palace. Past them moved palanquins carrying courtiers and ladies. Trees swayed, dappling the street with shadows. Kozeri walked with arms clasped around her begging bowl and her head bowed beneath her hat.

"I need to know about the last time you saw Left Minister Konoe," Sano said. "What did he say?"

"Nothing . . . That is, nothing except the same kind of things he said in his letters." Kozeri's voice was low but steady; perhaps she, too, felt more at ease with an impersonal subject between them. "I haven't had a real conversation with my former husband in years."

Sano sympathized with her unwillingness to discuss a painful subject, but instinct told him that the encounter was important to the case. "Let's go over everything that happened," he said. "Start with the left minister's arrival at Kodai Temple."

The brim of her hat bobbed as Kozeri reluctantly nodded. She kept her eyes on the ground as they walked, perhaps embarrassed by the curiosity of passersby who stared at the rare sight of a nun and a samurai walking together. In spite of himself, Sano wished she would look at him.

"It was early morning," Kozeri said. "Another nun and I were sweeping the veranda when he came. He said, 'Kozeri, you're as beautiful as you were when we married fifteen years ago. You never seem to age.' I dropped my broom and backed away, but he came up the steps toward me. He was smiling. I told the other nun to go get help.

"He said, 'I'm so glad to see you. Can't you at least act glad to see me?'" The memory of fear echoed in Kozeri's voice. "Then he started getting angry. He said he knew my heart better than I did, and I should realize that I loved him. He began talking about . . . things he wanted to do to me." Kozeri lifted a pleading gaze to Sano; her ivory complexion turned pink with shame. "Must I repeat them?"

"No, that's not necessary," Sano said hastily. "What happened next?"

Kozeri sighed. "This is very difficult. . . ."

"I understand," Sano said. "Take your time."

Too late he noticed that they'd left the busy streets and were nearing the river. Willows lined the bank. Their arching boughs formed caves of shadow. Between the gnarled tree trunks, sunlight glinted on the water, but the foliage hid the far bank. The slope of the ground blocked Sano's view of the houses behind him; the ripple of the water drowned out traffic sounds. It seemed as though the city and everyone else in the world had vanished. Sano was about to suggest that they return to Sanjūsangendō when Kozeri descended the riverbank and set down her begging bowl.

"The left minister trapped me against the wall. He grabbed my shoulders." She stood with her back pressed to a willow, hands clenched at her sides, pantomiming her story. "Then some priests came and took him away." A sigh of relief eased from her; she ran her hands down her breasts and hips, as if to assure herself that Konoe hadn't hurt her.

Watching, Sano felt a shameful burgeoning of desire, and an unwelcome understanding of the left minister's obsession with Kozeri. She seemed so innocent, yet overwhelmingly seductive. Sano tasted danger and excitement. His heart was racing, his breathing quick. He smelled decaying vegetation and the river's marshy scent; mossy ground yielded beneath his feet as he went to stand by Kozeri. He felt the vague, uneasy confusion that he'd experienced during his first interview with her. What was he forgetting to ask?

Kozeri turned toward him. A nervous smile hovered upon her lips. Sano wondered whether she'd brought him here deliberately. Were her feelings as mixed as his own? Her eyes shone fever-bright, and under the loose robe, her breasts rose and fell with rapid breaths. She looked scared; she also looked like a woman erotically aroused. Sano felt his own body respond.

To hide his distress, he said, "What else happened?"

"That was all." Then a thoughtful look came into Kozeri's eyes. "Wait . . . I'd forgotten. When the left minister was forced to leave the temple, he shouted at me. I don't remember his exact words, but they went like this: 'Soon you'll realize that you made a terrible mistake by leaving me. I'm on the verge of the greatest accomplishment of my life. Soon every man shall do my bidding, every woman desire my favor. You shall be so impressed that you'll return to me at last!' "

"What do you think he meant?" Sano asked, intrigued.

"He always wanted to be imperial prime minister," Kozeri said. "I assumed that he was finally going to get the post."

A promotion would have given him greater prestige at court, but Sano believed Konoe had learned the murderer's secret and planned to apply it toward a different sort of 'accomplishment' that would win him power, wealth, and Kozeri's esteem. Yet once again, the sense of a gap in the case bothered Sano, although Chamberlain Yanagisawa had supplied much of the missing information.

Kozeri stood watching him. Her hand wandered up to pat her lips, then clasp her throat. Her sensual habit of caressing herself provoked in Sano an almost irresistible urge to touch her. "The other nuns will be wondering what happened to me," she said.

Sano noticed that the afternoon sun had descended in the sky, sheening the river with bronze. The shadows under the willows had deepened. Above the water's incessant rush hummed a prenocturnal chorus of insects. Sano had the evidence he'd come for; he should go back to the Imperial Palace and finish his inquiries, or find out what had come of Chamberlain Yanagisawa's raid on Lord Ibe's estate.

"Yes," he said, "we should go."

Yet neither he nor Kozeri moved. Her eyes filled with panicky anticipation. *Go on and have her,* whispered a demon inside Sano. *Other men do this all the time; there's no need to feel guilty. Reiko doesn't have to know.* Sano walked slowly toward Kozeri. She gave a frightened whimper, but made no effort to stop him. Now he stood close enough to hear her breathing in sharp hisses and see the saliva gleam on her quivering lips. His hands lifted. This was wrong. He loved Reiko, whom he'd already hurt badly by faking his death. He ached with his need for Kozeri.

Hands poised above her shoulders and their faces almost touching, Sano saw his inner turmoil reflected in her eyes. As a nun, she would have taken a vow of celibacy, but she was a sensual woman who'd lived fifteen years without a man. Sano could see her trembling with repressed hunger. Forcing himself to think of Reiko, he only realized a disturbing truth about his nature. A part of him was drawn to women with an aura of tragedy, whose spirits carried the same veins of darkness as his own.

Women like Aoi, the ninja spy he'd fallen in love with during his first case as the shogun's investigator.

And Sano knew that Reiko, with her bright personality, could never quite satisfy the dark part of him, no matter how much they loved each other.

Suddenly Kozeri moaned, a sound of utter, passionate submission. Tilting her head, she laid her cheek on Sano's hand, eyes closed and lips parted. The feel of her hot, moist skin thrilled Sano. With his other hand he stroked the nape of her neck, that most erotic visible part of a woman's body. Letting his fingers trail slowly down Kozeri's back, he drew her closer to him.

She moaned louder and pressed herself against him. For a moment, Sano swooned with pleasure. Then horror jolted him from dazed lust and into awareness that he'd taken the first step toward forbidden sex. Now his desire filled him with revulsion. With an anguished cry, he pulled away from Kozeri.

She stared in surprise. "What's wrong?"

Raising his hands in a gesture of helpless apology, Sano shook his head and said, "I'm sorry."

"Don't you want me?" Tears welled in Kozeri's eyes.

"I can't do this," Sano said. Turning, he fled as if pursued by an invading army.

25

At Kodai Temple, the afternoon had passed in its unvarying routine of prayers and chores; the nuns had returned from begging in the city, and evening rites had begun. While bells tolled across Miyako, the setting sun poured fiery light through the windows of the convent dormitory. There knelt the nuns, heads shaven, completely naked. In three rows, firm young bodies alternated with those of older women with sagging flesh. They faced the abbess, who sat upon a platform at the front of the room.

"Breathe deeply," intoned the abbess. She sucked air through her mouth. "In. Out. Gather the energy within you."

At her place in the middle row, Kozeri inhaled the musky smell of the women whose breaths echoed her own. She tried to let her mind drift and feel the energy kindle inside her. For fifteen years she'd practiced this exercise, designed to focus her mental power and bring spiritual enlightenment. Usually she slipped into a trance easily, but tonight the required concentration evaded her. The shogun's *sōsakan* had disturbed her inner harmony. Scenes from the past invaded the darkness behind her closed eyelids.

She saw the garden of her family's mansion, the secluded paradise of her youth. Again she ran laughing through the spring rains, hot summers, autumn leaves, and winter snows with her favorite cousin and playmate, Lord Ryōzen. As the years passed, Kozeri became a beautiful young woman, Ryōzen a handsome youth; friendship evolved into romance. Their families approved of the match, which would strengthen the connection between two noble clans. At age fifteen, Kozeri and Ryōzen knelt before the Shinto priest and sipped the ritual three wedding cups of sake.

Kozeri spent happy days making a home for Ryōzen, while he worked as secretary to Left Minister Konoe. In the evenings they entertained themselves with music, poetry, and lovemaking. Soon Kozeri was pregnant. Then, five months later, things went suddenly, terribly wrong. Kozeri was resting in her room one afternoon when her mother entered.

"Daughter," said the older woman, her face woeful, "I bring terrible news. Ryōzen is dead. Someone stabbed him."

Kozeri shook her head in disbelief. "But I just saw him this morning. There must be some mistake."

"There is no mistake," her mother said sorrowfully.

"No!" Kozeri stumbled from the house and met servants bringing in a blanket-covered figure on a litter. Tearing off the blanket, she saw her husband's still, pale face. She burst into a torrent of weeping.

Then an excruciating cramp convulsed her stomach. Kozeri screamed and fell. More pains wracked her. She heard her mother calling, "She's in labor! Fetch the doctor!"

Many agonizing hours later, Kozeri delivered a dead baby boy. She lost much blood; fever followed the stillbirth. Ten months passed before Kozeri rose from her bed. She sat listlessly in the garden, pining for Ryōzen. Then one day her father came to her.

"It is time to consider your future," he said. "Left Minister Konoe has asked for your hand in marriage, and I have consented."

Now the sonorous voice of the abbess drew Kozeri back to the present: "Feel the energy flow from your center to every part of your body. Let us seal the power inside us."

Kozeri opened her eyes and saw the abbess holding a long strip of cloth. She picked up a similar cloth from the floor beside her. Imitating the abbess's movements, she wrapped it tightly around her stomach. The other nuns did the same. In the dying sunlight, their faces shone with a tranquillity she envied.

"Lean forward, head and shoulders down," said the abbess. "Align your nose with your navel. Relax. And breathe, slowly. One, two . . ."

With the cloth compressing her muscles, Kozeri inhaled and exhaled, silently counting toward four hundred breaths. Briefly she resisted the memories, then let them come. . . .

She hadn't wanted to remarry, but it was her duty to obey her father, who craved the prestige the new match would bring to their clan. Hence, she wedded Left Minister Konoe. He was a virtual stranger; his rank and wealth awed her. During the ceremony, she dared not even look at him, and their wedding night proved an inauspicious beginning for the marriage.

In the bedchamber, Konoe tenderly undressed her. "Don't worry, I'll be gentle," he said.

Kozeri knew she should show gratitude toward him for rescuing her from widowhood, yet she couldn't help recalling Ryōzen, and their happiness together. Tears burned her eyes. Feeling no desire for Konoe, she endured his caresses; she let him mount her. But when he pushed his erection against her womanhood, her inner muscles clenched shut. Konoe thrust and panted, but couldn't get in. Pain overcame Kozeri's self-control. The tears spilled.

Konoe forced a smile and said, "It's been a strenuous day. Let us sleep now, and begin over tomorrow."

He spent all his free time with Kozeri, and much money on gifts and amusements for her. All the palace ladies envied Kozeri, but the left minister seemed so grand that she couldn't get over her shyness. When he talked, she could manage only timid monosyllables in reply. Further attempts to consummate their marriage failed, and Konoe began to express his dissatisfaction in frightening ways.

Every evening he would ask, "What did you do today? Whom did you see?" and make Kozeri account for every moment of their time apart. He forbade her to go anywhere without him. He dropped in on her during the day, as if to catch her doing something wrong. He would not allow her to receive guests. Besides Konoe and his staff, the only people Kozeri saw were her elderly music, calligraphy, and painting teachers.

Isolated and lonely, she began to resent her husband. He sensed her antipathy and punished her with cutting remarks, violent acts. Once, in a fit of rage, he tore up all her clothes.

"Ungrateful wretch!" he shouted, stripping her naked and throwing her out in the snowy garden. "Freeze out there until you can show some affection for your husband!"

The next day he apologized profusely and bought Kozeri a new wardrobe. Her husband seemed to be two different people: his normal, public self, and the monster who ruled her. Kozeri's fear worsened their marital relations. She would have gladly let the left minister enter her, if only to pacify him, but her womanhood closed up whenever he tried. Furious, Konoe abandoned the gentle, patient approach. He fed Kozeri aphrodisiacs. He slathered oil on her crotch, prying at the threshold with wooden implements. Her pained cries further incensed him. Muttering curses, he drove his organ at her like a battering ram.

One night, after another failure, he said, "It's no use. You don't want me. You don't love me. And you never will."

Rising, he donned his dressing gown and stood looking down at Kozeri, his face taut with angry frustration. While she cowered, he said, "For love of you, I committed a heinous act. I risked my position and my honor, sacrificed my tranquillity and freedom. All for nothing!"

He left the room, and a horrifying thought took shape in Kozeri's mind. His words showed her the past in a different perspective. Little things, hardly noticed at the time, now took on an ominous significance. She recalled Ryōzen remarking, "The left minister enjoys hearing about how we play music together." Indeed he seemed eager for any information regarding their personal life, and Kozeri had been pleased by what she thought was his interest in Ryōzen, whose career would benefit from Konoe's patronage. She remembered the left minister's frequent visits to their home, and ceremonies where his brooding gaze followed them. Now Kozeri understood that she, not her husband, had been the real focus of Konoe's attention all along.

He'd fallen in love with her while she was still married to Ryōzen. The police had never caught Ryōzen's killer; they couldn't find anyone with reason to wish him dead. Left Minister Konoe could have stolen Kozeri from Ryōzen by simply ordering them to divorce and commanding her to marry him; thus, no one had suspected Konoe of the murder, even though he benefited by her widowhood. But Kozeri knew his jealous nature. He wouldn't have wanted her first husband around as a rival for her love, so he'd "committed a heinous act."

Left Minister Konoe had murdered Ryōzen.

Now the four hundred breaths ended. The abbess began to chant: *"Namu Amida Butsu. Namu Amida Butsu."*

"Namu Amida Butsu," Kozeri repeated along with the other nuns. Their voices rang with joyous conviction; hers sounded hollow as she remembered the horror of her discovery, and the confusion that followed. Nobody would believe her if she accused Konoe of murder; he was too important and respected. The Imperial Court wouldn't let her go to the police. Her family wouldn't risk Konoe's disapproval by taking her side. Kozeri must hide her emotions and keep peace with the left minister.

But nothing she said or did pleased him. He grew more brutal in his efforts to penetrate her, and he watched her ever more closely. Then, shortly before their first anniversary, Kozeri's samisen teacher died. The new one who came to give her lessons was a courtier in his twenties, nicknamed "Saru"—Monkey—because of his talent for mimicry. With his lopsided smile and bulging eyes, he wasn't handsome, but he was kind. Perceiving Kozeri's unhappiness, Saru made her laugh at his imitations of animals and people. For the first time since Ryōzen's death, Kozeri found pleasure in life. She had a friend.

Then one evening Konoe stormed into her chamber, his face livid with rage. He grabbed Kozeri and threw her against the wall.

"Adulteress!" he yelled, slapping her face. "Dirty whore!"

Kozeri cried, "What are you talking about, husband?"

"Don't pretend you don't understand," he said. "Every day you whisper and laugh with him. I know, because I've listened outside the door. He's your lover. Don't deny it!"

He meant Saru! Kozeri was shocked. She had no romantic interest in the music teacher. Besides, Saru was happily married. "No," she protested.

"Liar!" Konoe kicked her stomach. She fell and curled up; he kicked her head. "I heard you two mocking me. I've thrown him and his family out of the palace. They'll starve to death in the streets."

Kozeri realized that her husband had eavesdropped on Saru's caustic imitation of him. "I'm sorry!" she cried. "Please!"

His fists battered her. Blood poured from her nose. She screamed as Konoe ripped handfuls of hair from her head. Cursing, he picked up her samisen and beat her with it. At last he stood back, hateful triumph in his face.

"I trust you've learned your lesson," he said.

Despair emboldened Kozeri. She said bitterly, "Why don't you just kill me, the way you did Ryōzen?"

For a long, awful moment she and Konoe stared at each other. She saw the truth of her accusation in his eyes. Anger flared in them, and she braced herself for another attack. Then he shook his head, turned, and walked away.

Kozeri wept. When the tears subsided, a calm clarity settled upon her mind. She understood that Konoe meant to continue trying to force her to love him. His cruelty would worsen until eventually he lost control and killed her. Kozeri's religious upbringing had taught her to accept fate; yearning for Ryōzen, she considered suicide to escape misery and hasten her reunion with him. But part of her didn't want to die. Bruised, bloody, and aching, she packed a bundle of the new robes Konoe had given her. She fled to Kodai Temple, where her family had once taken refuge during a fire in the palace. The convent was a haven for maltreated women with religious leanings. The nuns took her in, accepting her wardrobe as a dowry. Kozeri imagined herself safe from the left minister forever.

A month later, Konoe burst into the convent, interrupting the novices' prayers. "I've searched all over for you," he shouted at Kozeri. "Now you're coming home with me!" He would have grabbed her, had not monks overpowered him. As they dragged him out of the temple, he shrieked, "I'll get you. You can't hide!"

He came again and again, sending letters between visits. When the nuns begged for alms in the city, Konoe accosted her. Sometimes he pleaded, apologizing for his behavior. Often he threatened to kill her if she didn't return to him. Sometimes Kozeri heard nothing from him for months; just when she began to believe he'd given up, he would reappear and the letters resume. In spite of her gentle nature, Kozeri hated the left minister. He'd destroyed her life, driven her from home and family. Why couldn't he leave her alone? She longed for his death, and an end to her misery.

She'd gotten her wish. But now, worse troubles threatened. She was a suspect in Konoe's murder; *Sōsakan* Sano's questions had made it obvious. What if he found out how the left minister had treated her? Still, arrest wasn't the only thing she feared from Sano. His coming to Kodai Temple had shattered the calm she'd achieved through prayer and meditation. He'd awakened old emotions, suppressed longings.

In seeking a religious life, Kozeri had fled not just the left minister. Because her second marriage had overshadowed the happy memory of her first, she'd wanted nothing more to do with men. The need for peace outweighed all other desires. For years she'd been satisfied with having food, shelter, her faith, and the other nuns for company. But Sano had awakened a response in her; desire for him had stirred Kozeri's body to life. He'd aroused in her a powerful renewed need for the love of a man. She wanted to know Sano and continue the lovemaking they'd begun by the river today; yet although she longed to see him again, she dreaded the prospect.

"Now stand," said the abbess, rising slowly. "Mouth shut, chin drawn in, spine straight. Keep breathing; look straight ahead. Clear vision equals a clear conscience."

The nuns rose. Kozeri envisioned their consciences as clear water, hers as a dust storm. She possessed knowledge that could help Sano solve the case, but she also had dangerous secrets to keep. Telling the truth could jeopardize her life; love could destroy her hard-won peace. She'd not only lied to Sano, but this exercise she was performing had equipped her with a weapon that she'd used against him in self-defense. If he discovered the nature of the weapon, he would charge her with murder. Kozeri didn't know what would come of their acquaintance, but his duty, and their mutual attraction, had ensured one outcome.

Sano would be back.

Clad in a dressing gown, her freshly washed hair sleek and wet, Reiko walked from the bathchamber at Nijō Manor to her room and found that Sano had returned. He was seated on the floor, sorting through the boxes of papers from Left Minister Konoe's office that Chamberlain Yanagisawa had just sent. He greeted her with a quick nod, then continued perusing documents.

"I was starting to worry about you," Reiko said, kneeling beside him. Night had fallen; the inn's guests had already retired. "Shall I order your dinner?"

"No, thank you," Sano said, frowning at a letter in his hand. "I stopped at a food stall, so I'm not hungry."

"Well, I'm glad you're back." Puzzled by his curt manner, Reiko said, "Guess what: I've learned something about the fern-leaf coins." She described how she'd made inquiries and connected the coins to the Dazai gangster clan.

"That's a good lead," Sano said. He stopped his work and looked at her, yet Reiko would have appreciated a little more enthusiasm from him. "But Left Minister Konoe might have been spying on the Dazai for some purpose not connected to the imperial restoration plot, or his murder."

"That's true." Although she understood the need for objectivity, Reiko was disappointed by Sano's skepticism. "What did you learn today?"

"I just came from Nijō Castle," Sano said. "Chamberlain Yanagisawa raided Lord Ibe's house, but the outlaws and weapons were gone. He's leading a search for them. Unfortunately, he's located *Yoriki* Hoshina, as Marume and Fukida have just informed me. I've had Hoshina transferred to a new hiding place, but it may be just a matter of time before Yanagisawa finds him again. Earlier, I questioned Right Minister Ichijo, Emperor Tomohito, and Prince Momozono." Sano described the interviews, then said, "Either Ichijo or the emperor could have the power of *kiai*; either or both could be involved in the imperial restoration plot. They both have alibis that don't convince me, but would be hard to disprove."

"What about Lady Jokyōden?" Reiko said.

Sano's gaze strayed to the scrolls that lay in stacks around him. "I haven't had a chance to see her yet."

"Why not?" Reiko was surprised because he'd been gone long enough, and she thought he would have called on all the suspects while at the palace. She was also anxious to know whether Jokyōden could have committed the second murder. A solid alibi would clear Jokyōden of suspicion and ease Reiko's fear that she'd made a mistake by trusting the woman.

"I went to see Kozeri." Now Sano resumed sorting through papers with intent concentration.

"Again? Why?"

"I wanted to know about Konoe's last visit to her." Without looking up from his work, Sano said, "She saw Konoe shortly before his death. He told her he was on the verge of a great accomplishment. This suggests that he'd discovered the conspiracy and planned to report it to the *bakufu*, with the expectation of getting a big reward."

His reason for taking the time to see the nun seemed flimsy to Reiko, and the diversion uncharacteristic of Sano. "Yes, that does indicate that Konoe knew about the plot," she said, "but Kozeri's not really a suspect, is she? There were no outsiders in the palace during Konoe's murder, and when Chamberlain Yanagisawa set you up to be murdered, he didn't notify Kozeri of the opportunity to kill you."

"Kozeri's story substantiates my theory about the killer's motive, which is critical to solving the case. She's an important witness, so I went to see her. I'll talk to Lady Jokyōden tomorrow." Irritation tightened Sano's voice. "Why can't you respect my judgment?"

He'd been short-tempered the night before last, and for as little apparent reason as now, Reiko remembered. "Are you angry at me because I went around asking about the coins?" she said.

"I'm not angry," Sano snapped.

"Then what's wrong?" Now Reiko realized that he'd behaved this way after seeing Kozeri the first time. "Did Kozeri say or do something to upset you?"

"Of course not," Sano said in a defensive, unconvincing tone. "I already told you what happened. If I'm upset, it's because you question everything I do."

A sharp prick of suspicion disturbed Reiko. But no, she had absolute confidence in Sano's fidelity. Although other husbands took lovers and mistresses, he'd never given her reason to think him interested in another woman.

Shamed by her suspicion, Reiko said, "I'm sorry. I didn't mean to upset you."

Sano nodded, dismissing her apology. He compared the note she'd found in the charcoal brazier beside a letter from Konoe's personal files. "The calligraphy matches. Konoe did write the note about the activities at Lord Ibe's house. And here's something else." He read from a document: "'I, Nakane the Weaver, agree to sell my house in Nishijin to the Honorable Left Minister Konoe Bokuden.' There's a map showing the location of the house that Lady Jokyōden took you to. So Konoe did own the house." Sano gave Reiko a brief, forced smile before returning his attention to the papers. "Maybe Jokyōden isn't the killer and we can trust her."

"Maybe," Reiko said, uncomfortably aware that she hadn't told him about Jokyōden's affair with Konoe. She'd promised her discretion, and she must honor her promise unless the affair became vital evidence in the case, which it so far hadn't. She was afraid that Sano was keeping secrets from her, too.

They spent the rest of the evening in stilted, minimal conversation, and when they went to bed, they lay awake for a long time, facing away from each other.

26

"I hope you don't mind if I work while we talk," Lady Jokyōden said to Sano. "No matter what misfortunes befall us, we must still observe the rites of Obon."

"Please, go right ahead," Sano said.

It was morning, and they were in the Buddhist chapel of Jokyōden's residence. The rain doors were raised; the wind wafted a bitter tang of smoke into the room. On a platform in a recessed niche sat a gilded Buddha statue surrounded by gold lotus flowers. Many narrow alcoves each held a table containing a vase for flowers, an incense burner, and a *butsudan*—memorial shrine—in the form of a small cabinet. From the ceiling hung trappings of the Festival of the Dead: plaited white paper strips, toys once owned by deceased children, and a mask of Otafuku, a deity of fortune.

Lady Jokyōden knelt on the tatami floor amid supplies for her Obon preparations and untied the cord around a stack of straw mats. Sano, standing nearby, noted that Jokyōden seemed unperturbed by his unannounced arrival. She'd politely acquiesced to an interview and didn't seem to mind being alone with him, but she waited for him to speak first.

"Where were you during the murder three nights ago?" Sano asked.

Serenely indifferent, Jokyōden began setting mats under the *butsudan*. There was no hint of mystical power about her, and Sano thought it unlikely that rigorous martial arts training would have been wasted on a woman. While still on his guard, he felt less apprehension than while interviewing Right Minister Ichijo and Emperor Tomohito.

"I can't remember," Jokyōden said.

Perplexed, Sano said, "Surely you have some idea."

"I am afraid I do not."

"The murder happened just before midnight," Sano said. "What were you doing then?"

Busy with her task, Jokyōden gave him a demure glance from beneath lowered eyelids. "I really don't know."

Sano was more inclined to believe that she preferred not to say. She certainly wasn't the fool that she sounded. Whether innocent or guilty, why didn't she just present a plausible lie instead of such a ridiculous claim?

"Did you go near the kitchens?" Sano asked.

"Perhaps . . . perhaps not."

And why not just place herself elsewhere, away from the murder scene? "Did you see or talk to anybody?" Sano persisted. "Is there anybody who might have seen you?"

"I don't recall whether I saw or spoke with anyone." Having finished with the mats, Jokyōden filled the alcove vases with water from a spouted jar. Her movements were precise; she didn't spill a drop. "You will have to ask the other palace residents whether they saw me."

Nettled by her impervious calm, Sano said, "You can't really expect me to believe that you've forgotten everything about that night."

She turned to him with a bland smile. "I expect nothing. But I beg you to excuse this humble woman for her poor memory."

During past investigations, Sano had met suspects who'd obstructed him by pretending ignorance, but none had carried it off as smoothly as Lady Jokyōden. What a maddening woman! Still, he admired her nerve.

Then Jokyōden said, "In my opinion, the world is a better place with one less despicable Tokugawa samurai. Your treatment of the emperor was a disgrace." Frowning, Jokyōden arranged fresh lotus flowers. "You dishonored the entire Imperial Court. It was an insult that begged revenge."

Sano stared at Jokyōden in amazement. After refusing to tell her whereabouts at the time of the murder, she'd just handed him her motive for wanting him dead! What was she up to?

"It's understandable that you don't care for me," he said, "but perhaps you found Left Minister Konoe more compatible."

"Why do you say that?" Jokyōden said in a tone of polite curiosity.

"You knew about the house he'd secretly purchased, which indicates a more than superficial acquaintance with him." Sano ventured a bold guess: "Were you and he lovers?"

Jokyōden gasped and dropped the vase she was holding. It broke on the floor; lotuses scattered and water splashed. With a moan of distress, she grabbed a cloth and began cleaning up the water.

"Here, let me help." Sano gathered up the fallen blossoms, gratified to see that he'd shaken Jokyōden's composure at last.

"Thank you," she murmured. She inserted the flowers in a new vase and placed it carefully on an altar. Then she stood and faced Sano. "So your wife told you my secret, even though she promised me her discretion? No? But of course, you are clever enough to have guessed." Jokyōden's expression was strained. "Yes, the left minister and I were once lovers."

Then Reiko had known, Sano thought; yet instead of telling him, she'd kept silent. Sano was furious at Reiko, but he welcomed the news of her duplicity, as if it somehow excused his own behavior with Kozeri.

Jokyōden said sadly, "My husband is not the most stimulating companion, and his nature requires me to perform many of his duties. My work brought me into close contact with Left Minister Konoe. He was attractive and unmarried. We had many interests in common. I was lonely. Eventually, friendship led to romance. But the romance did not last."

"Why not?" Sano said, making an effort to forget his personal problems and concentrate on Jokyōden.

"In the beginning, the left minister seemed wonderful. He praised me, brought me gifts, made me feel cherished and important. I fell in love with him. But soon he changed. He lost his temper if I disagreed with him on court policy. He pressured me to put my husband's official seal on documents that would give him more authority. When I refused . . ." Jokyōden blinked, swallowed, then said, "He had other women. And he was always busy with Tomohito, talking to him, supervising his lessons, rehearsing him for ceremonies, and playing games with him, while ignoring me.

"Finally I told the left minister that I wanted to end our liaison. I expected him to object, apologize, and ask for another chance, but he just said he'd never really wanted me; he'd used me to gain more influence over the court. And he didn't need me any longer because he'd won Tomohito's confidence. His affection had been a pure sham. I was terribly hurt and made a hysterical scene."

Abruptly Lady Jokyōden knelt by a tray of covered dishes. She lifted the lids, revealing traditional Obon foods: noodles, rice cooked with lotus petals, dumplings, sweet cakes, pickled eggplant, and fruit. With extreme care, she picked up a pair of chopsticks and divided the food onto small platters made of unglazed red earthenware. Sano thought he saw tears gleam in her eyes.

"So although I once cared very much for the left minister, it would be hypocritical for me to say that I regret his death. After our romance ended, I still had to work with him as usual. His presence was a constant reminder of my own foolishness. I wanted never to see him again." Arranging noodles on a platter, she drew a tremulous breath. "His death granted my wish."

Revenge on a cruel lover was a powerful motive for murder, yet something about Jokyōden's confession bothered Sano. Convincing as it sounded, he couldn't quite imagine her falling for such a transparent scheme, and once again, she'd volunteered information too readily. Dropping the vase had seemed too melodramatic for a woman as poised as Jokyōden. Now Sano wondered whether she and Konoe ever had been lovers, or quarreled. But if not, then why lie and incriminate herself further?

Sano said, "I understand that you manage the affairs of the imperial family. You must have a remarkable talent for business."

"You're too generous. My poor efforts hardly deserve praise." An air of waiting stillness came over Jokyōden, although her hands continued filling dishes.

"So it would be humiliating to fall under the domination of someone less worthy or capable than yourself."

"Humiliation was the ultimate result of my affair with the left minister, yes." Rising, Jokyōden began setting food platters on each altar as offerings to the spirits of the dead. She gave Sano an oblique glance, as if not sure what he was getting at, but sensing a trap.

"And now, with Left Minister Konoe gone, you're free from his interference," Sano said, walking beside Jokyōden. "But how free can you really be, while the Imperial Court is ruled by the *bakufu*? Do you ever resent its domination?"

"Why resent a circumstance that is beyond my control?" A note of puzzlement crept into Jokyōden's voice. "That would be a waste of energy."

"Not if you thought you could change your circumstances," Sano said, handing plates of fruit to Jokyōden. "Do you ever imagine ruling Japan? An entire country would offer a much wider scope for your talent than the small world of the court. Do you ever think you could govern better than the *bakufu* does?"

Jokyōden turned an acid glare on him and said, "Your mockery of this poor woman shows deplorable manners." Then, as she bent over an altar and set down the plates Sano had handed her, a glimmer of a smile lit her profile. "But perhaps a shift of power is overdue. In less than a century, many problems have plagued Japan: famines, a bad earthquake, the flood that washed away the Sanjo Bridge and drowned hundreds of people, the

Great Fire of Meireki that destroyed most of Edo, and two major fires here in Miyako. Such calamities are signs that the government is out of harmony with the cosmos. Only by transferring leadership to a worthier ruler can we avoid future disasters. Who better than a wise, capable member of the Imperial Court?"

Sano had begun to think that nothing Jokyōden said could surprise him anymore, but her declaration stunned him. She'd not only implied that she blamed the Tokugawa for Japan's bad luck, but that she considered herself qualified to take over the government! Was she responsible for the restoration conspiracy? Had she quarreled with Konoe over a love affair gone bad, or because he'd discovered the plot and meant to report her to the *metsuke*?

Or was this another move in some bizarre game of which she alone knew the objectives?

More baffled than ever, Sano said, "Have you already taken steps toward restoring harmony to the cosmos?"

"Perhaps . . . perhaps not."

Either she realized she was on dangerous ground, or she sought to confuse him further. Losing patience, Sano ventured a countermove: "It might interest you to know that a certain house in the cloth dyers' district was raided yesterday."

"Why should that concern me?" Jokyōden asked.

Sano couldn't tell whether his news disturbed her, or if she knew what it meant, but the atmosphere in the chapel seethed with Jokyōden's unspoken thoughts. He said, "Would you happen to know what's become of the weapons that were in that house two days ago?"

Jokyōden set the last dish on an altar. Standing, she faced Sano with an enigmatic smile. "Weapons are not always necessary for the overthrow of a regime. The murders in the palace prove that there is a force stronger than any army. You samurai call it *kiai* and think that you invented it, but the power to take life by an act of will developed before the Way of the Warrior. When your ancestors were primitive tribal chieftains squabbling in the dirt, the Imperial Court had an advanced culture handed down to us by the gods. We command the magic of the universe, and within the palace walls, ancient traditions continue."

A strange intensity lit Jokyōden's narrow eyes. As she glided out through the open doors, her layered silk robes fluttered in the wind. Curious, Sano followed, not knowing what to expect. An eerie disquiet infused the air. Above the garden, clouds and smoke drifted across the sky. Tiny waves rippled the pond; irises swayed; distant thunder boomed in the hills.

Jokyōden stood perfectly still on the veranda. She closed her eyes; her lips parted.

Moments passed. Sano waited, watching Jokyōden. Suddenly the boughs of a nearby pine tree rustled. From them dropped a small gray object, which landed on the gravel path with a soft thud. It was a squirrel with curled claws and a furry tail. For an instant the animal lay motionless. Jokyoden released her breath. The squirrel scrambled up and ran across the garden.

"Never underestimate your adversary's power, *sōsakan-sama*," Lady Jokyōden said.

Sano stared at her. Arms folded, she gave him a triumphant smile. Thoughts jumbled in his mind. Had the force of Jokyōden's will really felled the squirrel? Nature is full of small dramas; wait long enough, and something inevitably happens. Jokyōden's performance reminded Sano of magic tricks that depend on the belief of the audience. But the palace harbored an ancient evil. Suddenly Sano was afraid of Jokyōden. If she did have the power of *kiai*, she'd already murdered two men. She could kill him in an instant.

Backing into the chapel, away from her, Sano said, "Well, thank you for your time." His instincts warned against staying with Jokyōden a moment longer.

He thought he saw a flicker of relief in her tranquil gaze. As with Right Minister Ichijo, he had the sense of hidden secrets. Once more he wondered whether Chamberlain Yanagisawa had been entirely frank with him.

"Honorable Lady Jokyōden, you've given me a lot of evidence against yourself," Sano said, pausing at the door. "I could charge you with murder—and treason—on the strength of it."

She just smiled. "But you won't, will you?"

Now Sano understood that she'd accurately read his character, while hers remained a mystery to him. She knew she could play her bizarre, dangerous game with him because he wouldn't make another arrest without solid proof. He'd lost control over the interview at the start.

Exasperated, Sano burst out, "Why are you doing this? To make me think that your candor means you must be innocent? Do you want me to believe that you're guilty and you deliberately helped my wife find evidence against you? Or are you encouraging my suspicion to protect someone else?"

Jokyōden laughed; her humor further mystified Sano. "You are the detective. It is up to you to answer those questions."

27

Alone in the chapel after the *sōsakan-sama* left her, Lady Jokyōden resumed her preparations for Obon. As she opened a box of incense, her hands began to shake, and she had to set down the box so it wouldn't spill. The tremors spread through her whole body. Her vision darkened around the edges; the room spun in dizzying rhythm. She knelt, buried her face in her trembling hands, and succumbed to the delayed reaction to Sano's visit.

Jokyōden had known Sano would come to question her regarding the second murder, and she'd employed against him a strategy designed to risk some dangers and avert more serious ones. She'd thought she knew how far she could lead him and still avoid harm, but some of his questions had caught her badly unprepared. Now aware of perils whose existence she'd never suspected, she feared she would regret what she'd told Sano.

Forcing herself to breathe deeply, Jokyōden willed anxiety away. At last the tremors and faintness subsided, but she desperately needed advice on how to prevent the destruction of her son, herself, and the entire court. Jokyōden rose and walked to the main altar, took one of the candles that burned before the Buddha statue, then knelt at an alcove in the corner and placed the candle in a stand on the table there. She opened the door of the *butsudan*. The little cabinet, made of teak that had darkened with age, contained a wooden tablet bearing characters that read, "Wu Tse-tien."

Wu Tse-tien, who had lived in China almost a millennium before, wasn't an ancestor of the imperial family. However, the women of Jokyōden's clan worshipped her as a patron deity. At age fourteen she'd become a concubine to Emperor T'ai-tsung of the Tang dynasty. When he died, Wu Tse-tien had won the affection of T'ai-tsung's son and heir, Emperor Kao-tsung. He was a weak, lazy fool, she intelligent and ambitious. Empress Wu Tse-tien became the only woman ever to rule China, in defiance of the Confucian code that prohibited female leaders.

Her example offered great inspiration to women who shared Wu Tse-tien's nature.

Staring at the wavering candle flame, Jokyōden concentrated on the hazy brightness that spread across her vision. Soon an image began to form there. First appeared the silhouette of a human head and shoulders; then swirling colors coalesced. It was Empress Wu Tse-tien. Her black hair, piled in a high, elaborate coif, sparkled with jeweled combs. Embroidered gold dragons snarled on her red silk robe. Scarlet rouge and lip paint enhanced the beauty that had seduced two emperors. Wu Tse-tien regarded Jokyōden through sharp, shrewd eyes. Her mouth moved; her voice resounded in Jokyōden's mind:

Greetings, my sister. The spirit of Wu Tse-tien spoke in Chinese, but Jokyōden understood every word. *Why have you summoned me?*

"I need your help," Jokyōden said.

Wu Tse-tien's image had appeared as a girl during Jokyōden's childhood and gotten older through years of visitations. Now the Chinese empress looked to be Jokyōden's own age of thirty-nine. Wu Tse-tien was her closest friend and confidante, as if they'd grown up together, although Wu Tse-tien possessed the wisdom of a lifetime. When Jokyōden described her meeting with Sano, Wu Tse-tien frowned.

It was foolish to provoke him that way. A woman in our position should polish her image until it shines like the sun, not tarnish it by throwing mud upon herself. Instead of compromising your own reputation, you must build it up.

This was exactly what Wu Tse-tien had done. She'd hired Buddhist priests to forge "ancient" documents that prophesied the coming of a great female ruler, the reincarnation of a bodhisattva. Then they'd declared Wu Tse-tien to be this ruler, legitimizing her controversial reign. But Jokyōden had troubles propaganda couldn't resolve.

"I had to do it," she said, then explained why she'd practically confessed her guilt to Sano.

Wu Tse-tien nodded. *A daring but sensible strategy,* she conceded. *Your son is key to your success, as my sons were to mine.* After Emperor Kao-tsung's death, Wu Tse-tien had placed two of her sons, one after the other, on the throne as her puppets and founded her own Chou dynasty. *Emperor Tomohito is a logical focus for the detective's suspicion. To shield him is to shield yourself.*

"But I dread what could happen if the *sōsakan-sama* investigates me," Jokyōden said. "There are things I cannot have him discover."

Yes . . . Wu Tse-tien's expression was fond, though stern. *However, you knew the risks when you started on your forbidden path. Now you must prepare to face the consequences, whatever they may be. To labor and fight, then ultimately triumph, is your destiny.*

The pursuit of destiny had dominated Jokyōden's life as it had Wu Tse-tien's. She'd been born into the Takatsukasa branch of the Fujiwara clan, from which came many imperial consorts. Other *kuge* families considered their daughters mere pawns for improving their status at court and breeding future emperors, but the Takatsukasa had followed a different tradition. For generations they'd schooled their daughters in reading, mathematics, writing, music, Confucian philosophy, military strategy, astrology, ancient mysticism, and the art of politics—everything an emperor needed to know. Once they'd wanted more than just control over an emperor who shared their blood. They'd sought to oust the current imperial family and found their own court, and they planned to achieve this through a woman who could follow Wu Tse-tien's example.

Fate had thwarted Takatsukasa ambitions, however. Many of the daughters weren't smart or strong enough. Better prospects often lacked the beauty to attract emperors. When the warrior clans had taken over the country five hundred years ago, the Imperial Court lost power, and the Takatsukasa lost hope of founding a dynasty that would rule Japan. Long before Tokugawa domination further diminished the possibility of the court's return to power, the Takatsukasa leaders abandoned as a waste of time the program of training future empresses.

Still, women are often keepers of faith. Jokyōden's female kin continued to pass on to their daughters the lessons on gaining power. When Jokyōden came along, they rejoiced: Here was the right combination of intelligence, will, and beauty for Japan's first reigning empress. Jokyōden remembered long days of studying, harsh discipline. The lessons infused challenge and excitement into a world that lacked both. From an early age she believed in the destiny predicted for her, and at first her life seemed a direct path toward it, with Wu Tse-tien her guide.

Eliminate the competition for the emperor's favor, Wu Tse-tien had told her.

As a new concubine, Jokyōden had identified her chief rival among the other court ladies: her cousin Myobu. A lovely, strong-willed girl, Myobu had been trained in the same manner as Jokyōden and instilled with the same ambitions. They were the emperor's two favorites.

The court is like a beehive with two queens, said Wu Tse-tien. *The most ruthless fighter will be the victor.*

Wu Tse-tien had eliminated all her own rivals, including Emperor Kao-tsung's mother, whom she'd ordered drowned in a wine vat. To clear the way for her new dynasty, she'd executed several hundred aristocrats and members of the old Tang imperial family. She'd even murdered her own infant daughter, whom she feared might supplant her as empress and fall under the influence of her opponents before Wu Tse-tien could bear a son and secure her position. Now came Jokyōden's turn to show how well she'd learned by example.

One day the palace ladies made a pilgrimage to a mountain temple. Before they left home, Jokyōden sent a note to Myobu, saying she had something private to discuss and asking Myobu to meet her in a secluded pavilion on a cliff above the temple. When Myobu came, Jokyōden was waiting for her. One push, and Myobu fell to her death. Later Jokyōden claimed that Myobu had tried to push *her* over the cliff, and she'd acted in self-defense. With no witnesses, everyone believed Jokyōden. She became the emperor's official consort.

Use his laziness to your advantage, Wu Tse-tien advised.

Lady Jokyōden gradually took over the emperor's duties. Soon she gave birth to Crown Prince Tomohito.

Before you take the next step, make sure he will live, said Wu Tse-tien. *The mother of a dead emperor is nothing.*

Jokyōden waited twelve years. Prince Tomohito flourished. She convinced the emperor to abdicate and turn the throne over to their son. The sacred mirror, jewel, and sword of imperial sovereignty passed to Tomohito. Jokyōden advanced to the highest rank for a court lady. With Tomohito still a child, she could mold him into a tool to serve her ambitions. However, a serious obstacle blocked her progress.

Through the years, she'd grown aware of the court's diminished circumstances, its nonexistent influence over the world outside. Tokugawa troops guarded the palace. The *bakufu* doled out meager sums of money that kept the court alive but dependent. The imperial family had millions of devoted subjects, but no army. Jokyōden had eventually awakened to the fact that she had reached the pinnacle of her world, but there seemed no way to expand her domain. Would all her education, all her scheming, result in nothing more than command over the petty affairs of a few individuals?

Disappointment is the mother of creativity, Wu Tse-tien had counseled. *Reassess your objectives. Circumvent the problem.*

At last Jokyōden found a new direction for her life. It was daring, unwomanly, and violated both tradition and law. She loved it. But unfortunately, her new venture coincided with another circumstance: Left Minister Konoe's appearance as her suitor.

Never allow yourself to fall under the power of a man! Wu Tse-tien warned. *Men are a woman's downfall!*

But the left minister had awakened needs that Jokyōden had suppressed in pursuit of her dreams. He made her realize how much she craved affection; his lovemaking taught her that sex had other benefits besides procreation. She'd fallen in love with him. Carried away by romance, she had confided in him, and he had betrayed her.

"You were right," Jokyōden said now to Wu Tse-tien. "I never should have trusted the left minister."

Never waste time on regretting the past, Wu Tse-tien said sternly. Her eyes, the ornaments in her hair, and the dragons on her robe glittered in the flame that surrounded her. *Concentrate on the present and the future. Hasn't the death of the left minister solved your problem?*

Once Jokyōden had believed that Konoe's murder had saved her from exposure, scandal, and punishment while protecting her great venture. Then Sano had revived the danger. "I thought Konoe had died before he could use the power he held over me, but he was involved in things I never guessed. The *sōsakan-sama* survived the attack, and his investigation continues. I didn't anticipate the direction it would take, or the stakes involved." She added regretfully, "I was a fool to help Lady Reiko, but I could not have guessed what would come of taking her to the left minister's secret house."

That was a grave mistake, said Wu Tse-tien. *Now there is only one way to protect yourself and your son. You must cease your activities so that the shogun's detective will not discover them. Until he is gone from Miyako, you must have patience.*

Wu Tse-tien had shown Jokyōden the value of patience. The Chinese empress had waited forty-one years to found her new dynasty, until Emperor Kao-tsung and her strongest opponents were dead. She'd accumulated power over a lifetime, gradually replacing the old bureaucracy with men loyal to her. Yet Jokyōden couldn't accept Wu Tse-tien's advice.

"I can't stop now," she said. "This is a critical time. I've invested all my effort and capital and hope in this venture. Unless I move forward, I risk utter failure."

Bitterness hardened Wu Tse-tien's expression, because she had suffered defeat in the end. At eighty-three, she'd been forced to abdicate by one of her sons, who dissolved her regime and reestablished the old Tang dynasty. This was the one example from her mentor's life that Jokyōden must not emulate.

"I shall continue as I began," decided Jokyōden. Then she asked humbly, "May I have your blessing?"

My blessing, yes: my approval, no, Wu Tse-tien said peevishly. Even from the grave she liked to be in control.

"May I ask what the future holds for me?"

The Chinese empress spread her hands in a mocking gesture of resignation. *Yours is a perilous path, which you have chosen to walk without my guidance. The future is uncertain; good and evil are equally possible. I wish you luck, because you are on your own now. Good-bye until we meet again in the afterlife.*

"Wait," Jokyōden cried. But Wu Tse-tien's image vanished; the candle had burned out. Jokyōden sadly closed the *butsudan.* The world had changed since Wu Tse-tien's day. Jokyōden must go where Wu Tse-tien couldn't guide her. It was her destiny.

She prayed that her destiny would not lead to execution for murder and treason.

28

The news came just as Chamberlain Yanagisawa was preparing to attend *Yoriki* Hoshina's execution.

Hearing a knock at the door of his private quarters at Nijō Castle, Yanagisawa called, "Come in."

The guard captain entered, bowing. "Excuse me, Honorable Chamberlain, but there's a problem that I must bring to your attention. *Yoriki* Hoshina is gone."

A wave of shock hit Yanagisawa; his heart began to hammer. "What do you mean, gone? Hoshina was locked up at police headquarters. He's supposed to die this morning."

"The *sōsakan-sama* had Hoshina moved last night," the guard captain said. "Two *doshin* took him to a secret hiding place. They were ordered to guard him, but they're both subordinates and friends of his, and he persuaded them to let him go."

"Why hasn't he been caught?"

"There are troops out looking for him now, but he made the *doshin* promise to wait until sunrise before reporting his escape. So he's got a head start on us."

Yanagisawa turned away, trying to sort out his emotions. Hoshina's flight enraged him. With his knowledge of Yanagisawa's sabotage against an investigation ordered by the shogun, Hoshina alive and free was a lethal danger. Yet even in the throes of anger and fear, Yanagisawa felt relief. If Hoshina got away, he need not die. Perhaps they would meet again someday. But Yanagisawa wanted Hoshina back now, even if only to see him one last time on the execution ground.

Turning on the guard captain, Yanagisawa said, "I want those *doshin* executed for dereliction of duty!"

"They're already dead," said the captain. "They just walked into the *shoshidai*'s office, confessed that they'd set Hoshina free, then committed seppuku."

"I want troops combing the city, nonstop, until Hoshina is found," Yanagisawa said.

"Yes, Honorable Chamberlain."

After the captain left, Yanagisawa leaned against the wall, shaken. Then he forced himself to forget Hoshina. He still had to solve the murder case and triumph over Sano. They'd arranged to meet here at the hour of the rooster to share their findings, and until then, he would let the *shoshidai*'s troops continue the search for the outlaws while he followed the leads he'd kept to himself when he and Sano had agreed to work together.

Yanagisawa hastily shed his black ceremonial robes and donned the faded indigo cotton kimono, blue trousers, and straw sandals he wore for martial arts practice. The clothes were right, but he looked too clean. Going outside to the garden, he rubbed dirt on his garments. And he needed something to conceal his face. Then he noticed a gardener staring at him in puzzlement. The gardener wore a frayed wicker hat, bleached by the sun.

"Give me your hat," Yanagisawa ordered.

The gardener obeyed. Yanagisawa put on the hat, went back into his room, fastened his swords at his waist, and stood in front of the mirror. He gave his reflection a sardonic smile. With his battered face and raffish costume, he looked like a disreputable *rōnin*.

"Perfect," he murmured.

He slipped out the back gate of Nijō Castle. His pulse quickened with the same thrill he'd experienced during the raid on Lord Ibe's house yesterday, which had whetted his appetite for detective work.

Once out in the street, however, Yanagisawa began to doubt the wisdom of his venture. He felt small and defenseless without his entourage. Passing samurai gave him disdainful glances. Commoners made way for him, but no one offered the lavish displays of respect usually accorded him.

"Clear the road! Clear the road!"

The tramp of hooves and marching feet accompanied the shouted orders. Pedestrians scurried to the roadside. Yanagisawa looked down

221

Marutamachi Avenue and saw a procession coming toward him. Soldiers and mounted officials escorted *Shoshidai* Matsudaira, who rode a black steed.

"Get out of the way! What's the matter, are you deaf?"

A soldier pushed Yanagisawa aside. As the procession passed, angry consternation filled him. That the troops of a subordinate should treat him so rudely! And the *shoshidai* hadn't even noticed him. His disguise negated his rank and power. Chastened, he hurried on his way, hoping he wouldn't encounter anyone else he knew.

When he reached the Imperial Palace, he walked east on Imadegawa Avenue to a rear gate used by tradesmen. At a guardhouse, a sentry received deliveries. This, according to Hoshina, was where Lady Jokyōden's mysterious visitor brought messages every day at this time. Not that Yanagisawa trusted Hoshina's word. Not that he believed he would actually see the elusive young man known only as Hiro, who probably had nothing to do with the murders or conspiracy even if he existed. But the visitor represented one of two clues that Yanagisawa had and Sano didn't.

Yanagisawa strolled, mingling with other pedestrians while covertly watching the gate. Porters delivered loads of charcoal and produce. Across the street from the palace, Yanagisawa went to a tiny restaurant that offered a good view. He sat on the raised wooden floor, as far from the other customers as possible; they were all filthy laborers who might have fleas. A toothless old woman hobbled over to wait on him.

"A bowl of noodles and some tea," Yanagisawa said without taking his gaze off the palace gate.

More porters brought more goods to the imperial compound. Soon Yanagisawa's meal came. The tea tasted like weeds in stagnant water; the noodles were mushy. How could anyone eat such slop? Yanagisawa pretended to sip his tea while time dragged, other diners came and went, and more provisions arrived at the palace. The steam and food odors from the restaurant kitchen made him hot and queasy. Then, just when he was ready to give up hope, a lone figure approached the gate.

It was a dapper young man dressed in a brown-and-black checked kimono, his hair in a topknot. As Hoshina had said, he looked to be a member of the lower merchant class. He carried a cylindrical red scroll case. Yanagisawa leaned forward for a better look. The man stopped at the guardhouse and spoke to the sentry. Yanagisawa, who had excellent vision and had mastered the art of lipreading, easily discerned the man's words: *I have a message for the Honorable Lady Jokyōden.*

The gate opened, and a noblewoman of elegant, dignified appearance came out. She took the scroll case, bowed, and went back inside the palace. The gate closed.

Yanagisawa could hardly contain his elation. Hoshina hadn't lied to him about this, at least. He concentrated on the messenger, who leaned against the palace wall, awaiting Jokyōden's reply. Who was he? A secret lover? Maybe Jokyōden had killed Left Minister Konoe because he'd discovered the affair and intended to tell her husband. The man had an intelligent expression, but his face was homely, with protruding teeth. Yanagisawa hoped that the mysterious visits had nothing to do with love and everything to do with the conspiracy to overthrow the Tokugawa regime.

After a short while, the gate opened again. The woman handed the scroll case back to the messenger, who bowed his thanks. Yanagisawa resisted the impulse to rush across the street, arrest the man, and confiscate the message. If it turned out to have nothing to do with the murder case, he would look a worse fool than he did already.

The messenger trotted down the street. Yanagisawa rose to follow, but the toothless crone who'd served his meal hurried over to him. "You owe five *zeni*!" she screeched, blocking his way.

Yanagisawa stared blankly at her. He never carried money; his staff always paid his expenses. Now the crone's shrieks were attracting an audience. He saw the back of Lady Jokyōden's messenger rapidly moving away. Yanagisawa drew his sword and waved it at the woman. "I'm not paying for that garbage. Get out of my way!"

The woman obeyed, but shouted curses at him as he ran down Imadegawa Avenue. His quarry ducked into a side street. Dodging a peddler laden with baskets, Yanagisawa followed. The messenger entered a maze of alleys where hanging laundry bridged the narrow gap between balconies. His route zigzagged, avoiding main streets. He constantly looked sideways and backward. Was he carrying orders from Jokyōden to the outlaws? Would he lead the way to their hiding place?

As he threaded between food stalls around a shrine, chasing the messenger, Yanagisawa's blood raced with an intoxicating energy. Anonymous, unhampered by a huge entourage or formal garb, he felt as swift and invisible as the wind. Anyone else would have lost the messenger by now, but Yanagisawa had no trouble keeping up. With the same intuition that helped him predict other men's moves in the game of politics, he anticipated the abrupt turns that had foiled the palace guards who had tried to follow the messenger. He'd always had a good sense of direction; he could picture the route superimposed on a map of Miyako. They were in the main commercial district. Wherever he ended up, he could guide troops there to arrest the rebels. In this secret pursuit, he unexpectedly achieved the heightened awareness sought by devotees of Bushido. The samurai spirit in him expanded, and the search for clues seemed more gratifying than sabotaging a rival.

The messenger ducked into a passage barely wide enough for three men to walk abreast. Vertical signs protruded from shops. Many bore crests featuring the scales used for weighing gold: This was a district of bankers. Merchants strolled, accompanied by samurai bodyguards and clerks carrying ledgers and cash boxes. Suddenly the messenger vanished into a shop. Puzzled, Yanagisawa halted. This didn't look like a place where outlaws would gather, or hide illegal weapons. Jokyōden's messenger must have spotted him and run through the shop to evade him.

Yanagisawa hurried forward. The shop's sign read "Daikoku Bank"—named after the god of fortune. Yanagisawa peered into the narrow storefront. He heard the jingle of coins, rapid clicks, and loud conversation as clerks counted money, totaled sums on the beads of their *soroban*, and negotiated with customers. The clerks wore the same brown-and-black uniform that Yanagisawa had followed from the Imperial Palace. With relief he spied his quarry showing the scroll case to the elderly proprietor, who sat on a platform, weighing gold ingots on a balance. Proprietor and messenger walked through a doorway leading to the back room, with the scroll. Yanagisawa sped around the block and down the alley behind the shop. He had to find out what the scroll said and what the bank had to do with Lady Jokyōden.

The alley was lined with malodorous privies; stray dogs rooted in fetid garbage containers. Wrinkling his nose in distaste, Yanagisawa edged up to the back window of the bank. Inside he saw a dim office furnished with shelves and iron chests. The messenger and proprietor were seated on the floor.

Opening the scroll case, the messenger removed a document, spread it on a table, and scanned columns of fine calligraphy. "She's pleased with our service."

"She should be," the proprietor said. "By paying better exchange rates than other shops, we've attracted more customers. Our investments in local businesses have paid an excellent return. We've been hired to handle the Miyako finances of the great Matsui merchant clan, for a large commission. We store the rice stipends of Lord Kii's retainers in our warehouse, and we'll collect large fees for converting the rice to cash. Profits are up ten percent over last year. By next year, we'll be ready to open a branch in Osaka."

Yanagisawa wasn't interested in the bank's performance or the money-grubbing ambitions of its owner. The smell in the alley nauseated him. He strained to read the scroll, but the writing was small and the distance too great.

"What are her orders?" the proprietor asked.

Now we're getting somewhere, Yanagisawa thought. Perhaps the bank served as an intermediary between Jokyōden and the rebels. He waited to hear her plans for a siege of Miyako.

The messenger read aloud from the scroll, " 'Buy two hundred loads of lumber. Buy a thousand loads of coal, two thousand of soybeans, and three thousand vats of oil.' "

Jokyōden must be laying in supplies to build a fort and provision an army.

" 'Buy ten loads each of copper and silver.' "

She would also need to pay her troops, Yanagisawa guessed. Exhilaration filled him. Even if he hadn't located the outlaws or weapons, he was collecting evidence that tied Jokyōden to the conspiracy.

"A wise decision to buy now," said the proprietor. "I predict that the prices of those commodities will rise soon."

Maybe Jokyōden was also speculating on prices as a means of raising funds for the revolt. Yanagisawa savored the fact that he, not Sano, had made this discovery. *And if Jokyōden was guilty, then Hoshina was not. . . .*

" 'Transfer five hundred *koban* to her personal account,' " read the messenger.

Was this a loan to finance the revolt? If Jokyōden would incur such a large debt in addition to her lavish spending, she must be seriously committed to restoring the Imperial Court to supremacy. Her nerve impressed Yanagisawa. Had she killed Left Minister Konoe because he'd discovered her illicit deals?

Still, her gender prevented Yanagisawa from believing in Jokyōden's guilt. Although he knew she managed court affairs with the authority of a male official and he'd found this new evidence of her bold, unfeminine ambition, he couldn't picture Jokyōden stalking him through the palace compound. He couldn't imagine any woman possessing the power of *kiai*.

Suddenly two huge samurai came running down the alley toward him from opposite directions. They seized Yanagisawa, ripped off his swords, and flung him facedown on the filthy ground. A heavy foot pressed down on his neck. The door opened, and the proprietor's voice demanded, "Why were you loitering around my office?"

"Let me up!" Yanagisawa ordered, furious. The bank's staff must have spotted him out front, become suspicious, and sent guards after him. "Do you know who I am?"

"A would-be bank robber, I bet." A pair of sandaled feet, topped by bare legs and a short kimono, came into Yanagisawa's view. This man carried a *jitte*—the parrying weapon used by the police. "You're under arrest."

The *doshin*'s assistants bound Yanagisawa's wrists, dragged him to his feet, and hustled him down the alley. "If you don't release me at once," Yanagisawa raged, "you'll be sorry. I'm the shogun's second-in-command!"

"Sure you are," the *doshin* scoffed. "We'll just take a walk down to police headquarters and sort this all out."

29

After leaving Lady Jokyōden, Sano went to the imperial consorts' residence. Lady Asagao was no longer a suspect, but he needed to resolve some unfinished business concerning her.

He found Asagao reclining on cushions on the shady veranda of the residence. Ladies-in-waiting plied large fans to create a cooling breeze around her. Clad in layered pastel robes, Asagao wore her hair in a limp plait. A physician dressed in a long dark blue coat fed her potions from ceramic bowls. When Sano climbed the veranda steps, she turned toward him. Apprehension pinched her round face, which looked sallow and plain in the absence of her usual makeup. Her attendants eyed Sano with distrust. The physician glowered.

"Lady Asagao must not be disturbed," he said. "The ordeal of imprisonment has weakened her health. To recover, she needs rest and quiet."

Sano knelt by Asagao, bowed, and said, "Your Highness, I apologize for your ordeal. It was an abominable mistake, and I beg your forgiveness." That Chamberlain Yanagisawa had manipulated them both into the false arrest hardly diminished the guilt he felt toward Asagao. "However, I must request your assistance. Will you be so kind as to answer a few questions?"

The emperor's consort pouted. "Why should I?" she said sullenly.

Why indeed, thought Sano. She didn't need to defend herself against further accusations, and she had no reason to voluntarily help someone who'd torn her away from her home and imprisoned her. The law permitted intimidation and torture to extort information from witnesses, but Sano didn't want to inflict more suffering on Lady Asagao or further antagonize the Imperial Court, so he must give her a different incentive to cooperate.

"I've discovered a plot to overthrow the Tokugawa regime," Sano said. "The plot is almost certainly connected with the murders. It's imperative that I catch the killer before he or she can kill again or bring war upon Japan. His Majesty the Emperor and your father are still under investigation."

Sano paused to let Asagao absorb his words, then said, "More mistakes could occur. Another innocent person might be subjected to the same treatment as yourself. Wouldn't you like to prevent that?"

Asagao squirmed on the cushions; her eyes darted like minnows trying to escape a fishing net. She might not possess great intelligence, but Sano perceived in her a natural cunning. She'd understood his implied threat to punish her kin unless she cooperated. Now she cast a pleading glance at her companions and made a weak attempt to sit up.

"I don't feel well," she whined. "Take me inside."

The physician and ladies-in-waiting moved to help her, but Sano steeled himself against letting Asagao use her illness to escape him. "Leave us," he told her attendants.

They reluctantly obeyed. Asagao cowered on the cushions, fearful yet defiant. Sano said, "Let's talk about the night Left Minister Konoe died. You told my wife that you were with your ladies-in-waiting. Later they admitted that you'd sneaked out to meet someone. Which is the truth?" Although he didn't really believe that determining Asagao's whereabouts would solve the case, unanswered questions bothered Sano. "Where were you?"

Asagao said, "I was in the tea ceremony cottage. With my father."

Sano recognized the story that Right Minister Ichijo had told Chamberlain Yanagisawa. He also knew that *Yoriki* Hoshina had established that the cottage had been occupied by a pair of lovers, and therefore not by Ichijo and Asagao. Obviously, Ichijo had instructed his daughter to corroborate his lie. She'd provided her father with the alibi she no longer needed. The probable reason behind her deception gave Sano an idea how to turn Asagao's motives to his advantage.

"Were you ever present when your father counseled the emperor?" Sano asked.

"Sometimes." A puzzled frown wrinkled the consort's brow.

"What did they talk about?"

"I don't remember. Court business, I suppose. I didn't pay much attention." Asagao spoke with eager nervousness, as if hoping that ignorance would safeguard her until she could figure out where the conversation was heading.

"Did His Majesty talk about past emperors who had tried to overthrow military regimes?" Sano said. "Did he ever express the desire to do the same?"

Shocked comprehension dawned in Asagao's eyes. She sat up and blurted, "No. Never."

"His Majesty wants to rule Japan, doesn't he?" Sano said. "He not only fights make-believe battles; he's planning a real one. Did he tell you that he's been bringing weapons into Miyako and recruiting soldiers for a war against the Tokugawa?"

"He wouldn't do that!" Asagao cried.

"Wouldn't he?" Sano said, wondering if Asagao was really surprised, or if she'd already known about the conspiracy. "His Majesty is bored by his sheltered life. He's puffed up with conceit and dreams of glory. But plotting a coup is treason. For such a serious crime, not even an emperor can escape death."

"I don't know what you're talking about." Panic shone in Asagao's eyes. "Tomo-*chan* would never try to overthrow the *bakufu!*"

Whether she was lying didn't matter; it wasn't Sano's intention to gain evidence against Tomohito right now. The emperor was just bait for a trap. "Yesterday the soldiers and weapons were in a house belonging to Lord Ibe of Echizen Province. Did His Majesty ever mention it?"

"No!"

"Did Left Minister Konoe discover His Majesty's plans?" Sano said. "Did His Majesty know that Konoe was a spy, and fear that Konoe would report his crime?" Now came the time to spring the trap. "Where was His Majesty on the night of Konoe's murder?"

"Tomo-*chan* wasn't in the garden. He didn't kill the left minister!" Asagao's desperate gaze sought help, but the courtyard was empty and still in the hot sunshine, and the building behind her as silent as if everyone had deserted it. In the trees, insects shrilled; a bird shrieked.

"How could you know where His Majesty was, when you were in the tea cottage with your father?" Sano rose and stood over Asagao. "That same story can't provide alibis for both men. It looks as though I'll be charging one or the other with treason and murder. You can help me decide which."

"No!" Asagao tried to rise, but her legs tangled in her robes, and she fell against the cushions, helpless.

"Of course you want to save your father," Sano said, hating what he must do to the consort. "He gave you life; he fed and sheltered you during your childhood. You wouldn't like to see him hurt, and it's your duty to protect him. But what about your duty to the emperor? His alibis for both murders are weak. He needs you to point my suspicion away from him . . . toward somebody else."

"Please leave me alone," Asagao implored. Sweat beaded her face; her pale lips trembled. "Don't make me do this!"

Suppressing his pity for her, Sano said, "If His Majesty is found to have committed treason, a new emperor will take the throne and select a new chief consort. You'll lose your status and special privileges. You could become a lady-in-waiting to your replacement, or marry a noble who's willing to accept a cast-off consort as a wife. Or you could enter a nunnery." These options represented utter humiliation to a woman of Asagao's rank. "If that's what you want, then by all means cast your lot with your father. If not, then perhaps you should reconsider the wisdom of protecting him at the emperor's expense."

Sano let the echo of his harsh words die. He waited for Asagao to choose which of the two most important men in her life she would betray. Loath to incur the consequences of implicating Japan's sacred sovereign in the crimes, Sano didn't want it to be Emperor Tomohito.

Asagao whimpered, hugging herself.

"Where were you when Left Minister Konoe died?" Sano asked.

For a long while he thought Asagao's loyalty to her father would prevail. Then defeat drained the tension from her body; she began to weep. "I was in the tea cottage," she said, "but my father wasn't. I was with my friend Lord Gojo. We didn't want anyone to know about us, so when the policeman came around asking everybody where they'd been that night, Gojo said he was with a friend he bribed to lie for him."

A connection clicked in Sano's mind. Lord Gojo was the man whom Reiko had watched flirting with Asagao in the Kabuki play. She'd been having an affair with him, not Left Minister Konoe. Asagao and Lord Gojo had been the two lovers in the tea cottage. She'd had an alibi she hadn't wanted to use because it would have exposed her infidelity to Emperor Tomohito.

"I only said my father was with me because he asked me to." Tears streamed down Asagao's face; she wiped them on her sleeve. "I never saw him that night."

She'd rejected the ties of blood for those of sex and power, sacrificing her father to protect Tomohito. Yet Sano felt no pleasure at breaking Right Minister Ichijo's alibi. He hated himself for manipulating Asagao. The pursuit of justice too often required the basest means.

"Thank you, Lady Asagao," Sano said, adding, "I'm sorry."

Her bitter glare burned him. Shamed and depressed, he went to the door and called Asagao's attendants. As they led her into the building, she turned to Sano. Between ragged sobs, she said, "My father wasn't in the Pond Garden when the left minister died, but I know who was."

A desperate guile shone in her reddened eyes. Sano had half-expected her to shield Ichijo by accusing someone else. Now, as she gasped for breath, he waited to see whom she would incriminate.

"It was the left minister's former wife."

"What?" Shock resonated through Sano. Kozeri, in the palace on the night of Konoe's death? But Kozeri had an alibi—or did she? She hadn't been at the scene of Aisu's murder—or had she? Now Sano realized that this was the vital information he'd forgotten to obtain from Kozeri. Had his attraction to her rendered him so negligent? Sano unhappily acknowledged the possibility, but a kernel of doubt formed in his mind. It burgeoned into suspicion, then anger as he realized what Kozeri had done.

Asagao laughed, an ugly chortle. "Kozeri fooled you, didn't she? Before the left minister died, I overheard him giving orders to his assistants. Ask Kozeri why he wanted the Pond Garden to himself that night. Ask her why she was there."

Sano grabbed Asagao's shoulders. "You tell me!" he commanded.

She looked disdainfully up at him. "Ask Kozeri how her first husband died. Ask her if she killed the left minister. Then ask her where she was when that other man died." As the attendants bore Lady Asagao away, her mocking laughter drifted back to Sano.

30

Sano wanted to rush off and confront Kozeri with Lady Asagao's allegations, but first he went to the imperial guardhouse to check the records of comings and goings at the palace on the dates of the two murders. Afterward he visited Kozeri's family, a noble clan who lived in the *kuge* district of the palace. He learned enough to convince him that he'd made a grave mistake that he must redress after the meeting he and Chamberlain Yanagisawa had scheduled to share the results of their inquiries.

By the time he arrived at Nijō Castle, the sun had turned orange over the western hills; gongs signaled the onset of Obon rites. The smoke from altars diffused the light, so that the air seemed filled with scintillating topaz dust. The gate sentry told Sano, "The honorable chamberlain went out early this morning and hasn't yet returned."

Across the street, Sano saw Marume and Fukida loitering outside a teahouse. He'd assigned them and some other men to spy on Yanagisawa. Now he hurried over to the detectives. "Yanagisawa's gone," he said.

The pair looked surprised. "We never saw him come out," Marume said.

Sano and the detectives checked with the men assigned to watch the other gates, but none of them had seen Yanagisawa.

"He slipped right past everyone," Sano said in dismay.

Yanagisawa's disappearance was more trouble on top of the problem of Kozeri. Sano didn't want to believe Kozeri had deceived him, although he knew she had. Nor did he want to think about what might happen when he saw Kozeri again. Would he bring a killer to justice, or make matters worse? What in heaven was Yanagisawa up to now?

In the barracks of Nijō Castle, the guard captain told Sano that the chamberlain had been detained.

"Where?" Sano asked. "By whom?"

The captain looked nervous, as if wondering how much to tell Sano. "Uh, I just received news that the honorable chamberlain is at police headquarters. I sent some men to fetch him. He was arrested."

Baffled, Sano said, "Why?"

"I don't know."

Sano and his detectives rode to police headquarters. Around the main room, Yanagisawa's troops stood guard. A score of *yoriki* and *doshin* lay prostrated, hands extended. *Shoshidai* Matsudaira knelt before the clerk's platform, gazing fearfully up at the man standing there. With a shock, Sano recognized Yanagisawa. His clothes were dirty and disheveled. His bruised face wore a fierce scowl.

"This is a gross insult!" he yelled at the *shoshidai*. "If one of your *yoriki* hadn't recognized me, I would be in jail now." With scathing fury he chastised the assembly for treating him like a criminal.

"A thousand apologies," the *shoshidai* whimpered. "Please forgive my staff's terrible mistake. They will be punished severely. I assure you this will never happen again."

"See that it doesn't," Yanagisawa said, "or you'll lose your post." He added, "And you'd better find *Yoriki* Hoshina by morning. Dismissed!"

The police fled. "He's in disguise," Fukida marveled. "That's how he got past us. Who would have guessed he'd do that?"

Sano approached Yanagisawa and *Shoshidai* Matsudaira. "Why were you arrested?" he asked the chamberlain.

At the sight of Sano, anger darkened Yanagisawa's expression; he didn't answer. The *Shoshidai* said timidly, "For attempting to rob a bank in the merchant district."

"I told you, I wasn't," Yanagisawa said with icy emphasis. "I was walking along, minding my own business, when three thugs attacked me. The police took the word of the merchant who accused me of trying to steal his filthy money."

"Yes, of course," the *shoshidai* said apologetically.

"What were you doing in that part of town?" Sano said. "Why are you dressed like that?"

"My mishap has nothing to do with the case," Yanagisawa said. "I owe you no explanations."

Sano followed Yanagisawa out of the building. "What was that about finding *Yoriki* Hoshina?"

A sardonic smile came over Yanagisawa's face as they reached the street and his retainers helped him onto his horse. "Your hostage has escaped."

More trouble! Sano hid his dismay. With Hoshina gone, he had no way to hold Yanagisawa to their deal. He'd better find the *yoriki* before Yanagisawa did. He and his men mounted their horses and rode down Oike Avenue alongside Yanagisawa. The sun's hazy crimson orb floated above hills obscured by smoke and mist. Ruddy light bathed the crowds. The heavy odor of hot grease from kitchens overlaid the suffocating atmosphere.

"Have you found the outlaws and weapons?" Sano asked Yanagisawa.

"Not yet." Yanagisawa's voice was tinged with defensive annoyance.

Disappointed at this news, Sano told Yanagisawa that Lady Asagao had retracted her father's alibi.

"So Right Minister Ichijo is looking to be a likely culprit, then?" An enigmatic smile played over Yanagisawa's mouth. "Interesting."

"That doesn't mean the other suspects are out of the picture," Sano said. The thought of Kozeri festered in his mind like a wound. "Lady Jokyōden refused to tell me where she was during Aisu's murder, and we still haven't connected Ichijo to the conspiracy."

"Not yet, anyway." Slapping the reins, Yanagisawa sped ahead of Sano.

"He wasn't just innocently minding his own business when he got arrested," Fukida scoffed.

"And he knows something he's not telling us," Marume said. Sano nodded in dismal agreement, thinking that he should have put Yanagisawa out of business when he'd had the chance. He gave Marume and Fukida new orders to deal with the problem, and then report back to him as soon as possible.

"Where will you be?" Fukida asked.

Now it was Sano's turn for evasion, because he hated to lose face by admitting his mistake with Kozeri. "If you need to reach me, leave a message at Nijō Manor," he said, then rode away.

Sano had intended to head straight to Kodai Temple, but Reiko would be eager for news. He rode to Nijō Manor, where he found Reiko in their room, at the table, nibbling at a dinner of rice balls, grilled fish, and greens, and sipping tea. Sano knelt opposite his wife. Her polite bow reflected the uneasiness that had shadowed their parting that morning.

"The outlaws and weapons haven't been found yet," Sano said.

"I'm sorry to hear that." Eyes downcast, Reiko gestured toward her meal. "Do you want this? I don't seem to be very hungry."

"No thank you; I'm not hungry either."

Reiko glanced at his swords, which he hadn't removed as he usually did when he came home. "Are you leaving again soon?"

"Yes," Sano said. Nervousness accelerated his heartbeat.

"Where are you going?"

"To see Kozeri." The name tasted like poison.

"Again?" Now Reiko lifted a troubled gaze to his face. "May I ask what for?"

"Lady Asagao claims that Kozeri was in the palace when Left Minister Konoe died," Sano said. "The imperial records don't show that she entered the compound on that date, but they do show that she was there when Aisu was murdered. She'd gone to see her family. According to them, she arrived in the evening, spent the night in their house in the *kuge* district, and left the next morning. It was her first visit since she entered the convent fifteen years ago.

"Lady Asagao also said to ask Kozeri how her first husband died. Her family told me she'd been married to Left Minister Konoe's secretary, a young courtier named Ryōzen—the man who was murdered by Konoe." Too late, Sano had connected Kozeri with the crime that had put Konoe under the *bakufu*'s power. "In view of these new facts, I need to question her again."

Reiko's expression turned quizzical. "I assumed you'd already questioned Kozeri's family to double-check her story about her marriage to the left minister. But even if not, wasn't the information on her first husband in the *metsuke* dossiers that Chamberlain Yanagisawa sent you?"

To his disgrace, Sano had been convinced enough of Kozeri's innocence that he hadn't bothered to read her dossier.

"You've already interviewed Kozeri twice," Reiko said, "and you've only just found out that she had the opportunity to kill Aisu, and possibly Konoe? Didn't you ask her where she was when they died?"

"No," Sano admitted, hot with embarrassment even though he had a good reason for his negligence. "Whenever I was with Kozeri, I got a peculiar, dazed sensation in my mind, and a feeling that there was something important I was forgetting to ask her. Now I know why. The nuns at Kodai Temple practice *shugendo*. Kozeri focused her mental energy on my mind and prevented me from asking her where she was during the murders."

To his consternation, Sano saw disbelief on Reiko's face. She said, "Kozeri used magical powers to manipulate you? Can that be possible?"

"If the power of *kiai* exists, then why not the power to control the mind?" Sano said.

Reiko regarded him with doubt. "It seems more likely that you didn't ask her important questions because you decided she's innocent. How could you favor a suspect and criticize me for trusting Lady Jokyōden?"

This was dangerous territory. Sano had to steer the conversation away from the subject of what else had blinded him to Kozeri's deception. He said, "Speaking of Lady Jokyōden, she and Left Minister Konoe were once lovers."

"Oh? That's interesting." Caution veiled Reiko's gaze. "How did you find out?"

"From Lady Jokyōden herself." Sano described his interview with the emperor's mother, then bent an accusing look upon Reiko. "She said you knew. Why didn't you tell me?"

Reiko sat up straight, lifted her chin, and said, "She asked me to keep it a secret. I agreed because I thought that her relationship with Konoe was less important than what she gave me. Without Lady Jokyōden's help, we would never have discovered the conspiracy. I think my reason for trusting her is more credible than yours for favoring Kozeri." Suspicion narrowed Reiko's eyes. "Is Kozeri beautiful?"

The atmosphere in the room stretched tight as sails filled with storm winds. Sano forced a laugh. "Kozeri is a nun. Her head is shaved, and she's not young."

"That isn't what I asked, but never mind—I can see the answer on your face." Reiko stood, regarding Sano with sickened comprehension. "It was your personal feeling for Kozeri, not magic, that made you forget to ask her for an alibi before you decided she was innocent." Reiko backed away from him, appalled.

Sano heard the hurt beneath the anger in her voice. Rising, he hurried over to Reiko, reaching for her clenched hands.

"It's not what you think," he said, stifling the guilty memory of caressing Kozeri. "Nothing happened."

Reiko clasped her hands behind her so he couldn't touch them. "How stupid do you think I am?" she cried.

Abruptly, she turned away from Sano. Her shoulders trembled; he heard her ragged breathing. Her pain stabbed his heart. Standing before the painted mural of mountain landscapes, she was so beautiful and proud. Sano experienced a surge of desire for her, which further complicated his emotions. How could he want anyone but Reiko? How could he regain her trust?

He said, "Kozeri interfered with my thoughts. That's all." The lie pricked his conscience. "It's you I love, and no one else."

"I don't believe you," Reiko said in a high, broken voice.

"You don't believe me because you haven't met Kozeri."

"No," said Reiko, "I haven't." Turning, she faced Sano, her tearful gaze hard, like a pond freezing into ice. "But it's time I did meet her."

Horrified at the thought, Sano said quickly, "That's not a good idea. If Kozeri is the killer, she's dangerous. She might hurt you. I already have the information about her relationship with Left Minister Konoe and his last visit to her. I only have to ask where she was during the murders. There's no need for you to . . ."

The contempt in Reiko's eyes halted his excuses. "But there is," she said. "No matter whether Kozeri deceived you by magic or by feminine wiles, she's done it twice, and she could do it again. I'll have better luck getting answers from her."

Sano saw two choices, equally unacceptable. He could give Reiko her way and risk the chance that Kozeri would tell her about the episode by the river. Or he could refuse, jeopardize the investigation, and destroy his marriage. With dread and resignation, Sano understood that he had no choice at all.

"All right," he said. "We'll go to Kodai Temple tomorrow morning."

"Not tomorrow," Reiko said grimly. "I want to go now."

Reiko in her palanquin, Sano on horseback, and their guards traveled along crowded streets bright with Obon lanterns. At Kodai Temple, they discovered that Kozeri wasn't at the convent because the nuns had gone to perform Obon dances at Gion Shrine. They journeyed there in silence. Since leaving Nijō Manor, Reiko had exchanged not a single word with Sano; her rage and pain were so intense that she could hardly bear to look at him. She couldn't believe that nothing had happened between him and Kozeri. She hated her jealousy; she hated Sano for causing it.

A sudden, heart-stopping thought struck her. In all the recent excitement, she'd forgotten to track her female cycle. Now Reiko calculated that her monthly bleeding should have started yesterday. It still hadn't. Missing twice in a row made pregnancy more certain. She became aware of a new fullness, a slight swelling, in her abdomen. She stared through the window of her palanquin at Sano riding beside her.

"Kozeri seems to spend as much time away from the convent as in it,"

Reiko said. "Apparently, religious vows don't restrict her movements or ban her from the Imperial Palace."

"Apparently not," was all Sano said, though she knew she'd stung him by implying that he shouldn't have assumed a nun lacked freedom of movement or access to the crime scene. Yet her spite shamed her more than it relieved her anger.

Night had fallen, but the moist, smoky air reflected the lights of the city; the sky glowed an eerie purple. Gion's teahouses glittered with parties. Boisterous drunks thronged alleys lined with "dog screens," bamboo barriers that kept stray dogs and rowdy pedestrians away from the buildings. Sano and Reiko left their guards outside the shrine and walked through the torii gate. Bright lanterns hung from trees above the gay, noisy crowds that milled among refreshment stalls; gongs chimed incessantly. Reiko heard drumbeats, which she and Sano followed to a courtyard outside the shrine's main building.

A line of women dressed in billowing white robes glided, swayed, and gestured with slow, ritualistic motions. In the light of lanterns strung across the courtyard, their shaved heads shone like pale moons. A rapt audience watched the nuns, who turned in unison, clapped, and formed a circle. Male dancers wearing loincloths and straw hats surrounded them. As the two groups moved in opposite directions, a melancholy song rose from the spectators.

"Which one is she?" Reiko said with deliberate calm.

Sano pointed. "That's Kozeri between the two elderly nuns." He added, "Please take care."

Behind his stoic expression, Reiko read his fear of what she might learn from Kozeri—and what she might do. "Wait here," she said.

She marched up to the dancers, watching Kozeri. The nun's figure was shapely and graceful. Her heavy-lidded eyes were somnolent as she dipped and undulated; her full lips curved in a serene smile. As Sano had said, Kozeri wasn't young, but she looked ageless rather than old. Her shaved head only accentuated her beauty. Reiko had always taken her own beauty for granted, but hatred and jealousy overcame her.

"Kozeri-*san*!" she shouted.

The nun turned. When she saw Reiko, a perplexed frown replaced her smile: She obviously wondered why a stranger should address her in such a peremptory tone.

"I want to speak with you," Reiko said, following Kozeri as the circle of dancers revolved.

Uncertainty clouded Kozeri's face, but she stepped out of the circle, joined Reiko, and bowed. "Yes, Honorable Lady?"

Her soft, breathy voice hinted at the allure she held for men. "I'm the wife of the shogun's *sōsakan-sama*," Reiko announced with all the imperious pride of her class.

"Oh." Kozeri looked dismayed. "I didn't know he was married. I didn't know he had brought his wife to Miyako."

Of course Sano wouldn't have told her, Reiko reflected bitterly. "I help my husband with his work," she said. "We're investigating the murder of the left minister together, and I want to ask you some questions." Needing to show Kozeri that she and Sano had a close, special relationship, she didn't hide her purpose behind the false pretense that this was a social call. "Come with me."

Kozeri hesitated, then said, "Very well."

As Reiko led Kozeri through the crowds, she saw Sano frowning and waving at her from across the courtyard, signaling her to stay. Reiko ignored him. She and Kozeri walked to a deserted garden behind the building. A lantern over the doorway shone through pine trees, casting a network of shadows across the grass. The chirp of crickets muffled the distant drumming and singing. Reiko and Kozeri faced each other. Kozeri folded her arms protectively across her bosom as she waited for Reiko to speak. Reiko was trembling inside, sick with a terrible curiosity.

What did he say to you? she wanted to ask. *What did you do together?*

Yet she did not, because she dreaded the answers. Instead she said, "Why didn't you tell my husband that you were in the palace during the murder three nights ago?"

Kozeri's face mirrored dismay at Reiko's belligerence. "I was just visiting my family. It didn't seem important."

"I don't believe that's your only reason," Reiko said coldly.

Kozeri darted a longing glance toward the lights of the courtyard. Then she sighed and looked at the ground. "I was afraid he would think I was the killer."

"Are you?"

"No!" Kozeri stared at Reiko, aghast.

"Did you know that my husband was in the palace that night?" Reiko demanded.

"Not until the morning after, when my family received the news of his murder. Later we found out that it was somebody else who'd died." Kozeri licked her lips nervously. "I don't even know who the man was. I never left my family's house that night." With a timid, beseeching smile, Kozeri said, "I never meant to cause your husband any trouble. You must believe me."

Reiko regarded her with scorn. "Your wiles won't work on me. Right Minister Ichijo, Lady Jokyōden, Prince Momozono, and the emperor were all told that my husband was coming to the palace. I imagine that the news spread rapidly around the Imperial Court. You could have heard it and decided to kill my husband so he couldn't arrest you for the murder of Left Minister Konoe. You sneaked out of your family's house and went looking for him. But you found Chamberlain Yanagisawa and his men, and you mistook them for my husband's party. You killed the wrong person."

"That's not so!" Kozeri cried in panic. "I didn't kill anyone. Ask your husband. He knows—"

Her protests faded under Reiko's glare; she sighed, bowed her head in defeat, and spoke in a low, forlorn voice: "All right. I'll tell you what happened. The left minister came to Kodai Temple the day before he died. He said he was going to close down the convent and force me to return to him. Then he ordered me to come to the Pond Garden the next night, to celebrate a special occasion." Kozeri swallowed hard. "I was terrified. When I was his wife, he beat me almost to death. I knew that if I had to live with him again, he would kill me. I had to save myself somehow."

This story, which contradicted what Kozeri had told Sano about her marriage and the time and nature of her last encounter with Konoe, only increased Reiko's distrust. "How could the left minister close down the convent, when the Imperial Court has no authority over religious orders?" Reiko asked.

Kozeri lifted her hands, then let them fall. "He said he could. I believed him."

Had she been so convinced of her former husband's power over her that she'd taken the threat seriously? Reiko wondered. Or was Kozeri lying again? "What was the special occasion?"

"He didn't say. I didn't ask. But I knew he meant to take his pleasure from me."

"Go on," Reiko said.

"I agreed to meet him," Kozeri said. "The next night his attendants came to the temple after everyone there was asleep. They took me in a palanquin to the Imperial Palace. We traveled to the imperial enclosure without meeting anyone. We stopped in the Pond Garden, and the attendants took me to the cottage on the island. They lit a lantern and left me alone inside."

Prince Momozono claimed he'd seen a light in the cottage just before he and Emperor Tomohito discovered Konoe dead, Reiko remembered; there had indeed been someone else in the Pond Garden besides them. The secrecy with which Konoe had arranged the rendezvous explained why the imperial records showed no outsiders in the palace that night and *Yoriki* Hoshina hadn't identified Kozeri as a suspect.

"There was a sake decanter with two cups on the table in the cottage," Kozeri said. "I sat and had a drink and prayed for the courage to kill the left minister."

Reiko couldn't believe what she'd heard. "Wait. You admit you went to the Pond Garden to kill him?"

"Yes." Kozeri moved into the shadows beneath a tree. A breeze riffled the leaves, casting patterns of light and dark across her haunted face. The pulse of drums punctuated the singing in the courtyard. "I had a small vial inside my sleeve. It contained a drug that I'd bought from a peddler. I was going to pour it into the left minister's sake. After he drank, he would fall asleep and never awaken. I hoped I could slip away and everyone would think he'd died of a sudden illness."

She'd planned to use poison, not the power of *kiai*? Reiko listened, dumbfounded.

"Then I heard him call out, 'Help!' First he was running, then it sounded as if he were dragging himself across the ground. His breathing was loud and strange. I looked out the window and saw him standing by the cottage. He cried, 'No. Please, no.' I was terrified. Then—"

Shuddering, Kozeri said, "There was a terrible scream. It went on and on. I watched the left minister writhing in agony while blood gushed from him. Then he lay still. The scream stopped." She fixed a strange, blurred gaze on Reiko. "The left minister was dead."

She'd wanted to kill him so he couldn't abuse her anymore, but the murderer had spared her the trouble. The explanation made sense to Reiko, and her skepticism waned. "What did you do then?" she asked.

"I knew that everyone in the palace would have heard the scream," Kozeri said, caressing the top of her bosom. "Someone would come and find the left minister. I didn't want them to think I'd killed him, so I blew out the lantern and ran away. In the *kuge* district, I found a watchtower with fire equipment underneath. I got a ladder and climbed the palace wall. I took the ladder with me and threw it in an alley so no one would know that someone had sneaked out of the compound. Then I walked back to Kodai Temple."

Reiko felt a pang of sympathy for the nun who'd suffered so long and witnessed a terrible murder. "Please forgive me for upsetting you," she said, taking Kozeri's soft, smooth hands in hers. "I'll tell my husband what you said. Attempted murder is a crime, but under the circumstances, surely he'll pardon you."

Tears of gratitude streamed from Kozeri's eyes. "A thousand thanks," she murmured, smiling gladly. "You're so understanding and kind."

Although Reiko had never been attracted to women, touching Kozeri gave her a sensuous pleasure. Her anger dissolved in hazy confusion. She couldn't remember why she'd hated Kozeri just a moment ago. Sexual arousal burgeoned inside her. Then realization jolted Reiko alert.

"You're doing to me what you did to my husband!" she cried, recoiling from Kozeri.

"What?" The nun gaped in surprise.

"You used mental energy to keep him from asking where you were during the murders. I didn't believe him when he told me, but I do now, because you're confusing me the same way!" Now Reiko regretted accusing Sano of lying to her.

Fear shimmered in Kozeri's eyes, but she said bravely, "Yes, but I meant you no harm. I just wanted you to believe me. I needed to make you like me so you wouldn't hurt me."

"And you made him want you." As enlightenment dawned, Reiko cursed herself for doubting Sano's love for her.

Whatever had happened between Sano and Kozeri hadn't been entirely his fault. If she could entice a woman, then what a strong effect her magic must have on men!

Reiko lashed out at Kozeri: "Liar! You didn't try to poison the left minister. You didn't just watch him die. You murdered him, and Aisu too!"

"I didn't!" Hurt indignation welled in Kozeri's eyes. "I wouldn't wish such an awful death on anyone."

"Not even the man who murdered your first husband?"

The blood drained from Kozeri's face, leaving her lips so white that Reiko could see red marks where she'd bitten them. "How—how did you know?"

"You were once married to Konoe's secretary. Konoe stabbed him to death. Then he married you. Somehow you discovered what Konoe had done. You plotted revenge."

Kozeri drew herself up; angry color blotched her cheeks. "All right. I knew. I hated the left minister for killing Ryōzen. I blamed him for the loss of the child I miscarried after the murder. But it all happened years ago. If I had wanted revenge against the left minister, I had plenty of opportunity when we lived together. Why would I wait so long?"

242

"Because you didn't have the ability to murder him back then," Reiko retorted. "Instead, you ran away. At Kodai Temple, the nuns taught you how to channel your mental energy through your voice. You acquired the power of *kiai*."

"That's ridiculous!" Kozeri laughed, a shrill, hysterical sound. "We do exercises that bring tranquility and enhance our prayers. We can influence people's thoughts, but we don't believe in violence."

"I don't believe you." Determined to implicate Kozeri in another crime, Reiko said, "Have you ever been to Lord Ibe's house in the cloth dyers' district? Do you know the outlaws who've been living there? Where are they now? Where have they taken the weapons?"

While her mouth soundlessly formed the words *outlaws* and *weapons*, Kozeri looked at Reiko as if she'd gone mad. But Reiko conjectured that she'd befriended the outlaws during her travels through the city and joined their cause as a way to gain power against her former husband. What if she'd learned that Konoe had discovered the plot and decided to kill him before he could report it to the *bakufu*? She could have contacted Konoe, pretended she wanted a reconciliation, and arranged the secret meeting in the Pond Garden.

"Don't pretend you don't understand." Fists clenched, Reiko shouted into Kozeri's terrified face, "Where are the weapons? What are the outlaws planning?"

"I have no idea what you're talking about!" Kozeri cried. Her eyes darted; she leaned away from Reiko, then blurted, "There's something I've been wanting to tell your husband. Something that will help his investigation." When Reiko only stared at her in speechless fury, she said, "As I was leaving the Pond Garden after the left minister died, I saw a man hiding in the shadows. It was Right Minister Ichijo."

Did Kozeri think her gullible enough to fall for another trick? Reiko felt angry blood suffuse her face.

Obviously daunted by Reiko's expression, Kozeri began to babble: "He didn't see me, but I recognized him from when I lived in the palace." Her eager smile didn't erase the fear in her eyes. "Don't you see what that means? There was somebody else in the garden besides me. Ichijo must have killed my former husband."

Reiko's emotions exploded. "I don't want to hear any more of your lies!" she shouted. "Ichijo wasn't there. Only you."

"I'm not lying," Kozeri protested.

Reiko grabbed her by the shoulders and shook her; Kozeri's head snapped back and forth. "You're part of the rebel conspiracy. You killed Konoe. Admit it!"

"Stop. You're hurting me."

Limp and unresisting, Kozeri began to sob. Reiko understood how Konoe's love for her had turned to murderous rage. So meek yet so contrary, she was weak despite her magic powers, pitiful but exasperating.

Was this what Sano wanted in a woman?

Reiko had an impulse to strike Kozeri until she confessed and begged for mercy. So much did she want Kozeri to be guilty and die for the crimes, she didn't care whether Kozeri could kill her with a scream.

The drums ceased with a burst of applause: The Obon dance had ended. Reiko heard Sano calling, "Reiko-*san*! Where are you?" She froze, immobilized by contrary urges. She wanted to run to her husband, but she dreaded facing him after what had just happened. She couldn't bear for Sano to find her and Kozeri like this, and she longed to flee, but not if that meant leaving him alone with Kozeri.

Then Kozeri said in a plaintive voice, "I can see why you think I'm guilty, but why do you hate me so much? Is it because you think your husband loves me?"

That her jealousy was so obvious humiliated Reiko. She turned and stumbled away, not wanting to hear more.

"I tried to get him to make love to me because I wanted him, not just to trick him," Kozeri called after her. "But he wouldn't. Now that I've met you, I understand why. He loves you. He wanted me, but he couldn't betray you."

Reiko halted in her tracks. How she longed to believe that! But many men did commit adultery; while she'd thought Sano was different from other husbands, perhaps her trust in him had been naïve. Besides, Kozeri had lied and deceived too often. Didn't her claim that she and Sano hadn't coupled indicate that in fact they had?

Then Reiko was running blindly. The speed of her flight chilled the tears that streamed down her cheeks. She didn't know what to think or do. Nor did she know whether to believe Kozeri's story about seeing Ichijo at the scene of Konoe's murder.

31

At the hour of the boar, business had ceased on Kawaramachi Avenue, except in a few teahouses. The wide avenue, which ran north and south past Miyako's main commercial district, resembled a long tunnel, with the high earthen wall of the Great Rampart on the east, rows of shops and houses lit by Obon lanterns on the west, and the purple-black night sky above. Gates in the rampart provided access to the Kamo River. At intersections, guards manned neighborhood gates. Although some residents already slumbered on mattresses spread on balconies to catch the river breezes, others sat in doorways, talking and smoking, while pedestrians drifted home from cemetery visits.

Through the thinning crowds walked Right Minister Ichijo, a solitary figure dressed in a modest gray kimono and wicker hat instead of his usual court costume. Leaning on his ebony cane, Ichijo maintained a brisk pace for a man his age, looking neither right nor left nor behind him. His elegant profile and stooped shoulders inclined forward as if he were impatient to reach his destination.

Chamberlain Yanagisawa followed at a discreet distance behind the right minister. Again he wore the garb of a *rōnin*. After chasing Lady Jokyōden's messenger, pursuing Ichijo was easy. Either the right minister didn't think anyone would follow him, or he didn't care if they did. Instead of weaving through alleys, he marched right down the middle of the street. He certainly didn't act like a man on a secret mission, but Yanagisawa believed that appearances lied.

His spies had turned up the interesting fact that Ichijo had told his staff he was going out alone tonight, without disclosing his plans. Did this herald one of the mysterious trips that *Yoriki* Hoshina had mentioned? Yanagisawa still yearned to believe that Hoshina had honestly tried to help him by unearthing genuine clues. He especially needed evidence against Ichijo because of what his spies had reported about Lady Jokyōden.

Servants claimed to have seen Jokyōden in her office shortly before hearing the scream that had killed Aisu. She'd also been there when the imperial watchmen went to inform her about the second murder. No one had seen her elsewhere. Although Yanagisawa didn't know why she'd refused to admit this to Sano, it seemed unlikely that she'd sneaked outside, killed Aisu, and gotten back to her office without anyone noticing her. If she hadn't murdered Aisu, then the probability that she'd murdered the left minister decreased; the messenger and the Daikoku Bank might have nothing to do with the conspiracy. Therefore, Ichijo was the prime suspect, now that Sano had broken his alibi for Konoe's murder. Yanagisawa hadn't told Sano about Ichijo's trips. If they revealed a connection between Ichijo and the rebels, Yanagisawa wanted to be the hero who arrested the killer and averted a civil war.

At the Gojo Avenue intersection, Ichijo stopped at a gate in the Great Rampart. Yanagisawa took cover in a doorway and watched Ichijo speak to the sentry, who opened the gate. The right minister vanished through it. Yanagisawa hurried over.

"Let me out," he ordered the sentry. "Quickly!"

"State your name and your business." The sentry regarded Yanagisawa's humble appearance with scorn.

This time Yanagisawa was prepared for encounters with officialdom. From his waist pouch he took a small scroll that gave his name and rank. He showed it to the sentry. The man was probably illiterate, but he recognized the shogun's personal seal on the document. He hastily let Yanagisawa through the gate.

Outside the Great Rampart, Yanagisawa spied Ichijo walking down the stretch of Gojo Avenue that sloped toward a flight of stone steps leading down to the river. Together yet far apart, Ichijo and Yanagisawa descended these, then crossed the Gojo Bridge. Beneath it the Kamo rippled, faintly luminous. Lights twinkled on the opposite bank; bonfires smoldered. The smell of smoke, the laughter of couples strolling the embankment, music drifting from teahouses, and the warm night all evoked in Yanagisawa the memory of his night with Hoshina. A wave of longing swept through him.

Where was Hoshina now? The search parties had turned up no trace of him. Through sheer will, Yanagisawa banished the thought of the lover who'd betrayed him.

Ichijo walked off the bridge and into a deserted neighborhood of densely packed houses. A few Obon lanterns still burned. Yanagisawa trod softly within the darkness beneath eaves and balconies so that Ichijo wouldn't notice him. He thought he'd conquered his fear of walking alone in the city, but now it revived. If Ichijo was the commander of the rebel outlaws, he would have to communicate with them somehow. He wouldn't let them come to the palace; nor could he send or receive messages that might be intercepted. He would have to meet his troops secretly. Was he on his way to their hiding place now? Yanagisawa wanted badly to locate it, but he dreaded an encounter with a band of *rōnin*, gangsters, and warrior priests. What if they caught him spying? And if Ichijo was the killer, Yanagisawa was in mortal danger.

The right minister quickened his steps. Buildings gave way to a gleaming moat. From a tall stone foundation in its center rose a grassy earthen mound as high as the nearby houses and perhaps a hundred paces in diameter. A fence of stone pillars ringed the top of the foundation, enclosing a tree-shaded plateau from which loomed the mound's retaining wall.

Lagging behind in an alley, Yanagisawa watched the right minister march around the structure. It was crowned by a stone monument shaped like a squat pagoda. Lights from below illuminated characters engraved there. Reading them, Yanagisawa recognized the structure as the Ear Mound. This was the monument to Toyotomi Hideyoshi's war on Korea more than a century ago. Although the invasion had failed, Hideyoshi's forces had slain many defenders. Distance had prevented his army from following the usual practice of presenting the severed heads of their defeated enemies to their commander. Therefore, the ears of some forty thousand Korean soldiers had been pickled in brine, shipped to Japan, and entombed in the Ear Mound.

A bridge spanned the north side of the moat. Ichijo stepped onto it. Yanagisawa hid in the entryway of a house directly opposite the bridge, which led to stone steps in the Ear Mound's foundation. Above these, beyond an iron gate and the trees, more steps climbed to the base of the mound, where an altar held flowers, burning lamps, and a smoking incense vat. Ichijo walked to the first set of steps. He eased himself down, laid his cane across his lap, and wiped his brow. Then he folded his hands and sat motionless.

Time passed. Yanagisawa grew impatient. Then he heard rapidly approaching hoofbeats. The right minister raised his head. He was meeting the outlaws here, Yanagisawa guessed. Ichijo was too crafty to go to the rebels' den and risk leading spies there. A meeting in a public place could pass for a chance encounter. Anticipation and fear gripped Yanagisawa. He wanted to see the outlaws, learn their plans. But if they should discover him here in this lonely place, they would most certainly kill him.

From an alley to his right emerged two samurai on horseback. They cast furtive glances around the Ear Mound. Ichijo waved. Yanagisawa peered through the bamboo lattice that screened his hiding place. The two samurai dismounted at the bridge, tied their horses to the posts, and walked toward Ichijo, who rose to meet them. A round of bows ensued, and greetings inaudible to Yanagisawa. Then the three men settled on the steps, their figures haloed by the light of the lamps on the altar behind them.

Yanagisawa slipped out of the entryway. Sidling past buildings and across alleys, he circled the Ear Mound until he was behind it. He tiptoed to the edge of the moat. Now he distinguished three voices speaking in turn—one gruff, one a high whine, and Ichijo's.

". . . took you long enough to get here," Ichijo was saying. "You were supposed to be waiting for me."

"We came as soon as we could," said Gruff Voice.

"With the trouble we've had, you should be glad we made it at all," whined the other man.

"I hired you to handle trouble," Ichijo said coldly. "I hired you to obey my orders, and I expect to get the service you promised."

"Well, we expect to be treated better than slaves." Belligerence harshened Gruff Voice's tone. "After all, we're risking our lives to do your dirty work."

"You knew the duties the job entailed. You knew the danger," Ichijo retorted. "If you're too lazy and cowardly to go on, then I've no use for you. I can't afford to leave such important matters in the hands of unreliable men. Unless you fulfill your part of the bargain, you won't reap the rewards."

Yanagisawa's heart began to race. The two samurai were *rōnin*, possibly the ones from Lord Ibe's house. If "trouble" meant the hasty relocation of troops and weapons, then "important matters" referred to the imperial restoration, and "rewards" to the spoils of war.

"All right, all right; we're sorry we were late," the Whiner said quickly.

Gruff Voice said, "This place makes me nervous. Let's hurry up so we can get out of here."

There was a brief silence. Then Ichijo said, "How are they?"

"Safe and well," said Gruff Voice.

Ichijo's allies, Yanagisawa thought; *secure in their positions, waiting for the command to march.*

"Has my merchandise arrived?"

"Yes. The last of it came twelve days ago."

The guns and ammunition, manufactured illegally and smuggled into Miyako a little at a time?

"Well, then." An odd sadness tinged Ichijo's tone. "I suppose you'd best be on your way."

There was a clink of gold coins.

"Is this all?" Gruff Voice said with disapproval.

Ichijo said, "You'll get more later."

When the emperor rules Japan and the Imperial Court commandeers the nation's wealth? A thrill shot through Yanagisawa. He was sure he'd just witnessed Ichijo advancing payment for mounting a war against the Tokugawa. With great relish Yanagisawa looked forward to arresting Ichijo. He could hardly wait to see the look on Sano's face when he . . .

A familiar sensation, like invisible hands on his skin, disturbed Yanagisawa: Someone was watching him. Instinctively he crouched, scanning the alleys and rooftops. In the darkness, he couldn't see anyone, but the menacing hidden presence revived the terror of the attack in the Imperial Palace. Was the killer stalking him again?

But that was impossible, with the killer sitting just around the curve of the Ear Mound. Yanagisawa heard Ichijo and the samurai talking, although his panic reduced their words to gibberish. Could there be more than one killer? Was it Hoshina? Yanagisawa wanted to learn more about the conspirators' plans, but he had to get away, fast.

Then he heard Ichijo say, "Farewell. We shall meet again soon. Until then, I place my faith in you."

Footsteps tapped across the bridge. The horses' bridles clanked as the samurai untied them. Yanagisawa guessed that Ichijo's parting words to the mercenaries meant that he planned to launch the revolt in the near future. He was entrusting them to deploy the troops and weapons, while he carried on his normal existence until the battle. Yanagisawa's samurai instinct, for so long buried beneath personal ambitions and torments, now challenged his fear for his own safety. A forgotten sense of duty spurred his determination to catch the traitors. Peering around the Ear Mound, he saw the two samurai ride off down an alley. He sprang up to follow.

But old habit persisted. Yanagisawa thought of the hidden watcher. *Only a fool tracks outlaws to their den alone!* warned his inner voice.

Hesitation cost him his chance. By the time he raced after the two samurai, there was no sign of them. He could hear their horses' hoofbeats receding into the distance, but although he spent hours looking for the outlaws, they'd vanished into the night.

32

"I'm going out now," Sano said to Reiko the next morning. When they'd returned to Nijō Manor last night, he'd found a message from Detective Fukida, alerting him to a matter that required action today. "Will you be all right?"

"Yes." Seated by the window of their room in Nijō Manor, Reiko was immaculately dressed and groomed, her face pale and drawn but composed. She did not look at Sano.

"Are you sure?"

Last night he'd caught her as she ran from Gion Shrine, wild-eyed and breathless. He hurried her back to Nijō Manor, where she'd calmed down enough to tell him that Kozeri had admitted being in the Pond Garden during Left Minister Konoe's murder, but claimed that she'd seen Right Minister Ichijo afterward. Sano didn't know whether to believe it, but he guessed that more had transpired than Reiko would say. In bed, she'd lain rigid and silent beside him, and this morning he'd awakened to find her brooding by the window. He desperately wanted to know what had happened between her and Kozeri, yet he was afraid to ask.

Now Reiko said, "I'll be fine. Don't worry about me."

"What will you do today?"

"I thought I'd finish examining the papers from Left Minister Konoe's office. Maybe there are clues somewhere."

Sano welcomed her interest in the case as a sign that they still had common ground. Always eager for the truth, he longed to break through her reticence. "Reiko-*san*," he began.

"Yes?"

He heard apprehension in her voice; she still wouldn't look at him. Forcing her to talk now would only make things worse. He said, "Marume has been questioning the associates of *Yoriki* Hoshina to find out where he might have gone, with no luck. Hoshina seems to have vanished completely. But Fukida had interesting news. He thinks Chamberlain Yanagisawa is on to something important that he doesn't want us to know about."

Rising, Reiko moved to the boxes of papers, knelt, and bent her head over them. "I hope you find out what it is."

"Thank you." Sano paused, then said, "Good-bye."

"Good-bye."

Things couldn't continue like this, Sano thought as he left the inn. Something had to break, and he hoped that when the air cleared, they would find happiness again.

Sano, Marume, and Fukida strode into the private quarters of Nijō Castle, where Chamberlain Yanagisawa was finishing his morning meal. Outside the open rain doors, the shady garden looked deceptively cool, but the glaring, hazy sky visible above the rooftops heralded another sultry day. And Sano's temper was as hot as the weather.

Without preliminary greetings, he said to Yanagisawa, "When were you going to tell me about Right Minister Ichijo?" He paused, then added accusingly, "Or weren't you?"

"Whatever are you talking about?" The picture of innocence, Yanagisawa wiped his lips on a napkin. The bruises on his face had darkened to a lurid bluish purple, but the swelling had gone down. "I've already told you all I know."

"Don't bother with denials," Sano said, furious. He heard Yanagisawa's bodyguards stir behind the sliding walls. "You followed Ichijo to the Ear Mound and listened to his conversation with two samurai he met there."

Lifting his tea bowl, the chamberlain's hand gave an involuntary jerk.

"I followed you," said Fukida.

Yanagisawa surged to his feet and glared at Sano. "Of all the low, silly tricks. With a killer on the loose and an insurrection brewing, you squander effort by sending a flunky to spy on *me*, as if *I* were the criminal! We're working together, remember?"

"I haven't forgotten, but obviously you have." Sano faced down Yanagisawa. "Don't try to confuse the issue. Putting surveillance on you turned out to be a good idea, didn't it? You wouldn't spy on Ichijo unless it was important to the case. I want to know why you followed him and what you learned."

Yanagisawa gave Sano an insolent smile. "Nothing."

"You were close enough to hear what Ichijo and those samurai were saying," Fukida said.

"Shut up," Yanagisawa ordered without looking at him. To Sano he said, "Even if I did hear something, why should I tell you? Many thanks for breaking Right Minister Ichijo's alibi, but you and I are finished. I know Ichijo is responsible for the murders and the imperial restoration conspiracy."

Marume and Fukida looked at Sano, who experienced a rapid, jarring sequence of reactions. First came dismay: Yanagisawa had solved the case, and with Hoshina gone, Sano had no proof of Yanagisawa's earlier sabotage and therefore no way to discredit his enemy's victory. Then he felt anger: The chamberlain had beaten Sano by using the results of his work, then pursuing leads behind his back. Next came fear of dishonor, loss of his post, and the destruction of his family. But Sano saw a glimmer of hope: If Ichijo was the traitor and murderer, then Kozeri wasn't. Maybe she'd told Reiko the truth. Could Sano and Reiko forget her and put their quarrel behind them?

Recovering his equilibrium, Sano said to Yanagisawa, "You let Ichijo's friends get away last night. If you'd told me about your plans, we might have captured them. And if Ichijo is the killer, then why haven't you arrested him?" The narrowing of Yanagisawa's eyes told Sano he'd hit a nerve. "Ichijo may very well be the leader of the conspiracy, but you're afraid you won't be able to make him tell you where the outlaws and weapons are. You need me, because you can't think what to do next."

"You're insane," Yanagisawa declared.

"You know I'm right," Sano said.

"Get out of here."

"Good luck." Sano nodded to Marume and Fukida, who followed him to the door. "I suppose you don't want to hear my plan for coercing Ichijo. Oh, and you'd better just hope that what I've discovered about him isn't the critical piece of evidence you need to get his cooperation."

Sano and his men had walked halfway down the corridor when they heard Yanagisawa call, "Wait." Marume and Fukida grinned at Sano. They all returned to the chamber, where Yanagisawa said, "Well? What's this critical evidence you have?"

"First I want to know what you learned from spying on the right minister last night," Sano said.

The chamberlain's expression turned murderous. Sano nodded encouragingly. At last Yanagisawa grimaced in exasperation. "The two samurai are *rōnin* who work for Ichijo." After describing their conversation, he said, "They must be part of the army he recruited to overthrow the Tokugawa. But they didn't mention when or where they'll attack, and I don't know where they are now."

Excitement coursed through Sano, followed by unwilling admiration for his enemy. Yanagisawa had established an apparent connection between Ichijo and the restoration conspiracy. Sano asked, "How did you think to spy on Ichijo?"

Yanagisawa's ominous look warned Sano off the subject. "It's your turn to talk."

"Before I say anything, I want you to reinstate our partnership," Sano said.

Yanagisawa nodded grudgingly.

"I also want you to agree that you won't sneak around behind my back again, sabotage me, or try to harm me in any way while we're working together."

"All right, all right!" Yanagisawa threw up his hands. "You have my word. Now tell me what you know about Ichijo. And it had better be good."

Although Sano didn't trust Yanagisawa's word, he had to be content with their pact if they were to go on together. "I have a witness who saw Ichijo at the scene of Left Minister Konoe's murder," he said, and told Kozeri's story, which Yanagisawa's news about Ichijo had convinced him to believe.

"A witness." Yanagisawa spoke with relief as well as satisfaction. Obviously he'd still harbored uncertainty about Ichijo. "The right minister's attempt to cover up Konoe's murder also supports his guilt. So what's your plan for him?"

"We confront him with the evidence," Sano said. "We give him a chance to confess and turn in his confederates. If he refuses, we lock him up and interrogate him continuously. He eats, sleeps, and bathes only when we permit him; he sees no one except us. We don't mistreat him, but he's a proud man who's used to being in control; imprisonment will break him eventually."

"But that could take forever!" Yanagisawa said.

"When Ichijo's mercenaries hear of his arrest, they'll worry that he'll turn them in," Sano said. "They'll run for their lives. The rebellion will fall apart." He lifted a hand, forestalling Yanagisawa's objections. "But we don't just wait for that to happen. While one of us is wearing Ichijo down, the other will be giving the same treatment to Emperor Tomohito."

Approval dawned on Yanagisawa's face.

"Ichijo must have told the emperor some details of the plot," Sano went on. "I think His Majesty can be persuaded to inform on Ichijo in exchange for keeping his throne."

"A brilliant scheme," Yanagisawa admitted with a calculating look in his eyes. "I'm glad I thought of it."

Though Marume and Fukida frowned at the theft of their master's idea, Sano nodded, willing to give Yanagisawa credit for his plan if it meant they could deliver a killer to justice and avert a war.

Yanagisawa said, "What are we waiting for?"

The brilliant plan crumbled as soon as they rode up to the Imperial Palace. Tokugawa troops had gathered outside the compound, along with a battalion of *yoriki, doshin*, and civilian police assistants. The commanders shouted urgent orders. While Sano, Marume, Fukida, and Yanagisawa watched in bewilderment, the whole army swarmed into the city.

Yanagisawa approached the gate, where two scared-looking watchmen stood guard. "What's going on?" he asked.

Bowing, they answered, "The emperor is missing!"

Stunned, Sano looked at Marume and Fukida. Their exclamations echoed his alarm.

"Where is *Shoshidai* Matsudaira?" Yanagisawa demanded.

"At the emperor's residence," chorused the watchmen.

"Can this have anything to do with the murder case?" Fukida asked.

"I don't know," Sano said, "but if something bad has happened to the emperor, it could mean disaster."

Any misfortune that befell the sacred sovereign heralded trouble for all of Japan: earthquakes, fires, typhoons, famine. And if Emperor Tomohito should die, even a temporary break in the continuity of the imperial succession would create disorder in the cosmos and evil among mankind.

Yanagisawa had already dismounted and marched into the palace compound. Sano, Marume, and Fukida leapt off their horses and followed. Watchmen and Tokugawa troops ran up and down the lanes of the *kuge* quarter. In the sun-baked courtyard of the emperor's residence, anxious court nobles and ladies stood apart from a crowd of angry samurai officials. *Shoshidai* Matsudaira hurried out of the latter group and flung himself on the ground at Yanagisawa's feet.

"Oh, Honorable Chamberlain," the *shoshidai* wailed, "I apologize for letting the emperor disappear. I've failed in my duty. I shall commit *seppuku* to atone for my negligence."

"Stop whining and tell me exactly what happened," Yanagisawa said. "How long has the emperor been gone?"

Right Minister Ichijo left the group of nobles and came over. "No one has seen His Majesty since he retired to his bedchamber last night. His attendants discovered that he was missing when they went to wake him for his sunrise prayer ritual. When His Majesty wasn't found after a search of the palace, I notified the *shoshidai*. But he could have disappeared hours before daybreak."

"Have you examined his quarters?" Sano asked.

"Yes," said Ichijo. "Everything was in order. A set of daytime clothes is missing from his wardrobe."

"Then he probably went voluntarily," Sano deduced. "How did he get out of the palace?"

"He must have climbed over the wall."

"Had he said or done anything recently that might indicate where he was going or why?" Sano watched Yanagisawa fuming over the catastrophe and the disruption of their plans.

"Not that I've been able to determine," Ichijo said. "His attendants say he acted perfectly normal; he told them nothing. And the idiot Prince Momozono is nowhere to be found. I suspect he went with His Majesty."

An imperial watchman ran into the courtyard, waving a scroll with gold chrysanthemum crests on the ends, bound in gold silk cord. "Here's a letter from His Majesty. I found it hanging in the Purple Dragon Hall."

"Give me that." Snatching the scroll, Yanagisawa opened it. Sano saw large, childish calligraphy scrawled upon the fine paper. Yanagisawa read aloud:

" 'To My Honorable Family and Loyal Court:

Don't bother looking for me. We shall meet again soon enough, and then the whole world will know what I've done. This is the dawn of a new era. Tonight I shall lead my army in battle against the Tokugawa oppressors who have subjugated the imperial throne for too long. I shall seize the capital and take my place as the rightful ruler of the land. No one can stop me. The gods have decreed my triumph. Until then, farewell.

                    The Divine Emperor Tomohito' "

A stunned silence hung over the courtyard, thick as the sweltering heat. Sano shook his head in confusion. This new development marked Emperor Tomohito as the instigator of the imperial restoration conspiracy, but what about all the evidence against Right Minister Ichijo?

The watchman said, "The sacred sword is missing from the treasure storehouse. His Majesty's suit of armor is gone, too."

A woman emerged from the mass of court ladies. At first Sano didn't recognize Lady Jokyōden. She wore a dressing gown, no makeup, and her hair loose; in the crisis of the emperor's disappearance, she must have forgotten to dress. Instead of a youthful Miyako beauty, she looked like a middle-aged woman ravaged by horror.

"My rash, foolish son!" Jokyōden cried, wringing her hands.

Chaos broke loose. Courtiers loudly disclaimed any involvement with the rebellion; sobs arose from the ladies. The whole group surged toward the courtyard gate. Sano understood their fear of being punished as unwitting parties to treason, but the last thing he needed was a disturbance in the court.

"Restrain them!" he called to the *bakufu* officials. "Put everyone in the palace under house arrest!"

The officials hastened to obey. Yanagisawa turned on Right Minister Ichijo. "You're responsible for this. You put the emperor up to the revolt. You recruited the army and planned the siege!"

With haughty dignity Ichijo said, "I have no part in His Majesty's actions. If I had known of his plans, I would have dissuaded him from going."

"Don't lie to me!" Yanagisawa shouted. "I saw you with those *rōnin* last night. They're your mercenaries. You paid them combat wages for the battle that the emperor thinks he's leading. Where will they launch the attack?"

Ichijo's face went ashen with shock. "You . . . saw me?" He staggered backward, leaning heavily on his cane. "But my business with those men has nothing to do with the emperor, or a conspiracy against the Tokugawa."

"Lady Asagao has admitted that you weren't with her when Left Minister Konoe died," Sano said, "and we have a witness who saw you in the Pond Garden immediately after the murder."

"Yes . . . I was there. But I didn't kill him." Ichijo spoke in a distracted tone, as if he neither knew nor cared what he was saying.

"Yes, you did!" Yanagisawa said. "You murdered Aisu, and you tried to murder me, too. Confess! Tell me where the emperor is!"

Ichijo's eyes were glazed as he murmured, "Konoe . . . Merciful gods. I should have guessed . . ." He swayed dizzily and collapsed in a faint.

"Wake up!" Yanagisawa slapped Ichijo, but the right minister remained unconscious. The *bakufu* officials herded the court nobles and ladies away. Yanagisawa glared at Sano. "What brilliant scheme do you propose now?"

The next hours passed in a blur. By afternoon, search parties had covered much of the capital without locating the emperor. Right Minister Ichijo had regained consciousness, but continued to insist that he knew nothing about the rebels. A distraught Lady Jokyōden insisted likewise. Both suspects were under house arrest along with the rest of the Imperial Court. Soldiers now guarded all approaches to Miyako; cannon had been mounted along the Great Rampart, and all samurai in the area drafted into service. Yet the local Tokugawa army numbered only the few thousand required to maintain a visible presence during almost a century of peace. The rebels might have recruited more than this, and could launch a violent bid for power even though the emperor's foolish announcement of his plans had lost them the advantage of surprise.

Nijō Castle now assumed its proper role as a military fortification. Troops occupied the guard turrets. Sano and Yanagisawa, like rival generals forced to unite against a common threat, shared a hasty meal in the private chambers.

"Maybe we already have the clue we need to find the emperor and prevent the revolt," Sano said, scooping noodles into his mouth with chopsticks.

Yanagisawa drank tea. "Not those mysterious coins? Even if we had time for them, I seriously doubt whether they would help us solve our immediate problem."

"I wasn't talking about the coins," Sano said, "although I have found out that they're linked with a local gangster clan, the Dazai. I meant the papers you took from Left Minister Konoe's office. If he was spying on the rebels, perhaps he knew where they planned to assemble and wrote down the information."

"I've already been through those papers, and I can't recall seeing anything that might be a reference to a siege on Miyako."

"It wouldn't hurt to check again," Sano said.

With a shrug, Yanagisawa conceded, "What have we got to lose?"

When Sano arrived at Nijō Manor, Reiko met him at the gate, her face vivid with anxiety. "I've been watching the soldiers march through the city," she cried as Sano dismounted from his horse. "The *shoshidai* has ordered all the samurai at the inn to report for military duty. Does this mean the revolt is going to start soon?"

"Yes." Sano explained about the emperor's letter and disappearance. "Unfortunately, we don't know when or where the rebels will attack."

"What are you going to do?"

At least they were speaking again, Sano thought. A stable boy took charge of his horse, and he went into the inn with Reiko. "You and I will review the papers from Left Minister Konoe's office."

In their room Sano discovered that Reiko had emptied the boxes; journals, scrolls, and loose pages lay sorted into piles around the room. Pointing at various piles, she described their contents: "These are the left minister's calendars, which list meetings, ceremonies, and holidays. Those are his notes on palace business. Drafts of imperial edicts. Letters from the *bakufu* and other court nobles. Banquet menus. His diaries include the history of his rivalry with Right Minister Ichijo, insults toward Lady Jokyōden, and complaints about Emperor Tomohito's bad behavior, but if there's anything here to say who killed him, I can't find it."

"That doesn't matter. Chamberlain Yanagisawa and I are almost certain that Ichijo is the murderer," Sano said.

Reiko stood perfectly still as Sano told her about the apparent link between Ichijo and the imperial restoration conspiracy.

"Ichijo admits he was in the Pond Garden during Konoe's murder," Sano finished, "and his alibi for Aisu's murder is weak. As a high court official and intelligent, ambitious politician, he's the likeliest instigator of the revolt, although he claims he's innocent and won't talk. What I hope to find in the papers is a clue to the rebels' strategy."

"Then Kozeri really did see him. She told me the truth." Reiko dropped to her knees. Wide-eyed, she pressed a hand to her throat as if choking.

"What's wrong?" Alarmed, Sano knelt beside his wife.

To his delight, Reiko leaned into his embrace. He felt her trembling as she spoke through sobs: "Last night Kozeri said she'd tried to seduce you, but you wouldn't let her because you love me. I didn't believe her then, but I can now. And I know that she did use magic to deceive and entice you, because she tried the same thing with me. Please forgive me for doubting you!"

Sano held Reiko tight. Almost weeping himself in the bliss of their reunion, Sano whispered, "It's all right now." He thanked fate for the way the threads of the case had woven together.

After a moment Reiko disengaged from him. "Enough," she said, wiping away tears. Her voice was brusque, but her face shone with relief and happiness. "We have work to do."

They began going through the papers she'd sorted. Even with a war looming on the horizon, Sano found a keen pleasure in their task. Still, as he pored over documents, his hope of a successful search waned.

"I'm not finding anything useful," he said. "Maybe the information is in code."

Reiko laid aside a scroll and took up another. "If so, I didn't recognize it. The meaning of all these writings seems perfectly clear to me. I can identify the purpose of each document, and there are no ambiguous phrases. I haven't seen anything that I would judge as not what it appears to be."

. . . *ambiguous phrases . . . the meaning . . . seems perfectly clear . . . not what it appears to be* . . . Reiko's words formed a mesh of sound that drifted like a net through Sano's mind and snared a dim, amorphous memory. Where had he recently read an ambiguous phrase whose meaning had seemed clear, but might not have been what it seemed? Instinct told him that the answer was critically important. Holding his breath, Sano concentrated. The memory crystallized into bright clarity.

"We're looking in the wrong place," he said.

Reiko glanced at him in surprise. "You mean you don't think the information is in Left Minister Konoe's papers?"

"Yes, I do," Sano said, "but these aren't his only papers." He hurried to the cabinet. "Konoe also wrote those letters to Kozeri." With trembling fingers Sano took out the last letter. "This was written seven days before Konoe's murder. Listen." He read the angry expressions of unrequited love, concluding with the passage he'd recalled:

" 'Soon the forces of defense and desire will clash upon the lofty, sacred heights where spires pierce the sky, feathers drift, and clear water falls.' "

"It sounds like a poetic allusion to sex between a man who wants it and a woman who doesn't," Reiko said, "which describes the relationship between the left minister and Kozeri."

"That's what I thought at first. But what if he's describing a different kind of struggle, at a real place? 'Forces of defense and desire' could mean the Tokugawa army and the rebels who want to take over Japan." Another inspiration struck Sano. "Didn't you say that Konoe had asked Kozeri to meet him at the palace to celebrate a 'special occasion'?"

Reiko nodded; comprehension sparkled in her eyes. "He asked her six days after he wrote the letter, and one day before his death. Maybe he was hinting in the letter that he'd discovered the rebels' strategy—"

"And where they planned to launch the attack," Sano said.

"The 'special occasion' was the revolt, which would fail because Konoe was going to report it to the *bakufu* in time for the army to—"

"Head off the siege of Miyako. Then the *bakufu* would—"

"Reward Konoe by granting his request to shut down the Kodai Temple convent and force Kozeri to go back to him," Reiko finished triumphantly.

Exhilarated by their shared reasoning, they laughed together. "I found the clue on our first day in Miyako, but I didn't recognize its significance," Sano said. "Now we just have to figure out where this place is."

"Lofty, sacred heights," Reiko mused. "Maybe Konoe was talking about a mountain, but if so, which one?"

"Spires could mean a temple," Sano said, "though there must be as many of those as there are mountains in the Miyako area."

"Drifting feathers and clear water?" Reiko shook her head. "That part doesn't make any sense to me."

"I've read something like that before, in writings about Miyako . . ." Sano thought hard, but couldn't grasp the memory. "My knowledge of the city is limited, but a local citizen might recognize the reference."

He rushed out the door and found the innkeeper's wife kneeling in the corridor, her ear to the wall. She gasped in alarm and said, "Hello, master."

"Please come in," Sano said, hurrying her into the room. He read her the passage from the letter. "Does that suggest anything to you?"

The woman smiled, obviously relieved because he didn't scold her for eavesdropping. "Oh, of course. It means Kiyomizu Temple—the Clear-Water Temple on Sound-of-Feathers Mountain. A very beautiful place. You must see it while you're in Miyako."

"I expect I will. Many thanks for your help."

Now Sano recalled what he'd read. Kiyomizu Temple, strategically situated on high ground, had been for centuries a favored spot for mobilizing troops and a secret rendezvous site of spies and rebels. He and Reiko exchanged jubilant smiles, but immediately sobered as their gazes moved to the window. It was nearly dusk.

There wasn't much time to head off the rebels' attack.

33

It was the last night of Obon. The time had come for the visiting souls of the dead to leave the world of the living. Throughout Miyako, people threw stones on roofs to drive the spirits away. As the pale pink sunset sky deepened to magenta, crowds converged upon the Kamo River. They launched small straw boats, each containing incense, a lantern to light the spirits' way to the netherworld, food for the journey, and written prayers. The water became a sparkling stream of lights. Huge bonfires in the shape of auspicious characters burned on the hillsides, guiding the spirits back to the cemeteries.

Marching southeast from Nijō Castle, the Tokugawa army, two thousand strong, made slow progress through streets flocked with citizens. "Make way!" shouted the banner bearers at the head of the procession. "Take cover. Go home!"

Gunners, archers, and mounted troops pushed through the heedless crowds. Sano, clad in full armor, rode at the end with the commanders. He said to Marume and Fukida, "The rebels probably chose tonight to attack because they thought the entire militia would be busy participating in the Obon rites."

"If not for the emperor's decision to announce his plans, they might have succeeded in capturing Miyako," said Marume.

"They might still cause mass destruction," Fukida said, "if we don't get to Kiyomizu Temple in time."

The army crossed the Gojo Bridge. Below, tiny bright boats floated downstream. For Sano, the scene had the atmosphere of a nightmare. The long Tokugawa peace had lulled the samurai class into complacency; never had he imagined riding off to civil war, except in fantasy. But fantasy had become reality. Beneath his metal breastplate, Sano's heart thudded like the urgent cadence of a war drum. He smelled the sharp odor of nerves and anticipation rising from his comrades. Would he fulfill the ultimate samurai destiny of dying in battle for his lord? Sano offered a silent prayer that he and Reiko would be safely reunited. She was in Nijō Manor, protected by her guards, and she'd promised that if the war reached the city, she wouldn't join the fight. Sano hoped she would keep that promise.

Someone rode up beside him. "Are you ready, *Sōsakan* Sano?"

It was Chamberlain Yanagisawa, mounted on a black steed. He wore a magnificent suit of red-lacquered armor and a golden-horned helmet. Since learning the rebels' plans, he'd applied his impressive organizing skills to the task of defending the regime. He'd marshaled the best fighters and gotten them under way in an impossibly short time, while leaving forces behind to guard the city. Sano had been amazed to discover that inside the corrupt chamberlain beat the heart of a samurai.

Now, as they rode through the eastern suburbs toward Kiyomizu Temple, Sano bowed to Yanagisawa, who looked the perfect general, ready to inspire his troops to victory. Never had Sano envisioned fighting under the command of the man who'd so often tried to destroy him. Yet the ancient mystique of great warriors like Tokugawa Ieyasu and Toyotomi Hideyoshi surrounded Yanagisawa like a magic spell. The warrior in Sano cleaved to it. He willingly placed his life in his enemy's service.

"You understand your orders?" Yanagisawa said. The gaze he swept over Sano, Marume, and Fukida was clear of animosity, focused on larger concerns than personal strife.

"Yes, Honorable Chamberlain. We three will find the emperor and capture him alive," Sano said.

"Good. I'm counting on you."

As Yanagisawa moved on to confer with his other commanders, Sano felt strangely uplifted by the encounter. Surely all the men present would fight their best for Yanagisawa tonight.

The approach to Kiyomizu Temple led the army up a steep incline, along a narrow lane of shops where craftsmen had produced pottery for generations. High above loomed the temple gate, its square arch and flaring roof stark against a landscape of forested cliffs. The sky was the color of a fresh wound.

A murmur rippled through the ranks of the army: "Listen!"

From beyond the gate came the thunder of hoofbeats. Torches borne through the temple precinct by the approaching rebel army cast an eerie glow. Sano felt battle lust consuming him and his allies like invisible flames.

Chamberlain Yanagisawa called, "Ambush them at the top of the hill!"

The army surged forward, reaching the crest just as several thousand rebels stampeded through the gate and down broad stone stairs leading to a plaza. Some were samurai in elaborate armor, but many wore ragged peasant clothes. Gangsters sported leather tunics over bare, tattooed skin. White hoods cowled the shaved heads of priests in saffron robes. Banner bearers waved flags imprinted with the imperial crest. Foot soldiers carried bows, guns, and spears; mounted troops brandished swords and lances. Their torches illuminated shocked faces: They hadn't expected such prompt opposition. Now they froze in ranks.

"You're trapped!" Yanagisawa shouted from his position behind his troops. "Surrender!"

Instead, a defiant yell came from the rebel general, a mounted samurai clad in full armor: "Stand and fight!"

Simultaneously the archers and gunners of both armies dropped to their knees, aiming bows and arquebuses. A storm of arrows whirred across the plaza. Volleys of gunfire rocked the night. Amid gunpowder fumes and smoke, men fell dead and injured. Conch trumpets and war drums signaled troop movements. Then a maelstrom of swinging blades and rearing horses engulfed the plaza as the troops fought. Pressing forward through the melee, Sano felt arrows clatter against his armor. A rebel samurai galloped at him, waving a sword. Sano cut his opponent across the neck. The rebel's horse galloped away, dragging a corpse. The glory of destruction horrified Sano, and thrilled him to the core of his samurai spirit.

"Come on!" he shouted to Marume and Fukida. "Let's find the emperor!"

They fended off attackers while their mounts trampled fallen bodies. Torches lay scattered on the ground. In their light, Sano scrutinized the rebel soldiers. He didn't see the emperor among them. He guessed that the rebels wouldn't allow Tomohito to join the battle. Tomohito represented their claim to power, and they needed to keep him safe.

"He must be in the temple," Sano said.

As he and his men urged their mounts up the stairs beyond the plaza, gunfire exploded behind them. Shots ricocheted off Sano's armor, jolting him. Marume's lance speared a swordsman who blocked their way, but another rebel dragged him off his mount. While they fought, a bullet struck Fukida's horse. It screamed and tumbled down the stairs. Fukida jumped out of the saddle, but his arm caught in the reins. Sano leapt from his own mount and jerked Fukida loose. They fought the enemy past twin statues of roaring lion-dogs and up the second flight of steps, leaving dead men in their wake. Marume joined them. They raced through the gate.

The temple precinct, built on terraces hewn from a steep hill, was enveloped in a darkness relieved only by flames in stone lanterns along the paths. The sounds of gunfire and clashing blades faded as Sano and his men sped up more steps, through an inner gate, past a pagoda. Pausing to catch his breath, Sano saw several low buildings to his left. All were apparently deserted. Moving cautiously, he led his men past a tinkling fountain, through another gate. Beyond stretched a covered passageway, and ahead, the main hall.

With its vast, humped roof, it looked like a giant outgrowth of the hill. Huge, square pillars supported lower peaked roofs above exterior corridors. The windows were dark, but Sano pointed to a glow emanating from the south side. He and Marume and Fukida advanced stealthily through the passageway and into the hall's west corridor, toward the light. It came from brass lanterns attached to the ceiling of a wide veranda that jutted over the Kin-un-kyō Gorge. Far below, in the distance, the lights along the river and in Miyako twinkled. Hearing voices from the veranda, Sano halted.

"I want to fight in the battle. Why do I have to stay here?" It was Emperor Tomohito, sounding petulant.

"Because you'll get killed if you go down there," said a man's stern voice. "We're protecting you."

Then came the sound of a scuffle, and Tomohito's outraged cry: "Let me go! I'm the emperor. You have to obey me!"

"If you want to live to rule Japan, you'll obey *us*," said a different voice.

Sano peered around the corner. The lanterns lit the veranda like a stage. Two samurai in leather armor tunics stood with their backs to Sano. Through the gap between them he saw Tomohito, dressed in his old-fashioned imperial armor, a long sword at his waist.

"This is the first time I've ever been outside the palace," Tomohito pouted, "but I haven't seen anything except this stupid temple. You wouldn't even let me look out the window of the palanquin on the way here." His voice quavered tearfully. "And now I'm missing the battle that I've dreamed about for so long!"

While the emperor raged and tried to push past the soldiers, they entreated him to be quiet. Sano could tell from their worried voices that they knew the coup attempt had gone wrong. Sano whispered to his detectives. Then he circled the hall. He stepped onto the veranda behind Tomohito.

"Surrender quietly, or you will be killed immediately," he said.

The emperor spun around, his babyish face startled beneath the ornate helmet. "You?" he exclaimed.

The two rebel samurai froze. When they drew their blades and started toward Sano, Marume and Fukida rushed them from behind. Then the four men were battling in a tornado of darting figures and flashing blades.

Backing away from Sano, the emperor blustered, "What are you doing here?"

"I've come to take you home, Your Majesty," Sano said.

"I won't go." Tomohito puffed out his chest and stood his ground. "Not until I've conquered the Tokugawa."

Sano pitied the boy's delusion, fostered by his isolated existence and the people who had spoiled him all his life. "I'm sorry, but that is not your destiny," Sano said. "The shogun's force is slaughtering your troops as we speak. Listen: You can hear the sound of defeat."

Diminishing gunfire resounded across the hills; the ring of fewer steel blades echoed. Marume and Fukida had driven the emperor's guardians off the veranda, down to the path beside the hall. Yet Emperor Tomohito shook his head in angry denial.

"We can't lose," he said. "I have the divine sanction of the gods. My victory is certain."

"It's time for you to face reality," Sano said. "The few rebels who get to the city will find more troops waiting for them, thanks to the advance notice that you couldn't resist giving. That was poor military strategy, but a good thing for you. The revolt will be crushed with minimum damage, and you can save yourself from punishment by surrendering."

"Surrender?" Tomohito laughed scornfully. "On my grave!"

Grabbing the gold-inlaid hilt of his sword, he unsheathed the weapon. Sano gazed in awe at the steel blade, etched with archaic designs and characters, that shone with an almost unearthly glow. This was the sacred imperial sword, passed down through generations of emperors, and taken from the palace treasure-house by this foolhardy youth. Now Tomohito sliced looping swirls in the air. He took a prancing step toward Sano.

"I'm off to war," he said. His eyes, filled with nervous jubilation, reflected the blade's gleam; he grinned at Sano. "And you shall be the first enemy I slay."

"Don't do this," Sano entreated the emperor. "You can't beat me."

Tomohito laughed. "I could have killed you yesterday. Now I will."

He swung the sword. Sano leapt backward, and the blade whistled past his chin. The emperor howled, lashing out furiously while Sano dodged. When Tomohito sliced at his legs, Sano jumped over the blade. Cuts battered his armor tunic.

"Your Majesty, the revolt wasn't your idea," Sano said. He darted behind a pillar, and Tomohito's sword stuck in the wood. "Right Minister Ichijo incited it, didn't he?"

Yanking the blade free of the pillar, Tomohito lunged after Sano. "Ichijo has nothing to do with this. I want to conquer the Tokugawa. And you can't stop me!"

"You couldn't have recruited an army or procured weapons by yourself," Sano countered, dodging more cuts. "Ichijo must have done it."

"Stop talking nonsense!"

The emperor's blade slashed at Sano's head, driving him toward the wall of the building. Sano knew that if he fought back, he risked hurting the emperor, but refusing to stand up to Tomohito would only confirm the boy's belief that he was good enough to take on the Tokugawa army and send him to his death in the battle. Drawing his sword, Sano parried cuts.

"When Ichijo found out that Left Minister Konoe was a *metsuke* spy who'd discovered the plot, Ichijo killed him," Sano said. His blade clanged against Tomohito's, forcing the emperor across the veranda toward the railing. But Tomohito only laughed; his attacks grew wilder. "If you'll implicate Ichijo, I'll persuade the shogun to pardon you."

"I don't care if Ichijo did kill Left Minister Konoe. I don't need him anymore. I don't need a pardon from the shogun, either. When I rule Japan, he'll be my servant!"

Sano's arm ached from blocking strikes; his head reverberated with the ring of steel. He was the far better swordsman, but a person who wants to win has an advantage over one who doesn't want to fight. Tomohito whacked Sano's left upper arm. The blade cut through the chain mail and padding of his sleeve. To his alarm, Sano felt searing pain, then the warm wetness of blood.

"Ha!" Tomohito exclaimed. "I got you! Prepare to die!"

Eyes bright with glee, the emperor raised his sword in both hands. He rushed Sano, bellowing. In desperation, Sano feinted a jab at Tomohito's groin. The emperor sprang backward and lowered his weapon. Sano brought his blade around, slashing at Tomohito's hands. With a cry of pain, the emperor let go of the sword. It clattered across the veranda. Tomohito stood paralyzed, gazing with horror at his outspread right hand.

A narrow cut traced a red line across the knuckles. He looked at Sano, his face aghast.

"I'm bleeding." His voice was a ragged croak. Probably he'd never been injured before, never seen his own blood. He must have thought himself invincible.

"I'm sorry," Sano said, horrified at wounding the sacred sovereign. Perhaps, though, the experience would teach Emperor Tomohito a lesson. "But this is minor compared to what will happen if you don't cooperate."

"The gods shall strike you down for this," Tomohito whimpered. Dropping to his knees, he cradled his bloody hand.

"The penalty for treason is death by decapitation." Sano kept his sword pointed at Tomohito, underscoring the threat. "Even your divine status won't save you—unless you agree to denounce Right Minister Ichijo."

Marume and Fukida hurried onto the veranda. "The guards are dead," Marume said.

"Go back to the battlefield," Sano said. "I'll handle things here."

The detectives left. Sano stood beside Tomohito. "The right minister manipulated you into believing that the plot was your idea and he was just carrying out your orders. He's a murderer who doesn't deserve your protection. Give up, Your Majesty. Save yourself and let Ichijo suffer."

Tomohito shook his head in dazed misery. "No," he whispered. His complexion was a sickly white; he seemed on the verge of fainting. "He didn't. I can't . . ."

"Look around." Sano swept his sword in a high arc that encompassed the mountains above Kiyomizu Temple, the lighted city below. "Japan is bigger than you can comprehend. The Tokugawa army is hundreds of thousands strong. Any rebels who escape slaughter tonight may straggle across the country, attracting a few followers, stirring up trouble, but they'll be defeated in the end. Ichijo's ambitions far exceed his grasp."

As the emperor gazed at the view, he seemed to see it for the first time. A shudder passed through his body. The shadows of dying dreams darkened his eyes. Sano sheathed his sword, overcome with sorrow for the boy. Tomohito wept.

"I wanted to rule Japan," he mourned. "I wanted to be someone besides a useless god locked away from the world. Now I'm afraid to die." The knowledge of his own mortality filled his voice with terror; tears streamed down his face as he looked up at Sano. "Right Minister Ichijo didn't mount the revolt, but if you want me to say he did, I will, if you'll spare my life."

His insistence upon the right minister's innocence disturbed Sano. Finally he had the testimony needed to convict Ichijo, but what if Ichijo really wasn't the instigator of the revolt? Did that mean he hadn't killed Left Minister Konoe or Aisu either?

Reluctantly, Sano entertained the possibility that the revolt and the murders were not connected, or else were connected in a way he'd never guessed. He began arranging facts into a new theory. Emperor Tomohito was the heart of the Imperial Court as well as the center of the revolt. The interests of everyone at the palace were linked to his. Therefore, someone other than the traitor could have killed to protect Tomohito from the punishment he would suffer if Konoe reported the conspiracy, then later tried to kill Sano and halt his investigation for the same reason. If the traitor and the killer weren't the same person . . .

A flash of enlightenment seared Sano's mind. The suspect he'd dismissed as incapable of mounting an insurrection fit this new logic as well as did the more likely culprits. Prince Momozono was the emperor's confidant, and must also be privy to the secrets of many other people who didn't bother hiding their business from an idiot. He could have known about the plot, and that Left Minister Konoe was a *metsuke* spy. Sano tallied other reasons that pointed to Momozono's guilt. Stricken by the certainty that this new theory was right, he marveled at the unexpected turn the case had taken.

Then, from the east side of the hall, Sano heard hooting sounds, followed by slow, stumbling footsteps. He recalled Ichijo saying that Prince Momozono must have run away with Emperor Tomohito.

"Help me, Momo-*chan!*" the emperor cried.

The killer was coming.

34

From astride his horse, Chamberlain Yanagisawa surveyed the battle. Gun muzzles spewed thunder; arrows flew. Swordsmen clashed, their blades glinting in the light of fallen torches and a tree that had caught fire. Hundreds of bodies lay strewn across the plaza and the steps leading to Kiyomizu Temple; riderless horses galloped free; blood stained the ground. Yanagisawa's army had suffered many casualties, but the Tokugawa forces now far outnumbered the rebels. Victory was near.

Yanagisawa rode back and forth along the perimeter of the battlefield. Waving his war fan, he shouted orders to the commanders, who conveyed them to the troops with conch-shell trumpet, war drums, and flags. His throat was sore and his voice hoarse, his ears deafened by the noise. Smoke and gunpowder fumes filled his lungs. He ached from the impact of bullets against his armor. The barbaric violence sickened him, yet he gloried in it. Battle had fully roused the samurai spirit that had awakened within him during the investigation.

Now his political feuds seemed like trivial substitutes for real war. When a mounted rebel soldier charged him, Yanagisawa swung his sword, slashing the man's throat. A soaring exhilaration lifted him above himself, to a rarefied plane where he could fulfill his true purpose in life: to lead his lord's army to victory, or die in the effort.

A pair of outlaw priests broke away from the combat zone. Clutching spears, tattered saffron robes flying, they sprinted down the sloping road toward the city.

"Stop them!" Yanagisawa called.

Before his troops could respond, a figure bounded up the dark street and waylaid the rebels. It was a samurai dressed in ordinary kimono. Wielding his long sword in his right hand and his short one in his left, he fought the priests.

Yanagisawa watched in puzzlement. Who had belatedly joined the defense? Then the newcomer cut down one of his opponents. As he drove the other up toward the plaza, he emerged into the light. Yanagisawa recognized familiar broad shoulders and a distinctive grace of motion. He blinked.

"It can't be!" he muttered.

The samurai finished off the second priest and loped up the hill, looking around him. It was *Yoriki* Hoshina. Suddenly he caught sight of Yanagisawa. He paused, a sword in each hand, as he and Yanagisawa looked at each other. The noisy chaos of battle faded from Yanagisawa's consciousness.

Then Hoshina advanced hesitantly up the road. Brimming with wonder, hardly aware of what he was doing, Yanagisawa dismounted and walked toward Hoshina. Had desire conjured up an apparition to haunt him? As they came together in the shadows beside a building, Yanagisawa's legs felt unsteady.

"What are you doing here?" he asked.

Hoshina stopped several paces away. On his cheeks were bruises Yanagisawa had inflicted during their fight—he was real, not a ghost. He said, "I've come back."

"Why?" Rage and pain erupted in Yanagisawa. "To play me for a fool again? To kill me for humiliating you in front of your police comrades?"

Hoshina wordlessly shook his head while Yanagisawa brandished his sword, then dropped his weapons and spread his arms in a gesture of surrender. "Because I had to see you again," he said, as though it were the most obvious reason in the world.

Increasingly baffled, Yanagisawa said, "But I condemned you to death. I could kill you now."

"I don't care." Breathing hard, glistening with sweat, Hoshina stood proudly. "To be with you makes death worthwhile."

The words filled Yanagisawa with an amazement that he hid behind scorn. "Well, if you're so eager to die, then why did you run away?"

"It was my only hope of proving that I'm not the villain you think I am. It was the only way to convince you that all I wanted was to help you."

How Yanagisawa wanted to believe the *yoriki*! But he couldn't bear to be hurt again. "This is another trick," he said. "You think you can escape death by worming your way into my affections again. You're too much of a coward to accept your fate and die like a samurai!"

With a rueful smile, Hoshina said, "If I were a coward, I wouldn't have come back. If I were still the schemer that I've been all my life, I would know better than to try a ploy that had already failed, on a man who recognized me for what I was. I want to atone for betraying your trust and prove my love for you." Hoshina took another step toward Yanagisawa. "Then I'll die gladly."

"You're a liar!" Even as Yanagisawa's spirit trembled at the ardent declaration, he pointed his sword at Hoshina, keeping the length of steel between them. "I'll kill you!"

"I don't think you will." Instead of picking up his fallen weapons, Hoshina moved closer to Yanagisawa. From the battlefield, sporadic explosions of gunfire continued. Hoshina's steady gaze transfixed Yanagisawa; the sword trembled in Yanagisawa's hand as he backed away. "You could have killed me yesterday," Hoshina said, "but you didn't even draw your sword. That's why I'm willing to gamble my life now. But even if I lose the bet, at least I'll have brought you evidence to help you solve the case and made amends for betraying you to the *sōsakan-sama*."

"What evidence? What are you talking about?"

"When I escaped, I took cover in the underworld of Miyako," Hoshina said. "I tracked down police informants and asked questions. What I learned will help your investigation."

"I don't want to hear it!" Yanagisawa took another step backward, clutching the extended sword. Hoshina advanced. He dipped his hand into the cloth pouch at his waist. Fearing a hidden weapon, Yanagisawa cried, "Stop. Don't move!"

Hoshina removed a small object from the pouch and offered it to Yanagisawa on his outstretched palm. "Do you remember this?"

It was a fern-leaf coin from Left Minister Konoe's office. Uncomprehending, Yanagisawa nodded.

"I've found out what it is," Hoshina said. When Yanagisawa didn't respond, anxiety sharpened his face. "I understand why you're suspicious, but please, just listen to what I have to say. Then decide if you can forgive me for the harm I've done."

Instead of running away, Hoshina had stayed in Miyako to continue the investigation! He'd kept his promise to investigate the mysterious coins. Confused and shaken, fighting to maintain his resolve against Hoshina, Yanagisawa continued backing away, his sword aimed at the *yoriki*.

"You're just trying to manipulate me into pardoning you!"

Despair slumped Hoshina's shoulders, and his face looked suddenly ravaged by fatigue. "If that's what you really believe, then so be it." Still, he kept advancing. Yanagisawa's back struck a solid wooden pillar, abruptly halting his retreat. Hoshina moved closer until his throat was touching the tip of Yanagisawa's blade.

"So kill me now," Hoshina said, "and I'll die satisfied with the knowledge that I did my best for the man who means more to me than my own life."

The sight of the sharp steel point indenting Hoshina's bare skin filled Yanagisawa with awe. No man dedicated to self-interest would ever offer up his life this way. Yanagisawa could finally believe in Hoshina's honesty. And he saw a chance to put a tragedy behind him and atone for his own sins.

Shichisaburō had died for love of him. Rather than do what was right and honorable, Yanagisawa had condemned the actor to execution. But he needn't relive the past. He drew a deep breath. If he could find within himself the mercy to forgive, the courage to relinquish pride . . .

Hoshina's steady gaze, filled with a mixture of faith and fear, compelled Yanagisawa's decision. The breath rushed out of him; the sword fell from his grasp. Hoshina's face lit with happiness. They exchanged a long, silent look that conveyed forgiveness and gratitude, affirmed love, and stirred desire, while jubilant shouts from the battlefield heralded the imminent Tokugawa victory.

Eventually, they picked up and sheathed their weapons, then stood side by side, watching the battle, uncertain what to say. Hoshina ventured, "Now can I tell you what I learned about the coin?"

"Yes, if you like." Yanagisawa's heart was soaring with such happiness that he hardly cared about the clue.

"The coin was minted by a powerful Miyako gangster clan by the name of Dazai," Hoshina said.

"That's interesting," Yanagisawa said, not wanting to admit that he already knew and let Hoshina think his effort had been wasted.

"My informant is a Dazai retainer," Hoshina said. "He told me that the gang trades in stolen goods. Usually the chief buys them outright from thieves and keeps the money he makes from reselling them. But when the merchandise is very rare or valuable, he pays after he's found the right buyer. He gives the thief one of these." Hoshina held up the coin, explaining, "The Dazai are former samurai. They have a sense of honor. The coin is their pledge that they'll either pay for the merchandise eventually, or return it."

274

The unexpected news revealed a startling new dimension to the murder case. "The coin was found with two others in Left Minister Konoe's house," Yanagisawa said. "That means he sold things to the Dazai. Things he'd obtained illegally, that he couldn't sell on the open market."

"And the fact that such coins were found among Konoe's possessions meant he'd never been paid." Eagerness animated Hoshina's face. "So I asked my informant if the Dazai still had the merchandise. He said yes. I talked him into letting me into the warehouse where they hide stolen goods. I saw what they got from Konoe: antique kimonos, with chrysanthemum crests on the fabric. I recognized them from when I inspected the imperial storehouses."

"Konoe stole from the palace?" Yanagisawa struggled to fathom the notion of the *metsuke* spy as a thief. "Why?" Then he shook his head. "The Dazai wouldn't have asked; all they would care about was the money they could make by selling imperial treasure to rich collectors."

"But I know why," Hoshina said excitedly. "The kimonos weren't all that Konoe had sold the Dazai. He'd been bringing them valuable artifacts for years, a little at a time. But here's the most interesting part: After selling the things, the Dazai didn't pay Konoe. Some of the gold they kept, as part of a secret deal they had with him. The rest they delivered to a priest at Lord Ibe's house, along with weapons and ammunition. Do you know what that means?"

It meant that he and Sano had completely misunderstood a critical element of the murder case, Yanagisawa realized. "Konoe was behind the imperial restoration attempt," he said, stunned by the revelation. "The troops were armed with money raised by stealing palace treasure." Not through loans from the bank to which Yanagisawa had followed Jokyōden's messenger; not with payments made by Ichijo during secret meetings at the Ear Mound. "Konoe's deal with the Dazai must have been a pact to combine forces to overthrow the Tokugawa. He got the revolt under way, and his allies carried on after his death. Merciful gods . . ."

"The spy was the traitor!" Hoshina exclaimed.

"Sano and I assumed that the revolt was the reason for Left Minister Konoe's murder." Chagrin overwhelmed Yanagisawa. "But if he was responsible for the plot, he didn't die because the killer wanted to keep him from reporting it to the *bakufu*."

"Therefore the plot had nothing to do with Konoe's death," Hoshina said.

"I just can't accept that!" Yanagisawa restlessly paced the street.

"We can't ignore the facts," Hoshina said. "As soon as this complication is out of the way—" he gestured toward the battlefield "—we can go back to the palace and find out the truth about Konoe's murder."

"I suppose you're right." Yanagisawa slowed his steps; yet he couldn't concede defeat. He devised a fresh theory around the conspiracy, like rebuilding a house to accommodate a giant piece of furniture that won't fit. He said, "Before, the question was, 'Who was the traitor Konoe had discovered?' But what if we turn it around and ask, 'Who knew Konoe was a traitor?' "

"I don't see where that leads," Hoshina said, bewildered.

Instinct told Yanagisawa that he was heading in the right direction. "Suppose Konoe didn't die because he had compromising knowledge about anyone. Could the murderer have killed Konoe because he—or she—knew about his treason?"

"Anyone who knew about the conspiracy could have destroyed the left minister by simply reporting it to the *bakufu*," Hoshina pointed out. "There would have been no reason for murder."

Yanagisawa recognized other flaws in his theory. He had no proof that Right Minister Ichijo or Lady Jokyōden had known about the plot. Emperor Tomohito had known, but as part of the conspiracy, he couldn't have betrayed Konoe without getting himself in trouble. But Yanagisawa could guess who had known . . . and couldn't have hoped to gain by reporting Left Minister Konoe's crime to the *bakufu*.

In a leap of thought and logic too rapid to express in words, Yanagisawa whispered, "Prince Momozono is the killer!"

Hoshina laughed. "You're joking." Then, seeing that Yanagisawa was serious, he said, "Why do you think so?"

Yanagisawa suddenly saw the personal ramifications of his discovery. He ran uphill to the plaza. There, amid trampled corpses, some hundred rebels still fought valiantly. Yanagisawa scanned the ranks of his army. Mounted troops rode down the enemy; teams of swordsmen battled each priest, gangster, and outlaw samurai. Yanagisawa didn't see Sano, who must have gone off in search of Emperor Tomohito. Sano hadn't heard Hoshina's story; he didn't know what would happen if he tried to capture the emperor.

Now Yanagisawa saw his dearest wishes hovering on the horizon like a radiant constellation: Sano gone forever; the solution to the murder case in Yanagisawa's hands, his victory over the rebels certain; a secure future in the shogun's favor. All he had to do was absolutely nothing. Yanagisawa inhaled the scent of blood and gunpowder as he savored his triumph . . . but somehow it wasn't as satisfying as he'd expected. With astonishment, he realized that something had changed inside him. Tonight he'd experienced the Way of the Warrior. The taste of honor had diminished his appetite for the feud with Sano. Deliberately letting one of his soldiers die seemed disgraceful behavior for a samurai general.

Yoriki Hoshina joined him. "What's wrong?"

Yanagisawa stared at Hoshina. Now he understood that their reunion had also changed him, had altered his vision of the world. For two years Sano had been the bane of his existence; yet Sano had always acted out of duty to the shogun and dedication to his work, not out of a desire to injure Yanagisawa. Sano had saved his life, spared him punishment. And Yanagisawa had promised not to harm Sano. Could he repay the good fortune of his happiness by dishonoring their bargain and abandoning a comrade in danger?

Looking up at Kiyomizu, Yanagisawa guessed that Sano had gone into the temple to find Emperor Tomohito. When he did, he would also find Prince Momozono. Yanagisawa took a hesitant step forward. But habit prevailed; a sudden change of heart didn't negate the goals of a lifetime. Yanagisawa backtracked two steps.

Should he let fate take its course, or rush to Sano's rescue? Should he serve ambition and self-interest, or comradeship and honor?

35

"Everything's g-going to be all r-right, Your Majesty."

Head tossing, body convulsing, Prince Momozono stumbled across the temple hall veranda toward his fallen, weeping cousin. Light from the ceiling lanterns splayed his ungainly shadow across the floor; his yelps punctuated the gunfire that boomed from the darkness down the hill. Knotted ropes circled his left ankle and wrist, the loose ends trailing; a cloth strip hung around his neck: The rebels must have bound and gagged him to keep him quiet.

Sano beheld the prince in amazement. Momozono looked as pitiful as ever, but he harbored the force of *kiai*, and Sano recognized the potentially lethal complications introduced by Momozono's arrival. He scented the cold breath of danger; his mind raced.

"I'm glad to see you safe, Honorable Prince," he improvised, anxious not to reveal that he knew Momozono was the killer. Getting the boys back to the city and Momozono into the custody of the *bakufu* seemed the best strategy. "Now that you're here, I can take you and His Majesty home."

"No! I can't bear for everyone to see me in disgrace!" The emperors's sobs dwindled to panicky gasps. "I never want to go home again!"

Prince Momozono lurched close to his cousin. He said, "We're n-not g-going with you."

The pair looked like frightened children defying a bully. Sano's heart sank. "Neither of you has anything to fear," he said, thinking fast. "Prince

Momozono wasn't party to the revolt, and Your Majesty will be spared the consequences of treason."

Tomohito gazed uncertainly at Sano, betraying his need to give himself over to authority, but Momozono cried, "D-don't believe him, Your Majesty. You must learn to beware of p-people who want to use you for th-their own purposes. Look at what happened because you trusted the l-left minister!"

Confusion disconcerted Sano. Did Momozono mean the right minister? Was Ichijo behind the conspiracy after all?

"The left minister was my friend," Tomohito protested. "I wanted to rule Japan, and he helped me. He bought weapons with the money from selling imperial treasure. He raised an army to overthrow the Tokugawa for me. Before he died, he planned the siege of Miyako."

Sano's jaw dropped. "Do you mean that *Left Minister Konoe* was responsible for the revolt?"

Despite his astonishment, he saw that the revelation made perfect sense. The motives and means he'd attributed to Ichijo also fit the murder victim. Konoe, too, had been an ambitious man who'd wielded influence over the emperor. His position, like Ichijo's, had allowed him the freedom to go about recruiting troops. And Konoe, as chief court noble, would have ruled from behind the throne if he'd lived and the coup had succeeded.

But his status as a *metsuke* agent had blinded Sano to these facts, and important clues. The notes from Konoe's secret house must have been his plans for organizing the coup, not observations scribbled while spying on Lord Ibe's estate. A man capable of murdering Kozeri's husband, then pursuing her for fifteen years after she repudiated him, was mad enough to attack the Tokugawa. Now Sano recalled Ichijo saying, "Konoe . . . I should have guessed," and understood that Ichijo had realized that Konoe was responsible for the plot. Emperor Tomohito had said he didn't need Konoe anymore, meaning that because Konoe had already launched the revolt, he was no longer necessary for its success. Sano silently cursed his failure to see what now seemed obvious.

Prince Momozono bent over the emperor; while one arm flapped like a broken wing, the other clumsily embraced Tomohito's shoulders. "It's t-time to face the facts, Your Majesty. Day after d-day I listened to the left m-minister praising your ancestors who commanded power over Japan. I w-watched his h-hired martial arts experts teach you s-swordsmanship and convince you that you were a g-great warrior. He d-didn't think I understood what he was d-doing. I heard him fill your h-head with dreams of glory until you agreed that you must lead an uprising against the *b-bakufu*."

"It was my idea." Tomohito's face puckered with doubt. "He was just helping me fulfill my destiny."

Prince Momozono shook his head. "Y-you were too c-caught up in the left minister's scheme to n-notice what he m-muttered to himself every time he d-described the wonderful future when the Imperial C-court was restored to supremacy. But I heard. He s-said, 'Then she will love me. Sh-she will be forced to obey m-me as her husband and l-lord.' Your Majesty, h-he planned a revolt to get power over the w-wife who left him!"

"He did it for me!" Tomohito insisted, drumming his heels on the veranda while tears spilled down his cheeks.

Then the siege of Miyako hadn't been intended as just a drive for political power, but to satisfy an obsessive love. The "accomplishment" that Konoe had mentioned to Kozeri wasn't his elevation to the post of imperial prime minister, Sano realized; the "special occasion" Konoe had wanted to celebrate with her wasn't a reward for turning in a traitor. Both euphemisms had referred to his takeover of Japan, which would place her and everyone else in his power. In his last letter to Kozeri, he'd alluded to the site of the revolt, which he knew because he himself had chosen it.

Momozono knelt beside the emperor. "I c-couldn't let the l-left minister get you in trouble. So I k-killed him."

Sano was horrified. He needed a confession, but not here, with nothing to deter Momozono from killing to protect the emperor and eliminate a *bakufu* official to whom he'd just admitted he was guilty of murder.

"*You* killed the left minister?" The exclamation burst from Tomohito. Then dismayed recollection came into his eyes. "The night Konoe was murdered, you were already in the Pond Garden when I got there. After we found his body, you asked where I'd been before we met. I said, in the study hall, alone. We agreed to say we'd been there together. When that other man died, I was alone in the worship hall, and you promised to say you'd been there, too. I thought you did it for my sake. But it was you who needed an alibi!"

He jumped up and began beating the prince with his fists, shouting, "You tried to ruin my future. How dare you?"

"I did it to s-save you! An anonymous l-letter telling what the left m-minister was doing wouldn't have b-been enough to convince the *bakufu*—he was too important and r-respectable. I had no choice but to k-kill him. I didn't know that the r-revolt would go ahead after h-he was gone!" Raising his unwieldy arms in self-defense, Momozono accidentally struck Tomohito's chin, further enraging him.

"I'll kill you!" Tomohito howled.

"Stop!" Sano dragged Tomohito away from the prince, fearful that Momozono would turn against his cousin for failing to appreciate what he'd done. Sano considered slaying the prince, whose crimes merited the death penalty, but he abhorred killing and hoped to arrest Momozono without violence.

On his knees, head tossing, Momozono cried, "If the revolt w-were to succeed and L-left Minister Konoe seize power, h-he would have exiled me, the way he tried to years ago. Were it to f-fail, Your Majesty would have b-been executed. And what w-would have happened to m-me then?"

"Who cares about you?" Tomohito demanded, trying to maneuver around Sano so he could get at the prince.

Selfishness was at the heart of every murderer's motive, Sano knew. Momozono had acted on the emperor's behalf, but he'd also been defending his own precarious position. He, of all the suspects, had the most to gain by Konoe's death and the most to lose by either his victory or defeat in a war with the Tokugawa. Only one question remained.

"Why did you kill again?" Sano asked the prince.

"I g-got the message that you were coming to the p-palace. I w-went to kill you so Lady Asagao would be f-freed and you wouldn't discover the c-conspiracy. On my way, I c-came upon four s-samurai, walking through the palace g-grounds. I heard them t-talking. A man with a drawling voice was p-praising the leader for framing L-lady Asagao and forcing her to confess."

Aisu and Yanagisawa and their guards, Sano thought.

"I r-realized that they were r-responsible for her arrest. They w-went on talking, and it was clear th-that they wanted to w-watch me kill you, then arrest me. It was a trap!" Momozono went into a fit of facial contortions. "I h-had to do what I'd set out to do, but I couldn't let them c-catch me. So I went after them. Two of the m-men ran away. I k-killed the one with the drawling v-voice and trapped the l-leader. But then I heard you c-coming. I couldn't recover my strength quickly enough to s-scream again, so I ran away."

A chance encounter had resulted in Aisu's death, Sano realized, and spared his own life. If he was clever enough, fortune might favor him again.

"I commend your loyalty to His Majesty, and I understand what a terrible ordeal you've been through," Sano said gently, while he sought a way to persuade Momozono to surrender himself and the emperor. What kind of favorable terms could he offer a confessed murderer? "Let's go back to the palace where you can rest, and—"

With an effort that ripped a yell from him, the prince stood. Distress clouded the twitching muscles of his face as he said to Sano, "You treated me with m-more respect than anyone else ever has. For that I offer you my humble th-thanks. But I c-can't let you take His M-Majesty, so I must kill you, too."

"Wait," Sano said, though fearfully aware that his luck had failed him. He appealed to the emperor, who stood staring at Momozono in panting fury. "Your cousin is dangerous. We have to go. Please come with me."

"No!" Tomohito lunged at Momozono again. When Sano caught him and tried to lead him away, he tore free, cursing.

Hysterical frenzy besieged Momozono. His shrieks echoed across the hills. His face contorted, while his arms and legs flailed in a bizarre dance. Then he threw back his head and clenched his jaws. The frenzy waned, leaving Momozono eerily silent and still. His manic energy, now harnessed, emanated from him in a pale aura that absorbed the sounds of battle and distant gongs.

An ominous, familiar tension tingled the air around Sano. Its soundless vibration pulsed through him. Sudden lassitude weakened him. He reached for the long sword at his waist, but his arm moved sluggishly, as if he were dragging it through water. His spirit recoiled from the ghostly, sinister touch of Momozono's will. Realization startled him. Contrary to popular wisdom, the power of *kiai* wasn't always the product of rigorous martial arts training. In Momozono's case, it was a symptom of his mysterious affliction. An accident of fate had made him an outcast and granted him the ultimate deadly weapon. He must have practiced his skill on those birds found dead in the palace gardens.

"What are you doing, Momo-*chan*?" the emperor asked. A queasy expression came over his face. "It's scaring me. What's that noise? Where's that light coming from? I order you to stop!"

"My apologies, Your Majesty." Prince Momozono had shed his stammer along with his tics; his voice was clear, steady, and full of regret. "There's no other way. He knows I killed two men. He knows you were a willing participant in the rebellion. He has to die."

Sano's fingers, grown thick and clumsy, fumbled his sword from its scabbard. The weapon seemed a hundred times heavier than usual, and Sano's hand too weak to bear the weight. The sword fell. The debilitating force radiating from Momozono dropped Sano to his knees; his fear turned to terror; his wish to serve justice gave way to the need to save his life.

"There's no reason to kill me," he choked out. "Left Minister Konoe was a traitor. By killing him, you demonstrated loyalty to the Tokugawa regime. The shogun will spare you the death sentence, maybe even pardon you altogether."

Momozono shook his head sadly. "Anyone with a power like mine would never be allowed to live. But I don't really care if I die. It's His Majesty I must protect. I can't let you capture him and execute him as a traitor."

"The emperor isn't responsible for the plot," Sano hastened to say. Keeping Momozono talking would prevent him from gathering the breath he would need for a spirit cry. "The *bakufu* will make allowances for his age and Left Minister Konoe's influence over him. They won't want a scandal, or a breach with the Imperial Court. If His Majesty repents, he won't be punished."

"Yes, I repent," cried Emperor Tomohito. "I'll never be bad again. Just stop, Momo-*chan*!" Backing away from his cousin, he stumbled, fell, then crawled between pillars toward the door of the temple hall. "Help! Somebody, please!"

As hot waves of panic coursed through him, and his heart pounded with accelerating thuds, Sano recalled a classic ritual practiced by ancient samurai in wartime: *kugi goshin-ho*, annihilating the forces of evil by evoking the nine magic ideographs. He closed his hands, then released the index fingers, pressing the tips together near his breast.

"*Rin! Rin! Rin!*" he chanted.

To his relief, he felt a slight relaxing of the tension. The heat in his blood began to subside; his heartbeat slowed.

"I'm not stupid enough to think His Majesty will be forgiven," Momozono said bitterly. "If I claim that Left Minister Konoe was to blame for the revolt, who will believe me? That's why I killed him. Can you picture me telling the *bakufu* that he was planning a coup?" The aura around Momozono brightened; the energy pulsed with quickening intensity. "I'd have been mocked and dismissed."

"But I believe you. I'll convince my superiors." Assailed by Momozono's invisible force, Sano fell back on his heels. With a huge effort, he brought his fingertips together, gasping, "*Sha! Sha! Sha!*" Even though the physical relief was minimal, renewed courage flared in him.

"I can see that you're sincere," Momozono said, "but if you think your support of my word will save His Majesty, you're more of an idiot than I am."

In desperation, Sano argued, "Have you thought about what will happen if you kill me? Without me to persuade the *bakufu* that His Majesty is innocent, he'll be condemned for treason. My detectives will come when they hear your scream. They'll find my corpse, and they'll catch you. You can't buy your freedom, or the emperor's, with my death."

Momozono's expression disdained this scenario. "His Majesty will tell the *bakufu* that the outlaws abducted us from the palace and brought us here. You attacked His Majesty because you thought he was a traitor. I defended him the only way I could. It won't matter that everyone knows I'm a murderer."

With wordless eloquence, Momozono gestured toward the dark, open space beyond the railing. Below the tall beams that supported the veranda, the cliff dropped off precipitously. No one could survive such a fall. "I'll be dead before the police can arrest me."

As his heart pumped currents of panic through him, Sano chanted, "*Jin! Jin!*" When he tried to form the ideograph, his fingers wouldn't intertwine and fold. "Please," he whispered, "have mercy!" His spine gave way, and he crumpled. Momozono's will constricted his lungs; his heart seemed ready to explode. His ears reverberated; he could barely hear Tomohito shouting, "No, Momo-*chan*, no!"

"Get out of the way, Your Majesty," ordered the prince.

Faint scuttling noises impinged on Sano's last vestiges of consciousness as the emperor crawled away. "Help!" Sano called.

His voice was a dying whisper trapped in his throat. Marume, Fukida, and the Tokugawa troops were far away at the battlefield. Momozono loomed over Sano and began breathing loudly, first in hisses, then wheezes, then huge gulps. Sano felt the last of his strength fade away. The power of *kiai* paralyzed him. He couldn't manage the slightest flinch of muscle or fragment of speech.

Momozono's voracious breaths stopped. He stood immobile, staring at Sano. Currents of energy swirled within the blackness of his eyes. The force radiating from him grew until the night thrummed and the whole cosmos seemed on the brink of shattering. Then Momozono's mouth opened, stretching so wide that all his teeth showed around the gaping dark hole of his throat. Helpless, Sano watched Momozono inhale a huge breath. As Sano's thoughts dissolved in a turmoil of pain and terror, he fought desperately to remain lucid. The Way of the Warrior decreed that a samurai must face death with dignified courage, and Sano couldn't die without a final prayer.

Reiko! I love you! My spirit will watch over you until we are reunited in the netherworld!

The inhalation swelled Momozono's thin chest as he prepared to

284

release the full force of his power. With stoic tranquility, Sano resigned himself to the inevitable.

But instead of a deafening scream, Momozono emitted a grunt. The tension in the air snapped like a burst bubble; the vibration ceased. Alarm replaced the wild ferocity in Momozono's eyes. He staggered forward a step. Then his expression went blank, and he crashed facedown on the veranda. On his back, a red stain spread from a slit in his kimono. Over his lifeless body stood Sano's savior: Chamberlain Yanagisawa.

Yanagisawa bent at the waist, breathing as hard as if he'd run all the way from the battlefield. The blade of the sword in his hand dripped Prince Momozono's blood. Sano was overwhelmed with gratitude and relief. Yanagisawa's complexion was deathly pale between the livid bruises; his body shook with tremors induced by what must have been a fierce struggle to approach and slay the man with the power of *kiai*. But his face wore a brilliant, sardonic smile.

"You once called me a back stabber," he said to Sano. "Aren't you glad I lived up to my reputation?"

36

The day before Sano left Miyako, he and Chamberlain Yanagi-sawa bid official farewell to the Imperial Court. Obon had ended, and a fresh wind had swept away the bonfire smoke. Clouds diffused the sun's glare and cast shifting shadows upon the courtyard outside the Purple Dragon Hall. Nobles lined the yard, kneeling still while drums beat a slow, ritual cadence. On this morning two days after the Tokugawa army had quelled the revolt, the Imperial Palace basked in serenity. To Sano, walking behind Yanagisawa as guards, palace functionaries, and *Shoshidai* Matsu-daira escorted them across the courtyard, the scene had the quality of an ancient painting: eternal, untouched by the hand of fortune. Yet Sano knew better.

The procession mounted the steps to the hall, whose raised doors revealed the imperial throne room. Inside, Emperor Tomohito sat in his canopied pavilion. Sano and Yanagisawa knelt on the veranda opposite him, with their escorts flanking them. They bowed in solemn reverence.

Shoshidai Matsudaira said, "The honorable chamberlain and *sōsakan-sama* have come to take their leave of the Imperial Court." His voice trembled; he looked ill. Yanagisawa had reprimanded him for allowing a conspiracy to foment right under his nose. Soon he would be demoted and another Tokugawa relative put in charge of Miyako.

From his place below the emperor's throne, Right Minister Ichijo addressed Yanagisawa and Sano: "We thank you for coming and solving the difficult problems of our capital."

Beneath his courteous manner Sano detected a combination of relief at seeing them go, and suppressed elation. Rumor said that Ichijo's promotion to the rank of prime minister would soon be announced. He'd achieved his lifelong goal.

"We thank you for your cooperation," said Yanagisawa, "and regret that we must depart so soon."

Sano offered his own thanks and regrets, but he guessed that their polite speeches fooled no one.

"I grant you my blessing for a safe journey back to Edo," said Emperor Tomohito.

All the arrogance had deserted him; his chastened expression lent him a new maturity. Sano predicted a long, peaceful reign for the young sovereign, who had finally learned his place in the world.

While priests chanted an invocation, Sano perceived a vacancy in the palace; there was a quietude formerly broken by hoots, yelps, and frenetic motion. The air seemed charged with the absence of Prince Momozono. Yesterday Sano had issued orders for the prince's cremation and burial. Perhaps his spirit would find peace at last.

The ceremony drew to a close, and Sano pondered the most dramatic effect wrought by the murder case: the change in Chamberlain Yanagisawa. Yanagisawa had offered no explanation for saving Sano's life, but Sano hadn't needed one. The chamberlain had brought *Yoriki* Hoshina with him when he'd rescued Sano. While Yanagisawa had described the discovery that had sped him to the temple, joy had lit his face as if he'd swallowed the sun. The investigation had made a detective out of him; the battle had turned him into a samurai. Love had redeemed his spirit.

Now the procession exited the courtyard. As Sano and Yanagisawa walked through the narrow streets of the *kuge* district for the last time, Right Minister Ichijo joined them.

"A private word, if I may?" Ichijo said.

Sano and Yanagisawa dropped behind their entourage and walked with the right minister. Ichijo said, "We all know that your investigation is not quite complete."

"True," said Yanagisawa.

"I will explain what you saw when you followed me to the Ear Mound," said Ichijo, "if you will keep the information confidential."

Yanagisawa raised an eyebrow at Sano, who smiled. Some things never changed. Ichijo was still a consummate politician. Loath to tarry in Miyako, Yanagisawa and Sano had agreed that they would return to Edo, leaving Detective Fukida behind to tie up loose ends. But perhaps Fukida needn't worry about this one.

"Very well," Yanagisawa said.

"I have a secret mistress and daughter in the village of Kusatsu," Ichijo said quietly. "I visit them whenever I can. I also send them money through intermediaries. That's what I was doing at the Ear Mound. I hired those two *rōnin* to protect my family from bandit raids and convey cash to them."

Sano said, "That's not illegal. Why the need for secrecy?"

"The woman is a peasant," Ichijo said. "For a man in my position, an affair outside the noble class is unseemly. It would have damaged my career. I was passing through the Pond Garden on my way to Kusatsu when Left Minister Konoe was murdered. I didn't want to be caught at the scene, so I continued on my trip." He added, "Konoe knew my secret. He was blackmailing me."

The procession reached the palace gate. "Thank you for the information," Sano said, glad to have a mystery solved.

"If you will kindly excuse me, I have business to attend to," Ichijo said, bowing.

"As have I." A bemused expression, tinged with worry, came over Yanagisawa's face.

"And I," Sano said, as foreboding stirred in him.

At the Palace of the Abdicated Emperor, Reiko sat on a veranda with Lady Jokyōden. They gazed at the sunlit park, where courtiers and noblewomen strolled. Wind chimes tinkled; dragonflies hovered over fragrant flowers.

"Everything looks the same," Reiko said. "It's as if nothing had happened to disturb the peace of this world."

"I must devote more effort to preserving that peace," Jokyōden said, "and more attention to His Majesty the Emperor."

This was the only reference they made to the revolt. Reiko contemplated Jokyōden's hint that she would keep her son under stricter control. Men dominated politics and waged wars, but a woman working behind the scenes could accomplish much. Reiko doubted if the emperor would dare defy his mother and misbehave again, and the Tokugawa regime was indebted to Jokyōden.

"Many thanks for your help," Reiko said, bowing.

With dignified grace, Jokyōden also bowed. "I am honored to have been of service."

"I wonder—" Reiko paused, eager to satisfy curiosity, yet hesitant about broaching a personal question. "May I ask why you decided to help me, when your interests opposed mine?"

"I saw myself in you," Jokyōden said with a wry smile. "Besides that, another woman aided me many times during my life. She is beyond my assistance, so I repaid her favor by helping you." As if to herself, Jokyōden murmured, "May that deed compensate for those less virtuous."

A chill passed over Reiko. By now she'd read the *metsuke* dossiers that Chamberlain Yanagisawa had sent Sano. She'd learned of Jokyōden's rivalry with another court lady whose fatal fall over a cliff might not have been accidental. Even if Jokyōden hadn't murdered Left Minister Konoe or Aisu, even if she didn't have the power of *kiai,* she was still dangerous.

Lady Jokyōden gave Reiko a faint smile. As though aware of Reiko's thoughts all along, she said, "Women are generally considered helpless, yet under the right circumstances, we are capable of great harm as well as good."

Reiko realized with an unpleasant shock that she herself was a dangerous woman. As the wife of the shogun's *sōsakan-sama*, she had more power than ordinary women, and she'd played a role in incriminating the innocent Lady Asagao. Would she, too, someday have sins to regret?

There was another reason for this visit besides bidding good-bye to her friend: Sano had asked her to solve a minor puzzle in the case. Knowing that Jokyōden would see through any subterfuge she tried, Reiko said bluntly, "I'd like to know what is your connection with the Daikoku Bank."

Jokyōden looked surprised, then recovered her composure and nodded. "I trusted your discretion once, and you did not fail me, so I shall tell you. As you may know, the imperial family has financial problems. I sold my valuable kimonos and used the money to establish the Daikoku Bank. Through my agents, I issue loans and speculate on commodities. The profits supplement the court's income."

"Astonishing," Reiko murmured. Surely Jokyōden was history's first noblewoman banker.

"I made the mistake of telling Left Minister Konoe," said Jokyōden. "He demanded a share of my profits in exchange for not revealing that I had crossed the boundaries of womanly behavior and trespassed on the purview of the merchant class."

"I'm sure that if I tell my husband about your business, he'll agree to ignore it because you're doing no harm and you led us to the conspiracy," Reiko said.

"I would much appreciate his generosity," said Jokyōden.

Reiko suspected that Jokyōden had chosen to reveal her secret because she'd predicted this outcome. The world of women wasn't so different from the world of men, Reiko observed. Favors were the common currency, and she owed Jokyōden a greater debt than she'd repaid. Perhaps she could pass along the favor by helping other women in need, and use her power to do good.

They rose and made their final bows of farewell.

"It may be that we shall meet again someday," Jokyōden said.

In spite of the distance from Miyako to Edo, Reiko had hopes that they might. So many unimaginable things had already happened: the discovery of a man with the power of *kiai*; Sano's return from the dead; a war averted. Anything seemed possible.

"Perhaps we shall," she said.

As her palanquin carried her out of the Imperial Palace, her thoughts turned toward another impending event—one more commonplace than her recent experiences, yet just as miraculous, and now a certainty. Soon she must tell Sano.

At Nijō Castle, troops and servants prepared for the trip to Edo, packing clothes and supplies, readying the horses. Chamberlain Yanagisawa paced the veranda of the private chamber. He inhaled on his tobacco pipe, hoping the smoke would calm his nerves. Hearing footsteps behind him, he stopped, turned, and saw *Yoriki* Hoshina standing at the far end of the veranda.

"You sent for me." The hesitancy in Hoshina's voice made it almost a question.

"Yes . . ."

Slowly they walked toward each other and stood at the railing, looking out at the stark, treeless garden. "So you're leaving tomorrow," Hoshina said.

Yanagisawa nodded. His spirit and body came alive with the exhilaration that Hoshina's presence inspired. After leading the victorious army back to Miyako and returning Emperor Tomohito to the palace, they'd spent much time celebrating their reunion with violent, physical passion. Yet so much had happened that neither had dared mention the future.

"There's something I want to talk about," Yanagisawa said, at the same moment Hoshina said, "I suppose this is our last day together." An uncomfortable silence ensued. Then, with a sense of leaping off a cliff, Yanagisawa spoke in a voice barely above a whisper: "It doesn't have to be."

"What did you say?" Hope battled disbelief in Hoshina's face.

Now Yanagisawa's voice came out clear and strong: "I want you to come to Edo with me."

That Hoshina also wanted it was apparent in his shining eyes and trembling mouth, but he didn't speak.

"I'll make you my new chief retainer," Yanagisawa said.

"You would do that? After I betrayed you?" Incredulity strained Hoshina's voice.

"After you proved your loyalty, yes, I would." Yanagisawa spoke with full knowledge of the danger of fostering a potential rival.

"If you'd proposed this a few days ago, I would have jumped at the chance. But now . . ." Hoshina smiled wryly. "Instead of planning my brilliant future, I'm thinking about how having me around could hurt you. I served you well this time. But later . . . what if I turn out to be the same man who once meant to take advantage of your generosity? How can you trust me?"

"Perhaps I'm still the same man who condemned you to death for disappointing me," Yanagisawa said. "If you trust me, I'll trust you."

They exchanged a long, questioning gaze. Then, with somber smiles, they nodded.

"You'd better settle your business in Miyako and start packing," Yanagisawa said. "We leave at daybreak."

Sano rode through Miyako, down streets now bare of the stalls that had sold Obon supplies, past houses no longer decorated with lanterns or incense burners. The city teemed with gay, bright life, and along the Kamo River, only piles of ash remained from the Festival of the Dead, but as Sano reached Kodai Temple, his mind was uneasy. Reiko had willingly agreed that he should pay a last courtesy visit to Kozeri, and knowing what he now did about the nun, he thought he could resist her . . . but he wasn't quite certain.

Wind stirred the pines that rose above the temple walls; clouds obscured the sun. Walking along stone paths, through tranquil gardens, Sano hoped to conclude his business with Kozeri in a businesslike manner, as Reiko trusted him to do.

In the courtyard waited a palanquin and four bearers. Down the steps of the nunnery came a woman dressed in a blue cotton kimono; she carried a cloth bundle. With a white drape covering her shaved head, Sano almost didn't recognize Kozeri.

She spied him, and her steps faltered. Eyes downcast, she walked to the palanquin, where Sano joined her.

"Where are you going?" he asked.

Kozeri gave him a shy glance from beneath lowered lids. "I'm leaving the nunnery."

"Why?" Even as Sano spoke, he guessed the answer: He had diverted Kozeri from her spiritual calling. Preoccupied with his own troubles, he hadn't thought about how their encounters might have affected her. Guilt stabbed him. "I'm terribly sorry," he said.

A fleeting smile crossed Kozeri's averted face. "It's not your fault," she said. "Meeting you only forced me to admit what I've known all along: I'm not suited to be a nun. Now that the left minister is gone, there's no reason to stay here."

She raised her head and looked directly at Sano. Desire flared between them even though he'd braced himself against her. He realized that sometimes an attraction arises between a man and woman regardless of their wishes, even without magic spells. He also knew he had better leave before he succumbed.

He said hurriedly, "The reason I came is to apologize for any trouble my investigation has caused you."

"Oh, that's all right," Kozeri murmured. "I shouldn't have deceived you. Please forgive me."

Her meekness irritated Sano. He discovered that he didn't really like Kozeri. Cloaked in passive martyrdom, she inspired not his admiration or respect, but his pity. She'd never breached the part of his spirit where his love for Reiko dwelled. While castigating himself for his weakness, he'd overlooked the fact that he *had* withstood temptation, and he could again. But what of Kozeri, at whose expense he'd learned his lesson?

"Where will you go?" Sano asked her.

"For now, I'll live in my family's summer villa. We agreed on that when I visited them a few days ago and told them I wanted to leave the nunnery. Perhaps someday a new marriage can be arranged for me."

In her eyes Sano read Kozeri's hope for a good husband to love, a child to replace the one she'd lost. Now she opened the door of the palanquin and stowed her bundle inside.

"Goodbye, *sōsakan-sama*," Kozeri said. "I wish you well."

"And I the same to you," Sano said.

With mutual relief, they smiled and bowed. Then they departed Kodai Temple, she in the palanquin and he on horseback, traveling in opposite directions.

292

The sun rose crimson over the misty hills above Miyako. While the imperial capital still slumbered, a procession of foot soldiers, mounted samurai, servants, and a single palanquin filed out the city gates, heading east along the Tōkaidō highway between lush green fields. The rhythm of hoofbeats and marching feet mingled with the waking cries of birds. Humid heat steamed from the earth, yet a hint of coolness in the air presaged autumn.

Riding beside Sano, Detective Marume said, "That was some adventure, but I will be truly glad to get back to Edo."

Detective Fukida recited:

"My native city—longing recalls
The winding streets, the castle on the hill."

Chamberlain Yanagisawa dropped back from his place near the head of the procession to ride alongside Sano. "Shall we congratulate ourselves on a job well done, *sōsakan-sama?*"

"You deserve much of the credit," Sano said.

"That's true," Yanagisawa said complacently.

"May I look forward to a continuation of our partnership when we reach home?" Sano asked.

The chamberlain favored him with a long, unreadable gaze that boded an uncertain future. Who could tell how long their truce might last?

Yoriki Hoshina joined Yanagisawa. Looking at them, Sano felt a qualm of unease. Where he'd previously had one enemy, would he now have two?

Yanagisawa's faint smile said he knew exactly what Sano was thinking. Then he and Hoshina rode ahead, leaving Sano to wonder.

CPSIA information can be obtained at www.ICGtesting.com
Printed in the USA
LVOW08s2046050516

486873LV00002B/166/P